Praise for

The Status of All Things

"Pop culture references and a healthy sprinkling of magical realism combine to make *The Status of All Things* a timely reminder that all is not what it seems. With a sparkling narrative that will have you turning pages at a breakneck speed, this is women's fiction at its finest."

—Tracey Garvis Graves, *New York Times* bestselling author of *On the Island* and *Covet*

"What a treat! *The Status of All Things* is a fun, clever and utterly engaging story of love, loss, the power of destiny and the importance of friends. A thoroughly enjoyable read. I loved everything about it, from beginning to end."

—Mary Kubica, *New York Times* bestselling author of *The Good Girl*

"A new twist on modern day women's fiction . . . the integration of magical elements works surprisingly well in this witty story that is much more than charming romance. A fun and fast read for fans of Meg Cabot and Jennifer Weiner."

—*Library Journal*

"I raced through *The Status of All Things* at a breakneck pace. A perfect blend of what-if and what-should-be, Fenton and Steinke have found a rhythm together that works. They bring that little touch of magic we could all use in our own lives to the page with vibrancy and wit."

—Catherine McKenzie, bestselling author of *Hidden* and *Forgotten*

"Written with heart and keen insight into the influences of social media, *The Status of All Things* tells the tale of one woman's quest to change the past. The story gives us magic, a touch of whimsy, and a reality that's hard to shake. Smart and true with a pitch-perfect ending, it will leave readers feeling satisfied and also asking 'what if?' "

—Michelle Gable, internationally bestselling author of *A Paris Apartment*

"With their razor sharp wit and astute social commentary, Liz Fenton and Lisa Steinke—two of women's fiction's brightest stars—tackle the question: Would you be truly happy if you could rewrite your own fate via Facebook? And the answer is definitely not what you expect."

—Emily Liebert, author of *When We Fall*

Praise for
Your Perfect Life

"*Your Perfect Life* has all of the ingredients that I love in a book—relatable characters who make me laugh out loud, a delicious, page-turning premise, and sweet and surprising insights about the perfect life may be the one you've already got."

—Jen Lancaster, *New York Times* bestselling author

"I loved this from the very first line (which will go down in history as the funniest, bravest first line ever). Hilarious, honest and truly touching, Liz Fenton and Lisa Steinke are two important new voices in women's fiction who write about life in such a real, relatable way."

—Sarah Jio, *New York Times* bestselling author

"For every woman who's ever wondered about the path not taken, Fenton and Steinke mine—with tremendous humor and insight—the mixed blessing of unexpected second chances."

—Emma McLaughlin and Nicola Kraus,
New York Times bestselling authors

"Liz and Lisa's voices are warm and comforting, like a relaxed chat with great friends while wearing cozy PJs and sipping wine. I highly recommend *Your Perfect Life!*"

—Beth Harbison, *New York Times* bestselling author

"Liz Fenton and Lisa Steinke blend their voices seamlessly and hilariously and remind us that even though the grass often looks greener under our friends' lives, nobody gets happily ever after unless they go after it. *Your Perfect Life* is clever, quirky, fresh, and ultimately, empowering!"

—Claire Cook, bestselling author of
Must Love Dogs and *Time Flies*

"*Your Perfect Life* puts a fresh twist on a 'Freaky Friday' scenario: What if you switched bodies with your best friend, and got the life you'd always secretly coveted? I adore Liz Fenton and Lisa Steinke's witty, winning style and gobbled up their debut novel."

—Sarah Pekkanen, author of *Things You Won't Say*

"Sassy, heartfelt, and smart, *Your Perfect Life* is a clever take on switched identities that will make you think hard about the choices you've made in your life and what matters most to us all in the end."

—Amy Hatvany, author of *Safe with Me*

the year we turned forty

a novel

liz fenton
and
lisa steinke

WASHINGTON SQUARE PRESS

new york london toronto sydney new delhi

Washington Square Press
An Imprint of Simon & Schuster, Inc.
1230 Avenue of the Americas
New York, NY 10020

Copyright © 2016 by Liz Fenton and Lisa Steinke

First Washington Square Press trade paperback edition April 2016

WASHINGTON SQUARE PRESS and colophon are registered trademarks of Simon & Schuster, Inc.

For information about special discounts for bulk purchases,
please contact Simon & Schuster Special Sales at 1-866-506-1949
or business@simonandschuster.com.

The Simon & Schuster Speakers Bureau can bring authors to
your live event. For more information or to book an event, contact
the Simon & Schuster Speakers Bureau at 1-866-248-3049 or
visit our website at www.simonspeakers.com.

Manufactured in the United States of America

10 9 8 7 6 5 4 3 2 1

Library of Congress Cataloging-in-Publication Data

Names: Fenton, Liz, author. | Steinke, Lisa, author.
Title: The year we turned forty : a novel / Liz Fenton and Lisa Steinke.
Description: First Washington Square Press trade paperback edition. | New York :
Washington Square Press, 2016.
Identifiers: LCCN 2015041738 (print) | LCCN 2015044930 (ebook) Subjects:
BISAC: FICTION / Contemporary Women. | FICTION / Family Life. |
   FICTION / Humorous.
Classification: LCC PS3606.E5844 Y43 2016 (print) | LCC PS3606.E5844
(ebook)
   | DDC 813/.6—dc23
LC record available at http://lccn.loc.gov/2015041738

ISBN 978-1-4767-6344-6
ISBN 978-1-4767-6345-3 (ebook)

For Shane and Riley—you are the very best part of me.

To my mom, Valerie—for telling me I could.

the year we turned forty

CHAPTER ONE

....

June 2005

"Push! Harder!"

The labor-and-delivery nurse belted out the command as Jessie shook her head defiantly in response, her entire body trembling, sweat and tears dripping down her face, pooling at the base of her neck. Even as the baby crowned, she knew she wasn't ready for its arrival.

"I can't," she finally managed, her mouth as dry as a ball of cotton. She'd kill for a drink of something that would quench her thirst—in fact, she could vividly picture herself strangling the nurse in exchange for a tumbler piled high with huge cubes of ice and filled to the brim with cold water.

"You *can* do this." Her husband Grant's breath felt like fire on her ear, his words fast and fumbled, desperation lacing every one. He and the nurse had been having a not-so-subtle conversation with their eyes for the last hour, their concern heightened with every raised eyebrow and pointed look at the baby's heart monitor attached to Jesse's protruding belly. "You have to. It's time. Please, honey." Grant's pale skin was glistening under the fluorescent lights, his dark hair matted against his head as if he was the one who'd been in labor for almost twenty hours. He rubbed the corners of his dark green eyes vigorously, and Jessie knew he was searching for the encouraging yet forceful words that would make her want to push the baby out, but his slumped shoulders exposed how close he was to admitting defeat.

Her pregnancy had been difficult for so many reasons, and Jessie wasn't one bit surprised that it was culminating in an arduous labor. In her mind, she deserved every painful contraction, every minute that clicked by without relief.

Jessie could feel her baby fighting its way out now, and she remembered why that severe burning sensation between her legs was called the *ring of fire*. She tried to concentrate on the hideous paintings of pastel floral arrangements adorning every wall, but the searing pain yanked her back to reality just as her doctor walked into the room, effortlessly releasing the commanding words Grant was having trouble articulating. "This baby is coming—*now*—and you have a job to do here, Jessie."

"Okay," Jessie huffed before taking a deep breath, gathering a current from deep inside her, and pushing with a force she didn't realize she had. The baby's first cries unleashed a tornado of emotions—of joy and sadness, relief and anxiety. As her newborn son was placed on her chest and she inhaled his smell, she was bewildered by how holding her baby for the first time could be both the best *and* the worst moment of her life.

• • •

"What do you think is taking so long?" Gabriela glanced at the clock on the wall, her long nails tapping the ripped navy blue armrest beside her, her makeup from the birthday party the night before smudged beneath her coffee-colored eyes. She was still wearing her skintight emerald green dress. Despite the amniotic fluid stain down the side—Jessie's water broke in a violent burst at Gabriela's house the night before, splashing off the travertine tile and onto her dress—it was attracting more than a few approving glances.

"I'm sure it will be any minute now," Claire declared calmly from behind a tattered copy of an old tabloid magazine. The couple canoodling on the cover had long since split up. "I actually thought because it's her third kid she'd push like one time and poof, we'd have ourselves a baby."

Gabriela glanced at the swinging doors once more, willing Grant to burst through them like a jubilant new father, dispersing candy cigars as he announced that the baby had arrived safely. When Jessie's water broke, something had cracked open inside Gabriela too—an incredible desire to hold the infant, to nuzzle it against her and marvel at its ten tiny fingers and toes. She'd never wanted children of her own, and had never wavered, not even when her husband, Colin, would place yet another of their friends' birth announcements in front of her with an expectant look in his eyes. She'd gently repeat her explanation—that she didn't feel she was meant to be a mother. Then she'd watch the range of emotions ripple across his face— first the frustration that she wouldn't change her mind *for him,* followed by the realization he'd never be someone's father. But ultimately, the love he felt for Gabriela always won out. She'd been honest about how she felt since early in the relationship, and until they had married, she'd thought he had been on the same page. But then he would drop a hint here, make a comment there, and she often wondered when *or if* he'd finally stop bringing it up. Until eventually, he did.

Which is when something unexpected happened.

Gabriela had recently turned forty. When she did, it revealed a hole inside of her she hadn't known was there. Now, she couldn't wait to see the look on Colin's face when she told him she was ready to be a mom.

• • •

Claire eyed Gabriela discreetly from behind her magazine, watching her carefully cross and uncross her long legs. Gabriela could be described as a lot of things: organized, practical, whip smart, even nurturing. But worrisome and anxious were not words Claire would ever use, and Gabriela's nervous behavior baffled her. She was surprised Gabriela had not only come to the hospital but waited here this entire time. It wouldn't have been at all out of character for her to have stayed at the party and visited the baby once it was cleaned, bundled, and sleeping soundly in a bassinet. Jessie had actually tried to convince both of them to do just that. Through clenched teeth and short, heavy breaths, while Grant was pulling up the car, Jessie had practically begged them not to ride with her to the hospital, to please stay and enjoy the party because it was theirs too, the urgency in her best friend's blue eyes taking her by surprise, almost enough to make Claire agree.

Gabriela's, Jessie's, and Claire's birthdays fell within a few months of each other—Gabriela in late May, Claire in June, and Jessie in July—and they'd made a vow almost twenty years before, while sipping beers at a dive bar in Newport Beach, their feet crunching the peanut shells covering the floor, to always celebrate together. Last night, they'd clasped hands as Colin toasted them, making a joke that forty was the new eighteen. Gabriela glowed as her husband captivated the crowd, Jessie shifted her weight, nervous and uncomfortable, her bladder signaling she needed to go *again*. And Claire only half listened as she popped a strawberry into her mouth, shyly making eye contact with a man different from any she'd met before, who'd made her heart flutter when they'd grazed arms and shared small talk at the chocolate fountain earlier.

Claire's phone vibrated in her hand and her stomach jumped as she realized the adorable guy she had bantered with last night was now calling. She pulled her magazine up slightly to hide her smile from Gabriela. Forty was starting off right.

• • •

Jessie squeezed her eyes, fighting the flow of tears that continued to gush from them, like a pipe that had burst inside her. She hugged her baby to her chest tightly, putting her finger inside his hand and watching as he gripped it. She studied her newborn son's scrunched face, searching for her own features, trying to calm her rapid breath as she instantly recognized the shape of his nose and jut of his chin. She glanced over at Grant. Did he see it too? She had promised herself that she would tell him today. That he deserved to know the truth. She even let herself believe that he might stay anyway, although she was smart enough to realize that it would never be the same, that she'd never again catch him looking at her like he'd just met her and was intrigued by all the things he didn't yet know.

Grant pressed his lips to her forehead and combed his fingers through her damp hair. She looked at him hard, trying to etch each angle of his face into her memory, so she could always remember what it was like to have him love her like this.

"I have something to tell you," Jessie said in a lowered voice as she glanced at the nurses busily cleaning up.

"Me too." Grant gently took the baby from her and cuddled him against his broad chest, his eyes glinting with tears. "I love the girls with all my heart, but I never knew it would feel this way to have a son."

Jessie swallowed the words that had been sitting on her tongue and made a choice. She had no idea if it was the right one, but it was the only one she was capable of making. "I'm so glad. He looks just like you."

CHAPTER TWO

. . . .

Ten years later, June 2015

"Mom?"

Jessie folded her new gold one-piece bathing suit in thirds and placed it carefully into her suitcase, already picturing herself wearing it poolside at the Aria Hotel with a skinny margarita in one hand, a *People* magazine resting against her thighs, and her two best friends by her side. *Heaven.* She'd try not to be envious of Gabriela in the string bikini she knew she'd be wearing— probably white, to show off her caramel-colored skin—or of Claire's freakishly youthful appearance—people often thought she was in her late thirties, even though she would be turning fifty tomorrow. When Claire had suggested Vegas as their destination, Jessie's first feeling had been panic, as she'd imagined all the twentysomething bleach blondes in tight miniskirts strutting through the casinos making her feel frumpy and out of place. But she couldn't tell Claire and Gabriela that. They both seemed to have the metabolism of fourteen-year-old boys and wouldn't understand.

Not that Jessie was overweight. But she was still carrying

ten extra pounds, her body not bouncing back from Lucas' birth as easily as it had with her now twenty-year-old twins, Madison and Morgan. It was a side effect of having a baby at forty, not thirty. Jessie wished she could've been one of those supermoms who went straight from the hospital bed to the gym, sliding effortlessly into her skinny jeans just weeks after giving birth. But she'd been so exhausted all the time, she was barely able to rouse herself out of bed at all hours of the night to feed Lucas before hauling herself into the shower to start each day, jam-packed with driving car pool to the girls' sports practices and games. Not to mention she'd always had a general apathy toward actual exercise. So before she knew it, the loose skin around her middle had taken permanent residence, as had the extra pounds that had attached to her hips and thighs. But Jessie had grown used to her new body, artfully disguising it under carefully cut tops and tailored jeans.

"*Mom?*" Lucas' voice was more urgent this time.

"In my room," Jessie answered as she took a selfie while wearing a fedora she'd purchased on a whim yesterday, before sending it to Madison and Morgan. *Can I pull this off?* She texted with the girls almost daily. It was the perfect way to keep in touch with them while still giving them their space.

"Dad's here," Lucas announced as he plopped down on her bed, his thick brown hair a sharp contrast against her pale peach comforter, the furrow between his emerald eyes deepening as he squinted at the soccer ball he was tossing in the air above him.

Jessie listened to the sound of the ball rhythmically hitting Lucas' palms as she placed her toiletries in the outside zipper pocket and released a sharp breath just as she caught her son's eye, not realizing he had been watching her. Quickly, she transformed her frown into a smile.

Dad.

"Okay," Jessie answered with forced cheer, picturing Grant sitting out front in his ancient Toyota 4Runner, tapping his hands against the steering wheel, strumming to the beat of some classic rock band—probably the Eagles.

Their relationship was fine, *now*. But it had taken them years, and most days, even fine was still an exaggeration, at least for Jessie. But in front of Lucas, and Madison and Morgan when they were home from college, they were like two politicians smiling for the cameras. Grant would kiss her on the cheek when he saw her, and even though it made her insides flop around like the clothes inside a dryer, Jessie would smile and ask him how Janet was doing. Great, he'd say. She was always so damn great.

It shouldn't have been a surprise when Grant moved out. Or when he asked for the divorce a year after that. Because that's what people do when you cheat on them. And it shouldn't have shocked Jessie that Grant couldn't get over it, that he didn't want to look her in the eye each day and recall how she'd betrayed him. That she wasn't the woman he thought she'd been. Yet she'd fallen to her knees anyway, begging him to give it a little more time. Deep down, she knew Grant had only delayed filing for as long as he had because he'd felt sorry for Jessie. She could tell by how he looked at her—like a bird with a broken wing, hobbling along, trying in vain to fly. She'd tried to convince him she'd been weak—that she'd let what began as a sliver of insecurity morph into a crater-sized doubt about him, about their marriage. She'd told him she was sorry, that she should've tried harder to talk to him about how lonely and rejected she'd felt. But he'd only looked at her with steely eyes and told her she was too late. She'd made the choice to turn to another man when she should've turned to him. And now he could never trust her not to do that again.

Grant had leased an apartment across town almost immediately after she'd told him what she'd done. Jessie still cursed herself for not pushing him to try marriage counseling. Instead, she backed off when he'd been against the idea, not feeling she had the right to demand it after what she'd done, too afraid to strain what had quickly become a very fragile union.

"Have a great time, honey!" Jessie walked over and kissed the top of her son's head as she pushed a tuft of hair out of his eyes and instantly regretted not getting him a haircut yesterday, knowing full well he'd return on Sunday night with a fresh cut that Janet had taken him to get.

"Dad's at the door, Mom. Says he wants to talk to you," Lucas said as he wiggled from her grasp and ran into his room to get his duffel bag.

As she headed downstairs, Jessie was thankful she'd gotten her dirty blond hair highlighted yesterday and that she was wearing her most flattering pair of jeans. And that she'd selected the navy blue top she knew not only brought out the golden flecks in her blue eyes but had always been Grant's favorite color on her. But she still wondered, as she often did, when she'd stop caring how she looked when she saw him. They'd been officially divorced for eight years, yet he always lingered in the background of her thoughts, just a heartbeat away from stepping out of the shadows.

She'd stood there helplessly after her confession, watching their entire future crumble, Grant's lip trembling as he fought back the tears. After he'd left, she'd clung to the memories of their wedding day like they were a thick tree trunk in a windstorm, remembering what they'd once been: deliriously happy newlyweds, him dabbing, not smashing, a tiny piece of cake on her nose; frightened new parents leaving the hospital with twins, Grant never accelerating above fifteen miles per hour; excited first-time homeowners, joking as they shared a bottle of wine that they hoped they'd make the mortgage each month. But just four words had changed everything. Four words had instantly trumped all the fights, the months without sex, the names they'd called each other. Just four words ruined their thirteen-year marriage.

Lucas isn't your son.

"Hi," Jessie said, her voice sounding too high pitched.

"Hey." Grant ran his hand over his smooth head. He'd finally been forced to shave it, his thin hair refusing to grow even with Rogaine. But somehow the baldness suited him. He'd started playing tennis in the past few years and he was tanned and toned. He looked better than he ever had. "Did Lucas have fun yesterday?"

"He did," Jessie said, thinking back on the birthday sleepover he'd had with his friends. "But be prepared, he might be up late tonight because he's so excited to officially be in double digits tomorrow."

"I'll be ready," Grant said. "And I wanted to talk to you about something real quick."

"Oh?" Jessie arched an eyebrow as she watched her ex-husband's eyes dart around the foyer. He probably wanted to ask her if Lucas could stay with him an extra night. He'd had to travel last week for work so he hadn't seen Lucas on Wednesday. She'd be tired from Vegas anyway, and a night alone would be nice.

"Where's Lucas?"

"Right here," Lucas said as he bounded down the stairs two at a time, his lanky legs curling up with each stride, reminding Jessie of a grasshopper's.

"Hey, buddy, will you go out front and kick the ball around? I need to talk to your mom for a minute," Grant said.

"Sure," Lucas said, smiling at Grant with pride. His club team had just won a national tournament and his dad's approval meant everything. Jessie couldn't help but smile on the sidelines, watching him search for Grant in the crowd each time he sunk the ball deep into the net of the goal.

But she stiffened as she watched Lucas bouncing the ball on his knee now. He still didn't know the truth. And with each passing day, every camping trip with Grant, every Father's Day, every time he asked for his dad—*Grant*—Jessie hoped she would never have to tell him. When she and Grant did argue, this was the hot topic. Should he or shouldn't he know who his real dad is? And if so, when? Jessie leaned toward no, Grant toward yes, arguing Lucas had a right to know, even if his biological father had made zero effort to be in contact. And while Jessie agreed that it was Lucas' right, she worried it might destroy him. Or worse, her relationship with him. And she couldn't even begin to think about how the girls would react.

Her infidelity had been a secret she and Grant had held close, blaming their split on having grown apart. And in many ways that was true. Their marriage had slowly shifted from giddy laughter on lazy Sunday mornings while they read the paper and sipped their coffee to strained voices and clipped tones from too many sleepless nights once they'd become a family of four. But that was okay. Jessie understood that they wouldn't always experience the highs of new love, that fervor that came with the knowledge you've found the person who completes you. She knew that time eventually wore passion down to its nub. But what she hadn't anticipated was Grant's declining sexual interest in her after the twins' arrival.

They'd always had an active sex life. Jessie had felt almost smug as she'd listened to her married friends with new babies complain about their husbands nagging them to do it when they just didn't want to. Jessie was sure that would *never* happen to her and Grant. She craved him the way someone might want chocolate or a glass of wine. She needed to feel him pressed against her, to smell his skin. They'd often joked during their first year together that they might be addicted to each other.

The changes in Grant were subtle, developing over several years. He stopped kissing her as deeply, his tongue no longer lingering, his hands no longer moving down her hips clearly wanting more. He stopped looking at her with a hunger in his eyes, and began almost looking through her. They stopped taking weekends away. Their sex, when they did have it, became predictable, then stale, and finally, infrequent. And at some point, it stopped altogether.

She remembered lying in bed, willing him to touch her, seething as she heard the sound of his first snore. She reached over and nudged him. Hard.

"Hey," Grant mumbled.

Jessie rubbed his naked back and worked her hands downward. "I think you forgot something before you fell asleep," she teased. She hoped she sounded confident. That she wasn't betraying the insecure corners of her mind—the same ones that had made her slightly obsessed with Sadie, his new assistant.

"Babe," Grant began, "I'm so tired. I promise I'll make it up to you tomorrow night. We'll get the kids to bed early."

Jessie snapped her hand back. "That's what you said last time. And the time before that."

Grant rolled over. "You really want to discuss this now? When I'm half asleep?"

"When the hell else are we going to talk, Grant? You're never here!"

Grant sighed. "Is that what this is *really* about? You're pissed off that I work too much?"

"No, this is about the fact that we haven't had sex in three months. Do you even realize that?"

Grant sat up. "There is no way it's been that long. What about after Claire's dinner party?"

Jessie remembered that night. He'd rubbed her thigh under the table while she'd stroked his leg. In the cab on the way home, Grant had slyly reached his hand up her skirt and she'd pushed herself into him, wanting to savor the moment. Yes, it had been amazing. But he hadn't so much as patted her ass since. "Grant. That *was* three months ago."

Jessie watched as he did the math in his head. "Really? I've been so busy at work, the time has passed in a blur."

"Because of Sadie?" Jessie asked, thinking of her gorgeous long red hair, her young fresh face. "Does she make the day fly by for you?" Jessie wasn't proud of it, but she'd recently Google-stalked her. It had been yet another night when she'd sat alone in their living room, the clock ticking past 8 p.m., her imagination running wild with reasons why Grant wasn't home. And when she'd discovered several images of Sadie modeling lingerie, her stomach dropped. Had he seen those? Of course he had.

"What does she have to do with this?"

"Well, you clearly don't want to have sex with me. So I'm wondering if it's because you're getting it somewhere else—if that's why you hired a model to get your coffee and make copies?"

"Do you really think I'm cheating on you? Because I'm not!"

"Well, you're hardly ever here. And when you are, you act like I'm invisible!" Jessie choked on the last part.

Grant reached for her. "I'd never do that to you or the girls. Do you really feel invisible?"

"Yes." Jessie wiped a tear away. "I do."

"I'm sorry, Jess. I feel so much pressure at work. And when I am home, it feels like survival, you know? Like in between sports and homework and baths and dinner, there isn't much room left for us."

Jessie nodded.

"I'll try harder. Okay?"

"Okay." Jessie brought her lips to his and hoped they'd stumbled back onto the right path.

But another three months went by without Grant reaching for her and she felt her insecurity turn to anger all over again. When he didn't even kiss her when he walked in, she would pick a fight about a crack on the countertop or the gas bill, all while shattering inside. He must find her lumpy and unsexy and boring. Otherwise, he would want to have sex with her. The constant rejection was like her shadow, following her everywhere, eventually leading her to look for that validation outside her marriage. And ultimately to Lucas. But never back to Grant.

Her life changed on the last Thursday of August 2004, Jessie's night to meet with her book club. They'd all had way too much wine as usual, and after they'd managed a short and boring conversation about the novel most of them hadn't read, a few of the women had walked to a bar close by for another round. That's when she'd seen him. Lucas' future father. But at the time, he was just Peter, a dad whose son was in the same fifth grade class as Madison and Morgan. She'd first met him when they'd both volunteered at a Halloween party at the school, Jessie reluctantly dressed as Cinderella after her daughters had given her a guilt trip about attending in costume. She'd had a laugh with Peter, who was dressed as Batman, and whose son had given him a similar spiel. A former semipro soccer player, Peter stood just a few inches above Jessie's own five-foot, six-inch frame. But she couldn't help but notice the way his broad chest was stretching the fabric of his costume and that his deep olive-green eyes sparkled through the small openings in his mask. She'd heard from the other moms that he stayed home with his son, but worked on the side coaching the local club soccer team and running a summer sports camp. As they crafted cobwebs out of cotton balls, he told Jessie that his wife, Cathy, was an investment banker who spent more time traveling to Tokyo, London, and New York than she did at home.

After the class party, Jessie bumped into Peter regularly, laughing as they'd slammed their car doors shut and clenched their dry cleaning bags or stood in line together at Starbucks. They'd often chat in the school parking lot long after drop-off had ended, Jessie leaning against her van as she spun her hair around her finger, wanting to prolong the moment. There was something about the way Peter remembered small details from their conversations, how he lobbed compliments effortlessly her way. The effects of seeing him would buoy her for hours after, making her step bouncier, her mood lighter. He made Jessie feel like she was interesting and sexy, that she could take on the world.

When she noticed Peter at the bar that night, shooting the eight ball into the corner pocket, and he'd looked up at her, she should have turned and gone home. They'd been teetering on a fine line between friendship and flirtation for months, Jessie forcing herself to push thoughts of Peter aside several times a day or to stop herself from emailing him with yet another wry observation on a topic they both found funny. But when he walked over with a vodka martini piled high with green olives, the drink she'd once told him she loved, and challenged her to a game, she agreed. She'd barely seen Grant lately. He'd been working thirteen hours a day and was so tired when he arrived home—long after dinner was eaten and the leftovers stored in neatly stacked plastic containers in the refrigerator—that he barely had the energy to listen to the girls practice their reading, let alone have a conversation with Jessie. She would often discover him asleep in one of their beds, a chapter book on his chest and one of his daughters snoring softly beside him. And she was sure that if she'd gone home right then, that's where she'd find him.

"Loser buys a round," she'd proclaimed as the other women she'd been with called it a night and started to leave.

"I'll give her a ride," Peter had said, smiling innocently at the moms, whom he also knew from school. He'd come up in conversation more than once among the women, everyone agreeing he was smoking hot, but also that he seemed very happily married. But Jessie knew from her private conversations with Peter—the ones that had eventually transitioned from light bantering about their kids' never-ending homework and rigorous sports schedules to heavier topics like politics and the fragility of marriage—that it was mostly for show, which was very similar to the one she and Grant had been performing lately. Together but not connected—a very precarious place for any marriage to perch.

• • •

Jessie understood now that she'd been a big part of the problem. That she'd let herself, and ultimately her marriage, become a victim of her own insecurities. At some point, she had shifted the responsibility to fix their relationship onto Grant's shoulders, making it even easier to think Peter was the answer to the question she had been secretly asking. At the time, she thought her marital problems were overwhelming, that her dissatisfaction was unique. But what she wished she could tell her thirty-nine-year-old self now was that even though their love wasn't as shiny as it used to be, it didn't mean that it didn't have merit. She realized too late that falling in love was the simple part—it was *staying* in love that seemed to elude most people.

After Jessie lost the third consecutive game of pool, Peter had whispered in her ear, "Want to get out of here?"

Jessie froze. It was one thing to flirt. To fantasize about this moment from the safety of her own bedroom. But to have it within her grasp? It felt surreal. She set her drink down and followed him before she could change her mind.

They drove in silence to a Quality Inn while his warm hand rested on her upper thigh. After securing a room, Peter had offered to buy her another drink in the sad little bar off the lobby, but Jessie shook her head and moved quickly toward the elevator, not wanting to lose her courage, the months of flirtation and lack of sex propelling her on.

Once in the room, she tried to ignore the worn carpet and peeling wallpaper as he did what she imagined him doing for months—ran his hands through her hair and touched his soft lips to hers. One kiss wasn't the end of the world, she told herself as she leaned into his full mouth. When he slipped his hand under her shirt, she reasoned that she wasn't going to let it go any further than that. And when he nudged her to the bed's edge, pulled off her jeans and underwear, and started to make his way inside her, she'd wanted to rip herself away. But she couldn't—not because of how he felt, but because of how he made her feel—beautiful. In that moment, she felt like the layers of her life had been peeled back, exposing the girl she used to be. She felt young and alive.

But that feeling vanished as quickly as it came. As she lay on the bed in Peter's arms, her jeans still bunched around one of her ankles, Jessie wiped a tear from her eye.

"This was a mistake," she'd whispered. Guilt was already fogging her perspective, and what had felt fantastic just moments ago now felt dirty and wrong. It was like a spotlight had just been switched on, a neon sign pointing out the obvious: she'd fucked up. "I need to go home," Jessie said as she frantically put herself back together, Peter watching her silently.

On the drive back, Jessie started making promises to herself. She'd be a better wife to Grant, a better mom to the girls. She'd become an active participant in her life again. Maybe she'd even confess to Grant. She'd read somewhere that telling your spouse you'd been unfaithful only alleviates your guilt, but can hurt them irreparably. And she didn't want to cause Grant any pain. Jessie made a pact with herself. She'd turn her marriage around. Starting the second she left that filthy hotel.

* * *

"Bye, Mom!" Lucas said, the front door slamming behind him.

"Bye, honey!" she called after him as he dribbled the soccer ball in the front yard.

"So what's up?" Jessie asked after the door closed, watching Grant shift his weight from the balls of his feet to his heels. Grant's face had always revealed his emotions, as if they were being painted on with brushstrokes. He knitted his brows and looked at his feet. "Janet and I are getting married."

Six words.

In just six words, Jessie felt her world collapse all over again.

CHAPTER THREE

....

Gabriela pushed her large sunglasses on top of her head as she approached the TSA agent, holding her driver's license in one hand and her carry-on in the other. She averted her eyes from the adorable little girl pulling a bright pink Disney princess suitcase in front of her, focusing on the date on her boarding pass instead.

Almost ten years ago to the day, Gabriela had rushed home from the hospital, her mind sharp and her body energized even though she'd been up twenty-four hours, Lucas' birth injecting new life into her. Something had happened when she'd nestled a swaddled Lucas against her chest for the first time and touched his nose lightly with her fingertip. She'd been hit hard by a thought, one that hadn't occurred to her when Jessie had the girls or when Claire gave birth to Emily twelve years ago. She realized that having a baby wouldn't be her biological choice for much longer. Soon, her body would be making that call.

As Gabriela rocked Lucas, twenty-one inches and seven and a half pounds, with a shock of dark brown hair sticking up from the top of his head, she smiled at an exhausted but radiant Jessie. Jessie had given birth when she was almost forty, so that meant Gabriela could too. But she didn't know how much longer she'd be able to carry a child inside of her. Her body could stop releasing eggs at any time and she could enter menopause. There was something about motherhood no longer being up to her that made her realize that in the back of her mind she'd held on to the small chance of it still happening. And it's what caused her to race home and burst through her front door where she found Colin resting comfortably on the white leather couch she'd already decided they'd have to replace with something sensible, like chenille or micro-suede or whatever stain-proof fabric parents were buying these days. He was holding the most recent issue of *People*, the one that had given her latest novel, *Back to You*, four stars. "Quite a birthday present," Colin said, pointing at the feature and smiling.

"Yes. But I have even bigger news," Gabriela said breathlessly as she threw herself down on the couch beside Colin, placing her head on his lap and looking up at him, noticing that his thick red hair was freshly cut. She hoped their daughter or son would inherit the deep color, along with his math prowess. Gabriela could barely balance the checkbook.

"Okay, I'm listening," Colin said with a laugh, the rich sound that had drawn her to him when they'd first met, immediately calming her. She remembered the first time she'd heard it, she'd been squinting at a map of the London Underground and he'd stopped to help, making a joke that she could navigate the tube a whole lot easier if she wasn't looking at it upside down. She'd glanced up at him, his lanky figure towering over her, his hair falling into his light blue eyes, and she'd giggled, mortified. She never told him, but sometimes, when she heard him offer his laugh to someone else, a small part of her felt betrayed, like he was granting access to a part of himself to which she wanted exclusive rights. "Let me guess. Jessie had another girl, didn't she?" Colin said before she could tell him what she knew he'd been waiting so long to hear.

"Nope, a son, Lucas. I love that name, don't you?"

Colin's face lit up. "It's a great name. Solid. I can't wait to get him out on the soccer field. We needed some testosterone in this group!"

"Maybe we could make one of our own?" Gabriela offered, wrapping her arms around his neck, then continuing before he could react. "I want a baby. I'm ready." The words spilled out faster than she could control them.

"Oh, honey," Colin sputtered after an excruciatingly long silence. Gabriela, with her ear now pressed against his chest, listened to the rapid thumping of her husband's heart and would later tell Jessie and Claire that his quickened heartbeat had answered her question long before he had. When he finally spoke, his slight British accent was almost a whisper, as he explained why he no longer wanted children. That he had waited years for her to change her mind and when she never did, he'd privately mourned the future he wouldn't have as a father and had slowly grown to accept his life without kids. And now he'd be almost sixty when his child graduated from college. Wasn't it too late?

Gabriela had listened in stunned silence to the same arguments she'd given him for so many years, her head spinning at the irony. Maybe that amniotic fluid on her dress had simply gone to her head, she heard him joke, in a desperate attempt to stop the tears she hadn't realized were even falling. And for the first time in their seventeen-year relationship, the sound of his throaty laugh didn't console her in the slightest.

She felt her chest constrict. She wanted a baby. She was ready. *Finally*. And she wondered if he was punishing her, if his resentment over the lost chances to toss a football with his son or go to father-daughter dances with his little girl was now rising to the surface.

"You're not even asking me why?" she heard herself saying, her voice distant. "Don't you want to know the reason I changed my mind?"

Jessie and Claire had often joked over the years that there was nothing Gabriela couldn't talk Colin into, and often credited the fast-talking Latina in her. Her perfectly carved dimples, long chocolate hair, and legs to match didn't hurt her persuasive skills, either.

When he didn't respond, she lifted her head up and forced a smile, feeling pathetic and desperate as she willed her dimples to work their magic. But Colin only shook his head slightly, his downcast eyes speaking the words he couldn't. *I'm sorry*. And in that moment, Gabriela knew he would never change his mind. She felt her insides twist so tight she had to use all of her energy just to breathe. A mixture of rage, disappointment, and fear consumed her as she tried to focus on something to steady the spinning room. Her eyes found their way to a picture of her and her mother, who had passed away when Gabriela was just sixteen, a car accident snatching the precious moments they should have celebrated together, from her college graduation to her wedding day, and now her success as an author. For so many years, Gabriela had convinced herself she was better off without a child, that she'd never want him or her to feel the crushing emptiness of losing a parent much too soon. But when she'd held baby Lucas, she was struck by how she'd let fear rob her of the incredible joy that would have come along with being a mom, no matter how short their time together.

She felt raw and hollow as she jerked her body up from the couch and stared at her husband. How could Colin do this to her? She heard herself yelling—angry, terrible words coming from somewhere deep within her, Colin's eyes wide and brimming with tears—before she finally stormed off, slamming the guest bedroom door so hard the walls shook.

For the next few months, Gabriela spent practically every moment holed up in her office overlooking the Pacific Ocean, where she worked on her latest manuscript about a woman who gets the opportunity to trade her future for just one day with her late mother. This book would change everything for her as an author, would separate her from the pack, would finally put her on the *New York Times* bestseller list, where she'd stay for six months, tripling her future advances, quadrupling the number of foreign countries clamoring for her books. Each day she'd rise before the sun, consult her meticulous outlines, printed on sheets of paper that she tacked to the corkboards lining the walls of her office, making sure no matter how much her heart ached that she hit her word count goal by the time she lay her head down on her pillow each night, vowing that she wouldn't let Colin's *no* take away her ability to express herself on paper.

She'd always been hyperfocused. Her editor, Sheila, had once remarked that she wished she could clone Gabriela, who didn't just meet her deadlines but always got her manuscripts in early. They were so clean the copy editors had an over-under bet to see just how many mistakes they could find, but Gabriela always stumped them with both her grammar and her research prowess. With this novel she threw herself into her writing in a

way she never had before, releasing her pain through her fingertips each day and letting it dance on the page, the stories in her
books always focusing on love, loss, and missed opportunities.

One morning Claire had arrived with two sugar-free ice
blended mochas from the Coffee Bean & Tea Leaf. "You have
not returned my last three calls. This is an intervention!" she'd
declared.

"I'm not avoiding you, I'm just busy," she said to Claire as they
walked into the kitchen, Gabriela slyly shutting her office door
so Claire wouldn't see the chaos: coffee cups stacked high, the
trash can overflowing with takeout containers, papers covering
every surface. Gabriela didn't want Claire to realize she was
practically living in there.

"I haven't seen you since Lucas' baptism," Claire said.

"You know how it is. Deadlines!"

"I get that you're in the middle of writing a book. But it feels
like you're hiding."

Gabriela shoved her sadness down so she could respond
without tearing up. "I'm not, I promise."

Claire reached her hand across the table. "Gabs, this is
me—you don't have to pretend to be strong. Just tell me what
you need."

Claire's steady gaze almost broke Gabriela. But there was
nothing Claire could do for her. She couldn't change Colin's
mind. And the last thing Gabriela wanted was to put another
burden on Claire. She was already spending nearly every day
with Jessie, who was devastated over Grant leaving. "Thank you
for being concerned, but I'm okay. The only thing I need right
now is a run so I can map out my next chapter!"

Most days Gabriela could wake up and take a long jog to
clear her head, plot lines coming together as the sand kicked

up under her feet. Then she'd sprint home to her computer and let the story tumble out of her for hours, the music she listened to on her headphones almost tuning out the sad song looping inside of her.

And it took a few more months after Claire came by, but eventually Gabriela pulled herself together, at least outwardly, rejecting her sweatpants in favor of tailored blazers and patterned scarves, and started meeting Claire and Jessie for coffee again, each time feeling a little less hollow, eventually able to bounce Lucas on her knee as they sipped their cappuccinos.

Gabriela handed her ticket to the TSA agent, who glanced between Gabriela's face and her driver's license rapidly, her eyes lighting up in recognition. "I love your books! They got me through a really bad breakup," she gushed as Gabriela smiled and thanked her for reading. She sensed the energy of the people around her shift upon hearing someone famous may be in their midst. This was LAX, after all. It wasn't uncommon to see Jimmy Fallon placing his laptop into a plastic bin or Emma Stone stumbling while trying to rebuckle the tricky strap on her wedge sandals. "Off to Vegas, huh?" the agent asked as she circled something on Gabriela's boarding pass, and Gabriela nodded. "Business or pleasure?" she pressed, clearly not wanting the conversation to end. And Gabriela had to force herself to engage, to remember there was a time when she would have acted just the same had she seen Judy Blume or one of her other favorite authors. She willed that earnest girl inside of her to claw her way to the surface now.

"Pleasure. I'm celebrating my birthday with friends," Gabriela said as she thought about seeing Claire and Jessie in just a few hours. Over the past year, they hadn't gotten together in person as often as they used to, and despite their constant communication online or over text, Gabriela had felt the distance grow between them. She knew Jessie and Claire were still as close as ever, but she had become busier with work, now under contract to publish two books per year, with daunting deadlines that loomed over her constantly. She hoped this trip would reconnect them and they would fall back into their old rhythms with ease and be reminded of the reasons they'd bonded while working in Gabriela's father's restaurant in college. Claire would engage them in funny stories, her speech slurring a bit more after each drink she consumed; Jessie would play mother hen, making sure they had a glass of water in between each cocktail; and Gabriela would do what she did best—keep the focus of the conversation on them instead of her.

Gabriela smiled, then quickly pulled out an advance copy of her next novel from her tote and handed it to the woman. "Here you go. It's not out for a few months."

"Oh my God. Thank you so much!" The woman's hand flew over her mouth. "By the way," the agent said, then dropped her voice to barely a whisper. "You don't look a day over forty!"

CHAPTER FOUR

....

Claire pushed the gas pedal harder and watched her speed accelerate on the odometer of her convertible, her hair flipping in the hot desert wind. She caught a glimpse of herself in the rearview mirror and laughed. She knew she looked a little ridiculous—like Thelma, or was it Louise?—with her scarf tied over her short blond hair and her round brown eyes hidden behind Jackie-O sunglasses, but she didn't care. She was thankful she not only looked young—her face practically wrinkle free, something she credited to the generous amount of sunscreen she'd applied daily since her teen years—but *felt* youthful too. And she was ready to give fifty a big, fat bear hug. Life was good, she thought as her engagement ring caught the sunlight.

Jessie and Gabriela hadn't been able to make the four-hour drive from Los Angeles to Vegas with her, even though they'd all planned to ride together, hence the rental of the garish, albeit gorgeous, bright red BMW, an homage to the midlife crisis they were *supposed* to be having. Claire had rolled her eyes as she'd scanned the incoming texts on her iPhone yesterday, full of halfhearted apologies and excuses from her friends. Gabriela claimed she had *another* last-minute deadline, something about copyedits and needing to fly so she could have extra time to work on them. Meanwhile, Jessie had just found out Grant was getting married to Janet, and from the moment she'd gotten the news, all she'd wanted to do was curl into a ball and watch Bravo reality TV on a loop.

"Exactly why you should drive out with me. The fresh air will do you good," Claire had argued when Jessie called to say she'd booked a last-minute airline ticket.

"I need some time alone to process everything." Jessie's voice was dull.

"Listen, woman—I've got Lady Gaga, Beyoncé, and Taylor Swift ready for you. We can sing at the top of our lungs about girl power."

"You know I can't hold a tune."

"True. Good thing the I-15 freeway is in the middle of no-where!" Claire joked, referring to the desolate highway to Vegas. When Jessie didn't respond, Claire softened. "Jessie. Come with me. Please. I promise I can make you feel better."

"I can't, Claire. Maybe on the way home?"

"Okay," Claire conceded. "But don't you dare listen to T-Swift without me."

"I promise."

Claire struggled to empathize with Jessie, that she could still hold on to so much pain from something that happened such a long time ago. Perhaps the reason Jessie didn't want to drive out with her was because she suspected Claire couldn't offer her the words she needed to hear right now. From the moment Jessie had confided her secret to her, Claire had been quiet yet supportive, listening to Jessie's *coulda, woulda, shoulda*'s over and over, feeling terrible for her friend as her marriage imploded and Lucas' biological father subsequently shunned all involvement with the son he wouldn't accept as his.

Dick, Claire thought. *There is no other word for that scumbag Peter.*

Claire would never understand how a man could turn his back on his own flesh and blood. Claire's own daughter, Emily, had been heartbroken when her father suddenly became too busy to show up for the important moments in her life. So Claire would always roll her eyes when Jessie would halfheartedly defend Peter's refusal to take responsibility—that he'd been scared shitless of losing the family he already had.

But Grant had raised Lucas as his own, when he could have easily turned *his* back on the boy. Jessie had been lucky in that way, Claire felt. She'd tried to delicately offer this silver lining to her friend more than once over the years, but Jessie seemed to be living in a time warp, unable to move forward. Especially once Janet entered the equation—all five feet ten inches of her. Since then, Jessie had been like a lone piece of luggage on a baggage carousel, endlessly circling around, with no hope of being recovered. Claire decided that this weekend she'd figure out a way to finally pull—no, yank—Jessie off that carousel, even if it meant using some tough love. She couldn't watch her friend waste one more minute of her life looking backward. It's not like she could change the past anyway.

Claire's phone rang and she scrambled to insert her earbud, hoping it might be Jared, her heart catching for a moment when she thought of him bending down on one knee in front of a crowded restaurant a few weeks earlier, Claire still feeling surprised each time she glanced at the ring on her finger.

"Hello?"

"Mom? Where are you? You sound like you're in a tunnel." It was Claire's now twenty-two-year-old daughter, Emily. Claire felt her body go rigid and exhaled slowly, reminding herself she no longer needed to brace herself for a knock-down-drag-out argument. Her relationship with Emily had been rocky over the years—they'd sometimes gone weeks without speaking, but had finally plateaued, the tension sitting untouched between them, like a sleeping snake they didn't want to startle.

"On my way to Sin City in a convertible," Claire yelled over the wind.

"You're so cliché." Emily laughed, and Claire could feel her rolling her eyes. "Is the car red too?"

"Might be." Claire laughed, then blushed deeply.

After a brief pause, during which Claire had decided she definitely looked like a total idiot driving down the freeway in a sports car, no matter how ironic she was trying to be, Emily finally spoke. "It's like you're giving fifty the finger! I like it."

Claire felt herself breathe again. Then let a quiet *fuck* escape from her mouth. Why did she still need her daughter's acceptance so badly?

"So what's up?" Claire finally asked, realizing Emily was waiting for her to respond. Their conversations were still so stilted, both of them trying hard not to trip over an emotional wire.

"I just called to say happy birthday!" Emily said brightly, and Claire felt her eyes get wet, then her warning sensors start to go off.

Was her daughter really calling with no ulterior motive? All signs would point to yes. They'd been in both individual therapy and counseling together for the better part of the last year and they'd made progress. Claire had accepted that Emily had given up on her education and her own responsibility in it. And Emily had become less selfish, more independent. But still. Had her daughter really changed? And even more than that, had Claire?

"And there's something else . . ." Emily's voice trailed off, and Claire gripped the steering wheel tighter. Here it comes.

"How much do you need?" Claire jumped in, working hard to push the sigh out of her voice. Claire could see her therapist's disapproving look so clearly, her pale lips downturned, her gray bob bouncing back and forth as she shook her head. But she didn't care. She wanted to enjoy her birthday weekend, and if loaning her daughter a few hundred dollars was what she needed to do, so be it.

"Are you serious?" Emily's voice turned cold.

"So you don't need money?" The tone of Claire's voice immediately matched her daughter's.

"No, I don't need any money. How could you say that?"

Claire fought her instinct to defend herself and explain that for years, her daughter had *only* called wanting cash, so could she really fault her for thinking that this time?

If you asked Claire, their conflict had started with puberty. If you asked Claire's therapist, it began when Emily's father walked out. And maybe, if Claire was being completely objective, it was a little bit of both. David had bailed when Emily was a newborn, although Claire had seen the signs from the moment Claire announced she was pregnant. They'd only been dating a few months when she found out, but they'd been madly in love, or so she'd thought. When she told him, his face flickered from a frown to a smile so quickly that she convinced herself she'd imagined it.

But then he'd been an hour late to register at the enormous baby department store that had made Claire's stomach turn, the endless aisles of bottles and burp clothes making her so nauseous she had run to the bathroom and splash cool water over her face, her chocolate eyes a stark contrast against her pale skin, her golden hair matted against her damp forehead. Then he'd let the crib box sit on the floor of Emily's nursery for months, Claire's hopes falling a bit more each time she walked by and glanced into the room to see it still there, almost sure at this point that it had become a metaphor for their relationship—a heavy burden no one wanted to deal with.

Eventually, she'd lured Gabriela and Jessie over with a good bottle of wine and they'd laughed as they pieced it together, Claire wearing a tool belt around her expanding belly, feeling more love in that room than she'd ever felt from David.

The final straw was when he'd almost missed Emily's birth, running in just as she gave a final push, excuses spilling from his mouth like someone trying to talk his way out of a speeding ticket. Right then, as he rambled on, she decided she *and Emily* would be better off without him.

"We're better off without you," Claire said as he walked through the door two hours later than expected, his breath reeking of beer and cigarettes. She was pacing the house, bouncing a two-week-old Emily in an attempt to subdue her cries. She'd been fussy all day and Claire was a mess, having slept only three hours the night before. But as she'd worn the carpet down trying to pacify Emily that evening, she'd decided that she'd rather do this alone instead of with someone she couldn't count on.

"I understand." David had nodded stoically and went to the closet to grab his roller bag, causing Claire to wonder if that had been what he wanted all along—for Claire to kick him out. For the guilt to rest at her feet.

Her therapist said because of the tremendous guilt Claire felt and her overcompensation for being a single mom, she had chosen to remove David from her life and then worked too hard to give Emily everything. And without meaning to, she had ended up enabling a very demanding and tantrum-prone child.

After Emily got her first training bra, and then shortly after her period, her behavior moved beyond crying fits at Target over wanting a Barbie doll to slammed doors when Claire asked her to clean her room. It was as if once Emily had breast buds she officially became entitled, demanding designer clothes like *all the other girls* at her school apparently had. Claire gave in, and her daughter dressed like the privileged girls in her class, the only difference being that Emily's expensive jeans and UGG boots were purchased on multiple credit cards that were nearly maxed out. Claire's real estate agent commissions came in like slow waves, and she was constantly strapped for cash, especially after the lending crisis. She often scolded herself for telling Emily's father not to bother with child support, or ripping up the checks he did send sporadically. Jessie and Gabriela had told her it was silly to be so prideful, but Claire insisted she didn't want his money.

"She finesses whatever she wants out of you—can't you see that?" her longtime boyfriend, Mason, asked when he saw Claire's bills piling up.

"I just want her to have the things her friends do. I don't ever want her to feel like she's not good enough."

"She has a mom who loves her so much she's willing to sacrifice pretty much everything for her. Shouldn't that be enough?"

"You don't understand," Claire said, blowing him off. Mason didn't have children of his own and could never fathom how Emily's joy was like a drug to Claire—it gave her a high that she'd do almost anything for.

Claire had been overjoyed when Emily received financial aid to attend Pepperdine, a college they could have never afforded otherwise. Emily's initial excitement over her acceptance was quickly overrun by her needs: an off-campus apartment because she just couldn't live in a dorm room with a stranger and wear flip-flops in a shared shower. She absolutely had to have a new car, because *how could she show up to such a prestigious campus in Malibu in her beat-up Honda?* Claire mentally calculated how much she'd have to take out of her retirement account to make this happen, and from the corner of her eye, watched Mason's jaw tighten as he listened. Later, as they'd gotten ready for bed, he told Claire that if she gave in to Emily's demands—and that had been the word he'd used, *demands*, despite Claire's insistence that Emily was merely *requesting*—their relationship was over.

"I can't sit back and watch you destroy yourself for someone who doesn't appreciate you." Mason sat on the edge of the bed, and Claire suddenly understood he wanted her to choose between him and Emily. "I love Em, I really do. But I hate how she manipulates you—how she uses your guilt as a weapon."

"Are you really asking me to choose? You or her?"

"No. I'm asking you to choose yourself. To free yourself from this ridiculous burden you've been carrying since David left. I'm asking you to let Emily stand on her own two feet and see what happens."

Claire sat down beside him and dropped her head. "What if she falls?"

Mason stood and wrapped his hands around her waist. "Then she'll have to learn how to get back up."

Claire didn't respond, nestling her head into Mason's chest. He always knew the right thing to say. It was what she would miss most when they broke up. Because for Claire, there was never a choice to make—it would always be her daughter. And a year later, Emily rewarded her mother's loyalty and sacrifice by dropping out of college.

"Mom? Are you there?" Claire snapped to attention at the sound of Emily's voice. It caught her off guard sometimes that her daughter still sounded so young.

"Yeah, I'm here. I'm sorry about the money thing."

"It's fine. I guess I could see why you'd go there," Emily admitted. "You know, I'm actually doing really well, in case you were wondering, Mom. I love my new waitressing job and I think I'm going to go back to school. That's what I wanted to tell you. That I found some of my old textbooks and it hit me. I really screwed up, Mom. I'm sorry," Emily said softly.

Claire tried to accept her daughter's apology at face value, instead of reading into it. Claire took a deep breath and said, "I know you are, honey. And I'm happy for you that you want to go back." Despite everything, that's all she wanted, for her daughter to be happy.

After they hung up, Claire thought about Mason. When he walked out, she was sure he'd return, that his love for her would ultimately win out. She'd missed him to the core, his absence creating a vacancy inside of her she wasn't sure she could ever fill. She regretted never letting him marry her, for her stubborn determination never to rely on a man again. After Emily dropped out of college, after Claire had raged at her own mistake— throwing dishes against the wall like someone in a bad television movie—she contacted Mason, chagrined. But it had been too late. He had moved on with someone else.

And she hadn't thought about Mason much since then, until she received his friend request yesterday. She'd stared at his picture for a while, deciding he looked basically the same aside from his eyes—were they sad? And even though she was curious about his life—*was he still living in Southern California? Had he bought that boat he was always talking about? Had he married that woman he met after me?*—she hadn't accepted his request. She was engaged to Jared now, a kind man with a warm smile, whose arms danced when he told stories. She'd met him the year before at a real estate convention, of all places, laughing, despite herself, at a bad joke he made about PMI insurance. So as far as she was concerned, turning fifty meant looking toward the future, not reliving the past.

CHAPTER FIVE

....

"Jessie just texted that she's on her way up to the suite," Gabriela announced to Claire. "Before she gets here, can you tell me how she's *really* doing with the whole Grant thing? And don't feed me some bullshit answer. I know she confides in you."

"Gabriela," Claire began.

"Listen, I know you two are closer than she and I are and that's okay. I'm not feeling left out or anything." Gabriela smiled, but Claire sensed that was exactly how she was feeling.

Claire grabbed the handle of her suitcase and pulled it behind her toward a bedroom and Gabriela followed her in. Claire had held Jessie's secret for years, since Jessie had broken down on the way home from her baby shower, confessing her infidelity as they sat in bumper-to-bumper traffic on the 405 freeway.

The day Grant moved out, Claire and Gabriela flanked Jessie in her driveway, literally holding her up as they watched him heave bags and boxes into his car, Gabriela flinching at the way Grant angrily slammed the trunk and barely glanced at them as he'd backed out of the driveway, thinking his sudden departure and aggressive attitude seemed like an extreme response to Jessie's explanation that they'd grown apart. Claire knew Jessie hated keeping the real reason from her best friend, but it wasn't her story to tell. Plus, she didn't know how she could tell Gabriela that even though a baby was the only thing she desired, Jessie had become pregnant by *mistake*.

Claire had often wished Gabriela knew the truth, so she could have offset some of the weight of the secret onto her. She'd always thought Jessie hadn't given Gabriela enough credit, that despite wanting a baby, she would have put that aside to be there for her friend. "She's not doing well," Claire finally offered as she pulled a sleeveless black blouse and red dress out of her suitcase, debating which she'd wear tonight.

Gabriela sat on the edge of the bed. "I get that he just told her he was marrying Janet, and that must stir a lot of feelings, but they haven't been together for almost *ten years*."

"Not everyone moves on from things the same way," Claire said diplomatically, and Gabriela's stomach tightened. Had her scars from a decade ago healed?

"I don't mean to sound insensitive," Gabriela said. "I just want Jess to be happy."

Before Claire could answer, they were interrupted by the sound of the door opening and Jessie calling out for them. Claire and Gabriela had to stifle their laughter when Jessie mimed an ass grab as she walked behind the cute bellman, only a tiny trace of sadness detectable behind her smile.

"He was so cute!" Jessie said after he left, pressing the pads of her fingers to her cheek. "Too bad I'm old enough to be his mother! I definitely look my age right now—especially after the bomb that got dropped on me yesterday."

"Will you stop? You look amazing!" Gabriela smiled as she handed Jessie a champagne flute, looking at Claire, both of them rolling their eyes, knowing Jessie would never understand how naturally pretty she was. "Do you want to talk about that bomb? Or do you just want to pretend it didn't happen? I'm flexible."

Yes, Jessie thought. *I do, so much. I want to tell you everything. But it's been ten years. Will you ever forgive me for not confiding in you? Or worse, will you hate me for what I've done?* Jessie took a long sip of her champagne and regarded her friend before finally answering. "No, I'll just bring you all down. Let's focus on having fun!"

Gabriela offered Jessie a warm smile to disguise the sting she felt, wondering if Jessie was always going to keep her at arm's length, never letting her all the way back in, but also knowing she only had herself to blame for pulling away so abruptly after Lucas was born. They'd never gotten fully back on track after that; there'd always been a gap between them no matter how hard Gabriela worked to fill it.

"So what are we doing tonight?" Claire asked as she kicked her bare feet up on the coffee table, her freshly painted red toenails shining under the light.

Gabriela rifled through her handbag and pulled out three rectangular slips of paper. "My agent sent these tickets over. Any interest?"

Jessie swiped them out of Gabriela's hand. "Blair Wainright!"

"You like him?" Gabriela smiled, surprised.

"Did you ever see any of his live television specials? He would levitate!" She clapped her hands together, ignoring Claire's eye roll.

"So you are voting yes, then?" Gabriela said as Jessie bobbed her head up and down. "Claire?"

Claire didn't want to go. She imagined them spending her birthday having a nice dinner, maybe going out to gamble after, not watching some celebrity magician.

But as she saw the light turn on in Jessie's eyes, she knew there was no way she was going to let her friend down. "Why not?" Claire forced a smile that turned sincere when she saw the delight reflected in Jessie's face.

Gabriela uncorked another bottle of bubbly. "My agent told me his 'people' sent these to me."

"How would he know you would be here?" Claire asked. "Isn't that sort of creepy? Even for a guy that levitates?" She smirked at Jessie and put her hands under her legs, pretending to lift her.

"Oh, who knows," Gabriela said dismissively. "We probably share a publicist or a manager or something. And for what it's worth, we're in the front row!"

"Woo-hoo," Claire mock-cheered.

Jessie laughed. "Don't be such a skeptic!" She pointed at Claire's champagne flute. "Just keep sipping on that. It will make everything seem fuzzy and magical."

Claire obliged, taking a drink, swiping a copy of *Las Vegas* magazine off the table with Blair's face on the cover, trying to ignore the way his onyx eyes seemed to see right through her.

• • •

Two hours later, the lights dimmed and Blair took command of the stage, levitating several feet into the air, the crowd's cheers almost deafening. He flung himself from trick to trick, pushing a cigarette through a coin, escaping a seemingly secure coffin, and reading the minds of several people in the audience. The theater erupted in applause as the curtain closed, and Gabriela had to admit, whether it was real or not, it had certainly been entertaining. She looked over at Claire, who was barely clapping, and Jessie, who was participating in the standing ovation, and smiled. Despite their difference of opinion about magic, she was glad they were all here together. She'd missed her friends.

A large man in a dark suit told them Blair would like to meet them backstage, then herded the three women into his dressing room. Gabriela scanned the ruby-red walls adorned with pictures of Blair with politicians, A-list movie stars, even Oprah. Several life-size wax statues of Blair were scattered throughout the room. As a famous author, Gabriela had met her fair share of egomaniacs—she'd even been accused of being one herself the other day on Twitter—but she quickly decided that Blair might just be in a league of his own.

Jessie perched on the edge of a butter-yellow leather couch while they waited for Blair. Unlike Gabriela, who was scrolling through her phone as if she were in the waiting room before a dentist appointment, Jessie had never met someone famous, unless she counted the time she literally *ran into* Cameron Diaz while getting into an elevator at Cedars-Sinai, spilling the contents of her purse all over the floor, looking up sheepishly as she grabbed for the tampon that had rolled away from the rest of her things.

Jessie turned to Claire. "So, what'd you think of the show?"

"Magical," she said sarcastically.

"You *still* don't believe?" Jessie asked, incredulous. "Did you not see what he did with that bird?"

"Sorry, Jess, I'm still not a Blair believer," Claire said.

"It's too bad I wasn't able to convert you."

All three women startled at the sound of Blair's voice, following it to the center of the room, where he stood.

Blair walked over and took Gabriela's hand, kissing it softly. "Thank you for coming, Gabriela. And you must be Jessie. And Claire."

Claire offered a nod, while Jessie smiled, her cheeks flushing.

"So, you're a fan of Gabriela's books?" Claire asked, and Jessie recognized her *you are full of bullshit* look that she usually only reserved for street-fair psychics and men who wore skinny jeans. "Because you don't really strike me as the kind of guy who lies by the pool with his nose buried in a novel about women and friendship."

Blair laughed. "You'd be right about that. I'm more of a John Grisham guy," he said unapologetically. "I'm afraid I haven't read any of your books, Gabriela. But my mom and my sister swear by you. Please, sit down, so I can explain why I wanted to meet you." Blair motioned to the couch. "Did you know the heavens gifted us with a solar eclipse tonight?"

Claire pressed her lips together and looked at Gabriela, who shrugged her shoulders. "No?" Jessie finally answered.

"Well, each time one appears, I'm given a special power. And I've chosen to share it with you."

"Isn't a solar eclipse considered a bad omen?" Gabriela asked.

"There are a lot of people who think because the sun disappears and the sky becomes ominous, that they are a bad sign, but they are actually quite magical. Sometimes things aren't always as they seem, Gabriela," he added pointedly. "But I think you already know that." Suddenly, Gabriela pictured her grandmother's face. Was he referring to her *abuela*?

Gabriela remembered how her grandmother would bring out her crystals and tell Gabriela stories about her childhood in Argentina, where they used the elements of the earth to heal their wounds—both the ones they could see and the ones they kept buried inside their souls. Gabriela's mother would walk by and roll her eyes, telling her mom in Spanish to stop filling Gabriela's head with nonsense. But her *abuela* would grab Gabriela's small hand with her own and whisper, "*Recuerde siempre, las cosas no siempre son lo que parecen.*"

Remember, things are not always as they seem.

Claire jumped in. "So what does this eclipse and the supposed power that comes along with it have to do with us?"

"I'm aware you're all here celebrating your fiftieth birthday. Although I must say, none of you look a day over forty-two, forty-three, tops."

"Gee, thanks." Claire shook her head. "So is that it? You want to use this *gift* to save us from getting older? That doesn't take magic. Just a good plastic surgeon."

"No. Aging is the most natural and beautiful thing in the world," Blair said as Claire stared at a framed picture of his barely legal wife posing on the cover of *Las Vegas* magazine. "This isn't about your age, *now*. It's about the year you all turned forty." Blair paused, and the women looked at each other as if to ask what he could possibly know about *that* year.

"What about it?" Gabriela spoke first.

"What if I could send you back there? To 2005?"

"Are you really suggesting you have the ability to make us time travel?" Claire folded her arms across her chest, trying to ignore the nagging feeling in her stomach.

Blaire nodded.

"If you really had that power, wouldn't *that* be what your show was about?" Gabriela asked, trying to steady her pounding heart as she and the other women gave him their best poker faces, none of them wanting to reveal that he was spot-on, that if they could go back in time, it would probably be to that year, when they'd each made choices that altered the course of their lives. Choices that had been weighing heavily on them ever since.

"It's not that simple. I can only use this gift each time a solar eclipse appears, every 177 days. But if you're not interested in this opportunity, we can agree to end this conversation right now and I'll suggest a hip new nightclub where you can spend the rest of the evening. There are a lot of really cute *young* guys there too." Blair gave them a knowing look as he walked to the door and started to open it.

Gabriela thought back to the bellhop. Could it be possible Blair was referring to him? What else did he know about them? Gabriela considered the baby she never had. Jessie's mind flashed to her one-night stand and the end of her marriage. Claire thought of her mother and clutched the edge of the soft leather couch in an attempt to squeeze the thought away, focusing instead on her daughter, Emily. 2005 had been the year when Claire had really started to lose her when their relationship had begun to unravel like a loose thread on a sweater.

"Wait," Jessie finally said, standing up quickly. "I would go back in a heartbeat." She thought of Grant. She wouldn't be able to take back what she did, but maybe she could convince him to stay?

Blair released his hand from the doorknob. "Okay. We have one taker. Claire?"

"No way," Claire scoffed, and looked at Gabriela for support, surprised when she wouldn't meet her gaze.

Gabriela thought about Colin. There had been so much gut-wrenching pain after he said he didn't want children. It had taken her so long to get over it. And even with ten years of experiences, maybe she somehow would be able to come up with the right words to convince him to have a baby the second time around.

"Why not, Claire?" Jessie frowned. "If we have a chance to make better choices, how could it hurt?"

Claire chose her words carefully. "Do I wish I had made some different decisions? Sure. And there are things I regret." Claire paused, meeting Gabriela's knowing look. *Many things.* "But, honestly, my life is finally where I want it to be. I'm getting married. Emily and I are in a good place. Why would I go back?"

"How about for me?" Jessie chewed on her lower lip.

"And me." Gabriela surprised herself. She hadn't meant to say what she'd been thinking. Or had she?

"You guys really want this?" Claire felt a pinch in her gut as they both nodded vigorously.

"What about your mom? Don't you want to see her?" Gabriela asked Claire gently. Claire felt her chest constrict. She was sure Gabriela would do anything for the chance to see her own mother again.

Memories piled on top of each other in Claire's mind. But with each thought, she felt only pain. She couldn't go through that again.

"Claire." Jessie said her name softly. "If you aren't sure, then stay. Gab and I will go."

"Actually, it doesn't work that way," Blair interjected. "If you don't all agree, then none of you can go."

"Why?" Jessie asked.

"This is a journey that must be taken, and *completed*, together," Blair offered, then added quickly, "And if you do all make the choice to go back, you'll have exactly one year—until midnight on Claire's forty-first birthday."

"And then what?" Gabriela asked.

"You'll have to decide if you want to stay and live the new life you've created."

"And what if one of us wants to stay but the others don't?" Jessie asked, already knowing the answer.

"You all have to choose to stay or I'll see you right back here again—in June 2015."

"Please, Claire," Jessie pleaded. "Think about the things we could change not just in our lives but in the world. Imagine all the disasters we can prevent."

"I have to stop you there," Blair said gently. "Unfortunately, that won't be possible. You won't have the power to make major changes to the course of history. Just your own." He glanced at Claire. "And of course, the people closest to you. Your choices will impact their lives too."

"Oh," Jessie said, frowning at Claire.

"And one more thing," Blair said.

"There's more?" Claire rolled her eyes.

"You can't use this ability to time travel for easy money."

"So I shouldn't run out and buy a ton of Apple stock?"

Blair shook his head. "Nope. And no lotteries or betting on sporting events either."

"Well that's no fun!"

"That's not the point anyway. Right, Claire?" Jessie said.

Claire sighed. She always had such a hard time saying no, especially to Jessie. But there had to be a *limit* of things she was willing to do for *other people's* happiness.

Blair's eyes bored into hers. "You are right, there is a limit. But maybe you need to go back to realize what that is."

Claire felt an electric current run down her arms and out through her fingertips. How had he known what she'd been thinking?

"So there's only one way to find out if this is real. Say yes," Blair said.

Gabriela took a deep breath. "I'll go."

"Me too," Jessie said, forcing the negative what-ifs from her mind, deciding to focus on the positive one. *What if* she could convince Grant to forgive her?

Claire looked at her friends. She had to admit her resolve was falling away, now that Blair answered the question she hadn't even asked out loud. She focused on her engagement ring. There was a chance she wouldn't meet Jared again. But she had no way of knowing that for sure. She might not repair her relationship with Emily this time. But what if she handled it differently, so that it never broke apart in the first place? And there was her mom. What if Claire could change *her* fate? And at the end of the year, she could be the holdout, the one who made them come back here. She looked at Jessie, who'd been her very best friend for three decades. She'd seen the remorse about what she had done with Peter eat her alive for years. And she knew that Gabriela, despite her career success, carried regret around with her like an extra limb. So she decided to do what she did best. Sacrifice. "Okay. I'll do it for you guys. Isn't that what friends are for?" she heard herself say, and squeezed Jessie's and Gabriele's hands tight.

CHAPTER SIX

·············

June 2005

"Jessie?"

Jessie heard her name but it sounded muffled and distant.

"Jessie?" the soft voice asked again.

Jessie's head was pounding, like someone was drilling a jack-hammer into her skull. She reached up to touch her temples, but her arms were like two deadweights at her sides. She must have had too much to drink last night. Blair Wainright's dark eyes suddenly materialized in her mind and she forced the image away. Had he drugged them? Maybe he'd given them roofies, or what was that other one? Special K? Where were Gabriela and Claire? Were they okay?

"Can you hear me?" The voice seemed closer now and was more persistent, firmer.

Jessie nodded, or at least she *thought* she was moving her head up and down. Then there was the weight of a hand on her wrist and something cold against her chest. And her eyelids were being pried open, a searing yellow light blinding her. "What are you doing?" Jessie's voice was hoarse and her mouth incredibly dry.

"I'm checking your vitals," a blurry figure responded.

"Gabriela? Claire?" Jessie asked the out-of-focus shape.

"No, my name is Cindy. I'm on the third rotation—morning shift. We met yesterday, but I don't expect you to remember. You were pretty out of it."

Jessie thought hard. Yesterday? Yesterday she'd been flying to Vegas to meet her friends. They'd had champagne, a lot of it. Then they'd been at the Blair Wainright show. And then after, they were . . . "Was I drugged?"

"Well, yes, that's what you said you wanted?" The voice responded as if it was the most normal thing in the world to request.

I asked Blair Wainright to drug me? Jessie tried to remember what happened after they'd all squeezed hands, but she couldn't.

"Where are Gabriela and Claire?"

"Oh, your friends? They were here last night, but they left," Cindy said, and as Jessie squinted at her, the lines of her face becoming more clear—it was heartshaped and her cheeks were covered with freckles. Who was this woman?

"Can you sit up?"

"Left? Where did they go?" Jessie tried to force her body into an upright position, but her muscles felt atrophied. How long had she been out? She closed her eyes then opened them again.

"I have no idea. Home maybe?"

Why would Gabriela and Claire leave her in Vegas? Jessie heard the sound of a motor and her bed began to move as items in the room started to take shape. She saw a poster with the numbers one to ten and a pain scale, then a dry erase board with several names listed—then balloons, and flowers, lots of flowers. She felt a pinch as she moved and saw a bag with fluid and followed it to an IV taped to the back of her hand. "I'm in the hospital?" Jessie's voice was shaking.

"I'm going to call the doctor," Cindy, presumably a nurse, said as she pressed a button. Her hair was pulled back with a clip and part of her bleached blond hair was sprouting out of the top of it. She was wearing light blue scrubs with tiny pink and yellow flowers on them that made Jessie feel dizzy if she stared at them too closely.

"I'm sorry, I don't understand why I'm here." Jessie felt her adrenaline start pumping. Blair Wainright had drugged them and then, had he . . . "Did something bad happen to me?" Jessie stammered.

Cindy poured water into a small plastic cup and held it out to Jessie, eyeing her skeptically. "You really don't know why you're here?" she asked as she pressed two pills into Jessie's palm. "Take these."

"What are they?"

"Just some Tylenol. We don't want your fever to return," Cindy said, frowning at her. "Jenny, the nurse who was with you on the night shift, said it spiked at one hundred and three, but"—Cindy flipped through some papers on a clipboard—"according to your chart, it seemed to break a few hours ago, thank goodness!" She laughed nervously.

"I don't remember that," Jessie said softly as a tear began to fall out of the corner of her eye, unable to mask the panicked feeling that was quickly consuming her. Why couldn't she remember anything and why had Gabriela and Claire left her? "I need my iPhone please—it has a polka-dot case and a screen-saver of my twin daughters in the stands at a UCLA football game. And where is my purse? It had my wallet and my iPad in it."

Cindy gave her a quizzical look. "I'm not sure what you mean by an eye phone, but if you want to make a call, there's a phone right next to you on the table. And as for eye pads, I can get you a cloth to remove your mascara."

Jessie laughed. "Okay, is this some kind of joke? I said iPad not eye pads? You know, the tablet? Apple?"

Cindy bit her lower lip and thought for a moment. "Why don't you wait for the doctor and we'll get this all sorted out," she offered, and watched Jessie finally swallow the pills. She would have done anything to make the pounding behind her temples stop. "I want him to take a quick look at you."

"Jess? I didn't realize you were awake," Grant said as he walked into the room, placing a soft kiss on her lips. "Did I hear you talking about Steve Jobs?"

"What are *you* doing here?" Jessie asked, ignoring his question. "Oh God, you're still on my emergency contact list . . ." Jessie trailed off as another tear escaped from her eye, rolling over the side of her nose. Mortified that her ex-husband had to come bail her out, she wanted to crawl under the covers and disappear, suddenly sickened by her inability to move forward, at her naïveté last night. Tomorrow she was going to start therapy. Claire had a psychologist she swore by—she'd get her number. She was going to get over Grant *finally*.

"You doing okay?" Grant perched on the edge of the bed as he widened his eyes at the nurse and Jessie felt something familiar about the moment, as if she were experiencing déjà vu. "The girls want to see you, but I told them to wait with my mom."

"They didn't need to come home from college for this!"

Grant squinted at her as if he didn't understand what she'd just said.

"I've called the doctor," Cindy interrupted. "Your wife seems surprised she's in the hospital. Keeps asking for her friends, Claire and—" The nurse stopped as if she was searching for the name.

"Gabriela," Jessie and Grant said together.

"She's asked for some things too. Tablets and eye pads?" Cindy continued as if Jessie wasn't in the room.

"Ex-wife," Jessie said, embarrassed by the nurse's mistake. It had been a decade. And now he was marrying someone else. Janet would claim that title now. For years, it had been Jessie and Grant, Grant and Jessie. Now it would be Grant and Janet. She knew those words would never slip off her tongue easily, no matter how many therapy sessions she endured. The worst part? Jessie had a feeling Janet would never make the same mistakes she did—that she'd hold on to him tightly. If Grant didn't want to have sex with her, she'd sit him down and work it out, not let it fester like a tumor.

"I'm sorry, did you divorce me in your sleep or something?" Grant pressed his lips together, unsure whether to smile or frown. And as Jessie stared at him, she realized he had his hair—*all of it*. It was dark brown and full and slightly long around the ears, *not gone*. He wasn't bald. And he was also softer around the middle—the way he *used* to be. As she eyed the fabric of his golf shirt stretching over his belly, it triggered a memory—she remembered the way it felt to wrap her arms around Grant's doughy stomach, the way it cushioned her own imperfections. She had friends who complained about their husbands' bodies— why couldn't they go to the gym or play basketball? Jessie would always stay silent, bobbing her head up and down to support them, not ever revealing that she secretly loved Grant's imperfect physique.

As Jessie watched Grant, his khaki slacks wrinkled as if he'd slept in them, her hand flew to her mouth in realization. She lifted up the bedsheet and felt her belly, slightly deflated, but not as hard, just as another nurse pushed a bassinet into the room with a baby in it. It was wearing a little white long-sleeve T-shirt and diaper and had a blue-and-pink-striped hat on its head. On the side of the glass, a sticker read *Hi, my name is Baby Lucas: 8 pounds, 10 ounces. Born 6-02-05.* "Oh my God!" Jessie marveled at the sight of her one-day-old son.

"Jess?"

"I'm okay, just obviously a little out of it . . ."

"You started running a fever as soon as we got you into the room after the delivery. You were talking in your sleep the whole time."

"What was I saying?" Jessie eyed Lucas as the nurse picked him up, aching to hold him.

"Oh, mostly gibberish, but you did keep calling out for someone named Blair?" Grant let out a strange laugh and she couldn't tell if he thought it was funny or not. "You're not cheating on me, are you?" he added, his smile still resting on his lips.

Jessie felt the color drain from her face as she searched Grant's for more information. Did he know more than he'd let on last time? Was this his way of testing the waters? Satisfying that nagging feeling he'd been having all along? Or was she simply overthinking things because she really had been unfaithful? She'd wanted to come back here so badly, but she hadn't thought through how heavy the burden of her secrets would feel again.

"I am most definitely not cheating on you with someone named Blair!" Jessie said. "I was obviously delirious from the fever," she added before he could respond, pulling him in as closely as her IV would allow, digging her head into the cushion of his chest that she had missed so much, wondering why she ever thought she could replace him. As the nurse placed Lucas against her breast and she buried her nose in his neck, she thought of Blair Wainright again. For whatever reason, he had given her another chance. And she was determined to get it right this time.

• • •

Gabriela awoke in the darkness, her head pounding. Was this what a migraine felt like? She was thankful for the thick curtains on the window of her hotel room, knowing the fiery Las Vegas sun would *not* help the ache inside her skull. What time had they gotten back to the suite the night before? As she swung her legs over the edge of the bed, Blair's claims about time travel began to flash in her head like scenes from a hazy dream. She couldn't believe she had fallen for his story. *Magical solar eclipse my ass*, Gabriela thought as she heard a phone start ringing. She scrambled to grab it, but realized it wasn't hers. It was someone's archaic BlackBerry. She hadn't seen one of these in a long time. Gabriela pushed a series of buttons, trying to remember how to answer it, and finally heard Jessie's voice.

"I'm in the hospital!"

"What?" Gabriela stood up and nearly collapsed, her legs wobbly as she tried to find a light switch. But then she remembered how the cute bellman stressed that the hotel suite was high-tech—so much so that there were no light switches. Hadn't he showed them a remote control that operated *everything*? Where the hell was it? "What happened? Why are you at the hospital?"

"I'm fine. Better than fine, I'm fabulous. Gab . . ." Jessie paused, and Gabriela thought she heard a baby crying in the background.

"Jess . . ."

Jessie lowered her voice to a whisper. "It worked, Gabriela. We're back in the year 2005. I had Lucas yesterday. Do you hear him? God, I forgot how little his hands were. His smell is so delicious. And my girls, they're so young again!" She looked at her ten-year-old twins, sitting on the edge of her bed looking wide eyed at their baby brother, their long ash-blond hair pulled into ponytails tied with pink bands. She'd forgotten how girly they'd once been, wearing tutus or dresses no matter what the weather and never leaving the house without their hair accessories.

"But I'm still in Vegas?" Gabriela said just as she stubbed her toe against a hard object. "Fuck!"

"No, you're not. At least I don't think so. Wait. Why don't you know where you are?"

"Because it's dark as hell in my room. I'm trying to find the remote control for the lights, or even the door!" Just then her hand felt the knob and she turned it. "Okay, so you're saying—" Gabriela stopped midsentence and looked around squinting at the sunlight streaming in through a skylight in the hallway.

"Well?" Jessie asked.

"I'm at my house, well, my old place. The one we were living in before . . ."

"You made all that crazy money off your book and moved to The Strand in Manhattan Beach."

"Yes," Gabriela whispered, and slid to the floor, gripping the phone that she now realized was hers, her palm sweaty as her mind started computing. "You said Lucas was a day old, right? So that means I may have already told Colin I want a baby. I remember I slept in the guest room that night because I was so mad at him. And that's where I am now." Her voice broke. "It's too late—he's already said no."

"Gab. You don't know that. Maybe you haven't told him yet. Maybe you aren't remembering it right."

Gabriela knew she was remembering it exactly right. Still, to this day, she could recall every word, every look, every feeling from the moment she decided she was ready to the second he shook his head and said *I'm sorry.* "It's too late," she repeated.

"Gabriela, don't say that. Maybe you've been given this chance so you can figure out another way to convince Colin."

Gabriela felt a flash of hope spike in her heart. "Maybe."

"Not maybe! Yes! I don't think we would have been chosen to come back if we didn't have the ability to change things."

Gabriela nodded to herself. Jessie had a point—Gabriela was not going to take no for an answer this time, not when she knew what her future looked like. "So what was it like to see Grant?"

"Crazy! He looks so different, but I like it better. He's the old him." Jessie thought back, remembering that he was just making it big as a freelance architect, his work having been recognized in *House* magazine. He'd been so excited and it had created so many opportunities—ones that he refused to turn down. But that also meant he was home much less. "The one who used to love me." Jessie's voice went quiet.

"He will again," Gabriela said. "You'll see."

"God, I hope you're right."

"I'm scared to see Colin. What if I say all the wrong things to him and make everything worse?"

"You'll be fine. But be careful—don't rush the conversation until you figure out what's happened so far, because everything you say or do can impact our future. Remember that horrible movie with Ashton Kutcher?"

"*The Butterfly Effect?*" Gabriela scoffed. "That movie was two hours of our life we'll *never* get back!"

Jessie couldn't help but laugh.

"Although maybe we *can* get it back by not watching it this time!" Gabriela added.

"True, but maybe we could consider it research. Remember how anything he said or did differently changed everything else? Even the smallest changes had consequences?"

"Oh God. You're right. We need to be careful." Gabriela remembered the way Blair ran his hand over his slicked-back hair when he talked about magic. Blair had told them they could only impact their own orbit, but still. That pressure alone was frightening.

Gabriela let out a long breath, scanning the guest room, feeling much like a guest herself. The stark white linens on the bed, the angular side tables and empty dresser top—couldn't she have placed a vase, a picture, *anything* on top to personalize it?—made it seem cold, uninviting, the opposite of what the room should be. Was that the person she had been? She reached up for the necklace she always wore, the one that had belonged to her mother, and fingered it delicately, relieved it was still there. It was the only thing in her life that represented her; everything else was packed away in boxes in the back of a closet because she found it too hard to look at. She slowly stood up, her feet still unsure beneath her, and tiptoed down the hallway to the master bedroom, holding her breath as she looked inside. But all she saw was a neatly made bed.

"But don't worry, Gab, we won't screw our lives up, at least not any worse than we did last time!" Jessie announced, her chipper tone startling Gabriela, who had been so deep in thought.

"You're not scared?" Gabriela asked.

"I'm scared shitless. I'm not sure I remember how to do this," Jessie answered without hesitation. But as she looked at Lucas and her daughters playing with his tiny toes, she felt hopeful. "So far, the only downside I see is that I won't get to find out what happens next season on *Scandal*," Jessie said, a smile in her voice.

Gabriela exhaled, wishing that really was the only downside, because they both knew it wasn't. "So what is the hottest TV show this year anyway? *Desperate Housewives*?"

"I think so," Jessie answered, thinking those women with secrets might be able to teach her a thing or two.

"Wait! Have you heard from Claire?" Gabriela asked, suddenly frightened she hadn't made the journey with them. But then Blair's words replayed in her mind—it was all of them or none of them.

"No, I haven't. I'm going to hang up and call her," Jessie said. "Do you know her number? I can't find it stored in this ancient BlackBerry of mine. How the hell did people function before smartphones? I feel like I'm in the Middle Ages!"

Gabriela laughed. "No clue. I can't even remember the last time I dialed an actual phone number! Colin always told me it would bite me in the ass that I didn't have anyone's number memorized. Guess he was right."

"I only remembered yours because it's so easy. The last four digits being 4444." Jessie smiled as Lucas made a sound and she smoothed his thick patch of dark hair. "And I think there's something about the old-school way of doing things that I some-times miss. Maybe being back here will slow us down, teach us to appreciate the little things?"

"Uh-huh. You say that until you want to text someone, but realize you'll have to scroll through three letters each time you want to type one!"

"Whatever! You just get over here. I need you!"

"Remind me. What hospital did you deliver at?"

"Cedars-Sinai."

"Okay, see you soon," Gabriela said. She got dressed quickly then sighed with relief when she found her keys dangling from a hook in the kitchen, where she'd always kept them. She slid into the driver's seat and reached to select the hospital in her GPS, but found only a CD player, the black leather case filled with her favorite music resting on the passenger seat of her 2000 BMW. "Fuck it," she sighed. "I'll just stop and ask for directions like they did in the old days."

• • •

When Claire had first woken up with an intense pounding in her skull, she reached for the aspirin she always kept in her purse, but her bag wasn't there. She gasped as she felt movement beside her, her stomach twisting in fear. Had she slept with someone last night? No, she wouldn't have done that to Jared. But the last thing she remembered was standing in Blair's dressing room, squeezing her friends' hands tightly, sure they'd pop their eyes open moments later, their feet still firmly planted on the golden carpet, shaking their heads at their gullibility. As she adjusted to the darkness in the room, she started to swivel her head slowly to see who was lying next to her, her heart thumping so hard she was sure whomever was beside her could hear it. She'd felt something catch inside her as she took in Mason's profile.

Was she really back here?

The last time she'd seen him had been a few weeks after he'd given her the ultimatum regarding Emily, when he'd come back to retrieve his things from her house. Their conversation had been brief and distant, like two strangers on an elevator discussing which floor they needed to get off on. And that had been it.

And now he was back in her bed, snoring softly. She looked at him again, taking in the dimple in his chin and his slightly crooked front teeth, just visible between his lips. He hated them, but she thought the flaw gave him character.

She slipped out from under the floral comforter and looked at it with fresh eyes. Why had she ever thought a pattern that looked like her grandmother's curtains had been a good idea? And then it hit her. *Emily*.

She was about to see her daughter as a young girl again, with braces and dots of acne sprinkling her forehead. She felt a surge of excitement as she hurried to Emily's bedroom and flung open her door. Then she heard herself scream. *She's not here.*

"What happened?" Mason materialized at her side, wearing only a pair of white boxer briefs.

Claire looked away quickly. "Where is Emily?" She started shaking and ran her hands over her bare arms. Had traveling through time screwed up her life in such a way that she wasn't Emily's mom anymore? But Emily's room was still the way Claire remembered it. A pink-and-turquoise-blue-striped comforter covered her four-poster bed. A *High School Musical* poster was taped to the wall. A CD player sat on her nightstand with a stack of discs a foot high next to it.

"You said she was at your mom's?" Mason's statement came out more like a question and Claire felt herself start to breathe again. She hurried back to her room and searched for her cell phone. She needed to see the date, to be sure this was really happening, that it wasn't some terrible dream. She did a double take when Mason walked over and handed her a silver Nokia phone with a tiny screen and a small keypad, the skin between her eyes creasing as she stared at it.

"Are you okay?" Mason studied her face.

Claire nodded dismissively and pressed a button.

"You're acting like you've never seen that thing before. Which is funny, because you had it glued to your hand last night!" He laughed. "Do your clients ever give you a moment of peace? Or your mom, for that matter? She must have called three times to update you about Emily."

Claire was hit with a memory of the night she'd first slept with Mason, also their first date. It was the same evening Jessie had Lucas. Claire had left the hospital and called him after listening to the sweet voice mail message he'd left only hours after the party, asking her out.

And Claire had thought, why not call him? Emily was at her grandma's. And he was so cute—tall and sturdy with deep dimples and soft brown eyes that made her knees wobble. They'd met for a drink, which led to several, and then she'd boldly invited him over.

She caught her reflection in the mirror hanging on the wall. Her hair was much longer and blonder than she remembered and sticking out in several directions. When she reached up to smooth it, she squinted at her appearance. Ten years had been stripped off her face, and as she ran her hand over her toned arms, she couldn't believe how strong she felt. She remembered how *old* she'd felt at forty, how much energy motherhood had taken when Emily was younger. After she and Mason broke up, it had been all her again, and she hadn't realized how much she'd leaned on him. How many lunches he'd packed and homework assignments he'd helped Emily complete when Claire had been working late. Even though she told him she didn't want to marry him and they didn't live together, he was almost always there. It was the hardest right after he left, when Claire would have to haul herself out of bed, averting her eyes from the side Mason used to sleep on, and help Emily get ready for school, pulling the refrigerator open and realizing they were out of lunch meat, noticing her daughter's open math book resting on the table, only half the problems finished. Then, finally, after Emily's bus would pull away, Claire would often crawl back into bed and sleep for another hour before she'd have to show her first house.

"What's today's date?" she asked Mason.

"June third," Mason answered as he pulled on his jeans and Claire tried not to gape. She'd forgotten how tall he was, how when she'd rest her head against him, she'd barely graze his chin.

"What year?" Claire frowned.

Mason cocked his head to the side. "I think you had a bit too much to drink last night."

"Just tell me—is it 2015? Is the president Barack Obama?"

"Who?" Mason frowned. "Claire, you know it's 2005, right? And the president is George W. Bush."

Claire felt her stomach sink to the floor. *This is real.*

"Claire?" Mason walked over to her. He'd put on a shirt, but it was still unbuttoned, exposing his toned stomach. She used to love running her hands over it, feeling the ridges of his abs. She eyed it now, her fingers buzzing, wanting suddenly to touch it again. But then she thought of Jared. What would he say if he could see her, standing next to her ex-boyfriend wearing nothing but an old faded LA Lakers T-shirt?

"Yes, of course," Claire managed. "Sorry, just a little out of it."

"Well, if I hadn't witnessed you taking that final double tequila shot when they announced last call, I'd be worried I might have hooked up with some crazy chick! But I'd be out of it too, if I were you." Mason laughed and wrapped his arms around her, kissing her deeply before running his hands up under her shirt.

Claire wondered if it was still considered cheating if she technically hadn't met Jared yet in this life.

Her phone rang and she pulled away from Mason gently, smiling shyly and tugging her shirt back down. "Sorry, I need to answer this."

He flashed her a smile, his eyes dancing with anticipation. "Hello?"

"Claire! It's so good to hear your voice! Are you okay?" Jessie asked.

Claire looked at Mason and she felt fluttering in her stomach and attempted to picture Jared's wiry, sandy-colored hair and mint eyes. The same ones she'd peered into the morning she left for Las Vegas right before he loaded her luggage into the backseat of the convertible. "This is crazy," she answered, and stepped into the bathroom, stealing another glance at Mason before she closed the door behind her. "Where are you? Where's Gabriela?"

Jessie filled Claire in on all she knew.

"So what now?" Claire whispered as she pulled down the toilet seat and sat on it.

"We try to fix the things we broke the first time."

"I don't know, Jess, I'm not sure it was the right choice to come back here." Claire looked down at her bare legs, grabbed her robe off the back of the door, and wrapped it around her, cinching it tightly. "You two wanted to change your own fate. But what if I'm here because I'm tasked with changing someone else's?" Claire sighed, thinking of her mother, Mona. When presented with the opportunity last night, she found she couldn't resist the chance to see her again. But now that she was perched on a toilet in the house she'd lived in ten years ago, she had no idea where to begin.

"Well, you're here now, Claire. And maybe changing your mom's fate is the first step in changing your own."

"I don't know. I think a few more sessions with my therapist rather than time travel would have sufficed," Claire joked, but underneath her laugh she was worried.

"Okay," Jessie conceded. "I get that this is super complicated. But personally, I'm grateful for this chance to rewrite my past."

Claire thought back to Mason's kiss, how it sent shockwaves to her toes. It felt so good, and so bad, all at the same time. "If we are trying to make things right, then why does it already feel so wrong?"

CHAPTER SEVEN

....

Gabriela waved good-bye as she backed out of the hospital room. Jessie held Lucas tightly against her chest, as if she were afraid he'd be snatched out of her arms, literally, by the hands of time. For the past hour, Gabriela had studied Jessie's wide grin as she brushed Madison's bangs away from her face and Morgan leaned across her lap, their newborn brother between them. Gabriela couldn't remember the last time she'd seen her friend smile so sincerely.

Gabriela had finally made her way to the hospital. It had taken her an hour, but with the help of an old map in her glove compartment, she was able to chart her route. She'd rushed from the car to the front doors, but then she'd slowed her pace, tentatively making her way toward the maternity ward, down the maze of long hallways, all identical with their gleaming white floors and fluorescent lights. She'd willed herself not to look in the open doorways, feeling like a voyeur spying on private moments she shouldn't see.

She'd been both scared and excited to see her friends again, knowing that laying eyes on them and *the baby* would prove that this *had* really happened. She'd finally found a sign pointing toward Jessie's room number, just past the hospital nursery lined with bassinets full of tiny swaddled babies. Gabriela had expected to keep walking, but her feet had other ideas, firmly anchoring her in front of the glass wall, forcing Gabriela to look inside. She'd studied the newborns, instantly imagining her own daughter, a long dark braid dangling down her back as she maneuvered across the monkey bars. She'd always had a feeling she and Colin would've had a little girl, and she'd have named her Bella. But she'd never told Colin, or anyone, about that premonition. Saying those things out loud would seem desperate and borderline crazy. Instead, she'd buried the thought, pushing it down until it finally settled in the place where she hid the things that hurt her most. But it worked its way to the surface today, and the name Bella echoed through her mind.

As she stared at the newborn babies, Gabriela began to feel daringly hopeful about her second chance. Instead of shutting down when she didn't get what she wanted, what if she *showed* Colin why having a child was so important to her—and why it would be so good for *them*?

She already knew how the next ten years without a baby were going to play out—they wouldn't involve biannual trips to places like Morocco and Johannesburg as Colin had predicted, her writing deadlines often making it impossible to leave the States for any stretch of time, unless it was to visit briefly one of the countries that had published her book. And they definitely wouldn't include regular sexcapades on the kitchen floor as he'd also promised. She remembered at one point when she'd been begging him to reconsider the baby, long after they should've gone to bed, their red eyes burning, their voices hoarse, Colin had brought their sex life into it. It had always been good, but predictable: once a week on average, missionary, sometimes spicier if he'd had a couple pints of Guinness beforehand. He'd looked at her and said, "And don't forget, another benefit of being kid-free is we can have sex *anywhere!*" Then he'd thrown his hands into the air, adding, "even on the kitchen floor." He'd been referencing one of Gabriela's favorite movies, *When Harry Met Sally*. But he'd gotten the context wrong and Gabriela's eyes had been so clouded with tears she could barely see him, her voice so dry from crying she couldn't speak. She'd just stared at him. *But they never did "do it" there. That's the whole point. The guy broke up with Meg Ryan's character and married someone else.*

When she had walked into the hospital room, she found Grant sitting on the edge of the bed as Jessie breast-fed Lucas. Gabriela leaned against the doorframe, shocked to see the years peeled away from both of them. Jessie's eyes were brighter and her hair was shorter and a darker blond. She remembered when Jessie made the rash decision to chop seven inches off her long locks in her sixth month of pregnancy, then immediately regretted it, sobbing that it was a "mom cut" that made her bloated face look like a bowling ball. But it had grown out since then and really suited her petite facial features. And Grant's face was fuller, and his hair—it was still years before his hairline would begin to recede—was all there. Grant caught her staring, his unlined eyes taking in the look on her face, thinking it was meant for Lucas. "He's pretty amazing, isn't he?"

Gabriela nodded. When she first saw her own younger face that morning, she'd been mesmerized, studying it from every angle, feeling as if her reflection was a picture of herself she'd posted on Facebook for throwback Thursday. She'd run her hands over her smooth, supple skin, still untouched by Botox or fillers, things she would come to rely on in just a few years, often scrutinizing herself to the point that Colin would hide the magazines when she appeared in them and accidentally "delete" her TV appearances off the DVR, always stressing that she was aging gracefully and there was no reason to be comparing herself to women in their twenties. But she couldn't help it, especially because her mother had been the most naturally stunning woman in the world to Gabriela, her beauty freezing in time when she died at thirty-eight. Gabriela sometimes stared at her photo and tried to picture her mother aging, but couldn't imagine so much as a line on her face.

Gabriela had nearly collided with Claire at the hospital entrance, the bright sun momentarily blinding Gabriela as she'd searched for her sunglasses. They'd regarded each other with quiet awe, whispering and giggling like two teenagers with a secret. Gabriela filled her in on what was happening in Jessie's room. That they hadn't been able to get more than a few minutes alone because Grant was hovering over the baby. Finally, they sent him on a mission to find a tabloid magazine Jessie said she just *had to read*, agreeing they'd meet up to talk in more detail after Jessie was released the next afternoon. Claire quickly brought Gabriela up to speed on her own morning—waking up next to a very naked and (how had she forgotten?) well-endowed Mason. Then her smile faded and she confided to Gabriela that she thought coming back had been, pardon the pun, a *huge* mistake, and she needed to get the hell out of there fast. That she hadn't thought things through when she'd agreed. She had let Jessie's unbridled enthusiasm get the best of her in the moment.

As she listened, Gabriela felt her unborn baby start to slip away. If one of them wasn't resolute in being here, did that mean they would all have to go back? But Gabriela didn't want to push Claire. She thought of Colin, and decided that wasn't the approach she wanted to take with *anyone* this time. She'd have to be more subtly persuasive. So she reassured Claire that she understood her anxiety and encouraged her to be open-minded when she saw Jessie.

By the time Gabriela got home, she was emotionally exhausted. She laid her handbag on the kitchen counter and looked for a bottle of her favorite coconut water in the fridge, before remembering it would be years before that drink hit the market. She settled on some spring water instead. Last time, the morning after Colin said he hadn't wanted a baby, she'd woken with a dry, scratchy throat that no amount of water she consumed could seem to repair. She'd taken a long run on the beach, the sound of her heavy breathing pumping through her ears. Then she'd hidden in her office the rest of the day, staring blankly at her computer screen, willing the words for her next novel to come while refusing any offers of food or drink or apology from Colin, who'd called in sick to work.

This time, she decided to put the baby discussion on the back burner. She wanted to see Colin again, to take him in as he was. She pushed through the swinging door that separated the kitchen from the living room and found him on the leather chair, staring out the window. Their view in Hermosa Beach really had been spectacular. Gabriela had forgotten how the two palm trees outside had politely bent apart, as if knowing they'd block the distant strip of Pacific Ocean otherwise.

"Hey," she said softly, and offered him a shy smile when he turned, thinking how unfair it was that he looked nearly the same now as he would at fifty-five, still tall and naturally thin with a full head of red hair that would become only subtly speckled with gray. Colin's agelessness seemed effortless.

"Hey," he echoed cautiously, trying to evaluate Gabriela's state of mind as he stretched his toned arms over his head, exposing rings of sweat. She noticed his running shoes kicked off next to him, realizing he'd just returned from a workout on the beach. Gabriela hadn't thought about the boot camp class he used to take in a long time, the one he'd tried to coax her into joining. But she'd said no, not just because she had zero desire to be screamed at by a drill sergeant instructor at 6 a.m., but also because she was a solo exerciser needing the time to work out plot points in her head.

She perched herself on the wide arm of his chair and smiled wanly. "So," she began. She knew from experience what *not* to say. But she still wasn't sure what the right words were that would unlock the man who had wanted a baby for so long. So she decided to apply one of the rules of writing: to show, not tell.

"Here he is," she said, holding up her BlackBerry with a tiny picture of Lucas she'd finally figured out how to take on her phone, his red, scrunched-up face now staring at them.

"Will you look at that," Colin said, cradling the phone gently as if it were an actual baby.

"The name Lucas fits him perfectly, don't you think?" she remarked as she studied Colin's face for more of a reaction. Although what did she expect? She knew he wasn't going to burst into tears and tell her this grainy image of a baby would change his mind.

"It suits him," he said, his answer sounding clipped and tentative, as if he were afraid to expound on it. Or maybe he didn't want to.

"Jessie's doing well," Gabriela offered, filling the silence, realizing her voice sounded a bit forced, like a salesperson who finally had a customer. She cleared her throat before continuing, choosing her words carefully. "And Grant, he was beaming. He kept saying he was so happy he finally had a son."

"That's great," Colin said as he handed the BlackBerry back to her. The purple shadows under his eyes showed the toll the argument had taken. She knew he was deliberately being cautious, unsure if Gabriela was going to lash out at him again at any second. She didn't blame him. She'd always had a temper, but she barely recognized herself the night they'd fought about the baby. As the hours ticked by and their fight continued to move in circles, she'd screamed, she'd thrown things, she'd become a version of herself she'd never seen before. But she'd been in such a hysterical rage that she hadn't been able to stop herself. And now, with ten years of reflection, she almost laughed. Did she really think that kind of behavior was going to encourage him to change his mind? That after she'd shattered their wedding picture against the wall, he'd scoop her up in his arms and make love to her right then and there without using protection? She let her gaze fall to the spot on the hardwood floor where the picture had landed, but there was no trace of it. Colin must have already cleaned up the shards of glass.

"About last night," Gabriela started, then stopped when she noticed Colin's shoulders stiffen. She put her hand over his before continuing. "I'm sorry, so very sorry."

Colin blinked at her several times. The last thing she'd spit at him before barreling toward the guest room had been hateful, and she'd instantly regretted it. But still she'd continued forward, as if her anger were wheels beneath her feet, and slammed the door behind her. *Maybe it's for the best—you'd make a lousy father anyway.*

"I didn't mean what I said," she said softly. "I was just so upset."

Colin stared at the ceiling for several seconds, as if replaying Gabriela's hurtful words in his head. "I know," he finally replied in a tone that made Gabriela feel as if he didn't know anything at all.

Even in her anger, she'd never been one to wield insults like weapons, especially with Colin, but she'd felt something snap inside her that night, a fissure that caused her to spin out of control. She was shocked by how fresh the argument seemed now, how the words prickled her skin as if she'd really screamed them just the night before. "If I could take it back, I would." Gabriela inched her body closer to him. "Because I know you'd be a great dad." She followed Colin's gaze outside, both of them watching a neighbor plant something in her herb garden. "That's actually why I think I was so upset."

"I'm sorry too," Colin finally said. "That I can't give you what you want."

"I know you are," Gabriela said, thinking of the last decade of their marriage. It had been solid. While so many of her friends had suffered through terrible, heart-wrenching divorces, suddenly only able to see their children part of the time, she and Colin had not only stayed together, they'd stayed happy together. Sure, the baby they never had had always been there, just under the surface, like a cyst about to burst. And Colin had tried in so many other ways to make up for the *no* he'd given her that night. He'd said yes to building the enormous house they didn't need and diligently stood by her side as her star rose higher and higher, never blinking when it overshadowed his own successful career as a lawyer. And even now, she wanted that version of their marriage to be enough for her. But she couldn't get it out of her mind that she'd settled when she'd accepted his answer. That there was a reason she was chosen to come back and change things.

"So what now?" Colin asked her, and she watched his Adam's apple jut out as he swallowed hard.

"Well, I was hoping you'd come with me to buy a gift for the baby," Gabriela said, surprising herself as she said it. She'd practically shunned Lucas the first time and had let Colin turn his back on him too, the pain too raw for both of them, their union too fragile to be reminded of what they would never have. And she wasn't going to let either of them make that mistake again.

"Sounds good. I look forward to meeting the little man," Colin said. "Oh, and your dad called about an hour ago."

Gabriela smiled at the thought of seeing her father's round face. He'd squeeze her the same way he had since she was little. She could swear he still saw her as a sixteen-year-old girl. And that was okay with Gabriela. She had always been in constant awe that he was able to recover from Gabriela's mother's death in a way she never could. She decided she'd call him back first thing tomorrow.

As Gabriela and Colin walked into the baby boutique an hour later, she was almost afraid to touch the chenille blankets and the adorable pacifiers, hoping that being there wouldn't be too much for them. She stopped and picked up a polka-dot onesie, marveling at how small it was. She rubbed the soft fabric against her cheek, wondering what joy or pain the next year would bring.

CHAPTER EIGHT

....

Claire sat in the driver's seat of her champagne-tinted Honda Accord, picking at the peeling leather on the steering wheel as she replayed the conversation she'd just had with Jessie. The hot June sun was beating through the front window, and the skin on her cheeks grew warm as she stared at the stucco building, picturing Jessie still walking laps around the maternity ward, her printed hospital gown flapping behind her as she pumped her arms. Her frenetic energy had reminded Claire of Emily on her fourth birthday, dancing around their living room after she'd eaten a giant piece of vanilla cake, the remnants of thick bubble-gum-pink frosting lining her lips. Today, Claire had shuffled alongside Jessie, nodding with a smile as she rambled in a hushed voice about how this was the most exciting opportunity any of them had *ever* had. But as Claire listened to words like *magical* and *life changing* and *second chances*, she felt the knot in her stomach tightening. She didn't agree. *Life wasn't meant to be played like a game of chess, moving the people you love like pawns to win the game.*

Claire turned the key and the car coughed and sputtered before finally roaring to life. When she'd started it at her house earlier, she'd been shocked by how familiar the loud sound of the transmission had been, even though she hadn't heard it in a decade; it had finally given out just before she'd turned forty-one. She was instantly reminded of calling AAA because she was stuck—always somewhere hugely inconvenient, like the parking lot of Ralph's grocery store on a hot day, as the dairy products she'd already loaded into her trunk soured while she dialed the number on the back of her membership card. Or worse, when she'd strand herself and her clients while showing a property, watching helplessly as their confidence in her fell with each turn of the ignition, most likely wondering why their real estate agent couldn't close enough deals to afford a Lexus. After the Honda's transmission finally died, she'd taken it as a sign, marching into the dealership and begrudgingly leasing a new car, only to discover that the beautiful midnight-blue sedan really didn't help her commissions at all, it only added to the monthly bills she was already struggling to pay.

As she drove toward her mom and dad's house to pick up Emily, her breath quickened and she willed both her nerves and her battered automobile to hold it together. Her dad would be easy. But seeing her mother and her daughter for the first time was going to be difficult. Her relationship with each was so complicated.

As they'd circled around the nurses' station during their walk earlier, Jessie had asked Claire if she was excited to see Emily as a twelve-year-old again. *Remember those knobby knees of hers?* she'd said as she offered a sympathetic smile to a new mom being wheeled toward the exit, her baby nuzzled against her chest and a look of panic in her eyes. Of course Claire remembered Emily's knees, and her lanky body, and the braces that never failed to surprise her when Emily opened her mouth, Claire always seeing her as a seven-year-old with two missing front teeth, and marveling at how fast she was growing up, her face and body in a perpetual state of change.

She wasn't sure she was ready to see her daughter that way again. She didn't know if she had the strength to relive this year, to parent a tween, which had felt like wading out into the ocean when the waves were fast and steady, fighting the undercurrent that threatened to pull her down at any moment.

She wasn't excited to remind Emily to set her alarm for school, to ask her if she'd finished her homework, to try and pry information out of her about the goings-on of middle school, all while Emily offered only mumbled yeses and nos. When she'd mentioned this concern to Jessie, she'd grabbed Claire by the shoulder and shook her softly, as if she was trying to wake her up from a nap.

"I know you're not looking forward to reliving the bad things, but you can change how it all turns out this time, we all can. We're getting a do-over!"

Claire chewed on the side of her lip as she thought of her mom and Emily. Even with the gift of hindsight she wasn't sure she could significantly alter anything, and more important, she wasn't sure she could handle it if she failed again. "That's not why *I* agreed to come back here. I did it so *you* and Gabriela could have a second chance."

"So that's it? You're going to sit on the sidelines while we try to fix our lives? It's not just Emily who needs you, you know." Jessie let her words hang in the sterilized air, nodding at a nurse passing by in pastel pink scrubs, squeezing Claire's hand.

Grant's eyes lit up when he saw Jessie reenter the room,

the innocence and joy reflected in them making Claire wonder if change really was possible. She'd always told herself it was Emily's stubborn personality that had shaped her choices. But there had been a small voice in her head, whispering to her late at night, that maybe things would've been different if she hadn't acquiesced when she should have stood her ground.

As Claire exited the 134 freeway, she felt her heartbeat quickening, like she was heading to a first date, and hoping that the guy even slightly resembled his profile photo and wouldn't visibly flinch when she mentioned she was a single mom. She'd learned right away it wasn't something you should *wait* to reveal—like your dating history or your desire to get married—after she'd gone on three dates with a man she really liked, before finally working up the courage to say she had a little girl. He'd been stunned, stammering through an explanation about how he wasn't ready to be a dad, fumbling as he tossed some cash onto the table and giving her a weak apology before leaving. She'd ordered a shot of whiskey, sipping it and feeling terrible as she tried to pretend she didn't have someone at home who relied on her for survival.

Walking through the front door of her parents' condo in Glendale, Claire removed her shoes and placed them next to her mom's gardening clogs. Her heart caught in her chest and she reached down to pick one of them up. Was she ready to see her after all this time? Through therapy, she'd finally accepted everything that had happened, that things had turned out the way they were supposed to. And now here Claire was, about to see her when she never thought she would have the chance again. Claire hugged the forest-green clog to her chest and beelined for her mom, finding her in the kitchen and hugging her tightly.

"Mom!" Claire buried her head in Mona's shoulder and sobbed into the soft lavender smock she always wore when she was tending to her herbs out back.

"Are you crying? And why are you holding my Croc?" Mona pulled back and Claire quickly wiped her tears, surveying the peeling wallpaper where the walls met the ceiling, the yellow refrigerator that was practically as old as Claire, and Shaggy, her parents' golden retriever, sleeping soundly under the dining room table.

Claire nodded. "It's just so good to see you," she said, taking in her mom's short silver locks pulled back in a ponytail that she'd secured with a rubber band meant for binding papers, not hair. Claire reached up to touch it, remembering the times she'd scolded her for not using the proper elastic.

"I know what you're going to say, but my hair is sixty-two years old; a little breakage won't matter," Mona said, rolling her eyes.

"You're right, who cares what you pull your hair back with." Claire smiled, her eyes filling with tears again.

Mona put her hand on her daughter's forehead. "You just admitted I'm right? Okay, now I know something's definitely wrong with you!" Mona grabbed Claire's upper arms and gave her a once-over. God, how she had hated when her mom did that, Claire always desperate to know the thoughts in her head as she appraised her, if she was passing a test she didn't know she was supposed to take. She would swallow hard and cross her arms over her body, wishing she didn't so desperately want the approval of a woman who seemed so reluctant to give it. Only later would she learn that her mom had meant nothing by this, that she loved Claire more than she ever gave her credit for. But by then it had been too late to reciprocate. "You look tired. Did you get any sleep last night?"

Images of her and Mason intertwined under her floral comforter flashed through her mind, and Claire suppressed a guilty smile.

"You're flushed, sit down." Mona guided Claire to a wooden spindle chair and filled a glass with tap water. "Drink."

Claire obeyed, letting the cool liquid rush down her throat while reaching down to pet Shaggy. She ran her fingers through his soft fur, remembering when he'd passed away in his sleep when he was fifteen. She bent down and kissed him and studied her mom. Claire noticed the blue circles outlining her eyes and her frail body beneath her smock, which appeared oversized. Mona had taken up golf and had been walking more in the past year, but it was more than that; now she could see the weight was vanishing in places it shouldn't have been.

"Do you have a picture of the baby?" Mona asked as she sat next to Claire.

Claire held out her phone to her mom, who frowned as she studied a photo of Jessie and Lucas. Claire already knew what her mom was thinking, and rightfully so. Mona was surprised at how happy Jessie looked. And that was an emotion Jessie hadn't shown much in the months leading up to Lucas' birth.

"I'm glad to see her smiling. I figured once the little one arrived, she'd come around," Mona said finally. "Motherhood is complicated."

Claire nodded. She and her mom were never as close as Claire had wanted them to be. She'd always felt surges of jealousy whenever Gabriela talked about her mom. In the sixteen years Gabriela knew her mother, she'd been closer to her than Claire had ever felt to Mona. That just wasn't Mona's way. She wasn't a nurturer, she was more of a guide, wanting Claire to stumble so she could teach herself how not to fall. Claire had learned from the hours of sitting on the soft leather couch across from her therapist that by trying so hard to please Emily, she was trying to manufacture a relationship like the one she'd wanted to have with Mona. Claire had become the lenient, easygoing mom she'd always wished she'd had, but she'd been too eager, trying to engage Emily in topics like boys or music, and was often met with eye rolls.

"Speaking of the complications of motherhood, where's Em?" Claire quipped.

"Finishing up her math homework," Mona answered proudly, and Claire knew by her satisfied smile what she was thinking, that Emily had given her no resistance, had done exactly as she was told, because she was with Grandma. And it was true, she did listen to Claire's mom—because Mona was willing to say no to the things Emily asked for, unlike Claire, who tragically underused the word.

"What took you so long?" Emily shot as she walked into the kitchen.

"Hi!" Claire chimed, ignoring Emily's accusatory tone and throwing her arms around her daughter, then stepping back and looking at her before squeezing her hard again.

"Okay, weirdo!" Emily said, wriggling from her grasp.

"Whoa, Jessie's new baby has made your mother quite emotional!" Mona said. "Are you running a baby fever?"

Claire laughed lightly and swatted her mom's hand away. "It's just so good to see you, Em," Claire said as she took in her daughter's loose-fitting jeans and Converses. She was still so young, so naïve. Maybe she could help Emily hold on to that innocence a little longer this time around.

"You're late. I was supposed to meet Anna at the mall," Emily whined, pressing her hand into her hip, and Claire's neck immediately stiffened.

Anna. Claire released an audible sigh, a visual of the wispy girl with white-blond hair and a row of perfect teeth freshly released from their braces coming to mind. Claire thought back to meeting her for the first time, smiling as Anna offered pleases and thank-yous to Claire at every turn, even asking to help with the dishes from their after-school snack. Claire later lingered outside Emily's room to listen in on them talking about a boy they both thought was cute. "I'd hit that," Anna said, and cackled loudly. Claire had flinched and grabbed the doorjamb, unsure whether to burst into the room and mortify her daughter or pretend she hadn't heard it. She'd chosen the latter, telling herself Anna was just going for shock value, repeating something she'd heard on TV. But over the next year, Anna proved to be problematic, interested in pushing every boundary and determined to take Emily with her. Claire finally had to forbid Emily from hanging out with her. This time, she'd stop that friendship in its tracks immediately.

But as she looked at Emily's pouty lips, she felt the familiar rise of guilt.

"I'm sorry." Claire uttered the beginning of an apology. But then, as a smile appeared on her daughter's lips, Claire thought of Anna again and the hell she'd gone through with Emily. Because she'd wanted to be a friend when she should've been a mom. She had to be different this time, or why did she bother coming back at all? She could tell herself it was only for Gabriela and Jessie, but deep down she did have some hope she could make her own life and Emily's better too.

"Actually, scratch that. I'm not apologizing to *you* because I made you late for a shopping trip—especially not one with *Anna*, who I'm not a fan of by the way. It's you who should be saying sorry for taking that tone with me," Claire said sharply, and Emily's large eyes widened.

"Sorry," Emily said obediently, and Claire felt a surge of hopefulness as she made eye contact with Mona, who was nodding her head in approval. Maybe taking a stand against Emily's attitude was exactly what her daughter needed. "So, Aunt Jess had a boy, right? What did they name him? I bet the twins are excited to have a little brother!"

"Lucas," Claire responded, taking a strand of Emily's hair and playing with it the way she used to, wrapping it into a knot, and Emily shaking it free reflexively. Claire had forgotten how beautiful her long dark blond hair had been at this age, cascading down her back in natural waves. In just a few years, Claire knew Emily would spend the night at a friend's house, hack off several inches, and cut severe, uneven bangs that fell into her eyes, then color it black in a tiny pedestal sink, the ugly green undertones of her cheap dye job always a reminder to Claire that she had completely lost control of her daughter.

"Will you stop? I *hate* when you do that!" Emily yanked her head away, and just like that, Claire's hope was sucked out of her.

Claire stepped back and watched as Emily pulled a pink Nintendo DS from her pocket, her eyes dropping away from Claire as she stared at the tiny screen, remembering how she'd regretted the purchase, wishing she'd been firmer when Emily had whined that she was the only kid in her grade that didn't own one.

"Please put that thing away. It's time for us to go."

"Wait a sec, I just started a new race on Mario Kart."

As Claire watched Emily's metallic purple nails rhythmically move over the arrows, she knew if she said nothing, Emily would continue to play the game for as long as it took, never stopping to do what she'd been asked.

She pried the device out of Emily's hands and stuffed it into her purse. "I said, it's time to go. Now say good-bye to your grandmother and thank her for taking care of you. *Now.*"

Claire raised her hand as Emily began to protest. "One word and you won't get it back for a week."

"Whatever," Emily huffed, finally squeaking out a bye and thanks and stomping toward the front door past Claire's father, who was clearly tuning them out as he watched TV in his leather La-Z-Boy.

Claire smiled at her father, who winked at her when he caught her eye. Claire hadn't realized how good it would be to see him like this, when ignoring the squabbles of his female family members was his biggest problem.

"What's gotten into you?" Mona said, coughing loudly as she appraised her daughter.

"I don't know, I guess I'm just tired of her attitude," Claire responded, thinking she was actually exhausted by it, having dealt with it for the better part of a decade, gently rubbing her hand in circles on her mom's back as she hacked. "You okay?" she asked, even though she already knew the answer.

Mona nodded. "Just a bad cough I can't seem to shake. I'll be fine."

"You should see a doctor," Claire said, trying to sound nonchalant, willing the tears in the back of her eyes to disappear.

"Don't be silly. It's nothing."

"Probably. But let's get it checked out anyway. Please?"

"Fine. I'll think about it. Are you sure you're okay? First, you bring the hammer down on Emily and now you're acting like I have cancer or something?" Mona laughed deeply and waved good-bye as Claire made her way down the steps of her child-hood home, the tears she'd been holding exploding from her eyes like missiles.

You do *have cancer, Mom. I'm just hoping this time we can catch it before it's too late.*

CHAPTER NINE

....

Jessie shot up in bed as a baby's cries woke her, her heart pounding, disoriented as she tried to figure out where she was. She squinted at the clock—it was just after 1 a.m., and as she started to drift back to sleep, she realized it was Lucas who was wailing because he needed to be fed. She'd forgotten how hard it was to make that transition from hospital to home, where you aren't just taking care of your baby, you're caring for your entire family. And there's no kind-eyed nurse to take your bundle to the nursery whenever you need a break. Jessie had been looking forward to the benefits of being ten years younger, but had conveniently forgotten how exhausting a newborn could be—how her bones would ache from lack of sleep, how her breasts would throb when they got too full. That even though her skin glowed and her metabolism was still working properly, she was just as exhausted as she'd been at fifty, maybe even more so.

She rose to feed Lucas, rocking in the yellow chenille glider, calming her breathing to match Lucas' as she lifted his mouth to her breast, closing her eyes and attempting to melt the past away.

When they'd returned from the hospital and Grant swung the front door open as the handle of Lucas' car seat pulled on the crook of her arm, she'd gasped. She hadn't seen her home, *their* home, the way it was with Grant, in years. After he'd been gone six months, making it very clear he had no plans to move back in, she'd redecorated, not wanting the house to resemble *them*. It was too painful to look at anything—the worn oversized chair they'd once made haphazard love in, the framed watercolor painting they'd purchased while on a weekend at a bed-and-breakfast, and even the dishes. Every mug, every plate, every spatula had a memory attached to it. Whatever Grant hadn't taken with him, she'd replaced. But it wasn't until the twins had returned from a weekend at their dad's, and she showed them the final transformation, that she'd regretted what she'd done. Instead of giggling and jumping up and down when they saw their new rooms, their eyes had gone cold. Their dad was gone, and now their familiar surroundings were too. Again, Jessie had failed them.

That first night home from the hospital with Lucas in a sling against her chest, Jessie had run her fingers across picture frames, tabletops, and tchotchkes throughout the house. She bit back the tears as she remembered frantically calling Goodwill and Salvation Army, where she'd sent most of their items, only to be told they were either purchased or shipped away to another location. Jessie winced as she ran her hand over the oak desk that she'd once sat at signing thank-you cards for the baby gifts she'd received for the girls. That was one of the many pieces she'd asked the movers she'd hired to put on the curb along with a cardboard sign with the word *Free* written in black Sharpie. It was her way of distancing herself from the person she had been. If only her heart could be mended as easily as replacing furniture.

Grant had caught her staring at a lamp and pulling at the fringe on a rug, and laughed. "You've only been gone a few days."

She hugged him. "It feels like years. I missed you."

Grant laughed again and kissed the top of her head. "You sure all those meds are out of your system?"

"Just promise me you won't go anywhere. I need you," Jessie said, keeping her grasp tight.

"I've got the whole week off," Grant said.

That hadn't been what Jessie was asking, but she stayed silent.

Jessie struggled to settle back into a routine she'd forgotten long ago; jogging through the aisles of Vons like a contestant on *Supermarket Sweep*, tossing whatever she could into the cart knowing Lucas could wake at any moment and scream for his milk; preparing the girls' lunches and filling their cereal bowls while Lucas yelled from his vibrating chair, his arms outstretched for her. She had assumed her baby memory would kick in the way a muscle might after it healed from an injury. And in some ways it had—like how she could clean up a diaper blowout with only one wipe, or the way breast-feeding felt like second nature. But there were still things she felt like she was relearning, like how to keep from getting pissed off at Grant when he wasn't around to help after that initial week at home with her. She realized being back here again just how much she'd romanticized her relationship with Grant in his ten-year absence. She'd buried the memory of how the deep lines around his eyes and slumped shoulders kept her from thrusting Lucas at him the second he walked in the door, so she could get a few minutes of reprieve. She was tired too, but he didn't seem to notice.

It was a miracle she survived after Grant left, still postpartum and grieving his alienation. Each day felt like climbing a mountain, finally reaching the peak every night, only to do it all over again the next day. She'd become a hard, hollow shell, smiling on cue when the girls jumped into the car after school, when their teacher asked if she was okay, when she and Grant showed up to parent-teacher conferences separately then shoved themselves into the child-sized chairs, something they used to laugh about. Jessie had tried to make a joke the first time, but Grant had remained stoic, refusing to acknowledge their shared history.

The divorce hadn't just been hard on Jessie, but on the twins too. Madison had always been an overachiever—reading more books than required and reluctant to stay home from school even when she had the flu—but she started refusing to do her homework and turning in incomplete tests in class. Her grades had dropped steadily, and Jessie had tried to get her to open up about it. "Talk to me," Jessie would plead. "Tell me what's going on in your head."

"Trust me, Mom. You do *not* want to know," Madison would yell before slamming her bedroom door—the poster of a spiky-haired Drake Bell from Madison's favorite Disney show staring her in the face. But Jessie did want to know—no matter how ugly her daughter's thoughts were. She'd knock lightly, waiting for Madison to answer, wishing she could make everything better, but knowing she was responsible.

And Morgan—their sweet little girl who wanted to help every stray animal she came across and was constantly setting up lemonade stands or offering to pull a neighbor's weeds so she could make money to donate to charity—had become sullen since Grant's departure. She didn't argue with Jessie the way Madison did. In fact, she didn't say much of anything, and that silence was almost worse. Morgan would come out of her room at night and see Jessie standing in the hallway between their two rooms, and simply shake her head at her mom. Sometimes Jessie wondered if she knew the truth, if she was silently scolding her for what she'd done to their family.

Jessie was petrified that the twins' initial response to their parents' breakup would become even more serious. They were already so mad at her and Grant. Every time she thought of the possibility of them knowing that she had been the one to shatter their family into shards of what it had been, a shiver ran through her.

She'd gone to Claire for advice. "How do you do it? I feel like the guilt is going to kill me." Jessie had just dropped the girls off at Grant's and they'd exited the car without saying good-bye, ignoring Jessie when she called out that she loved them.

"You're asking me?" Claire chuckled. "You know how much I struggle to say no to Emily."

Jessie pondered how to respond. Emily was bitter and treated Claire like a doormat and Jessie feared the twins could do the same to her. She hoped Claire hadn't noticed that she'd kept the girls away from Emily recently, coming up with excuses for why she couldn't go over to Claire's. She knew it was ridiculous, that Emily wouldn't corrupt them, but she was desperate to hold on to the frayed connection she still had with her daughters.

"You're doing your best," Jessie said gently. "But if you could do it all over again, what would you change?"

"Everything!" Claire said, and they erupted in laughter.

Jessie had finally called Grant late one night and begged him to move back in just for their daughters. He'd only released a long sigh, his silence speaking volumes. She knew it was a desperately bad idea—that even if he had come back home, his anger toward Jessie would have slowly infected them all. But she would've done anything to help her twins become the carefree children they had been just months before. After she'd hung up with Grant, she'd walked into the nursery and stared at Lucas fast asleep with his thumb in his mouth, and she'd thought, *I wish I could go back and fix this mess, but then I'd lose you. And how could I live without you?*

When she found out she was pregnant with Lucas, it was a steamy afternoon, rain uncharacteristically pooling in the streets in Redondo Beach. After missing her period, then throwing up for the second morning in a row, her breasts tender, her body exhausted, *she knew.*

But still, she had dragged herself into Rite-Aid, purchased four different tests, then frantically peed on stick after stick in a Starbucks bathroom after downing two venti green teas. She'd said a prayer with each new test she opened, that the line would fade from pink back to white, from *yes* to *no*. She knew in her gut that if she was pregnant, it was most likely Peter's. She and Grant had sex a few weeks after she'd slept with Peter, when she'd stayed true to the promise she'd made to herself to be a better wife. One night after she'd talked to Grant about his stress at work, he'd grabbed her and started kissing her in a way he hadn't in a very long time, and her chest had tightened. Had that been all he'd needed? For her to listen? But still, she knew the baby couldn't be his. Because once she'd missed her period and started feeling those symptoms she remembered all too well from the twins, she'd frantically done the math and figured out her night with Peter had occurred smack in the middle of her ovulation—and that he must have pulled out just a second too late. At the time, Jessie had been sure their lack of protection wouldn't matter. Her lazy ovaries had made it difficult to get pregnant with the twins, and that had been ten years ago.

When she'd finally broken down and confessed the truth about Lucas' paternity to Claire, several months into her pregnancy, her first question had been if she'd told Peter. Jessie nodded.

She'd asked him to meet at a diner in Venice Beach, where she was confident they wouldn't run into anyone they knew. She'd slid into the booth, the frayed vinyl seat scratching her bare leg as her skirt rode up underneath her. She pulled at the hem and ordered a cup of herbal tea and waited. She hadn't seen Peter since that night, when he drove her home from the hotel, the silence in the car making Jessie's internal dialogue about how she'd just made the biggest mistake of her life louder. She had fantasized for months about what it would feel like to be with Peter, but she'd never thought through to this part—to the *after*. She could have never understood the intense desire she'd feel to turn back the clock to make a different choice earlier that night. How she'd leaned away from him in the passenger seat and clung to the handle of the car door like it was an escape hatch, ready to eject herself at the first opportunity. At a stoplight, she'd even contemplated peeling off her heels and running the last half mile home. When he'd finally pulled up in front of her house, she looked up at her bedroom window and whispered, even though it would have been impossible for Grant to hear, that it couldn't happen again, that she was going to fix her marriage and he should too.

She knew it would be nearly impossible to avoid Peter forever, but Jessie attempted to with an intensity that bordered on obsessive. She deleted his number from her phone. She started arriving extremely early or annoyingly late to the drop-off and

pickup at school, waving quickly to all the other moms as she
herded the twins in and out of the car with such urgency they
would often ask why *she* was in such a hurry—wasn't she just
going home or to run errands? She changed dry cleaners and
started going to a different Starbucks. But then she woke up
one morning with that familiar tingle in her stomach that she
instantly recognized, and she realized she could no longer avoid
Peter and what they had done.

Peter wore a smug smile as he walked toward Jessie—he had
most likely interpreted her cryptic call as an invitation to pick up
where they'd left off. He leaned into the booth to hug her and
she stiffened.

"Okay. So I'm guessing you didn't ask me here because you
missed me?" Peter slid in across from her.

"I'm pregnant." The words tumbled from her mouth and it
took only seconds for Peter's expression to change, going from
shock to disbelief to anger, his lip finally snarling into a frown.

"It's mine?"

"Yes, and before you ask, I'm sure you're the father."

"So we'll take care of it then."

"This is not an errand we have to run or a household project,
Peter. This is a baby. You're a father. How could you even say
that?" Jessie's hand moved to her abdomen and she tried to conjure the man who'd made her feel so desirable that she started
blowing out her hair each morning and buying designer workout
clothes she couldn't afford, who'd looked at her when she spoke
and listened to every word that came out of her mouth like it
meant something. Where was he? Probably in the same place
her flirtatious, lululemon-wearing alter ego was, deeply buried.
And truthfully, even though she could never walk away from her
own child—she'd known that from the moment she stared at the

pink line on the white plastic stick—she was not that surprised by his reaction. She knew he was scared. She was too.

"I'm not an idiot, Jessie. I know we're talking about a baby. But you already have two daughters and I have a son. It would never work to have this child too."

Jessie didn't say anything and watched Peter as he realized that she'd already made up her mind. She was having this child.

"You can't be serious. Do you think Cathy and Grant are going to welcome this bundle of joy with open arms?" He shook his head. "We'll both lose everything."

"That's not his or her fault." Jessie looked down at her stomach.

Peter was silent for several minutes. Finally he spoke. "If you're really moving forward with this, then I'm sorry, but you'll be on your own. I need you to understand that."

Jessie studied Peter's face, hoping to see a glimmer of sadness, a flicker of angst, *any sign* he felt bad for turning his back on this child. But there was nothing. "I understand perfectly," Jessie answered. *I understand that you are a total asshole.*

After he stormed out of the restaurant, the waitress offered Jessie a sympathetic smile and she'd nodded, feeling a mixture of disgust and relief. She played with an unopened sugar packet, squeezing it between her fingers, feeling the hard granules press against the paper, and thought about her decision to tell Peter. She'd placed a hand over her still flat belly and knew she'd done it for the baby. She couldn't keep this secret from its biological father. If one day her child ever did find out the truth, at least she would be able to say she had told him. That he'd had a choice. Because she *would* have this baby, despite the complications he or she would bring to all of their lives. She could never let her unborn child pay the price for her mistake.

Jessie had waited three more weeks, the longest of her life, and finally, when she was nearly ten weeks along, she'd pasted a smile on her face and announced to Grant that he was going to be a father one more time, shrugging her shoulders when he asked her how it had happened. They hadn't been careful in years. She deflected with a joke about her lazy ovary deciding to get a work ethic, hoping he wouldn't question her further. And of course he didn't. His face had lit up and he grabbed her, pulling her in tight and kissing her hard, whispering that he was hoping for a boy. He'd always wanted one. And as Jessie nodded, the tears began to fall. Grant mistook them for joy, and they stood there while the night turned from dusk to dark, just holding one another so tightly that Jessie had let herself believe that it might all turn out okay.

"Hey." Jessie felt someone nudging her gently and opened her bleary eyes to find Grant staring back at her. "You fell asleep in here last night again," he said as he gently took Lucas out of her arms and set him in his crib before offering his hand to help pull her out of the chair.

"Thanks." She shuffled into the kitchen and started the coffeemaker, the aroma from the grounds filling the air. Even after Grant left, even when it had been so hard to get out of bed, she'd always loved the mornings—the way the sun rose so optimistically in the east filled Jessie with slices of hope that kept her going. "What are you up to today?"

"I've got to meet with the contractor on that place up in the hills, and then I'm going to look at a property in Palos Verdes. Apparently the owner is bored and wants a new kitchen."

Jessie took a deep breath. He hadn't been home before eight in weeks. She understood that his working allowed her to stay home, but she also missed him. And she couldn't let them fall back into old patterns, couldn't allow him to slip away from her again. This time, she had to be part of a solution.

"I understand. But sometimes I wish there was more time for you and me. I miss you. I miss us," Jessie said, and grabbed a mug, hesitating for a second as she realized it was one that Morgan had hand painted for her fortieth birthday. She ran her hand over the numbers four and zero, still bright and new, not yet faded and peeling after ten years of being put in the dishwasher. She made a decision to hand wash it from now on.

Grant wrapped his arm around her shoulder and guided her toward him. "You know I can't turn down work, Jess," he said, frowning. They had always agreed that Jessie would stay home after having the girls, so she'd happily walked away from her job as a kindergarten teacher to care for them. But even though Grant earned a nice income, it could be inconsistent, and the cost of living in Los Angeles was high, propelling Grant to accept every job that came his way, even if it meant he was absent for back-to-school nights and soccer practices.

"I would never ask you to. But I feel so disconnected from you sometimes." Jessie bit her lip and tried not to cry, the words so true, not only in this moment but for the last ten years, when she'd watched Grant live his life from afar, grabbing tidbits from the girls here and there to keep tabs on him as best she could. "I'm just asking you, when you're here, to be *here*," she said, taking a sip of coffee. "And maybe change a diaper once in a while." She smiled to show she was mostly joking at the last part.

Grant laughed. "Well, don't get all crazy now," he said as he tightened his grip around her. "But I hear you, Jess. I know it's been hard on you, and on us. I'll try to do better."

"Thank you." Jessie let out a deep breath, then planted a kiss on his lips. "Are you sure you have to go right this minute? The kids are still asleep." Grant's eyes had widened as she'd grabbed his belt buckle and kissed him deeply. He'd pulled back a few seconds later, asking her if she could have sex so soon after the baby. She'd giggled. "There are other things we can do," she'd said as she pulled him into the bathroom and shut the door.

• • •

"So? How was it?" Claire suppressed a laugh as Jessie recounted her conversation with Grant as they sipped their coffee drinks a few hours later, Jessie absentmindedly rocking Lucas' car seat, his tiny hand balled into a fist as he slept.

"Like riding a bike!" Jessie laughed. "And it made me realize how stupid I was for not making more of an effort last time," she said, and tried to push down the image of Janet's face flashing through her mind: the way her hair's soft layers framed her face perfectly, her hazel eyes sparkling when Jessie met her for the first time at Lucas' soccer game, Grant standing sheepishly behind her as Jessie tried desperately to act like she didn't care that he'd brought her. Or that Madison and Morgan seemed to like her. There was still a part of Jessie that felt like she was stealing Grant from her now.

"What? What is that look for?" Claire admonished.

"I was thinking of Janet."

"While you were giving Grant a blow job?"

"No!" Jessie exclaimed. "Just now. I just think Grant seems really happy with her. Maybe more than he ever was with me."

"Well, she doesn't exist in this world. At least not in yours and Grant's."

"For now." Jessie took a long sip of her latte, the hot liquid burning her tongue.

"Are you ready to talk about your game plan?" Claire inquired carefully as she poured a packet of raw sugar into her coffee. She'd tried broaching the subject more than once already, but each time she brought it up, Jessie had shushed her, telling her she wanted a little more time to enjoy being with Grant and the kids—as a family. But Claire had continued to push because she felt Jessie owed it to her to change her life for the better, especially if she expected Claire to do the work on her own. Jessie had been the driving force in the three of them returning here, and Claire wanted to help her make the right choices this time. She'd already been brainstorming better ways Jessie could tell Grant the truth, ways that might soften how he might react. Claire would even help explain it to Grant if Jessie wanted her there.

Lucas made a gurgling noise and Jessie smiled at him, pushing his pacifier back into his mouth and watching as he drifted to sleep again. "I've decided what I'm going to do." Jessie leaned forward, her hands cupped around her mug, her eyes focused on Claire's. "I'm not telling him this time."

Claire responded before she meant to. "Really?"

"What do you mean, *really*?" Jessie fired back. "What did you think I was going to say? That I'd tell him all over again? And have the same outcome? What would be the point of coming back here?"

"I don't know, Jess." Claire wasn't sure what she had expected, or what she'd do if she were in Jessie's shoes.

"The only thing I know for certain is that telling the truth doesn't always serve the right purpose. Maybe some secrets aren't meant to be revealed."

Claire sipped her coffee, mulling over Jessie's declaration, thinking about the times in her own life when she'd held secrets close in the best interest of others. "Okay, I hear you. And I get that you want to keep your family together, but I just have to ask, do you really believe it will turn out better if you lie to him?"

"I have no idea," Jessie said with a sigh. "But I've thought about this a lot. And *not* telling him is the only option if I want a different outcome. I just can't take the risk he'll leave us again," Jessie said as she lightly touched the little blue sock on Lucas' foot. "Now that I have him back, I'm terrified to lose him."

Claire nodded. To hold the truth inside probably *was* the only way to guarantee the marriage stayed together. And there was a likeness in Peter's and Grant's appearances—both had dark brown hair and green eyes. Without any reason to doubt her, Claire was sure Grant would always believe Lucas was his. The last time around, she'd thought keeping the lie inside during Jessie's pregnancy had been difficult, remembering the relief she felt once Grant knew the truth. She'd been heartbroken for Jessie, but there was a sliver of her that had also exhaled. Now Claire would have to lock the secret away permanently.

"If that's what you want to do, I support you." Claire put her hand on top of Jessie's, hoping Jessie would have the happy ending she wanted.

"And also . . ." Jessie paused. "I still think we need to keep this from Gabs." She looked down at her coffee cup as she said this, because she knew she was asking a lot of Claire to lie to their best friend, someone perfectly capable of keeping the secret. "It's just that she's already dealing with so much right now." They shared a knowing look. "And I see the way she stares at Lucas. I just don't want to hurt her."

"She'd understand," Claire said, echoing the same words from ten years ago.

"Maybe. But I can't take the chance that she won't. Besides,

I don't want her worrying about me. She has her own problems right now. Okay?"

"Okay," Claire agreed, pushing away the flicker of uneasiness that passed through her chest. They were here to make different choices, and something told her they *should* tell Gabriela. They already shared the biggest secret imaginable: that they were all reliving this past decade. Claire was about to tell Jessie just that when she froze, her eyes darting from Jessie to the door of the café.

"What?" Jessie asked when she saw Claire's face fall.

"Don't turn around. Peter just walked in. With his wife."

CHAPTER TEN

....

Gabriela tried to press the air out of her lungs, but she felt breathless, like she'd just sprinted down the beach. But she hadn't been running, she'd been in a stare down with her computer, her mind as blank as the screen, willing—no, begging—the words to come. She was supposed to be writing *the* novel, her fourth, the critically acclaimed book that landed her on the *New York Times* bestseller list.

She used to joke to Claire and Jessie that her memory had practically vanished the day she turned forty, and now the irony in that statement haunted her. If only she could recall what she'd *already* written. That's exactly what Jessie had naively pointed out yesterday—that she'd done it once, so wouldn't it be easier the second time?—which had made Gabriela want to smack her. She knew Jess meant well, because, logically, to someone who didn't write books for a living, rewriting one should be a piece of cake. But it wasn't that simple. Gabriela had twelve novels to her name, and keeping track of all of that information—four thousand pages, sixty main or supporting characters, and almost a million words—was a job in itself. She only knew the names she'd given her secondary characters because she kept them logged in a notebook in her office. She had her outlines and kept detailed notes, but still, she repeated herself more often than she wanted to admit—whether it was a character's physical description, an illness someone had been diagnosed with, or even a phrase—her editor would be the one to point out those things already existed in one of her other books.

She had been back in the year 2005 for just three weeks, but was acutely aware that her time was running out, not just to re-create her novel, but to re-create the life she should have chosen the first time.

She had been visiting Lucas regularly, bringing him overpriced gifts—pint-sized pairs of designer jeans and a black leather jacket. "Gabs!" Jessie had rolled her eyes in mock outrage after Gabriela revealed the price.

"I can't help myself—his little red lips and cherub cheeks send my biological clock into overdrive!"

Jessie smiled. "Do you think you're any closer to convincing Colin to have a baby?"

"I don't think so." Gabriela hadn't slept most of the nights she'd been back, her mind racing to think of ways to change Colin's mind. But she'd discard each idea quickly, deciding it felt either forced or desperate. Like when she'd taken him to the boutique to buy a gift for Lucas. She wasn't naïve enough to believe asking him to go with her to the baby store was going to make him have a lightbulb moment right there in front of the cloth diaper display, but she'd thought it would help gently nudge him. It hadn't.

"Didn't babysitting Lucas help? I have to say, no matter your motive, I was thankful to get out of the house."

Two nights ago, Gabriela and Colin had watched Lucas so

Jessie and Grant could go to the sushi restaurant they loved. She'd planned to casually ask Colin to hold Lucas for her while she used the bathroom, or feed him two ounces as she poured them some wine.

"Not really." Gabriela laughed. "No offense, but your son acted like a big ol' blob—he slept the entire time!"

"Yes—he is in that stage. Maybe wait until he's a little older? When he can smile and drool all over Colin?"

"Yes, I'm sure the drool will convince him," Gabriela said wryly.

After Colin told her he didn't want a baby last time, Gabriela had not told most people, not even her dad, blaming her depressed attitude on a looming writing deadline. Only Jessie and Claire knew the truth. People never suspected that she was mourning the loss of a child she'd never have, a loss that felt as great as the canyon in her heart that was formed when her mom died.

Her dad had long ago stopped asking for a grandchild. Gabriela had finally confessed to him years before that she didn't think she was cut out to be a mom.

She'd been sitting with him at the bar in his restaurant, Francesca's, named after her mother, sipping rich coffee laced with Kahlúa and dining on the tender chicken tamales it was known for. They'd been reminiscing about how Gabriela's mother would slave over the tamales each Christmas Eve and then hand deliver them to their friends and family.

"Remember how she would always say 'food is love' when I asked her why she went to so much trouble to make these?" Gabriela asked her father, motioning toward her plate.

He finished his bite and smiled. "And you'd roll your eyes and tell her it would be so much easier to get a gift certificate."

"God, I was such a brat." Gabriela blushed at the memory. "But she'd just shake her head and tell me that one day I'd discover my own way to show love. Because saying those three little words wouldn't be enough."

Gabriela hadn't understood then, but she did now. Writing was her version of her mother's chicken tamale—whether it was a short poem for Colin or a handwritten letter to her friends, it was her way of spreading happiness to others.

Gabriela took another bite, savoring the flavor of the masa. "You know what? I can still taste the love."

"It's the secret ingredient," her father said. "And one day you can pass it on to your own children."

She put her hand over his. "I know how much you want grandchildren, but I don't think that's going to happen."

Her dad's face fell. "Why not?"

"I don't think I'm cut out for it." Her voice caught as she confessed she hadn't tried to get pregnant because she was worried she wouldn't be as good at showing love as her mother had been.

"That's not true. You'd be a wonderful mom. I'm sure Colin feels the same way."

Gabriela thought about how Colin had finally stopped asking her if she was ready. "He has said that. But he's supportive of my choice."

Colin's mom, Rowan, had also given up, but only after Gabriela had forced her to stop prodding. Early in the marriage, Rowan would casually ask when Gabriela planned to have her first grandbaby. And Gabriela used to think, *First? She's assuming not only that I'll have one, but that I'll birth multiple kids.* But because Colin was an only child, and Gabriela hadn't wanted to cause conflict, she'd make excuses that weren't exactly lies and say things like, *Now isn't the right time,* or, *Maybe I'll be ready after I finish my next book*, never dreaming she'd one day change her mind.

But his mom couldn't seem to let it go, becoming like a woodpecker methodically pecking away at a piece of timber, taking notice of each of Gabriela's passing birthdays as if it were her own eggs that were diminishing in quality each year. Gabriela sometimes wondered if she and Colin were in cahoots, tag-teaming her until she finally gave them both what *they* wanted.

Gabriela decided that she'd had enough when she turned thirty-six. Rowan had made a comment about Gabriela's reproductive abilities, mentioning an article she'd read about women who'd frozen their eggs and how it could be like an insurance policy in case they needed them later. She wasn't sure if it was the two glasses of wine she'd consumed beforehand or the years of built-up defensiveness that had finally bubbled over, but she blurted out that she was not going to freeze her eggs *ever* because she *never* planned to have a child, which her precious son, Colin, had been very aware of from their third date. The shattered look on her mother-in-law's face had instantly made her wish she could take back each word. Gabriela had apologized for lashing out, but she never felt like her mother-in-law truly forgave her, and a silent tension had always remained between them.

But now, as she stared at the blank Word document on her computer screen, she knew she couldn't let their tentative relationship keep her from reaching out this time around. So she grabbed her purse and headed toward Rowan's home in Malibu before she could talk herself out of it.

"Gabriela?" When Rowan said her name, the inflection in her voice made it sound more like a question, her mother-in-law clearly surprised by her visit. Save for the requisite birthday or holiday get-together, they hadn't seen much of each other since the night Gabriela had snapped at her.

"Rowan, it's so good to see you," Gabriela said, meaning the words more than she realized she would, then stepped forward and kissed her on both cheeks and pulled her into a tight hug, feeling Rowan's shoulders tense. Gabriela had forgotten how tall her mother-in-law was, close to five nine without heels, and how beautiful, her shoulder-length auburn hair pinned back at her neck, the lines around her pale sapphire eyes only adding to her beauty.

"Please, come in," Rowan said as she swept her long arm in the direction of the sitting area off the kitchen, a room that Gabriela had memorized, with not so much as a lamp or a rug having been replaced in two decades. Gabriela remembered sitting perched on the edge of the white sofa with the pale yellow floral print, Colin next to her with a strange smile painted on his face, the teacup shaking slightly in her hand as she made conversation with her future in-laws for the first time. Colin's dad, Aidan, a lanky man just like Colin, with dark red hair and a nose slightly too large for his thin face, hadn't said much after they were introduced—the only sound had been spoons clinking against their tea saucers. But when he made a joke about British people's teeth, they'd all released hearty laughs that didn't at all match how funny the anecdote had been. Gabriela felt herself relax, knowing immediately where Colin had gotten his similar sense of humor.

Colin's family came from a long line of wealthy entrepreneurs. His great-grandfather started a charming pub over one hundred years before that still stood today, and was run by one of Colin's uncles, and boasted the best fish-and-chips in West London. Colin's father had left the family business to start up a software company that had eventually brought them to the States, working fourteen-hour days for years before it was sold for more money than they could ever spend in their lifetime. Gabriela loved that none of them, including Colin, ever talked about their wealth—his father still driving the old BMW that he'd had when she met Colin.

The skin between Rowan's eyes was knotted and Gabriela could practically see her mother-in-law's thoughts imprinted across her face. She feared something was wrong with her son, silently pleading for Gabriela to put her mind at ease. She had nothing to worry about: Colin was as healthy as ever, working out daily in their tiny home gym or with his boot camp class, eating protein diligently as a disciple of the Atkins diet. But were she and Colin okay? Gabriela didn't know.

"Rowan, I just have to say I'm sorry I haven't been around more, that things were never the same after that night," Gabriela said before she'd even lowered herself into the burgundy leather chair opposite Rowan's.

"It's okay, I'm just glad you're here now." She pressed her thin lips into a smile. Gabriela wasn't sure if Rowan meant the words, but she could tell she was trying, that she wanted to. "And I'm just hoping that everything is okay." Rowan picked at a loose thread on her cardigan sweater.

"Everything is fine," Gabriela said, her instinct to put up a wall to protect herself instantly kicking in. "Actually, it's not," she added quickly, the tears falling before she could stop them.

Rowan rose from her chair. "I'm here," is all she said before taking her daughter-in-law into her arms. Gabriela felt herself collapse into Rowan's chest, her sobs echoing in the cavernous house.

Once Gabriela had calmed down, they moved out to the

backyard that overlooked the Pacific Ocean, Gabriela inhaling the ocean breeze. They sat for several minutes on a bench before Gabriela finally spoke, the words spilling out almost faster than she could process them, Rowan listening intently, her hand squeezing Gabriela's. They talked for hours until the sun went down and the chilly air drove them back inside. Gabriela felt more relaxed than she had in a long time, opening up to Rowan about not just the baby but also her mother's death. She never realized how badly she'd needed Rowan, and she wished she'd let her in sooner. Rowan had revealed that it had been incredibly difficult for her to get pregnant with Colin, that she'd wanted a house full of kids and had been devastated when she couldn't conceive again. She and Aidan finally accepted that was God's plan for them. "We didn't have fertility treatments back then, and only a doctor could tell you that you were pregnant; there were no drugstore tests." Gabriela had never known this story, and she wasn't sure Colin did either. Her mother-in-law had always been fiercely private—or perhaps she had just been waiting to be asked the right questions.

"I'll talk to him," was the last thing Rowan promised before Gabriela got into her car to drive back home.

"Thank you," she'd whispered. "For everything. And I'm sorry, I really am."

Rowan had waved it off, told her she'd been wrong too, that she'd been overly aggressive about wanting a grandchild and hadn't wanted to hear it when Colin all but told her it was highly unlikely it would happen. She was sorry they hadn't talked it through sooner, wishing she hadn't been so stubborn for so many years. For her part, all Gabriela hoped now was that Rowan would have the influence over her son that only a mother could have.

CHAPTER ELEVEN

....

Jessie's shoulders tensed and she resisted the urge to crane her neck toward the door, to meet Lucas' father's eyes for the first time since she'd given birth to their son. She was terrified that if they saw each other, the secret they shared would be as transparent as a piece of glass.

Claire's heart lurched as she watched Cathy and Peter head toward their table, and she reflexively put her hand over it as if it were going to pop out of her chest. This hadn't happened last time. In the other version of their lives, Jessie and Peter's wife had never crossed paths after she'd had the baby. And Claire had never met either of them. The closest she'd come had been when she and Jessie stalked Peter's Facebook page just a few years ago, in 2012. There had been something about the way his green eyes pierced through his profile photo—on the beach with his arms wrapped tightly around his teenage son's shoulders, the son he hadn't denied—that made her stomach tighten, and she'd been grateful she would never have to meet Peter in person. *Until now*.

Claire noticed Jessie's breathing had intensified, her chest rising and dropping rapidly from beneath her loose-fitting top as Cathy approached them, her face devoid of expression. Claire slid her chair closer to Lucas and held her breath as she watched Peter shuffling behind his wife with his hands shoved deep into his pockets.

"Jessie, hi, it's good to see you!" Cathy exclaimed, and both Jessie and Claire released their breath as Cathy gawked at Lucas' striped blue onesie with My Mom's a Hottie printed across it in bold lettering. Claire noticed Jessie force a smile and wrap her arms across her middle section as she looked up at Cathy's rail-thin physique. "How precious is your new little guy!" Cathy turned back toward Peter, whose face was losing color rapidly, his eyes darting around trying to find something to focus on. "Isn't he adorable? Kind of makes me want another one," she said as she poked her husband playfully. He offered a stiff smile but said nothing, causing Cathy to shoot him a quizzical look. "Are you okay? You look pale."

Of course he's not okay. He's staring at his child for the first time, Claire thought as anger began to course through her. Watching Peter refuse to look in the direction of his son made her think of Emily's father. She wondered for the billionth time how a man could turn his back on his own child. She watched Peter reading a sign tacked to a corkboard about a beer and wine festival and considered something else she'd pondered after Emily dropped out of college, but hadn't wanted to face: *maybe she should have made different choices with Emily's dad, David.* It was easy for Claire to blame her strained relationship with Mona for her issues in parenting Emily. But what had David's absence in Emily's life done to her daughter? Claire had reasoned that no involvement was better than a sporadic influence, but what if she had been wrong?

Claire knew that if Peter took responsibility it could actually create more problems than not. And she also knew that Grant was going be Lucas' father, regardless. But from what Jessie had told her about Peter, he was a former pro soccer player and stay-at-home dad who ran sports camps in the summer. By all accounts a good father to the son he already had—but she couldn't shake the feeling that now that Peter had seen Lucas, it could change everything. Claire glanced at Jessie. There were no traces of the giddy girl who used to talk about Peter like he was a high school crush. As she studied Jessie now, all she saw was a woman who would shrink into herself if she could, wanting nothing to do with a man who had once filled her up and made her float like a helium balloon.

For a moment it felt like everything in the coffee shop was moving in slow motion as Jessie rearranged herself in her seat and Cathy ogled baby Lucas and Peter fidgeted with his Black-Berry. Claire knew it was up to her to break the awkward silence.

"Hi, I'm Claire." Claire extended her hand to Cathy and gave Jessie a pointed look.

"I'm Cathy," she said, shaking her hand firmly. "And this is my husband, Peter. We both know Jessie from Jefferson Elementary."

Peter offered his hand to her and she reluctantly took it, holding his gaze for a beat, wondering if he knew Jessie had told her the truth.

"Nice to meet you," Claire chimed, channeling her real estate agent persona. "I think I need to order Jess another double espresso, she's such a zombie this morning. Even though this little guy is sleeping peacefully right now, he's been a terror at night. Right, Jess?" Claire said, pulling a pale blue blanket up around Lucas' chin.

"Right . . . a terror." Jessie forced the words, trying to regain her composure. It had been years since she'd seen Peter. She was almost hypnotized by him, unable to look away, surprised how he knocked the wind out of her all over again. After she'd told him she was pregnant and he'd stormed out of the restaurant, she'd never spoken to him again, and managed to avoid him the entire time she carried his child, quickly turning the other way whenever she caught a glimpse of his profile in the elementary school hallway.

Shortly after Lucas was born, she'd found out Peter and Cathy had moved away. She'd driven by the sold sign in front of their ranch house, feeling conflicted—relieved because now she could finally breathe, but also devastated on behalf of her newborn son, that his father would leave without so much as a forwarding address.

Finally, she met Cathy's eyes. "Sorry I'm so out of it. Claire's right, sleep has been nonexistent in my life since this little guy was born. He's cute now, but you should have heard him at 3 a.m.!" Cathy laughed, and Jessie studied her face for any signs she knew the truth, but she seemed genuine—sweet, even— which only tightened the knot in Jessie's stomach.

"Those days seem forever ago, don't they, Peter?" Cathy said, giving him a sideways glance until he finally cleared his throat and spoke.

"Right, can't believe it's already been ten years," he said, only looking up from his phone for a few seconds.

Lucas chose that moment to open his eyes, nearly a perfect match to Peter's, and let out a small squeal.

"Oh, look at those eyes!" Cathy reached her arms toward

Lucas and Jessie froze, wondering if Cathy was going to see the resemblance. But she only asked if she could hold him.

Jessie felt an involuntary shiver ripple through her.

She didn't know Cathy well; she'd seen her in passing at school functions, and she'd only talked to her twice before she'd slept with Peter. The first was at a school bake sale, where they'd made small talk about a home renovation Cathy and Peter were doing. Jessie felt immediately intimidated by this beautiful woman—her rich brown hair fell to the middle of her back, her limbs seemed to go on forever, and her caramel-colored eyes were shaped like almonds. Not only did her high-powered job send her jetting across the globe, but she still managed to oversee the work done on her house *and* make it to school events. Jessie could barely get dressed before driving the twins to school.

The next time they ran into each other was in the school parking lot. Cathy was running late for her parent-teacher conference and looked considerably more frazzled than she had at the bake sale. She made a halfhearted joke to Jessie that it was hard to do it all, and Jessie felt a pang of sympathy for Cathy, knowing from Claire how hard it was to miss so many important moments in Emily's life because she had to work.

"Of course you can hold him," Jessie said finally, and tried to steady her trembling hands as she slowly unbuckled the straps on Lucas' car seat.

"Maybe you should hold off on that second double espresso. You're shaking." Cathy laughed and Jessie pressed her lips into a smile, placing Lucas gently in Cathy's arms. While Cathy bounced Lucas, Jessie looked at Peter, watching him recognize how the jut of Lucas' chin matched his own, the way his eyes turned from green to hazel as they caught the light. Sensing her gaze, he glanced at her for a second before looking away.

As Cathy cradled Lucas, swaying her hips unconsciously while she rocked him, Jessie's lip began to quiver and she knew if she didn't speak immediately, she would start crying. "Cathy, I'm surprised to see you here in the middle of the day," she finally managed.

"I took a new position at work." She didn't take her eyes off Lucas. "I won't be traveling anymore."

Jessie forced herself not to look at Peter for his reaction. "Congratulations." Last time, Jessie heard that she and Peter had moved because of Cathy's job. She'd been promoted and was making more money, and their new house had apparently been closer to the prestigious private school where they'd enrolled their son. Jessie had been patiently waiting for them to move away in this life too.

"Thanks. My company actually offered me a promotion. And believe me, it was hard to turn down because it came with a giant raise." She laughed. "Peter really pushed for me to take it. He said I'd worked so hard, that I deserved it." Cathy paused and gave him a smile. "He's always been so supportive."

Jessie's eyes locked on Peter's and he averted his gaze quickly. Jessie had wondered if he'd pushed Cathy to take the promotion so he could escape what he'd done. Jessie wondered why he hadn't been able to convince her this time.

"But the thing is," Cathy continued, "I would have been traveling even more, and I just had this epiphany. And here's the really funny part, I didn't even tell Peter this yet."

"What?" Peter and Jessie asked at the same time. Jessie laughed awkwardly.

"*You* were part of the reason I turned it down."

"Me?" Jessie asked as she caught Claire's eye. This was it. Cathy was about to slam her for the affair. Jessie suddenly wanted to pull Lucas from her arms and run, but she couldn't move.

"I saw you and your kids a few days ago, on Tuesday. You didn't see me. You were heading into the grocery store and I was driving to a lunch meeting and I thought, I could never do that. Spend a day with Sean during the week."

Jessie felt an intense pressure in her chest, as if someone were sitting on it. She remembered that day. She hadn't even thought twice before heading out of the house. They were picking up deli sandwiches and going to the park for a picnic. Last time, she'd avoided going anywhere in public with the baby, petrified she might run into Peter or even Cathy. But this time, she'd decided she needed to focus more on her relationship with her kids than worrying about a chance encounter.

Cathy was still talking and Jessie forced herself to listen. "And I thought, why am I wasting the best years away from my family? Peter gets to be around, and I should too. So I turned it down and demanded they find a spot for me that required no travel. And not only did I get that, but they said I can also work from home a few days a month." She looked at Peter again as she said this. Jessie suddenly wondered if his wife knew but was playing some sick and twisted game with both of them. Or maybe it really had been a coincidence that seeing Jessie with her kids prompted her into action.

"So you'll probably see me in here more often!" Cathy smiled and handed Lucas back to Jessie. "He's gorgeous. It's funny, he looks so much like Sean did as a baby," she said, handing Lucas back to Jessie.

Jessie tried to formulate a response but the words caught in her throat as she realized this had only happened because she'd come back. Last time, she'd lost Grant, but she'd also been free of any tangles with Peter and Cathy. She hugged Lucas tightly, suddenly worried that this change could somehow take him from her.

"All babies kind of look the same, small and squishy, right?" Peter said briskly. "We should probably get going, Cath; we're meeting the contractor at ten."

"Contractor?" Jessie asked before she could stop herself.

"Oh yeah. When I thought I was taking the offer, we were going to move, but now we're staying put and doing an add-on!" Cathy said brightly as Peter guided her by the arm toward the counter. "Nice to see you. And thanks for inspiring me!" she added with a smile as they walked away.

"You're welcome," Jessie said, her chin starting to quiver.

"Hey," Claire said firmly. "I know you're upset. But you need to hold it together right now, Jess," she said through gritted teeth as she eyed Peter and Cathy ordering their coffees.

Jessie nodded her head in agreement.

"You can cry when they leave, I promise." Claire squeezed Jessie's hand. "Jess, I know you were caught off guard, but you can't act like that around Cathy and Peter if you see them again or she'll figure out something is going on. She isn't stupid."

"No, she's not." Jessie smiled wide and waved good-bye to Cathy as Peter held the door, the silver bells that hung from the handle jangling as they left.

"Claire, what have we done coming back here?" Jessie looked at Lucas. "Cathy has now met the child her husband had with *me*. She didn't take the promotion because she saw me with the kids, *and* they aren't moving? Why would the universe want us entangled in each other's lives?"

"Remember, it's the butterfly effect. Even small changes can create a drastically different outcome." Claire thought about how easily she'd slipped back into her old patterns of letting Emily get away with things she shouldn't. They'd recently had an argument about her watching too much TV. Emily had screamed so loudly that Claire was afraid someone would call the police. She'd been too distraught to react, simply going in her room and closing the door behind her. Why couldn't she be stronger with her daughter even when she knew what the outcome would be if she wasn't? Claire took a drink of her now lukewarm coffee.

"Do you think Cathy suspects something?" Jessie leaned toward Claire.

"I don't think so," Claire answered. "She was really wrapped up in the baby."

"I know," Jessie said as she watched Peter and Cathy get into their black Suburban. "That's what makes me nervous."

CHAPTER TWELVE

. . . .

Gabriela thumbed mindlessly through an issue of *Good House-keeping* and waited for her name to be called, her heart thumping so hard she could hear the pounding in her ears. She pressed her thumbs against her temples and breathed in deeply.

"You okay?" Jessie asked, putting her magazine facedown in her lap.

"Yeah, I'm just nervous," she said as she scanned the waiting room full of women—some with swollen bellies, some without, some with other kids in tow, some young and a few older—like her. "I'm scared they're going to tell me"—she lowered her voice and leaned toward Jessie, who was sitting in the pale green vinyl chair across from hers—"that I'm too old."

"Don't be ridiculous! If that were the case, I wouldn't have been able to conceive Lucas at thirty-nine! You're only a year older than I was when I got pregnant with him." Jessie watched a four-year-old come whizzing by, his arms outstretched like an airplane, his mom sternly warning him that he'd better come back and sit down or there would be no ice cream for him after they left.

"Then why hasn't it happened yet?" The circles under Gabriela's eyes looked almost white against her olive skin.

"It will." Jessie moved into the seat next to Gabriela. "You should focus on the fact that you've been trying, that Colin changed his mind. Didn't you say that in itself is a miracle?"

Gabriela thought back to the day Colin came home early from work, finding her in what had begun to feel like a perpetual haze, staring at her computer screen, silently praying for the words to come. She wished she could have blamed the lure of Facebook or Twitter, but sadly, she didn't even have those distractions.

Colin had swiveled her chair around so she could face him and knelt down on the floor, his hands resting in her lap as he looked up at her. "I've changed my mind," he said, letting the words linger for a moment, watching as Gabriela processed the sentence she'd waited *years* to hear.

"You want a baby?" she said, tears and quiet laughter mixing together, but fear also lingering as she worried she'd misunderstood, that he was talking about something else.

"Yes," he'd answered. "I'm sorry it took me so long."

If you only knew how long it's really been, Gabriela thought as she hugged him to her chest, knowing instantly that Rowan had talked to him, feeling a sudden love for her mother-in-law she hadn't known was possible, and a slight twinge of regret, wishing she hadn't let her pride stop her from involving her last time.

"Thank you," Gabriela said, then listened quietly as Colin explained how his mom had sat him down and made him see it in a way he hadn't before. He struggled with the story, obviously feeling bad that his mother had been the one to convince him, not Gabriela. But she didn't care. All she was focused on was that he'd said yes.

They began trying immediately, but after she'd gotten her period for the second month in a row, she looked at the calendar and decided she couldn't waste any more time, that she and Colin should see a reproductive endocrinologist who could tell her if there was something wrong.

Colin had his sperm tested first and, as their doctor put it, he definitely had swimmers that were ready to race. So that had left Gabriela, who needed to undergo blood tests to determine hormone levels and an ultrasound, so any easily identifiable problems with her ovaries, uterus, or fallopian tubes could be ruled out. Then they'd start discussing assisted reproductive technologies. Gabriela had all the terms memorized now, having spent much of the last month studying everything from in vitro fertilization, or IVF, to gestational carriers, scouring message boards where she chatted with women about the best doctors, the latest technologies, staying up until all hours working on her pregnancy when she knew she should be working on her novel. Today she'd find out what this future held, if she'd be able to conceive on her own or if she'd need some help.

"Gabriela?" a nurse called out as she propped the door open with her hip, looking at her clipboard and then at the people in the waiting room.

"Want me to come in with you since Colin's not here yet?" Jessie asked.

"I'm here, I'm here," Colin said, rushing in just as the nurse called Gabriela's name again. "Thanks for waiting with her, Jessie. It was bumper-to-bumper on the 405!" he said as he loosened his tie and clamped his hand over Gabriela's and walked her toward the nurse. Jessie knew he'd been coming from his law office in Westwood, just fifteen miles away, but with Los Angeles traffic everything took forever, especially at 4 p.m. She admired him for ducking out of work early, showing that he really was invested in having a baby.

As Jessie watched the door swing shut behind them, she thought about how she'd gone to her first ultrasound appointment for Lucas alone. Grant didn't know she was pregnant and Peter was out of the picture. She'd felt loneliness cover her like a heavy blanket as she'd followed the nurse into a tiny room and was instructed to put on the gown and leave it open in the back. She'd draped the salmon pink quilted paper over her thighs and tried not to cry. Her mind had flashed to the first time she and Grant had seen their twin daughters, just two tiny fetuses floating inside of her, curled around each other. She'd been scared shitless—twins didn't run in either of their families—but also excited to do it with Grant at her side. They were only four years into their marriage and still madly in love.

There was a part of her that went to that appointment alone because she thought the doctor might tell her she'd imagined the whole thing, that the blood test results had been a false positive (she read that could happen) and she would float out of the doctor's office, and the one-night stand with Peter would stay buried deep inside of her where no one would ever find it. But instead, she'd seen the black-and-white image of her baby on the monitor, so tiny, tinier than she'd remembered they could be, and she'd started to cry. It didn't matter who the father was, she had a life growing inside of her.

As Jessie waited for Gabriela, she said a silent prayer for her friend, hoping the doctor was giving her good news, racked with guilt that she'd gotten pregnant so carelessly with a baby that belonged to the wrong man, while Gabriela was struggling to have a baby she wanted more than anything with the right one.

• • •

"I still don't see why we needed to come all the way down here," Mona complained as Claire pushed the elevator button with more force than was necessary, attempting to stay calm as she shepherded her mom toward Dr. Lee's sterile office. It was just a few miles from where she knew Gabriela was also awaiting critical news, mentally preparing herself for the stiff chairs and nurses to match. But the lack of comfort was nothing compared to how it would feel to sit by her mother *for the second time* as she received her cancer diagnosis.

Before, Mona had dragged her feet for over a year before seeing a doctor, unknowingly letting the disease fester inside her lungs like mold in a damp cellar. After they'd learned she had stage-three lung cancer, Claire and her father had second-guessed the hell out of themselves. They'd all heard the cough. They'd seen her color slowly drain from her face, the weight drop from her frame. But they'd all been too busy with their day-to-day routines to notice that she was literally dying right in front of them from a smoker's disease, even though she'd never held a cigarette to her mouth.

This time, she'd insisted her mom see a doctor, and when she balked, claiming it was probably just a respiratory virus, Claire had picked up the phone and made the appointment herself.

Claire held her tongue as Dr. Lee examined Mona, waiting for the spark of clarity in his eye as he pressed his stethoscope to her chest and listened, watching for the furrow of his brow that would indicate that he suspected this was much more than bronchitis. Claire nearly cried with relief when the doctor nonchalantly said he'd like to take some X-rays because Mona had mentioned she'd coughed up some blood, knowing from experience that this was a side effect of the disease. If he hadn't, Claire had planned to pull him aside and tell him she suspected lung cancer and that he *had* to order an X ray. She didn't know what she'd say if he questioned her reasoning—obviously not the truth, that she'd already lived this, that she'd already lost her mom once, that she'd do anything for more time with her. Claire prayed that they'd catch it early enough this time, but the unknown kept her up at night as she tossed and turned, fretting that she was too late again.

Mona's death had been long and painful, or at least that was how Claire remembered it, each day feeling as if it were moving in slow motion. Claire had been conflicted toward the end, wanting more time with her mom, but also recognizing how much she was suffering and wanting her pain to be over.

Their relationship had been complicated since Claire was young, even more so after Emily was born. Claire felt the weight of her mother's disappointment. A large sigh when Claire had opted to get a real estate license instead of finishing college. Downcast eyes when Emily's father left. Shaking her head when Emily acted out and Claire seemed unable to calm her. Claire became so used to these subtle gestures that she too saw herself as a failure. It wasn't until the very end of Mona's life that Claire and Mona came together, the shadow of death finally removing the layers of guilt and anger that separated them. Afterward, Claire went to her grave once a week and knelt beside Mona's headstone, sharing stories and asking her for advice, the way she wished she had while she was alive.

As Claire's mom changed back into her clothes, a bittersweet smile formed on Claire's lips. She could say those things *this time*, while her mom was alive. She had a chance to show her that she was a success, that she was a good mother, that she was a good person. And she sure as hell wasn't going to waste it.

"I can't wait for you to meet Mason!" Claire broke the silence as they made the long walk back to the car. Her mother seemed lost in thought, and Claire wondered if a part of her already knew there was something seriously wrong.

"Tell me about him," Mona said, seeming genuinely interested.

The corners of Claire's lips lifted involuntarily. She'd forgotten how easy things had been with Mason, how intently he listened when she spoke, even if she was just complaining about a client refusing to accept an offer that was only a few thousand under the asking price or dissecting the convoluted storyline on the latest episode of *Lost*. Or how her stomach did little cartwheels when he woke up and pulled her close to him, planting tender kisses on her neck that she wished would never stop. Claire loved how much he cared about his job as a furniture maker, searching for the perfect wood to create a custom dining room table or shelves for a child's room. She tried to put Jared out of her mind, tried not to think about how she'd burst into tears when he'd asked her to marry him, not sure if her stomach had butterflies because she was excited or scared or maybe a little bit of both. She was realizing that she wasn't completely over Mason, her heart opening for him again reflexively.

She told herself that if she was meant to marry her fiancé, life would lead her back to him, wouldn't it? If she looked for him now, she'd find him living in Anaheim with his first wife and children, the idea that he'd eventually find love with someone else, let alone marry her, the furthest thing from his mind. The timing would be off if she interrupted his life now and she knew from what had happened to Jessie that if their worlds collided, she could be changing their future together.

"Just be careful," Mona said as she dug in her purse, pulling out a piece of gum and popping it into her mouth, snapping it loudly as Claire navigated the morning traffic. "You have a daughter to consider." Before, Claire would have interpreted Mona's warning to mean she didn't think Claire was capable of making good decisions when it came to men. (Which, if she was being totally honest, had always been a little bit true.) Before, Claire's blood pressure would have risen with each smack of Mona's gum until she would eventually explode like a firecracker after the fuse had burned down, attacking her mom with a fierceness that would often dissolve as quickly as it came, but still causing damage that took far longer to heal. They always bounced back, but each argument would take its toll, further widening the gap between them.

Claire understood now that Mona only wanted Claire to be careful. In fact, Claire had said similar things to Emily as she'd gotten older and started dating more seriously, petrified she'd choose a guy like her father, one who'd bail at the first sign of responsibility. But Emily interpreted Claire's concerns as bullets to dodge, as judgment rather than concern. She'd tried to explain to Emily that she meant well, but she'd responded tightly that there was a fine line between care and criticism before hanging up on her. Claire had looked at the phone and laughed, thinking that Mona must be watching down and smiling now that Claire finally understood the complexities of raising a daughter.

"I will be careful," Claire answered quietly, wishing her mom could know she was trying to make better choices this time. She suspected that if they returned to 2015 on her forty-first birthday, any work would be erased like a chalkboard on the last day of school. Going back to her old life was still Claire's game plan—even though she'd made mistakes along the way, she didn't want to undo the many great things that came in the years *after* turning forty, like meeting Jared. She hoped Jessie and Gabriela would feel the same way, although she worried with each passing day that they were getting more attached to this life. Gabriela was closer to becoming a mother and Jessie, despite her run-in with Cathy and Peter, was reveling in having Grant back. But Claire knew a lot could happen in ten months, and she just hoped Blair would agree to let her go back on her own if necessary. And that her friends would understand why she wanted to.

"How's the market?" Mona asked a few minutes later. "Are you really going to buy *two* properties? Aren't you worried the bubble will burst?" Mona frowned.

"I think we have a few more years," Claire said expertly. She'd always loved her job, but when she'd watched so many of her clients get strapped with mortgages they couldn't afford, with lines of credit they'd regret later, eventually losing their homes and savings, she'd blamed herself and almost left the field altogether.

Before, she'd always let fear hold her back from investing in the market, her mother's conservative voice ringing inside her head. But now, with her gift of foresight, and her plans to buy and flip two houses, she had a chance to make enough money to actually be able to afford the Lexus she knew she'd have to purchase soon. She thought of Blair's warning, that they couldn't use time travel to make easy money. But she still had to see the right investments, manage any necessary renovations, and be able to sell them—and that all required expertise.

Claire slowed as she approached her mom and dad's peach

stucco town house, noticing how the roses planted out front were beginning to burst into bloom. "When is your next doctor's appointment?"

"Oh, let's see," her mom said, fumbling through her purse for the appointment card the nurse had given her. Claire thought how much easier it would be if Mona had a smartphone with a calendar, knowing she'd lose the card and have to call the office, which was precisely why Claire was asking her for the date now. "Next Tuesday. He wants to do a CT scan and some bloodwork. Seems like a lot of rigmarole for a bad cough," Mona said, but Claire noticed a flicker of concern in her mother's eyes. Her mom had always put up a tough front, but Claire knew she was hurting, that the pain in her chest was worse than she was letting on.

"I'll come with," Claire said, and laid her hand on her mom's shoulder, remembering how her life had been divided into two categories after Mona's diagnosis: *before* and *after*. Before, when she'd send her mom's calls to voice mail. After, when she'd fumble to take her call. When she would have done anything for just another day together. She would have let her smack her gum as loudly as she wanted.

"You don't need to. You should be working, right?" She opened the car door. "I'm a tough cookie. I'll be fine. I love you," she finished before blowing a kiss and walking toward the house.

Claire put the car in gear quickly and drove away, tears crashing down her face. Her mom had uttered the same words to her the day she died.

CHAPTER THIRTEEN

. . . .

December 2005

"I've got it," Gabriela snapped, and Colin threw his hands up and went into his walk-in closet, letting a long exaggerated sigh pass through his lips on the way in.

Gabriela twisted her right arm over her shoulder and tried with all her energy to reach the zipper on the back of her dress, her pride now refusing to let Colin help, even though she knew it was physically impossible to accomplish without him. She gave up and plunked down on the bed. She had so many fertility drugs coursing through her she felt as if she could fly into a rage or break down in sobs at any given minute. Just yesterday at Target, she'd seen a plaque about motherhood and started bawling, deserting her cart and ducking into a restroom before anyone spotted her.

In the six months since Colin had agreed to try to make a baby, she'd already undergone one intrauterine insemination and one IVF cycle and neither had resulted in a pregnancy. And despite Gabriela's fertility doctor's *cautious optimism*, that after she adjusted a couple of drugs, her odds of conception would increase, Gabriela was concerned. Time was running out. She knew from the TTC (trying to conceive) message boards she scoured nightly that she was ahead of the curve, that you weren't supposed to start seeking help until it had been a year of trying naturally, but she didn't have that kind of time.

Colin had raised his eyebrow when Gabriela insisted on starting a second round of IVF immediately after the last cycle failed. "Don't you want to give it some time? You're putting so much pressure on yourself. Remember, Dr. Larson said stress can actually make it harder to get pregnant."

Gabriela squeezed her hands into fists. She knew Colin had tried to deliver his sentence as gently as possible. Even still, she felt that anger start to burn inside of her and she had to shut herself in the bathroom so she wouldn't lash out at him. Gabriela hadn't been prepared for the snowball effect of devastation that happened after she had to tell everyone there was still no baby. With each phone call to her father and her mother-in-law, the sad words exchanged as she delivered the news to her friends, the pain inside her grew larger and larger.

Ten days after the only viable embryo created had been implanted in Gabriela, she'd rushed to the drugstore and bought several boxes of pregnancy tests, her hands shaking so much as she hovered over the first stick that she'd peed all over it. Dr. Larson had narrowed her blue eyes and cautioned her to wait until the blood test to get the most accurate results. The store-bought test had been negative and so had the three she'd taken after that, but still, she'd felt hopeful as she waited for the nurse's call, sure she could feel something different was happening inside of her. When her phone rang, she answered breathlessly, only to be told by Jan, a nurse she'd come to know fairly well after countless office visits for everything from blood work to ultrasounds, that she wasn't pregnant. Gabriela cried for hours, because it hadn't worked, because Jan didn't seem sympathetic, because of so many things, until the tears finally dried up and she felt numb. Colin tried to find the right words, but nothing he could say would change things. He didn't understand, he had no idea what she was feeling. The fear, the loss, the failure.

"Are you sure you're okay going tonight? Maybe you can tell Sheila you aren't feeling well? She'll understand," Colin said, emerging from his closet as he buttoned his blue dress shirt.

Gabriela shook her head. "I can't do that to her. She's already been incredibly patient considering I haven't sent her the pages I've been working on. I know she's nervous that I'm not going to deliver my manuscript on time." Gabriela thought about her last call with her editor, how Sheila had taken a long pause when she'd told her she missed her deadline because she'd been trying to conceive, no doubt shocked by Gabriela's change of heart, remembering the many times Gabriela had told her she was never having children for this very reason—they made life more complicated, and suddenly things like book deadlines seemed less important than your ovulation.

Colin's eyes asked the question he wouldn't. *Well, are you going to meet your deadline?* She didn't know the answer.

And it didn't help that she'd stopped doing the one thing that would help her when she had writer's block—running. Her once taut body had slowly become softer. Some of the women on the message boards had convinced her that yoga was a better option, so she'd purchased a mat and carried it down the street to the serene-looking studio and tried to blend in with the lithe women who were twisting themselves into pretzels while taking deep breaths and thinking about their intention. But all she could focus on was that time was slipping through her fingers. The in-structor had walked over and repositioned Gabriela's shoulders, whispering for her to loosen up. Gabriela smiled tightly and wondered, as she bent herself into a downward dog, if she had just given up her entire life to travel back ten years, only to fail at producing a book or a baby.

"I'm sorry I bit your head off earlier," Gabriela said, wrapping her arms around him. "It's the damn drugs. I feel like a crazy person!"

"I know, I understand," Colin said carefully, searching Gabriela's eyes before he continued. "But are you sure—"

"Yes, I'm sure I want to move forward with the egg retrieval on Saturday," Gabriela said, turning her back toward him so he could zip her up. "I have fourteen follicles this time, twice as many as last. So the chance of getting more eggs is consider-able. Plus I've been doing the acupuncture and I've eliminated gluten and dairy." She smiled, thankful she had insight from her previous life to help her, but also scared that it wouldn't make a difference. That's how it was now. It was like she was standing in the middle of an emotional scale, able to tip it in either direction at any moment, the only problem being she couldn't control it, or anything else for that matter—her body betraying her in a way she never thought possible.

Colin didn't answer, just kissed her on the forehead and started looping his black leather belt through his pants. She knew he was worried, that he was doing a lot of reading of his own. She'd found his laptop open recently to an article about how infertility could destroy a marriage. Her almost manic desire to conceive frightened Gabriela when she let herself go there, because Colin had been content without a baby, and their marriage had been fine without one, so now by trying to get pregnant, she could be putting their relationship at risk. But Gabriela wouldn't let that happen to them. She refused to accept that they could end up without a baby *and* more fragile than ever.

• • •

As Colin knotted his tie, he thought about how hard it had always been to say no to Gabriela. He knew the word wouldn't come easy from the first day he met her on that rainy street corner in London and she'd insisted on trying traditional English Yorkshire pudding, which Colin knew she would find tasteless because most people did—even him. But something about her left dimple, the curve of her mouth, made him acquiesce and then suppress a smile when the bowl of puffy batter was set before her. He'd watched as she scooped up a runny bite, her nose scrunching up just slightly as she swallowed. But she finished the bowl, never admitting she didn't like it. He spent the day listening to her stories—how she'd convinced a notoriously strict professor to let her take another shot at her midterm after she'd slept through her alarm; how she talked her way out of a speeding ticket when she'd been going fifteen miles over the limit—and soon realized that not only did she not take no for an answer, from anyone, she also didn't enjoy being wrong.

So when she came to him out of the blue to ask for a baby—*a baby, he still couldn't believe it!*—saying no was the hardest thing he'd ever had to do. Even though he hadn't actually spoken the word, his silence had. What he couldn't explain to her was how deeply she'd hurt him when she wouldn't change her mind. Yes, she'd been clear from the beginning that she didn't want children. And as a lawyer, even he couldn't argue with that. It was like they'd had a gentleman's agreement. He loved Gabs so much more than the child he didn't have, but still, it had taken him years to get right with it inside. To stop the knots from twisting in his stomach when he saw other dads with little girls riding on their shoulders or tossing a football with their sons.

He'd dulled the ache of not having his own kids by taking Madison and Morgan swimming or Emily to the park. But it wasn't the same. They weren't *his*. And that's what he'd tried to tell his mom when she'd brought it up recently. But she'd put her finger to her lips and asked him to open his heart and listen. And because his mom had never been this bold with him before, simply arching an eyebrow his way when Gabriela repeated she wasn't ready, he found himself agreeing. But he'd still been unsure. Worried Gabriela might change her mind again. It had never occurred to him that she'd become this laser focused, almost manic. The websites he'd been reading were helpful in assuring him they had a problem—*gee, thanks*—but didn't tell him how to fix it. He was the type of guy who liked his routines, who liked to keep things simple. He'd worn the same brand of running shoes since college, he liked to eat at the same Thai restaurant every weekend. But there was nothing simple about this.

And now, as he watched Gabriela slipping into her heels, he wondered what his *yes* was costing them. The seemingly endless fertility treatments were taking over their marriage, taking over Gabriela's work. When they did talk about another subject— a rarity—he could tell by the vacant look in her eyes that she was barely listening. Somewhere, in the corner of her mind, she was tracking her ovulation or thinking about the size of her follicles. He didn't recognize his wife anymore. She used to be a spark plug. Up without an alarm clock, writing a thousand words before the sun rose. Now she slept all the time and he could tell by the dust collecting on her laptop that she wasn't writing. And by the clean soles of her Nikes that she wasn't running. Her desire for a baby had trumped her want for anything else—*even him*. Their sex life was practically nonexistent. The last time was over a month ago and he could tell she wasn't into it. She'd been sleeping in the guest room most nights, claiming she was up late writing. But he knew that was a lie. He could tell she just didn't want to be near him. That he reminded her of what they weren't creating.

He wondered how much more of this he could take, how much more *they* could handle. Gabriela was the most competitive person he'd ever known—once holding up a game of Scrabble for twenty minutes, challenging the couple they were playing on their use of the word *quo,* and ultimately winning because she was able to convince them it was not a word used on its own, only as part of a phrase, and therefore not allowed. The lawyer in him had beamed with pride at her unwillingness to back down, finally Googling the answer to make her case. But now, this need to win was bordering on recklessness, and that scared him. What if they couldn't get pregnant? What would that do to her? The woman he loved more than anything in this world, the woman he knew he was going to marry from the first moment he met her, was slipping from his grip right in front of him, and there didn't seem to be much he could do about it.

• • •

"Gabriela, over here." Jessie waved at Gabriela and Colin through the crowd and they made their way to where she, Grant, Claire, and Mason were standing near a display showcasing several copies of Gabriela's third book, *Back to You,* which had recently been released. Gabriela felt a wave of gratitude that her friends had all come to support her tonight, at a holiday party a popular independent bookstore was throwing for Gabriela and a few other local authors who wrote books in the same genre. It was Sheila who'd convinced the owner of the store to include Gabriela in the event even though she'd failed to show up to a signing at the store two months prior. It had been the day after she found out she wasn't pregnant and she couldn't pull herself out of bed, Colin pleading with her to try, Gabriela looking up at him with bloodshot eyes begging him to please leave her alone.

"Sorry we're late," Gabriela said, giving Jessie a look that she understood instantly. Jessie had been fielding calls from Gabriela at all hours, Gabriela wanting her advice on what she could do to calm her hormones. Jessie asked Gabriela if she thought she was an expert because she'd been a beast during her pregnancy with Lucas. Gabriela offered only a *hmm* in response. Jessie had hung up wondering if she had been wrong not to tell Gabriela the truth about Lucas, that as Gabriela shared the rawest parts of herself, that Jessie should too. But after seeing Gabriela's emotions rise and fall like a roller coaster, she convinced herself that now was definitely not the right time to confide in her.

"Don't even worry about it. We just got here ourselves," Jessie said, pulling Gabriela toward her and Claire. "Sorry, girl talk for a minute," she said to Colin, Mason, and Grant, who shrugged, already engaged in their own conversation about some basketball player who was out for the rest of the season. "I got *so lost* trying to find this place. Grant just stared at me and asked why I hadn't printed the directions off the computer. I wanted to say I haven't done that in like ten years! I know it's already been six months, but I'm not sure I will ever get used to not having my apps. I miss my smartphone—it was so much smarter than me!"

"It sucks, doesn't it? Having to rely on ourselves again makes me realize how stupid technology makes us!" Claire said and laughed, thinking about how her daughter barely looked up from her portable video game, knowing full well what would happen when the iPhone hit the market. "But even so, I really miss Facebook. Now I have to actually call people to find out what's going on with them!"

"I miss my Yelp app the most," Jessie countered. "I can never decide where to eat!"

"Right now, if we said app, that waitress would offer us pigs in blankets or a shrimp skewer!" Gabriela said, and rolled her eyes. "This is so fucking weird, isn't it? In a few minutes, I have to go up there and talk about a novel I wrote over a decade ago. I had to reread it just to remember everything so I'm ready for the Q and A with the audience. I really wish I'd had Goodreads earlier, so I could've cheated and gotten some awesome reader's synopsis of the whole story!"

"I've almost called Mason *Jared* so many times lately and I'm terrified he's going to accuse me of having an affair!" Claire whispered, then caught Jessie's eye, instantly regretting her choice of words. She knew Jessie was finally feeling better about running into Peter and his wife. She'd been worried for months that she'd be getting a phone call from Cathy, demanding to know why Jessie's son looked so much like her own. But Claire had assured her that wasn't going to happen, even though Claire wasn't entirely convinced herself.

"Well, I never thought I'd say this, but I have to admit a lot of good has come out of this for me. Things I didn't expect," Claire said as she plucked a puff pastry off a passing waiter's tray.

"Like with your mom?" Jessie asked. Claire nodded. Since Mona's diagnosis, there had been many tears shed, but there was also hope. They'd caught the cancer an entire six months earlier, and Mona's doctor seemed much more optimistic than he had last time. But Claire was still scared to get too attached, to have to go through losing her mom all over again, so she didn't let herself read too much into it. Instead she was focused on making the most of their time together. Claire had started joining her in the garden, letting some overzealous but gorgeous Lowe's employee named Jake, with dimples for days, help her spend a fortune in the gardening department. The money had been worth it when Claire surprised her mom. She'd told her the story of the hunky employee as she'd emptied the contents of her shopping bag where Mona was kneeling by her rosebushes, and then retrieved her final purchase from the back of her car, Mona roaring with laughter as Claire pushed it into the backyard.

"You actually bought a wheelbarrow? Even *I* don't have one of those!" She'd put her hands on her hips as she studied its cherry red finish. "That, combined with these knee pads, will at least give me a good chuckle as we work side by side back here."

Claire couldn't help but laugh at herself as she looked at the pads adorned with a ladybug print that hadn't seemed so ridiculous when she was in the store.

"The sales guy must have been even cuter than you said!"

Claire smiled at the memory—she couldn't remember the last time they had been that happy together.

"What about you, Gabs? Are you still glad you came back?" Jessie asked tentatively, already knowing part of the answer— that trying to get pregnant had been tearing her apart.

"Things aren't going exactly the way I thought they would. But we still have plenty of time." She looked at her watch as she said it, as if it held the answers to when a baby would form in her belly. "It's all going to work out."

"It will." Claire grabbed her hand and squeezed it, trying not to think about how she hadn't been completely honest with her friends, that there was no way she was staying here, in this life, that once she did what she needed to do she was determined to return. "Just stay positive. We'll get through this together," Claire said, and smiled before walking over and draping her arm around Mason's shoulders.

Gabriela found herself wondering what it must be like for Claire, to be with Mason after two years of no contact with him. Gabriela had always liked Mason and was bothered when Claire let him walk away. She'd always questioned why Claire had let Emily come between them, when it was clear he was good for both of them. But she already felt so bonded to the *idea* of a baby that she knew she could imagine what being a mother actually felt like. She smiled as she watched Mason kiss Claire lightly on the lips, hoping it would work out for them, and for her.

It had been a long time since she'd been with anyone but Colin, but there were so few boyfriends before him, they were easy to remember. There had been Tim in high school, with burnt orange hair and freckles, fluent in French and a water polo player. And then there was Murphy, a stocky frat boy studying engineering whom she dated on and off for her freshman and sophomore years of college. And then she'd met Sam, a quiet chemistry major who used to take her to English pubs that served authentic fish-and-chips and was probably the reason she ultimately wanted to travel abroad, where she would meet Colin. The boyfriends before him had all tried so hard to get to know Gabriela. But after her mom died it was as if the elevator door closed and she was trapped inside. She would go through the motions of being the girlfriend, but struggled to understand the things her friends talked about, the way they'd feel a kiss down to their toes or how their stomachs would flip when their boyfriend would walk into a room. So she'd always been careful to end things just when she could see the change in their eyes, when they started looking at her differently, as if they were beginning to fall for her.

The crackle from the microphone jarred Gabriela out of her thoughts. She heard the owner of the bookstore make an announcement to welcome her and the other authors and guests. As Colin's warm hand wrapped around hers, she couldn't imagine any of those boyfriends standing next to her now, couldn't picture herself with anyone else but the man with the British accent and the raunchy sense of humor who had pried those elevator doors open and taught her to love. She began to walk up to the podium, hoping she wouldn't make a mistake when answering questions about her novel, not wanting to disappoint her loyal readers, who were the reason she loved writing so much. It was their support, more than anything else, that drove her to keep creating stories all these years. She turned around and smiled at Colin, who was clapping along with the rest of the crowd, and found herself wishing that her love for him would be strong enough to outweigh everything else, especially if she failed to get pregnant again and it was just going to be the two of them for the rest of their lives.

• • •

"Did you have fun tonight?" Jessie asked Grant as she pulled her sweater over her head.

"I did," he said simply as he got into bed. "I'm just tired."

"So I noticed." Jessie thought about how she had to nudge him during Gabriela's talk, his eyelids drooping.

"I'm sorry. The library remodel is killing me." He laid his head on the pillow and reached for the remote control. Jessie walked over and put her hand over his. "What?" he asked. "You don't want to watch TV?"

"I want to finish talking to you." Before, she would have silently steamed as he cut her off to turn on sports highlights, only to fall asleep minutes later, still gripping the remote. She would have let him off the hook, and given herself license to feel like a victim. But she understood that by letting him do that, she was just as much at fault. She crawled into bed, laying her head on her pillow and turning toward him. "I get that your job is stressful. And I'm thankful your business is thriving." She tried to find the right words. "But sometimes, it feels like you aren't really participating in your own life. *In my life,*" she corrected. "Tonight was important to me, to someone I love, and you fell asleep during her talk."

"I'm so exhausted, Jess," he said warily. "Look, I'm sorry I dozed off. But I think Gabriela will get over it."

"She will. But this isn't about her. It's about us."

His head shot up. "What do you mean?"

Jessie held her breath before responding. "Don't you ever worry that we could grow apart? If things don't change?"

"What do you mean? Are you unhappy?"

Jessie thought about his question. The truth was that she was happier now than she had been in ten years, years she'd wasted bemoaning the loss of Grant. But as much as Jessie was thrilled to have him back again, their problems hadn't magically disappeared.

"I'm not unhappy," Jessie started. "But we hardly see each other, and when we do, you can barely keep your eyes open. We need to remember to take care of our relationship and ourselves just like we do the kids." Jessie looked down as she said the last part, thinking about how she'd stopped nurturing her love for

Grant before, focused on the girls and not much else. "One day, they'll all be gone and it will just be us. I want to make sure we still like each other when that happens," she added, and prayed she'd still be with Grant when the twins left for college, instead of having to go back and forth via email about their tuitions and logistics, to stand next to Grant and Janet as they waved good-bye to the girls in the driveway of the home she used to share with him.

"What, are you saying you don't like me?" Grant asked teasingly, but there were shards of worry in the back of his eyes.

"No, silly. But life is busy, and is only going to get busier. I just want to make sure we don't lose each other along the way."

"Come here," he said, and pulled her face to his. "I'm sorry about tonight. I'm going to try harder, okay?" He placed a soft kiss on her lips. "And for the record, I still like you." He smiled.

Jessie kissed him deeply, sealing their connection. "Let me show you how much I like you too," she whispered before reaching her hands underneath the sheets that separated them. She hoped that even if the truth eventually came out again, they'd have a stronger foundation—one that would keep them together.

Jessie stayed awake long after Grant's heavy breathing had turned into a light snore. She heard Lucas gurgle on the baby monitor and smiled, scooting herself into the crook of Grant's strong arm, nudging him until he opened up to embrace her, the warmth of his body enveloping hers. Because now that she had the life that she wanted, she'd do just about anything to make sure it never slipped away from her again.

CHAPTER FOURTEEN

....

Claire pressed the damp washcloth lightly against Mona's forehead, avoiding her cheeks that had sunken from her weight loss. Mona had her good days, but she also had her bad ones, usually directly following the chemotherapy treatments, which were destroying not just the cancer cells but also her appetite.

"No?" Claire said, motioning toward the carne asada burrito with guacamole and cheese seeping out of it, resting on the plate in her lap. Claire had sat in bumper-to-bumper traffic for over an hour to get it, because Mona had a craving, one that Claire had been desperate to fulfill. But when she offered it to her mom, Mona had made a face like she'd smelled something sour.

"I can't." Mona turned her head and Claire placed the plate on top of Mona's dresser where Shaggy tried unsuccessfully to jump up and retrieve it.

"At least someone wants it," Claire joked as she watched the dog, but Mona didn't smile.

Claire grabbed her mom's hand. "Does *anything* sound good? I'll drive to San Francisco if that's what it takes."

Mona shook her head. "Sleep. Sleep sounds good."

"Okay," Claire said, watching as her mom drifted off and pulling the comforter up around her.

Later, Claire and her father sat in the kitchen, the plate with the uneaten burrito resting on the table between them. They'd absentmindedly picked at it with their forks, both of them refusing to discuss how Mona's body was quitting on her.

Since the diagnosis, Claire had been a permanent fixture at her parents' house, her and Emily regularly sleeping side by side on a sofa bed in the guest room, Mason coming by occasionally to take Claire to dinner, but always returning her to her mother's doorstep as if she were sixteen. Each time he kissed her good-bye, she could see him strain to see past her through the slightly ajar front door, knowing he wanted to come inside and have a beer with her dad or say hi to Emily. But things were different this time. Even though there was a strong chemistry between them, she knew they weren't going to end up together. And she needed to focus on the precious little time she had left with her mom. And then there was Emily, who seemed to be rebelling even more than she had the first time they'd lived through this.

More than once, Claire had berated herself for Emily's behavior, usually as she sat in the Los Angeles traffic that refused to move, Claire trapped with her self-degrading thoughts as the cars inched along the 101 freeway. Last time, Claire had shielded Emily from Mona's suffering, partly because she was in denial about the prognosis and hoped she'd make a full recovery, but also because she was afraid Emily wouldn't be able to handle watching her grandmother slowly succumb to the ravages of cancer. She'd often regretted her decision after Mona died. Emily hadn't really understood how dire the prognosis was until the doctors had said things like "make her comfortable" and "hospice." So this time she'd involved Emily more, letting her know the truth about her grandmother's disease, hoping it would motivate her to try to connect with her family, but that too seemed to be backfiring. She'd only retreated more.

At first, Claire attributed it to Emily being sad about her grandmother, but the more time that passed, the moodier Emily became, saying she was bored—complaining they didn't even have HBO, that she missed her friends, that she felt like she was being held hostage at an old folks' home. Claire would often catch her having hushed conversations on Mona's home phone, quickly hanging up when she heard her mother enter the room. Claire wondered if she was talking to Anna, whom she'd followed through on banning from Emily's social circle. Emily had also lied about not having homework on several occasions, then Claire had received phone calls from two of her teachers asking why she hadn't turned in not one, but multiple assignments. She had just listened to a voice mail from a teacher today that she needed to return, hesitant to hear the disappointment in her voice that her daughter wasn't delivering academically. Claire had already begged Emily to finish her assignments, to study for her tests. But short of doing the work for her, she didn't know how to form the words that would convince her daughter to care about her grades, especially now that her grandmother was sick. She knew she needed to sit down and talk to her, *really* talk to her, but between taking care of Mona and trying to sell the several houses she had listed, she hadn't had the time or energy for another argument.

• • •

"When are we leaving?" Emily's voice broke Claire away from her thoughts and she turned to face her daughter, who was leaning against the archway in the kitchen.

"Not for a while," Claire said, looking over at her dad, who was staring blankly at the burrito. "I want to be here when she wakes up from her nap."

Emily rolled her eyes. "I'm hungry."

"There is a ridiculous amount of food in this house. Help yourself."

Emily let out a huff and stomped over to the refrigerator, pulling at the handle with much more force than was needed, the contents banging against the door. "There's nothing in there I want," she stated without even looking at the food inside.

"I guess I could go grab you something," Claire said, exhaustion creeping into her voice. She swallowed her tears, the small tickle in her throat that had been threatening all week finally getting to her. She avoided her father's eyes now as he watched her from his chair at the kitchen table. Her dad had always been quiet, often letting Mona do the talking for both of them. Claire couldn't count how many conversations with Mona that had begun with, *Your father wanted me to talk to you about.* Ten years ago, he had faded into himself as Mona's condition worsened, almost as if he was trying to figure out how to live life without her before she was gone. After her mother's death, Claire tried to engage him, inviting him over for dinner once a week. But the truth was, she had never really known how to communicate with her father, and her mother's death had only made that more obvious. Claire had thought of how Gabriela's mother's death had bonded her to her father. She wanted the same thing, but didn't know how to achieve it, once admitting to her therapist that she'd been dreading the silence if she stopped at her dad's house on her way home from work so much that she'd deliberately missed the exit. She never dreamed that she'd get a second chance.

This time, Claire had inserted herself firmly into her father's quiet, retired world. Sometimes the relationship felt more like it was Claire who was the parent, her dad the sullen teenager, reluctant to share. She'd ask him to tell her stories about Mona while she was in the other room sleeping off the poison streaming through her body—discovering more about her father in the last six months than she had in her entire life, a fact that made her both deliriously happy and somewhat sad. *What else had she missed last time?*

"Your mother is tired," her dad said to Emily. "Eat something here."

Claire smiled shyly at her dad. They had slowly formed a united front since Mona's diagnosis. Against Emily's bad behavior. Against the insurance companies that were constantly trying to deny their claims. Against the cancer that was consuming not just Mona, but their entire family.

"Grandpa, all you have is leftover junk that even Grandma doesn't want to eat. It's gross."

Claire's phone rang before she could deal with Emily and she recognized the number as Sandy, a needy client to whom she had just presented an offer on her house. Claire held one finger up to Emily and walked into the other room to take the call. Sandy hadn't received the counteroffer that Claire had faxed before meeting her mom at the infusion center. "Goddamn fax machines!" she said under her breath, wondering how the hell she got any business done before she started using DocuSign, a program that allowed her clients to receive and sign all documents electronically. She wished she could invent it while she was here, but Blair had been very specific about what they had the power to do, and she was pretty sure making millions from stealing someone else's idea wasn't included in the deal. "I need to head over to the office to grab a contract," she announced as she stepped back into the kitchen, Emily standing against the counter, her hip jutted out.

"Good, let's get out of here," Emily said as she began to round up her books and folders and shove them haphazardly into her backpack.

"Hold on a minute." Emily's lack of compassion toward what was happening right in front of her made Claire furious. Couldn't she see how much pain her grandmother was in, the same woman who had given so much of her time to help raise her? She caught her father's eye, and like a lightning bolt had hit her, she suddenly knew what Emily needed. What had been missing for so many years. What Claire, even though she had it in spades herself, had never instilled in her daughter.

Empathy.

"You're staying here. I'll be back in under an hour."

"What? No! I'm coming with you!" Emily cried, throwing her bag on the floor, the contents splaying across the tile, Claire instantly flashing to Emily as a three-year-old when she'd done the same with a box of crayons at a restaurant.

"Tell you what, Em. I'll grab you In-N-Out on my way back. But on one condition." Claire hoped that dangling Emily's favorite hamburger place in front of her would make her more amenable to her idea.

Emily crossed her arms tightly over her chest, blocking the words silk-screened across her pale blue sweatshirt: As If. Claire almost laughed out loud at the symbolism and made a note to throw it out next time she did laundry. "What?"

"You stay here and sit with Grandma," Claire said softly. She pointed at Gabriela's latest book sitting on the counter, remembering how Gabriela had pressed a copy signed for Mona into Claire's hand as she was leaving the event, Claire fighting back the tears as Gabriela wrapped her arms around her, the hug saying more than words ever could. "Can you read that to her when she wakes up? We're on chapter ten, and it's getting really good."

Emily's eyes shot to the doorway of Mona's bedroom. Suddenly she wasn't twelve with long hair and braces. Her cheeks were soft and round, her wispy strands of hair sticking to her face, her tiny arms wrapped around her favorite doll. She was scared, Claire thought, and still a little girl in so many ways.

"Please," Claire pleaded. "I can't do this without you. Grandma needs you," she said, and watched Emily soften.

"She does?" Emily asked. Claire had never directly said those words until now, wanting to protect Emily from the day-to-day realities of cancer—the emotional roller coaster they had ridden last time, one that often left Claire feeling dizzy herself. But looking into her daughter's eyes now, she realized she might have finally struck the right chord. Everyone wanted to be needed.

"Of course. You know how much she loves you." Mona had always been the one person who understood how to walk Emily's tightrope, balancing discipline and love with such ease that Claire often wondered why Mona had never done the same with her. She had confessed to Claire, days before she died, when Claire had finally worked up the courage to ask. "I'll tell you a secret," she had rasped, Claire leaning in closer to hear, the machines in her hospital room threatening to drown out the words Claire had waited so long to hear. "You make all your mistakes with your own children, so by the time your grandchildren arrive, you know how to get it right. Plus, once you turn fifty, you kind of stop giving a shit what others think," she said, laughing weakly. Claire thought about her mother's words, and how horrible it was that she was finally ready to hear her mom's advice now that she was almost out of time to give it.

Emily took Gabriela's novel off the counter and flipped through it. "There aren't any R-rated scenes in here, are there?" She half smiled and walked into Mona's room, sat in the chair beside her grandmother's bed, and began to read as she waited for Mona to stir. Her voice was strong, a stark contrast to Mona's fragile one. Claire picked up her keys and headed toward the door. It was a small victory, but she'd take it.

As she drove to the office, Claire was feeling optimistic. Emily could help take care of Mona, and maybe doing so was just what she needed. And she hoped Emily would gain some perspective. Maybe she'd start being kinder. More understanding. Maybe.

She rolled down the window slightly, letting the warm Santa Ana wind blow through her car, and returned the call to Emily's teacher.

"Mrs. Marks. Hi, it's Claire Harris. I'm so sorry you had to call, but I wanted to let you know I'm going to make sure she turns in whatever assignments are missing."

Mrs. Marks cleared her throat. "I'm sorry, did Mr. Randall not talk with you yet?"

Claire struggled to conjure an image of a stout man with a comb-over. "The vice principal?"

"Yes, he said he was going to fill you in on what's happened."

"What do you mean on *what's happened?*" Claire asked, turning on her blinker as she exited the freeway.

"Well, this would probably be better discussed in person," Mrs. Marks said tentatively. "Can you come by the school first thing tomorrow and we can talk about the situation?"

Claire knew herself. She wasn't going to be able to wait until the morning to find out what the *situation* was. "We recently found out my mother has cancer and we're all struggling a little right now, so do you think you could give me more information tonight? You've got me worried here." Claire felt terrible playing the cancer card, but her heart clenched as she wondered what had happened to Emily.

"I'm so sorry to hear that." Mrs. Marks paused. "I can tell you there's been a serious incident involving bullying."

"Oh my God," Claire said as she imagined Emily pinned up against a locker or worse. Was that why she'd been so upset, so reclusive lately? Claire's stomach contracted—she had been too hard on her. "What happened to Emily? Who's been bullying her?"

Claire heard Mrs. Marks exhale. "I'm so sorry to have to tell you this, but you've got it mixed up. Nothing has happened *to* Emily. It's actually your daughter who's been the perpetrator."

Perpetrator? Emily definitely had an attitude problem, but she was also almost a teenager, going through puberty and navigating middle school—the trifecta of hardships for any adolescent. Not to mention her grandmother was dying. Claire pulled her car into the parking lot and turned the engine off. Emily wasn't a mean girl.

Was she?

CHAPTER FIFTEEN

....

Jessie watched Lucas as he rocked back and forth on his knees, the blanket gathering beneath him and his face full of marked determination as he tried to move his body forward into a crawl. As he blew bubbles through his tiny pink lips, she smiled, remembering the day she was leaving for the fiftieth birthday trip to Vegas, when Grant came to pick him up, how long his legs looked as he cascaded down the stairs. She'd wondered where the years went as he wriggled from her grasp when she tried to kiss him good-bye.

Last time, after Lucas was born, she'd been convinced she needed to keep him on a strict schedule, refusing to let even Morgan and Madison's busy activities dictate his nap or bedtime, often watching their softball games from the car as he slept. She was religious in her approach to when he slept and ate, while also trying to squeeze in the right amount of *time*—whether tummy or story.

But now, if Lucas refused to sleep, she'd scoop him from his crib and let him be awake, his large green eyes drinking in his surroundings. If he wailed in anger until she picked him up, she'd give in. If the girls wanted to hold him or feed him, she didn't hover over them in case they lost their grip. She just let life happen, as it should. And she'd worked harder this time to create a bond between the twins and their new baby brother. Just that morning, she'd asked the girls to feed him and watched as they both tried in their own way to get him to eat his strained peas. She'd felt so much more like a family this time than she had before. When Grant was able to get home for dinner and they all sat around the table together, the twins talking about their science-fair projects—Madison was calculating the density of fruits and vegetables and Morgan was doing a data analysis of the most popular animals—turns out kittens beat out puppies two to one!—while Lucas mashed his food, she could almost pretend Grant had fathered all three of them.

She leaned back on her wrists as she waited for Gabriela at the park, letting the sun dance across her face as she soaked in all these moments, willing them to replace the ones she'd like to forget.

"Jessie?"

Jessie snapped her head around at the sound of a familiar voice. She sat forward and pulled Lucas into her lap as she looked up, putting her hand over her eyes to see Peter standing above her.

"What are you doing here? Is Cathy with you?" She looked around, feeling a pit in her stomach. It was the first time she'd been alone with Peter since the day she'd told him she was pregnant. Jessie hugged Lucas against her chest and he squirmed. But she pressed him closer anyway.

"No, she's at work," Peter said without elaborating. "May I?" Peter pointed to the grass beside her.

"Actually, I was just about to leave." Jessie started to rise from the blanket.

"Jessica—"

"Please don't call me that." Not even Grant used her given name. And something about Peter saying it made her skin crawl—at least this time. Before, he'd mistakenly called her that and then it had morphed into an inside joke that for the life of her she couldn't remember why she'd ever thought was funny.

"Okay, *Jessie*." He put his hands up as if showing her he wasn't holding anything. "Listen, can I please talk to you?"

"Did you follow me here?"

"No . . . well . . . sort of," he stammered.

"What do you mean *sort of*?" Jessie started tossing squishy blocks and rattles into her diaper bag while perching Lucas on her hip.

"Just hold on a sec. I know how this looks, but I'm not stalking you. We need to talk and I couldn't think of another way to get you alone," Peter began, wedging his hands into the pockets of his khakis. "I haven't been able to get Lucas out of my mind since we ran into you."

All the sound around her quickly faded as if she'd shoved earplugs into her ears. She could see Peter's lips moving, but she couldn't hear him.

"Are you listening to me?"

Jessie scrambled for something to say, for the words that would make him retract his statement. When he'd refused to have anything to do with her pregnancy, she'd quickly settled into the idea. It would have been too complicated for him to be in Lucas' life. And she'd never told anyone, but when she used to rock Lucas to sleep while alone in her empty house, the twins with Grant for the weekend, she would thank her lucky stars that he was gone. His presence would have only reminded her of that night.

"What do you mean you can't get him off your mind? Where did he fit into your brain during the nine months I was pregnant? For the six months since he was born?" *And what about the ten years after that?*

"I don't know. There was something about seeing him, the way Cathy held him. Like, maybe we could work it all out somehow." He sighed loudly. "Maybe that's a crazy thought. But I *felt* something. And now I can't pretend I didn't."

"You could barely bring yourself to look up from your damn BlackBerry!" Jessie's voice rose and two speed walkers looked over as they passed.

"I know," he said sheepishly. "I'm sorry, I think I was in shock. But I did. Look at him, I mean. He has my eyes." Peter started to peer around Jessie's shoulder at Lucas' face, but she turned to block his view.

"So what are you saying?" Jessie could see her vein throbbing through her wrist.

"I don't know, exactly. Maybe I could spend a little time with him here and there?"

"Here and there?" Jessie snapped. "What, you want to take him to his Mommy and Me tumbling class? I'm sure that won't raise any eyebrows."

"No. Not like that. No one could know," Peter said, ignoring her dig. "Obviously, we'd need to keep this from Cathy and Grant. For now."

"What do you mean, *for now*?" Jessie said, shifting Lucas to her other hip and slinging her bag over her shoulder, panic rising inside of her.

"I mean, I think we should consider that one day we may

need to tell them the truth. Now that I've seen him, I don't think I can live with myself, knowing I have a son out there who doesn't even know who I am."

Jessie felt bile rushing up to her throat. All along, she'd banked on the fact that Peter would be the same uncaring jerk he'd been last time. But now that she'd made different choices, Peter seemed to be following suit. She felt a burst of rage. Why couldn't the universe just let her be content? Had her one mistake been so awful that she would forever be denied happiness? She had hated herself for years after what happened, and now she realized that the karma gods might be hating her too.

"No," she spit out.

"No what?" Peter looked at her incredulously

"I said *no*. Like you mentioned, you have a wife. And you also have a son, named Sean. You need to go back to *that* life," Jessie said as she started walking away.

"I have rights," Peter called after her, but she refused to stop, putting one foot in front of the other, nearly colliding with Gabriela as she turned the corner to where her minivan was parked, her breathing coming in short, desperate spurts.

"Are you okay?" Gabriela eyed Jessie as she tried to catch her breath.

"I'm fine," Jessie said as she took in the gauze and bandage on Gabriela's arm, remembering that she'd just come from the doctor, that today was the day she'd had the blood test that would determine if she was pregnant. "There was a swarm of bees over by our blanket and they kept following us wherever we moved." The lie fell off Jessie's tongue effortlessly. "Can we just have lunch at my place?"

"Of course." Gabriela stretched out her arms to hold Lucas.

Jessie handed him over and searched the park until she saw

Peter walking in the opposite direction, his shoulders hunched. Changing her own outcome had altered Peter's as well, and now, possibly Lucas'. She bit her lip hard, suddenly desperately regretting being back here, angry with Blair for leading them to believe they'd all get their happy endings by returning. Or had she just assumed that a second chance would automatically be a better one?

Peter had said he *had rights*, and she'd heard something in the undertone of his voice, that he was making her a promise. That he wasn't going anywhere. Until this moment, she'd had zero plans to return to her old life. But now, when she considered which was the better option—losing Grant but keeping Lucas, or losing Lucas but keeping Grant—she honestly didn't know what to think. But she was painfully aware that she had less than six months to figure it out.

"Let's ride together, then I'll bring you back," Jessie said to Gabriela as she popped the van's side doors open. "Sorry it's such a mess—just push the Cheerios and whatever else is on the seat to the floor before you slide in."

"I can't wait until there are mystery things ground into my car's seats," Gabriela said, smiling.

"Do you think you're pregnant?" Jessie asked as she buckled Lucas in.

"You know, I hate to say it out loud, but I do. I really feel different this time," Gabriela said, putting her hand over her stomach. "Plus, I got acupuncture before the implantation and our doctor said the embryo was grade-A quality, so . . ." Her voice trailed off.

"Oh, Gabs, that's such great news!" Jessie slid into her seat and reached over the armrest to hug her. "I knew with both of my pregnancies before I took the home tests. I think it's like a mother's intuition or something." Jessie forced herself to bury the image of her sobbing hysterically in the Starbucks bathroom after she peed on four tests, the pink lines confirming what her body had already confessed to her the week before.

"I have tons of the symptoms. Breast tenderness, tightness in my abdomen, exhaustion." She looked sideways at Jessie. "I've become an obsessive Googler."

"Thank God for Google," Jessie said.

"I'm so happy it had already been invented. Not sure I could go through this without it."

"When do you officially find out?"

"They're going to call me by tomorrow at the latest. And in the meantime, I'm *not* going to buy a home pregnancy test. So don't allow me to stop at CVS and get one, even if I beg you! I'm just going to find out the good old-fashioned way and then we can celebrate."

"Yay!" Jessie cheered as they started driving toward her house.

Gabriela's phone started vibrating in her lap and Jessie looked at her expectantly. "Is that them?"

Gabriela shook her head and frowned. "It's my editor."

"Lucas, do not have a meltdown. Auntie Gabriela needs to take a very important call," Jessie said over her shoulder.

"Hello?"

Jessie listened for several minutes as Gabriela offered a lot of *hmm*s and *okay*s, unable to piece together what the conversation was about. "I did get my itinerary, thanks," Gabriela said right before she hung up.

"What was that all about?" Jessie asked.

"I have to go to New York City tomorrow morning."

"Lucky! I love it there this time of year!"

"I don't think this trip will be about pleasure," Gabriela said.

"I'm behind on my deadline and Sheila is not happy. At least Claire is going with me as moral support."

Jessie stuck out her lower lip. "I wish I could go."

"It's not too late if you want to come."

"No, I can't. Grant's work schedule is crazy this week. But that doesn't mean I'm not insanely jealous of your girls' trip."

"He seems really tired."

"I know you saw him doze at your reading. I'm sorry." Jessie shook her head. "This project he's been working on is kicking his ass. If it makes you feel any better, he falls asleep on me quite often too."

"Oh, I wasn't offended! Those things bore me to tears too," she teased. "Is everything okay with you guys?"

"It's fine. I'm fine." Jessie smiled.

"Jess, I know that you really want to make things work with Grant this time," Gabriela began.

"I'm *making* things work this time. It's different," Jessie insisted, and told Gabriela about her recent talk with Grant. And how after, she'd set up a sitter and asked him out on a date. As she pulled on her jeans and placed huge dabs of concealer below her eyes to hide the signs of the sleepless nights from Lucas' teething, she thought about how she fell in love with Grant so swiftly. They'd met when he'd come to pick up her post-college roommate, Michelle, for a date, the chemistry between them instant as they'd listened to the hum of the blow-dryer, speculating how long it was going to take her to get ready. It hadn't worked out with Michelle, who'd quickly moved on with a personal trainer, and she happily gave Jessie her blessing when Grant had called to ask her out, joking that he hoped she air dried her hair.

She had made a reservation at one of their favorite restaurants in Marina del Rey, and as they watched the sunset, Jessie remembered the talk they'd had in their alternate life, the night she'd asked him about his job, how the stress had practically melted from his face as he explained, and then how he'd made love to her after. So this time, she vowed to keep the communication lines open, asking Grant about his latest project. He'd talked through some problems he was having with a beautiful old building in Long Beach that was being converted into a steakhouse. And Jessie filled him in on how Claire's mom was doing and about how Gabriela was still trying to get pregnant. And as he'd wrapped his arm around her as the sun fell into the ocean, her exhaustion had disappeared.

"Enough about me." Jessie changed the subject as she braked at a stoplight. "How far behind are you on your manuscript?"

"Yes, I've barely written a fourth of the book." Gabriela paused and looked out the window. "In fact, you owe me some feedback, girl. What do you think of it so far?"

Jessie swallowed. She had read the pages Gabriela gave her and had been avoiding giving her a critique. There hadn't been anything specifically wrong with them and she liked the storyline and characters so far, but the chapters weren't anything like the last time she'd written the same book. It was as if something was missing, the pages lacking Gabriela's trademark charm and magic. Jessie had always been able to give her an honest opinion, but now she worried it would be too much for Gabriela to take. And now that Jessie's destiny was changing drastically for the worse because of the things she had done differently, she worried what this might mean for Gabriela and her career.

She studied her friend's profile as Gabriela reached back to tickle Lucas. The newfound roundness of her face still couldn't soften the extra worry lines that had formed since she'd returned.

Gabriela had always been so driven, so much so that Jessie used to feel envious of the way she seemed to take the world by storm. She didn't just write, she was a bestselling author. She didn't just jog on the beach, she had completed several half marathons, beating her own personal records each time. She didn't just wear a stylish outfit, she'd pair it with the perfect cuff bracelet and matching necklace. So Jessie wasn't quite sure who this new Gabriela was, the one that came to meet her wearing yoga pants that had a stain on the thigh and a baggy T-shirt, who slept until noon on some days, and for some reason just couldn't get her natural sparkle to dance upon the pages of her manuscript.

It was true that there was a part of Jessie that felt closer to this version of Gabriela, her own imperfections now more reflected in her friend. She may have even confided her infidelity to this Gabriela, who seemed so broken that she might have understood how completely Jessie had lost herself too. She certainly wasn't happy her friend was struggling. In fact, she would have done anything to take her pain away. But there was no doubt their bond seemed tighter in this life, and Jessie was thankful for that.

"Well?" Gabriela prodded. "Did you hate it? Because I need to know if I'm going to get my ass handed to me in New York." She laughed hollowly.

Jessie had a feeling her publisher wasn't flying her across the country to congratulate her on what she had written so far. But as she searched Gabriela's face, she decided that she needed to be supportive, even if that meant lying. "I thought they were good, Gabriela. Really, really good."

CHAPTER SIXTEEN

....

Claire had always been a nervous eater. Whenever finals rolled around in college, she'd find herself power eating Tootsie Rolls until her stomach begged her to stop. As she grew older, she was smart enough to realize that even though she couldn't control her anxiety, she could control what she binged on. When Emily's dad had left her, her snack of choice became spicy corn nuts, popping them into her mouth, letting them burn her tongue and lips, the momentary pain they inflicted a welcome distraction from her emotional distress. When her mom was diagnosed last time, she'd become obsessed with dried fruits, carrying bags of dehydrated peaches and apricots in her purse, the vigorous chewing required to swallow them absorbing some of the aggression she felt at the universe for taking her mother far too soon. And when Emily dropped out of college, Claire had discovered wasabi peas, obsessively crunching them until she cracked a tooth.

"Beef jerky?" Claire held out the bag to Gabriela. They were on their way to New York City and the flight attendant had just announced it was okay to pull out electronic devices. Gabriela hauled out her heavy computer from under the seat with purpose, but froze as soon as her fingers touched the keyboard. Claire knew Gabriela had downplayed what this trip could mean for her professionally, instead selling it to Claire as a long-overdue girls' trip, and a chance for Claire to take a break from caring for her mom. But Claire knew Gabriela also wanted her there in case her editor delivered bad news.

Gabriela shook her head. "Too much sodium. Not to mention it's full of nitrates!"

"More for me then," Claire replied, and popped a thick piece into her mouth, barely tasting the savory flavor as she tore through it.

"I've never understood how you don't gain a ton of weight, especially when something's bothering you," Gabriela said, looking pointedly at the half-empty bag of jerky.

"I think stress increases my metabolism." Claire paused to chew. "Plus, it's not like I'm downing M&M's. This stuff is pure fat-burning protein!"

"Fifty-year-old Claire would be shaking her head at you right now. There's more salt in that bag than you're supposed to consume in an entire day!"

"Maybe. But forty-year-old Claire was thrilled to discover they make it in southern barbecue flavor!" Claire laughed.

Gabriela grabbed the bag from Claire's hands and handed it to the flight attendant, who was passing through the cabin with a trash bag. "Can you throw this away, please?"

"Hey! I wasn't done with that!"

Gabriela shut her laptop. "You don't need more jerky. What you need is someone to talk to about what's *really* going on."

"I'm fine. Just a little stressed, but fine," Claire said, not

wanting to burden Gabriela, who was waiting nervously to find
out if she was pregnant and worried about her meeting with her
publisher. The last thing she needed was for Claire to offload her
own problems on her.

Gabriela pointed at Claire's swollen fingers. "Okay, then.
If you can pull that ring off your finger right now, I'll leave you
alone the rest of the flight. But if you can't, then I know you've
been binge snacking again. And we all know what that means,"
Gabriela said gently.

Claire glanced down at her own hand, observing the tiny
fold of skin hanging over the sapphire ring that sat on her right
index finger, the vision of shoving it on earlier that morning in
her head. Now that they were thirty thousand feet up in the
air, she knew there was no way in hell it was coming off. She
sighed loudly. "Fine. Where do I begin? With how awful it is
to lose my mom all over again? Or how I found out yesterday
that in addition to raising a spoiled brat, I've raised a certified
bully?"

Gabriela popped up the armrest between them, glancing
at her laptop. She had promised her editor she'd have a new
chapter for her to read by the time she walked into her office
tomorrow, but the words were stuck somewhere between her
head and her heart. "It's a five-hour flight. Start at the beginning
and don't leave *anything* out."

• • •

Claire leaned her head against the window of the town car
Gabriela's publisher had sent for them, letting the cold air that
permeated it soothe her. She felt relieved after spending most
of the flight revealing to Gabriela the things she'd been keeping
bottled up. Mason was the only other person she'd told that

Emily had been suspended from school after she'd been caught writing hateful notes to a girl in her grade.

Gabriela listened intently as Claire confided that she hadn't considered the notes *that* bad at first. She'd actually thought Emily might even be joking when she'd read the first one because the pig she'd drawn on it was cartoonish, cute even. But then she'd read the words she'd written beneath it: *fat pig, oinker, hog.* In the second note, she'd drawn a cow and had written *You heffer.* Claire's eyes had stung with tears, and she'd had to swallow hard so the vice principal wouldn't see. Her hands shook as she handed the crumpled pieces of paper back to Mr. Donavan, imagining the girl Emily had attacked scrunching it up in her fist as she'd sobbed. Claire couldn't make eye contact with him, feeling as if he was blaming her, and rightfully so. If Claire had been paying more attention, would this have happened?

Emily had been silent, staring at the floor while she played with the threads fringing a hole in the knee of her jeans, nodding or shaking her head when asked a yes-or-no question, repeating *I don't know* each time Mr. Donavan asked her why she'd targeted this girl. Claire had sat there, wishing Emily would communicate, even if it meant she'd stood and yelled the reason at the top of her lungs—at least then she'd have answers.

After announcing Emily's three-day suspension stoically, as if he were reading next week's lunch menu, Claire and Emily were escorted out of his office. As they'd walked to the car, the only sound Claire could hear was the roaring of the bus engines as they'd pulled up to the school. Claire had forced herself not to give in to her instincts as silent tears fell down Emily's cheeks, not to grab her hand and squeeze it, as if sending the silent message that what she'd done was okay. Because there was nothing okay about it.

Yes, Emily had always had her share of problems. But she had never bullied anyone before—all her destructive behavior had seemed to focus on herself. Gabriela agreed that the drastic change was curious. Had Claire's own choices this time affected Emily's?

"Please talk to me, Emily," Claire said after they'd driven in silence for several minutes, tightening her grip on the steering wheel.

Emily stared out the window.

"Are you at least sorry?" Claire tried again.

Emily half shrugged and half nodded.

"What for? That you traumatized that poor girl? Or that you got caught?"

Emily twisted a faded friendship bracelet on her wrist. "Both, I guess."

"And you *really* don't know why you did it?" Claire held her breath, both wanting and not wanting the reason.

Emily shrugged, another tear sliding down her cheek. "Well I guess you have three days to figure it out and come up with a damn good apology. Not that it will erase what you've done. But it's a place to start."

Claire waited until they arrived home to give Emily her punishment. She shocked herself as she said the words—barely able to believe she was speaking them—that she was grounding her and forbidding her from hanging out with any of her friends for an indefinite amount of time. She couldn't remember so much as sending Emily to her room the first time around, always paralyzed by fear that her daughter would hate her more than she already seemed to. Claire also decided they should move into her parents' house, so Emily could be around even more to help. Claire watched as Emily's eyes turned cold and her jaw clenched. Claire could practically see the words coming up through Emily's body before they shot out of her mouth—angry, hateful things she hoped Emily didn't mean. She knew her daughter was trying to break her down the way she had so many times in the past. And even though she'd never witnessed Emily throwing a fit of this magnitude, Claire held strong for the first time, feeling like an umbrella fighting against the wind. It was one thing if Emily was going to bully her. But she couldn't let her do it to other people. Claire shriveled on the inside as Emily raged, throwing all the books, CDs, and trinkets off her shelves into a huge pile in the center of her room, her crying finally subsiding several hours later. Claire discovered her curled up in a ball asleep on the floor and placed a blanket over her, hoping she was making the right decision.

She'd called Mason, and after explaining what happened, he seemed surprised, not quite sure the punishment fit the crime, reasoning that a suspension from school was already pretty harsh. He'd also brought up Mona, speculating that maybe Emily was acting out because it was hard to see her grandmother so sick. Where was the old Mason who'd broken up with her because she wasn't firm enough with Emily? Now he was the one making excuses?

Claire thought about how the discovery of Mona's illness earlier in her relationship with Mason had changed its entire dynamic. She hardly ever slept over at his house, and when he saw her, she was rarely with Emily, usually just stealing moments— a coffee date here, a late-night drink there. So he didn't have firsthand knowledge of how challenging she could be, and Claire hadn't confided in him the way she did before. She told herself it was because she was so much busier this time, but a part of her wondered if she was afraid to get too attached.

Claire stayed silent while he made his points. He was right in many ways, but what he didn't realize, what he could *never* realize, is that she already knew what *wasn't* going to work with Emily. Giving in or hoping she'd "grow out of it" wouldn't suffice. Claire wished she could disclose to Mason that if she didn't take a firm stance with her daughter, Emily would ultimately come between them as well, that her toxicity would eventually tear down everything they had built together. That they'd never speak again after they broke up, but according to the Google search she'd done after she'd denied his friend request on Facebook, he'd get engaged to a childless architect named Nancy that he'd met on Match.com.

• • •

Gabriela and Claire's town car jolted to a stop in front of the Sheraton, located just a few blocks from Times Square. Claire couldn't wait to explore the city while Gabriela met with her editor. She'd never been to New York and was excited to dress the part in tall leather boots and a cozy down jacket she had only worn a few times at home, the frigid December air a welcome contrast to the unseasonably warm temperatures in Southern California.

"What time is your meeting tomorrow?" Claire asked as she slid the key card into the door of their room. Claire pulled her suitcase behind her and scanned the simple double bed accommodations, a far cry from the spacious suites Gabriela had described staying in at the height of her career.

"Noon. I was thinking we could have brunch before?"

"Mimosas and Bloody Marys? I'm in! I need a new source of sodium since you snaked my jerky!"

"None for me." Gabriela patted her stomach. "I should be finding out very soon if I have a baby in here."

Claire looked at her watch. "Well, it's almost 5 p.m. back home, so I'm sure they will be calling any minute. And then I'll drink enough for both of us when we celebrate!" Claire walked over and pulled Gabriela in for a hug and hoped her words sounded sincere. Gabriela's life hinged on the next twenty-four hours, and Claire was crossing her swollen fingers that she'd get the news she'd been waiting to hear.

CHAPTER SEVENTEEN

....

Gabriela's cell phone vibrated in her hand. She'd been clutching it nonstop for the past hour, almost dropping it in the toilet earlier as she tried to balance while squatting over the seat. She'd even insisted she and Claire have dinner in the restaurant inside the hotel, much to Claire's chagrin, reasoning that she needed to be nearby in case the doctor's office contacted the hotel, which she'd left as a backup number.

Gabriela had picked at her chicken piccata while Claire went on and on about Emily, swirling her third glass of pinot grigio as she dissected her decision to punish her the way she had. Gabriela nodded in all the right places, but inside, she was wishing she had a daughter to complain about. She knew it was silly, that of course Claire had a right to be upset about Emily getting in trouble at school and deserved the chance to troubleshoot the situation from every angle. But still, Gabriela had a hard time listening to it when all she hoped for was a phone call to tell her she was going to have a baby, a baby that might one day bully someone, she didn't care. She'd deal with it then.

"Is it them?" Claire asked as Gabriela's phone started to vibrate.

Gabriela nodded. *Please*, she thought as she said hello and walked into the lobby of the hotel.

Claire watched Gabriela's face from afar, waiting for her to break into a grin, but instead, Gabriela's mouth turned from a forced smile into a grimace, her hand running through her hair as she paced back and forth, nearly colliding with a group of tourists returning from a day of sightseeing. Claire's throat constricted as she watched her hang up and throw the phone into the overstuffed leather seat next to her.

Claire walked over and wrapped her arms around Gabriela.

"It's not fair," Gabriela said into Claire's shoulder.

"You're right, it's not," Claire agreed. "It's not fair at all."

"What's the point of all this? Why are we back here if it isn't to get the things we wanted?"

Claire had similar thoughts when her mom's doctor had told her the chemotherapy wasn't working as well as they would have hoped. They had caught it months earlier. Shouldn't that have meant they had a chance to beat it this time?

"So what do we do now?" Claire asked tentatively. "Overpay for bad movies in our room that we already watched ten years ago? I saw Oreos in the minibar." Claire smiled hopefully. "And wine, if that's what you need."

Gabriela shook her head and pointed to the bar lined with bottles. "*That*," she said so softly that Claire had to lean in to hear her. "*That* is what I need. A stiff-ass drink."

"Anything you want." Claire steered her toward the bar.

The two women sat in silence after their dirty martinis were delivered, Gabriela absentmindedly chewing on a blue cheese olive. "Do you think I'm just not meant to be a mother?" Gabriela finally asked, then quickly looked away as if she was afraid of the answer.

"Of course not!" Claire said. "There's still time, Gabs."

"But think about it. For so many years, I didn't want kids. Maybe there's a reason for that. Maybe it was because I'm not supposed to have them, or because . . ." Gabriela paused and twisted her wedding ring around her finger. "I can't. Maybe my first instinct was the right one. That there was always a part of me that knew I couldn't, even if I tried."

"That's ridiculous," Claire said, hoping she sounded confident. "You didn't want them before for many reasons—the pain of losing your own mom and the writing career you were trying to get off the ground were both a big part of it. It's all about timing, and for whatever reason, your time didn't come before and it hasn't yet, but it will."

"Did you read that somewhere? In one of those self-help books I've seen at your house?" Gabriela teased, taking a vigorous swig of her martini. "You sound like Colin's mom, Rowan. I swear, every other day a different motivational book shows up on my doorstep! I know she means well, but . . ."

"Hey, don't forget you owe her—she's the one who changed Colin's mind."

Gabriela nodded in agreement, still very thankful to Rowan, then and now. She'd continued to be a huge advocate for Gabriela, sometimes to the point that Gabriela felt she wanted the baby more than her son did. But regardless, Gabriela was happy to have someone as obsessed with the process as she was.

"I don't mean to go all Rowan on you right now, but have you ever heard the expression *your baby will find you?*"

Gabriela nodded. "I want to believe that's true, but I think that's just an idea that women desperate to have children cling to."

"You could be right," Claire said. "But I really do believe that things happen for a reason."

"Okay, then what's the reason we're all back in 2005? Because I know it's not for the peasant skirts!" Gabriela said, pulling at her paisley printed fabric.

"Or the baggy jeans!" Claire laughed. "I miss my skinnies!"

They laughed for several seconds, a welcome break from the sadness Gabriela's mood had brought on, until Gabriela drained her glass and leaned toward Claire. "Were our lives really so bad the year we turned forty? Because we've been back here over six months, and I won't speak for you, but I'd say mine is a hell of a lot worse."

Claire thought about her next words carefully, remembering the conversation she'd had with her mom before she'd left for the airport. Mona was uncharacteristically energetic as she'd recounted an episode of *The Golden Girls*. And she'd laughed, a long, sturdy sound Claire had almost forgotten. "I don't know. Was it a good year for any of us? No. But I don't know if the point is to compare. Maybe we need to revise our definition of what *better* means," Claire said, surprising herself with her optimism. But her mom's health was responsible, she realized now, even more than before, for teaching her how fleeting life was, how fragile.

"You sure you haven't been hanging out with Rowan?" Gabriela smiled and Claire felt herself breathe. She wanted her friend to be happy again. "Because that's pretty insightful for the person who was most skeptical about returning. Is it your mom?"

Claire nodded.

Gabriela's eyes watered and Claire felt a surge of guilt.

"I appreciate it so much, I do. I feel terrible that I get to see mine again and you don't."

"It's okay," Gabriela said, feeling her heart knot the way it always did when she thought of her mother. "I'd have to be sixteen again, and, well, that would suck!" Gabriela smiled wistfully. "There's only so far back I'm willing to time travel."

Claire put her hand over Gabriela's. "Here's the thing, Gabs. This is our life, our *only* life, as of right now, and will be for the next six months." Claire prayed this would all make sense at some point.

"So there's still hope?"

"Of course," Claire said, meaning it. There was always promise if you wanted there to be.

Gabriela squinted at Claire. "I think you'd say just about anything right now to cheer me up." Gabriela grabbed a cocktail napkin and wiped away a tear from the corner of her right eye.

"Also true." Claire smiled. "So from where I'm sitting, it looks like you have three choices," Claire said, holding Gabriela's gaze.

"Okay, lay them on me."

"You could give up."

"I've never thought of myself as a quitter," Gabriela said thoughtfully, and signaled the bartender for another round.

"You could keep trying." Claire watched a light spark in Gabriela's eye and felt heartened. She still had some fight in her.

"It's just so hard. I feel like this is killing me."

"I don't want to sit here and pretend I know what this feels like, because obviously I have no idea. But I still have to ask, are you ready to give up trying for a baby?"

Gabriela looked down at her hands. "I think I need to hear your third option first before I make my decision."

Claire nodded at the new martinis the bartender had just placed in front of them. "You can drink."

Gabriela clinked her glass against Claire's. "Tonight, I choose number three."

"Okay. But will you promise to give option two some thought?"

"Yes," Gabriela said, sliding the full martini glass closer to her and taking another sip, the vodka spilling carelessly over the top. "Now for the really hard part. I need to call my dad. And Colin." She bit her lower lip. "I'll be back in a little bit."

"Good luck," Claire called after her.

"Thanks," Gabriela said as she headed back into the lobby and sat on a couch in the corner. As she dialed her father's number, she remembered the first time she'd talked to him after traveling back here, when she'd announced that she and Colin were going to try to get pregnant. The tears she heard in his voice buoyed her in a way she hadn't been expecting. And when he'd said, *Your mother would be so happy,* she knew then that she couldn't fail. She had to do this. Not just for herself and Colin, but for her father. She exhaled deeply now when his voice mail picked up, his heavily accented English, even after so many years in the States, comforting her. She closed her eyes and soaked in his deep voice before clearing her throat and leaving a message that the in vitro hadn't worked, then lied and said she'd be fine and would call him when she returned from New York. Next she dialed Colin's number as she absentmindedly rubbed the knot forming in her neck. He answered on the first ring. "Did you hear?" he asked before she could speak.

"We're not," Gabriela said, barely able to get the words out.

"I'm so sorry, Gabs."

Their connection was silent for several seconds, Gabriela observing a husband and wife and two young children bounding into the lobby, unwrapping their scarves and giggling about the double-decker bus they'd ridden on earlier, the younger child pulling on his father's hand until he lifted him effortlessly onto his broad shoulders. Finally, Gabriela spoke. "I'm not so sure we should try again. Maybe this has all been a mistake," Gabriela said, not sure it had been a mistake at all, but badly needing to know what Colin believed.

"Whatever you think. I support you," Colin said.

Did she hear relief in his voice?

"This isn't just for me, Colin. It's supposed to be for *us*."

"I know that." Colin sighed. "I'm just trying to be understanding. I know how hard this must be for you."

"And what about for *you*? You act like I'm doing this alone!" Gabriela accused.

"Of course you aren't doing this by yourself," Colin said. "But I had accepted a life without kids. So I think if it's meant to be, it will be. And if it's not, we'll be just fine."

"Do you really mean that?" Gabriela waited for Colin to respond, watching a little girl swirling a wand high above her head.

"We were happier."

"What did you say?"

"I said we were happier, things were better. Now you're stressed out all the time and constantly pissed at me."

Gabriela softened slightly. "It's not me, it's the—"

"The drugs, I know."

"You say that like me being on fertility drugs annoys you."

"Well, it's a lot to deal with."

"And so is trying to get pregnant!"

"Gabs."

"Just say it. Say you don't care if we can't conceive." Gabriela wished with every breath in her body that he'd deny it, tell her she had it wrong, that he wanted this as much as she did. But she already knew he didn't. And she was also certain that she cared more about having a child than *anything* else right now.

She had told Claire that she didn't know, but she did. She knew with every fiber of her being. Her choice was number two. To keep trying.

"I have to go. I'll call you tomorrow," she said quickly and ended the call, not wanting to decide right now what their fate was, not here in the lobby of the Sheraton as the perfect children she spied earlier danced in circles around their parents to music only they could hear.

• • •

"How did it go?" Claire smiled hopefully as Gabriela slid onto the bar stool.

"He seemed fine. Almost relieved!" Gabriela's eyes were brimming with tears. "I'm so sick of this. Sick of crying. Sick of being disappointed. Sick of arguing."

"I'm sorry," Claire said, not knowing what else to offer.

"He just doesn't get it. He acts like I'm doing this alone. Like it's *my* problem!"

"What did he say exactly?" Claire asked.

"That if it was meant to be it would be. Almost as bad as your, *your baby will find you* bullshit!"

Claire paused, not sure if Gabriela was joking or lashing out. "Maybe he was trying to be helpful?" she said carefully.

"Oh, God, Claire. Please don't defend him. I don't need you to be the voice of reason right now. I need you to be on *my* side!"

Claire drained the last of her martini before responding. She'd watched Gabriela slowly disintegrate the past few months, until she was just a hairline fracture away from a full break. "Listen, I'm not defending him, but clearly you're upset. He's probably just being cautious in case—"

"In case what?"

"I just mean he's probably trying to protect himself. He wanted kids for a long time."

"I'm aware, Claire," Gabriela said tightly.

"You said you needed me on your side, Gabs. And, I am. But I just don't want you to be angry with *him* because *you're* not pregnant."

"I'm not. I'm pissed at him because *he doesn't care that I'm not pregnant* and maybe that means something."

"What are you saying?"

"That if he doesn't want the same things I do, maybe I should just go at this alone."

Claire tried to smother the flash of anger she felt. Being a single mom was the hardest thing she'd ever done. If she'd had a man like Colin, she would have never let him go. "You don't mean that."

"I think I do."

"You have no idea how hard it is to raise a child alone."

"Oh really? It's pretty much all you've talked about since we got here. Your problems with Emily."

"Right. Because parenting is hard, it's really fucking hard. For one person or two. You have a rock-solid marriage, Gabs. Why would you trade that for a baby that doesn't even exist?"

"Because maybe I've changed. And if you can't understand that, then maybe you have too."

"If that's true, then I'm not sure it's for the better. For either of us," Claire said coolly before scooping up her purse and heading to the room, leaving Gabriela sitting in stunned silence.

• • •

Gabriela pushed the button for the fourteenth floor of her publisher's office the next morning and fingered her *abuela*'s necklace. As the elevator ascended, she clutched her laptop bag, wishing she could magically make the manuscript she was supposed to write appear. Last night, she'd deliberately waited an hour before heading up to the hotel room, when she knew Claire would be asleep. And when she woke up this morning, Claire was already gone, a note on the nightstand saying she was sightseeing and would be back in time to get a cab to the airport. She hadn't wanted to face her anyway, to think about the things she'd said to Claire, to consider she might have been wrong. To accept that she was lashing out at her even though it was Colin who'd disappointed her. And her body—it had always been a pillar of health, pushing through the wall she hit at mile twenty-one during her first marathon. Even as her lungs expanded as she heaved, her legs feeling like dead weight, she still was able to will herself to the finish line. But now her body had betrayed her in this last stretch, and her personal finish line was starting to look further away than ever. So, yes, she was angry with Colin. But she was also pretty damn pissed off at herself.

She'd sat up in bed until 2 a.m. with her computer on her lap, willing the words to flow from her as effortlessly as they had the first time she'd been forty. She'd never struggled with writer's block, her characters always leaping onto the pages and almost writing themselves, often taking her in a direction that was better than the one she'd plotted.

But this time, writing felt like trying to run while waist deep in the ocean—*impossible*. And even after struggling to come up with the ten thousand words she had, she knew her pages were amateurish at best, coming off exactly as she'd feared, like she was trying to copy herself. But she obviously couldn't tell Sheila the truth—that she must have lost her talent while traveling through time. *Now* that *would make a good book*, she thought.

Not that she could write it. Or if she was being completely honest, had the desire to write it. Because she was starting to realize that perhaps she no longer wanted to be a bestselling author. While she'd enjoyed telling stories that resonated with people, she'd always hated the rest of it. The pressure of meeting deadlines, the stress of pleasing her editor, the lack of control over her creativity. She hadn't been able to articulate it when she was in the thick of it. But now, with some distance and perspective, she understood. Aside from her readers, the only thing she liked about being an author was the actual writing. And for some reason, the universe had decided to take that ability away from her too.

"Gabriela!" Sheila exclaimed, hurrying around her desk and hugging her tightly. Gabriela inhaled her Chanel perfume, the smell instantly taking her back to the countless lunches they'd shared, parties they'd attended. She'd always considered Sheila one of her closest friends, but today she felt distant, like an old acquaintance she hadn't seen for ages. It felt like another life, someone else's life. And maybe it was.

"Hi, Sheila. You look great!" Gabriela said, regarding her toned arms in her sleeveless shift dress, her glowing complexion.

"Thanks. It's Pilates! It's becoming really popular out here. Is it big in LA too?" Sheila said. And Gabriela noticed immediately that she didn't return the compliment. But she didn't blame her, she knew she looked tired, bloated, miserable.

"How's Colin?"

"He's great, thanks." Gabriela thought about the dozen or so calls from him she'd ignored since she'd hung up on him last night. "How's Jim? The kids?" Gabriela glanced at a framed picture of Sheila and her family at the beach—their last Christmas card photo. Gabriela remembered how she'd tacked it up on the corkboard in her kitchen alongside all the others, never feeling a pang in her gut as she studied the grins of the children. Now she could barely look at it.

"They're doing well! Can I get you a bottle of water?"

"Sure," Gabriela said as she took in the floor-to-ceiling bookshelves lining the wall of Sheila's office, filled with the many novels and memoirs she'd edited, some of which hadn't been published yet. Gabriela fingered the spines of several, finally resting on her debut, *The Life Not Taken,* a book she'd written just after graduating from college, about a woman who discovers her mother has been leading a double life. She'd completed the first draft in just three months, but then worried it wasn't right, spending the next several years writing and rewriting it at night and on the weekends, while working her day job at an independent bookstore, until she'd finally been ready to find an agent. Hands shaking, she'd mailed her query letter to her dream agent, Angelina Cross, on a Friday afternoon, with Colin gently warning her she might not hear anything—he'd had a friend who'd queried fifty agents and never gotten a single response—but one week later, Angelina had called to request the full manuscript and asked to represent her after reading it.

"Your first book, still my favorite," Sheila said, clutching two bottles of Evian.

"You say that to all your authors." Gabriela smiled, turning the novel over in her hand and examining her image on the back. She remembered that shot. Colin had taken it in their backyard. The wind had blown her thick hair just so and the light had been beautiful. They'd laughed when the finished copies showed up on their doorstep and Colin was given the photo credit, because he'd never taken a decent picture before that, usually shaking the camera so a photo ended up blurry. She recalled holding her novel for the first time in her living room, beaming, and she'd began cradling the tome like an infant. "My book baby," she'd said with a giggle. "I'll only birth from here," she'd pointed at her head. "Not here," she'd added, gesturing at her abdomen, pretending not to notice that Colin wasn't laughing with her.

"No! It really is your best," Sheila said, interrupting her thoughts. "You had such raw talent." Sheila paused when she caught Gabriela's frown. "Not that you don't still have it!"

The room fell silent, Sheila shifting her weight awkwardly. "Sit, please!" she finally said as she settled into a sleek leather chair.

Gabriela sank into a plush sofa across from Sheila, her first novel now resting in her lap. She stared at the cover, pale blue with a distant image of a woman standing at a fork in the road, remembering her reaction when she'd first seen it. She'd closed her eyes and said a silent prayer that she'd like it before ripping open the envelope Sheila had sent with a picture of the cover inside. She'd finally opened just one eye and squealed with excitement. She'd been so invested back then, in all the parts of publishing, emailing her agent and Sheila constantly with ideas, from publicity to sales and marketing. What had happened to that earnest young author?

"So, Gabriela, I wanted you to come to New York so we could talk in person. The way we used to." Sheila took a breath and Gabriela remembered back to the beginning of their relationship, when she'd call Sheila about a book idea she was trying to flesh out and they'd end up gossiping for hours like a couple of schoolgirls. "I feel like things have been different between us in the last six months. I can't explain it exactly, and maybe it's all in my imagination, but I've felt a shift in our friendship, in our working relationship, and I'm wondering if that has something to do with why your pages aren't ready. Did I do something? Was it our last phone call? I didn't mean to come down on you so hard about missing your last deadline."

"You were just doing your job!" Gabriela tried to sit up, but sank back into the couch. "You've been great. You've always been great. It's not you, it's me."

"You sound like you're breaking up with me." Sheila let out a nervous laugh.

"No!" Gabriela smiled. "But isn't that what *you're* doing? Aren't I here so you can tell me in person that the publisher is dropping me?"

"Not at all," Sheila said, and Gabriela felt herself exhale in relief. Maybe she wasn't ready to give this up after all. Maybe she was still that hungry writer with the raw talent who'd simply been distracted by trying to have a baby, and if she stopped stressing so much, she would regain her writing mojo.

Sheila shifted in her chair. "You mentioned you've been trying for a baby. How's that going?"

"Unfortunately, not very well," Gabriela said with a sad smile.

"Do you think that's distracted you a bit?" Sheila asked gently.

Gabriela put her hand over her abdomen, her eyes welling with tears as she tried to formulate a response.

"Oh, God, I'm so sorry. I shouldn't have brought it up. I've probably violated dozens of HR policies." Sheila pulled a tissue from a box on the table next to her and handed it to Gabriela.

"It's okay, we're friends too. And you have a right to ask." Gabriela wiped under her eyes.

"I'm here for you if you need anything."

"I know you are," Gabriela said. "And I'd be lying if I told you it hasn't been a distraction. But I promise, moving forward, it won't be."

"This explains a lot. Because the first chapter you sent me just seven months ago was brilliant, like the beginning of a book that would get you number one on the list and, please don't take this the wrong way, but what you've sent me since reads like someone else wrote it. It's not your voice at all."

"I know," Gabriela said solemnly, removing her debut novel from her lap and noticing a coffee stain on her skirt from when she bobbled her coffee as she crossed the street earlier.

"What can I do?" Sheila asked.

"Give me some more time?" Gabriela said, praying Sheila could actually grant this request.

"So here's the deal. I've already talked to the publisher and I can give you an additional six months, but not a day more. The manuscript would be due on June 11, and hopefully it won't require major edits or we might have to push the pub date. I've already told Angelina and she agreed."

June 11. Gabriela almost laughed out loud. What were the odds? That's Claire's birthday. The day they were supposed to decide whether to return home or stay here. *Of course.*

"Why are you frowning? I thought this would be good news. Do you need even more time?" Sheila smiled, but her eyes pleaded with Gabriela to say no.

"I'm sorry. Thank you so much for the extension. That's plenty of time."

"You're welcome," Sheila said. "Now that you have extra time, I'm counting on you to write me the bestseller I know you have in you. Don't let me down!"

Gabriela's heart started to pound. Could she write a bestseller and get pregnant in just six months? This was her one chance to have a baby. If she returned back home, she'd be fifty again and her fertility would be nonexistent. But this was also her one chance to write *the* bestseller, *the* book that would cat-apult her into another stratosphere of authors. So the question was, which version of her life did she want more? Because she was quickly realizing it may be impossible to have both—which meant at some point she'd have to choose.

CHAPTER EIGHTEEN

....

Jessie lay in child's pose on her mat, fiercely willing her body to give in to relaxation, jealous of the peaceful looks and spaghetti-like limbs of the other people in the class. She breathed deeply and attempted to let in the light the way the instructor had directed, but each time she tried to imagine a blank space where her thoughts lived, fear and anxiety, not to mention her huge to-do list, seemed unwilling to vacate.

Claire had suggested yoga. They were supposed to meet here every Tuesday and Thursday at 8 a.m., but Claire had made it only once, the rest of the times canceling at the last minute, blaming her clients, her mom, her issues with Emily, and most recently, her trip to New York with Gabriela. But Jessie had seen Claire's face during that first class, grimacing while trying to hold her body in a tree pose, and she'd realized then that Claire had just wanted to get Jessie there, never intending to follow through and become a yogi herself. Jessie should have known. Claire had never been one to work out. Her idea of breaking a sweat was having a heated negotiation with another Realtor. But she'd appreciated her friend more than ever since then, realizing that sometimes someone who loves you knows you better than you know yourself.

Jessie had found it almost impossible to stay present the first time she'd been forty, so she was even more determined to find her inner Zen this time around. Before the affair, when she'd felt the small fissures in her marriage turn into a gaping crevice that Peter had slipped through, she would barely notice life happening right in front of her. She would daydream while Morgan and Madison shouted her name as they climbed across the monkey bars. She and Grant talked, but it never felt like they were *listening* to each other.

Sure, she was *living*, waking up and smiling and even enjoying things. But somewhere along the way she'd started to feel like her best moments were behind her. She missed when Grant's bourbon-laced kisses felt naughty instead of sloppy, when she felt like there were still stories he hadn't told her yet, when their flaws were endearing to each other rather than grating.

But after their recent talk, the world glowed in Technicolor once more. Grant's touches made a little shiver run up her back. The twins' high-pitched squeals telling her to "turn it up" when Jesse McCartney was on the radio made her nostalgic rather than annoyed, and she drank in each milestone Lucas achieved, knowing she'd long for his innocence later. When she spied a beautiful sunrise, she'd stop and say a silent prayer of thanks to the universe, often wondering if the powers that brought her back here were the same ones that painted the sky each morning.

But when Peter surprised her at the park two weeks ago, it had changed everything. Now she was once again easily distracted, but this time out of fear, not boredom. She'd left her purse in the cart at Costco yesterday, not even realizing she was missing it until she ran through the Starbucks drive-thru. Her mind was cluttered with anxiety. Did she deny Lucas his real father, his bloodline, to save her marriage? Jessie was terrified that it might not be her choice to make anymore.

The yoga instructor, Solange, walked over and patted her shoulder as Jessie rolled up her mat. "Still struggling?" she asked, her gentle smile making her eyes twinkle.

"Yes," Jessie lamented. "Every time I try to clear my mind, it just fills back up again, like a boat with a leak."

"Interesting analogy," Solange mused. "Maybe you need to figure out what caused it."

"Caused what?" Jessie asked, digging in her purse for her keys, distracted again.

Solange reached into Jessie's bag and removed the key chain effortlessly, holding it just out of Jessie's reach until Jessie looked up and met her eyes. "The leak. If you want to find the inner peace you seem to be searching for, I'd start there."

• • •

Several hours later, Jessie grabbed her three-inch heels, still getting used to the idea that her post-pregnancy feet fit into them effortlessly. She smoothed her dress in the mirror, soft black and heather gray with a cowl neck that made her eyes shimmer, or at least that's what Grant told her a few minutes ago when he'd sidled up beside her while she applied her mascara. "You're going to be the hottest woman there," he'd added, referring to the school event they were attending that evening. Last time, Jessie had been there with Grant on her arm, just days before she'd confessed the truth and watched their marriage unwind like a spool of thread.

Jessie shook off the memory and smiled as she thought of Lucas now, almost seven months old. He'd just pulled himself up for the first time that morning, flashing a drooling grin at his accomplishment as Jessie and the twins applauded. And Madison and Morgan were thriving, bonding over their shared older sister status, playfully fighting over who could help give their little brother a bath. Just last night as the girls did their homework and Jessie and Grant were curled up together on the couch, Lucas made a noise that sounded like hi. Grant and Jessie exchanged a look—had that been his first word? They'd never shared moments like these after Lucas was born last time, not even a family dinner, Grant long gone before Lucas was old enough to sit in a high chair.

Jessie inspected herself in the mirror and thought back to how she'd felt seven months after giving birth to Lucas the first time, still struggling to fit back into her jeans, most days wearing her Lycra workout pants, but never making it to the actual gym, her depression over Grant leaving overpowering everything. She had to admit, she felt physically healthy and strong this time from her power walks at the twins' volleyball practices, Jessie huffing around the track as the girls spiked the ball inside the gym. She did enjoy breaking a sweat, and she was proud that she'd reclaimed her body. Now she just needed to reclaim her confidence.

Jessie felt her heart lurch as she thought of running into Peter tonight at the event, having seen his and Cathy's names on the list of attendees. She'd considered feigning illness, but she couldn't take the risk Grant would still go without her, leaving him a sitting duck for Peter to possibly target. Plus, the annual auction had always been one of Jessie's favorite nights each year. She'd drink too much wine and bid carelessly in the silent auction on baskets full of fancy skin creams and anti-aging serums, signed sports memorabilia, or a coveted spot for her minivan in the school's tiny parking lot.

Jessie suddenly flashed back to the bid she knew Grant had wanted to make at the live auction, the last one they'd attended as a married couple. There had been a six-week-old soft blond Goldendoodle puppy with big brown eyes and a playful kiss. Jessie had grabbed Grant's paddle before he could hold it up to make a bid. "Don't even think about it!" Jessie had cried out. "Do you think the puppy will even know who you are? You're never home!" The other couples at the table had laughed, but both Jessie and Grant had felt the underlying tension in her comment.

Tonight, Jessie waved to a few moms as she and Grant walked into the country club—Grant leafing through the book that listed the items for auction. "Uh-oh, there's a Goldendoodle on the list. Look at her," he said, showing her a picture of the dog with a bright pink collar. "I'm sure she'll be pretty popular!" He laughed. "I know that's the last thing we need right now. But how can you resist that face?" He gave Jessie a pointed look.

Jessie thought quickly. Maybe tonight was her chance to show Grant that she was listening. That what he wanted mattered to her. "I can't."

"I know," he said. "We can't get a dog."

"No," Jessie corrected. "I mean, I can't resist her face."

"What? Are you being serious? You've never wanted a dog," Grant said, and paused to write a silent bid on a football signed by Drew Brees.

"People change. You should bid." Jessie nodded her head across the grass, where the pup was chewing violently on a rawhide bone. "Just imagine the girls' reactions if we walked in the door with her later tonight. They would go crazy!" Jessie smiled and thought about how their faces would register shock, then joy when they realized Jessie had finally given in to their constant request for a puppy.

"But you'll be the one taking care of him most of the time. Are you sure?"

"We could use a little fluffiness in our lives. And a little more poop isn't going to kill me. Get the dog."

"What is this about? Because I know the girls will be excited, but they don't need a pet."

"I know. But this is about *you*. About what makes *you* happy."

"What makes me happy is our family," he replied simply.

"I know that, babe. But I can tell how much you want this. And I want to give you what *you* want," she finished, her throat constricting as she realized she'd never uttered truer words. She'd start with the puppy and figure the rest out as she went.

"Hey," Grant said as a tear slipped out of the corner of Jessie's eye. "Where is this coming from? I like dogs, but owning one isn't going to be like fulfilling some childhood dream."

Jessie shrugged, brushing the tear away with the back of her hand and turning to face the golf course as she saw Peter and Cathy arrive. "Please. Just bid on our furry friend." She realized the puppy was just a symbol of a life she didn't want to relive, but giving him this would make her feel like she was righting a wrong she'd made in her other life.

Grant stood behind her and wrapped his arms around her chest. "If you insist," he whispered into her ear. "But don't get too attached—she's going to be *my* dog! Even if you're the one that cleans up most of her poop. And feeds her. And does basically everything," he added, and Jessie could hear his sarcastic smile, the one where the right side of his mouth lingered upward a little longer than the left.

Jessie stared at the skyline, breathed deeply before silently asking for the answers she was searching for. Her eyes grew wide as a blaze of light lit up the sky. "Did you see that?" she craned her neck around to Grant. "The flash?"

He nodded his head. "I did. Do you think it's a sign we should get the dog?" he teased.

"I think that's exactly what it is." Jessie smiled, hoping that all of the magic in the world was somehow connected.

"I don't know what's gotten into you tonight, but I'm not complaining," he said as he pulled her in for a quick kiss. "Thank you," he whispered.

"You're welcome." Jessie closed her eyes, trying not to think of Peter, who she instinctively knew was watching them from somewhere at this event. She needed to savor this moment with Grant.

"Come on," Grant said, interrupting her thoughts. "Let's head over and finalize our silent bids. Then I'm going to check on Goldie. That's what I want to call her, by the way," he said, leading Jessie to the tent where the silent auction was taking place and also where Peter and Cathy were standing.

Peter straightened his wide plaid tie as they approached, his facial expression giving nothing away. Jessie held her breath as she met Peter's eyes, her heart pounding, waiting for his next move. But he simply smiled and extended his hand to Grant and shook it briskly. Cathy threw her arms around Jessie's neck, causing Jessie to flinch involuntarily, quickly covering it with a lie about being cold and wanting to find a heat lamp after seeing Cathy's startled expression. As Cathy began inquiring about who was watching Lucas that night, Jessie felt as if the walls of the tent were closing in around her. She couldn't do this. Stand here and talk about her baby with the wife of the man who had fathered him. It was wrong.

Jessie looked at her watch. "Oh wow, the silent auction is closing in five minutes. I'm dying to get the parking space this year!" Jessie said, grabbing a Sharpie off the table and hoping her plastered smile didn't look as fake as it felt as she tugged Grant's arm. "And Grant needs to warm up his paddle—he's bidding on the dog!" she said, and hoped Peter noticed that she and Grant were a united front. She felt herself breathe for the first time in minutes as she watched Cathy guide Peter toward the buffet.

"I'm going to pay Goldie a visit," Grant said.

"Go. You've got thirty minutes until the live auction begins. Plenty of time to get to know each other." Jessie smiled and pushed him toward where the dog was sitting in her crate, her tail wagging fiercely as he approached.

"We need to talk," she heard a voice murmur beside her, and she jumped slightly.

"I thought you were off getting a plate of chicken wings," Jessie said to Peter through gritted teeth without taking her eyes off Grant. "What are you thinking trying to talk to me *here*?"

"You won't answer my calls. What do you want me to do?"

Jessie forced herself to look at him and sighed loudly. "Fine. What do you want from me?"

"You know what I want. To see my son."

"Shhh," Jessie said, pretending to read a description card attached to a basketful of sweets. "And is that all? Just to see him?"

"For now."

"And if I don't allow it?"

"Then I'm not sure this is a secret I can keep."

Jessie shuddered. "You'd be willing to destroy your own life too? Because I'm not the only one with something to lose," she reasoned.

"Cathy and I haven't been happy in years." Peter let his eyes fall across Jessie's body. "Obviously," Peter said in a hushed tone, shaking his empty drink glass, the sound of the ice echoing in Jessie's ears as she wondered what happened to the guy who had charmed her so thoroughly.

"Well, we're working hard to be happy," Jessie said, seething. "I'm not ready to give up on my marriage. Even though you might be. So don't take me down with you."

Peter smiled like he thought she was bluffing. "Then give me what I want. And maybe I won't have to."

Jessie felt nauseous. "Fine. Thursday at two."

"That's a much better answer." Peter's voice grated on Jessie like the high squeal from a microphone when someone gets too close to it. "And by the way," he said, gesturing his empty glass toward Grant, who was letting Goldie lick his face. "Letting him get a damn dog isn't going to help him forgive you *if* he finds out."

• • •

Grant glanced over at Jessie, and she was scowling. And Jessie wasn't a scowler. She smiled even when she was sad, that reflex like a button that couldn't be switched off. Her lips curved upward into a grin when she was nervous too. In fact, she smiled so hard when he'd asked her to marry him that they'd joked he'd almost broken her face by asking. But she was frowning now. And as Grant watched her, he realized she seemed to be frowning at Peter, a man they barely knew. He was a stay-at-home dad from Madison and Morgan's class he'd remembered meeting at back-to-school nights and seeing at the soccer fields from time to time. He'd seemed like a nice enough guy. Maybe he was filling Jessie in on the latest drama with the class mom—Jessie had just been telling him on the way over here that this woman had been terrorizing all the parents who hadn't volunteered at the auction.

Just then, the puppy let out a sharp bark, demanding Grant's attention once more. "Sorry, girl," he said quietly, and gently stroked her fur. "I didn't mean to ignore you."

Jessie used to accuse Grant of ignoring her often. When they didn't fight about it, he could still feel it, could see it in the way her body stiffened when he entered the room. Like she was waiting to see what he'd do. Would he sweep her off her feet? Or would he prop his feet up on the couch? He hated to admit it, but he usually chose the latter. Not because he didn't love Jessie. Of course he did. But he felt so much pressure. Like if he did scoop her up in his arms, she'd think it was only because they'd argued about it for an hour the night before. If he pulled her in for a kiss and asked her about her day, he would feel like an actor performing the lines from a script she'd written. He wanted it to be organic, the way it used to be. And he'd been so tired. Not just physically tired. But tired of the guilt she threw at him like daggers each night. It weighed on him like a dumbbell he couldn't lift, no matter how hard he tried.

And then she got pregnant. Unexpectedly. Lazy ovary be damned. And he'd found himself conflicted. He'd finally earned enough that they'd had a nice cushion in the bank and the beginning of a college fund for the girls. He was thrilled by the idea of another baby—maybe it would be the son he'd always wanted. But he was also panicked. Could they afford another child? He knew they could, of course, but it would mean working even harder than he already had been. He didn't want to ask Jessie to get a job. He liked that she was home to pick up the girls after school and take them to their activities. He didn't want a babysitter to do that. Not when they could have their mom.

So he braced himself for what he knew would be coming when he started working Saturdays again and even later hours.

More daggers, more arguments, more resentment. But when Lucas arrived, everything changed in a way he could have never predicted. Yes, Jessie still wanted his attention, but she didn't seem so accusatory. She understood why he was working harder, that they had another mouth to feed. Grant didn't know why she'd had a change of heart. All he knew is that the weight had fallen off his shoulders. His wife actually seemed to like him again. She wanted to know *why* he was tired, rather than just being angry that he was. She initiated sex with him again, instead of huffing in the corner of the bed, thinking he was clueless to it all. Yes, he had known she wasn't happy. He just hadn't had the energy to fix it. But Lucas' birth had changed everything. Now Grant had it all—the son he'd always secretly wanted but didn't think he'd get. A happy wife who curled up on his shoulder each night. Two daughters who still thought he was a hero, who ran into his arms each night when he walked through the door.

He fed the puppy a treat and glanced over at Jessie again, who now stood by herself, her scowl replaced by a smile. Grant recognized it immediately—it was her sad one, where her bottom lip jutted out so slightly you almost wouldn't notice. But Grant always did. The question was, what, or who, had put it there?

CHAPTER NINETEEN

....

"Can you speak up? I can barely hear you," Claire said to Jessie as she handed sixteen dollars to the parking attendant at LAX, having just returned from New York. Claire thought she'd misheard the amount then remembered it was ten years ago, when things like airport parking were much more affordable.

"I'm freaking out!" Jessie whispered louder.

"Where are you?" Claire asked as a jet flew overhead, making it even harder to hear Jessie.

"In the bathroom stall, at the school auction."

"What happened?" Claire pictured Jessie crouched down by a toilet, cupping her cell phone with her hand.

"It's you know who. He's threatening me about you know what. *Here!*"

Claire released a drawn-out breath. She was conflicted about Peter wanting to be a part of Lucas' life. As his biological father, he had a right to be involved, and Lucas was lucky he wanted to be. But Claire hated that he was threatening Jessie. Claire thought about Emily's father, wondering if one of the reasons she'd been brought back was to handle that situation differently. If she should give him another chance and invite him back into Emily's life. He'd been unreliable when Emily was a baby, failing to show up to see her on most of the two Saturdays a month they'd agreed upon, then stopping entirely for months at a time. Claire dishing out ultimatums she never followed through on, him making promises to change he'd never followed through on. And it only got worse when Emily was a toddler and began noticing his absences, when he forgot to pick her up from preschool, and forgot about her second *and third* birthday parties, and basically forgot to be a father. Finally, when he forgot dads' night at her school, five-year-old Emily holding the card she'd made for him with tears streaming down her face, Claire called David. She warned him to never show his face in their lives again, not that it would be a huge difference. She scolded him and said Emily couldn't handle any more letdowns. He barely put up a fight. She imagined him yawning and shrugging on the other end of the line, as if she'd just told him they were out of eggs. After he coolly said good-bye, Claire had crept down the hall to Emily's room and peered in at her. Emily's tangle of butter-colored curls were wrapped around her ivory cheeks, her thumb wedged in her mouth. She'd sobbed silently: Emily was officially fatherless.

After that, David faded away and Claire had assumed that was because he was a deadbeat who really didn't want the responsibility. But when Emily turned nine, he began to send letters. One every three months or so, addressed to Emily in his steady hand. Asking for another chance. Saying he'd changed. Claire had read each one hundreds of times, looking for a sign in them that proved he really was different, that he would show up this time, but there was nothing that guaranteed he wouldn't let her daughter down again. She hid the letters in the back of her sock drawer, telling herself that he'd only fail Emily again if Claire allowed him back into her life. But now, watching Jessie deny Peter his son so she could protect herself, Claire wondered if she hadn't done the same thing. Denied someone who was ready to make the right choices for his child. "What did Peter say exactly?"

"He threatened to tell Cathy and Grant."

"So he's going to go public unless you let him see Lucas?"

"Yes. And I don't think he just wants to play in the sandbox with him. I worry he wants more."

"Where's Grant?" Claire asked.

"Signing the papers for our new puppy."

"Wait, what? Because I thought I just heard you say *puppy*, and you already have your hands full."

Claire heard Jessie exhale. "It's a long story, I'll tell you later. But I'm scared, Claire. Really scared. Please make me feel better. Tell me it's going to be okay."

"It's going to be okay," Claire echoed assuredly, but wondered if it would be. She remembered the last time Grant left. It was before Mona was diagnosed and she was able to be there for Jessie when she fell apart. But now Claire had her mother to take care of and she worried whether Jessie was strong enough to go through the pain of losing Grant—again. And then there was Gabriela, the two of them never fully reconciling after they'd argued at the hotel yesterday. They'd ridden silently, shoulder to shoulder in the cab to LaGuardia, listening to the driver chattering away on his cell phone in a language neither of them understood, Claire wanting to make a joke about the experience, but fearful that Gabriela would shut her down. The plane ride had been more of the same with nothing beyond polite exchanges. They'd gone their separate ways after they'd deplaned, Gabriela saying she hoped things worked out with Emily, Claire telling her she was sorry about the baby. But there were a thousand unspoken words floating in the space between them and Claire worried they might never be said.

"I don't want to lose my family, Claire," Jessie whispered, her voice sounding fragile, as if she would break if any more words came out of her mouth.

"That will not happen—*again*," Claire said, feeling her protective instincts take over, praying a solution presented itself, like maybe Peter would get hit by a bus. Then she immediately regretted the thought. He was still Lucas' father. And in this version of their life, the worst thing he'd done was freak out when he'd first heard the news. But once he'd seen his son, he'd come around. Even Claire had to acknowledge that. He was trying to do the right thing, even if he was going about it the wrong way.

"How can you be so sure?"

Because I can't even begin to consider the alternative. I can't imagine you without Grant again. You were a shell of yourself for so many years.

"Claire?"

"We're going to figure this out, Jess. I promise."

"So what should I do now?"

"Get the hell out of there and go home. Let's meet first thing tomorrow."

"Okay," Jessie said, and then Claire heard muffled voices in the background. "I have to go," Jessie said, hanging up quickly.

• • •

More than anything, Claire wanted to fall into bed the moment she got to her parents' house, but she knew she couldn't. She would need to resume her caretaker role and give her father a break. She'd spoken to her dad several times during the short window she was in New York, and he'd sounded exhausted as he'd updated her about Mona. She was depressed her hair had started falling out and she still had no appetite. And then there was Emily, Claire's dad assuring her that she had been very helpful, taking over for him several times so he could get some rest, even walking to the grocery store to pick up a list of items Mona needed. But when she'd gotten on the phone with Emily, she seemed even more distant than before, and Claire was only able to pull a word or two out of her. When they hung up, Claire questioned her decision to leave for the millionth time, and resented Gabriela—and herself—for talking her into it. Some girls' trip that had been.

Tomorrow was Emily's first day back to school since the suspension, and they were scheduled to meet with the vice principal about Emily's plan to apologize to her classmate. Emily had been tasked with writing a letter to the girl while Claire was away, but she suspected she hadn't. She worried they'd be up half the night bickering about how to craft the apology note, her shoulders tensing at the mere thought of it. As hard as mothering Emily had been last time, she didn't remember it being this difficult so early. Emily had begun to spiral once she hit high school, not while still in middle school.

"I'm home," Claire called out as she pushed the front door open. "Hello?" she said again after being met with silence. Not even the TV was on, and it was always on, blaring *Wheel of Fortune* or *Jeopardy!* "Dad? Emily?"

"Grandpa's asleep," Emily said as she rounded the corner, somehow looking much older than thirteen in just two days, her long hair pulled back into a ponytail, a pink hue to her cheeks.

"Oh?"

"I told him to get some rest, that I'd clean up the kitchen and help Grandma if she needed anything," Emily said matter-of-factly as she turned on the water and began scrubbing a casserole dish. Claire watched in disbelief, wanting to say, *Who are you and what have you done with my surly daughter?*

"Great," Claire managed, and slid into one of the chairs at the dinner table, as the dog nuzzled her leg, feeling bad for doubting her daughter. Maybe she had written the apology letter after all.

"So are you ready to go back to school tomorrow?" she said, bracing herself for a snooty response.

But Emily only shrugged, her back still to Claire as she rinsed the dish and grabbed a frying pan.

"We'll head over to meet Mr. Randall at eight thirty and show him the letter you wrote," Claire said, deciding not to directly ask if she'd written the apology note to the girl she'd hurt, hoping to show Emily she trusted her by assuming she had.

"What if she doesn't want to read it?" Emily said, her voice catching, and Claire felt her chest expand to let out the breath she'd been holding.

She rushed over to Emily, turning her around by the shoulders. "Of course she will."

"Maybe she won't want to forgive me."

"We all make mistakes. Everyone deserves a second chance."

"Dad didn't."

"What?"

"Dad didn't deserve a second chance. He asked for one and you refused to give him one."

"What do you mean?" Claire felt her heartbeat quicken. Had Emily's father contacted her directly?

"Is that why I don't have a relationship with my dad? Because you can't forgive him?" Emily's eyes blazed as they stared into Claire's. Emily hadn't brought up her dad in years. Where was this coming from?

"Em, it's complicated."

"So uncomplicate it for me," she said, sounding so much the way she did as an adult that Claire blinked several times to be sure this was the version of Emily who had just turned thirteen the week before and not the twenty-two-year-old one.

Claire took a deep breath, searching for the right words. She'd never said anything bad about Emily's father to her and she wasn't going to start now. But she wasn't sure how honest she should be. Last time, Emily hadn't asked about her dad when she was this age—in fact, he hadn't come up at all for years. Emily didn't mention him until her high school graduation neared, curious if he might attend. The letters that Claire had refused to acknowledge had finally dwindled away. Claire had felt a spasm of guilt when she had shaken her head, no, that she didn't think he'd be there for this milestone.

"He loves you, Em. But he didn't always follow through on what he said. It felt like we were better off without him."

"What do you mean?"

"When you were younger, he'd say he was going to come see you, but rarely did. I hated to see you disappointed, honey."

"But he wanted to see me, right?"

"Of course," Claire said. "But I guess things came up."

"Or was it that *you* didn't want him to see me?"

"Of course I wanted him to see you. Why would you say that?" Claire felt the heat rise to her cheeks, Emily's accusation hitting on the doubts she still had about her motives back then.

"Because that's what he said." Emily folded her arms tightly, and Claire wasn't sure if her mind was playing tricks on her, but Emily looked like her father so much in that moment. She had his dark brown eyes, framed by his equally dark lashes and eyebrows.

"Did he call you? Come see you?"

"No."

Claire breathed again. "Then where is this coming from?"

"Don't play dumb, Mom. I know, okay?"

"Know what?"

"Are you really going to stand there and act like you have no idea what I'm talking about?"

Claire searched for the answer her daughter was looking for, and then she noticed a sheet of notebook paper on the table with Emily's handwriting scrawled across it—her letter to the classmate she'd bullied at school.

And then she knew what Emily was talking about. *The letters.* She found the letters her dad sent.

Claire had come across them several months ago while searching for her favorite pair of fuzzy socks, finding the stack of white envelopes secured with a rubber band in the back of her drawer where she'd always kept it. She'd slid down next to the dresser and read them. And then she'd put them back, she was sure of it. There were ten of them, all one page and hand-written in black ink on a sheet of white printer paper. In the most recent one, he had mentioned Claire and that he knew she didn't want him in Emily's life. But that it should be Emily's decision. Claire had always planned to show Emily the letters at some point, and let her decide if she wanted to respond. But it never felt like the right time, and before she knew it, Emily was an adult and it seemed like it would take her backward to read them. And when he'd never sent another after she'd turned twelve or tried to contact her in any other way, Claire convinced herself she'd made the right decision not to show her at all, that he couldn't be counted on, that he'd just ended up retreating into his own world the way he had so many times before.

She'd been with Emily every time they'd gone back to their house to get more of their things, except once. She remembered now. They were having an eighties-themed dress-up day at school and Emily needed to borrow something from Claire. The letters hadn't crossed Claire's mind. She was preoccupied with a call she'd received from her assistant, telling her that the financing for the offer they'd just accepted had fallen through. So her father had offered to drive Em. She must have found them while looking for something to wear.

"I can explain, Emily."

Emily's eyes filled with tears. "What could you possibly say to make me understand why you didn't think I needed my dad?"

Claire opened her mouth to speak, but then closed it again when she realized she really didn't have much of an answer.

CHAPTER TWENTY

....

Gabriela threw the box of tampons against the wall, the contents spilling out across the ivory rug, anger-filled teardrops splashing down her face. She'd gotten her period almost the second she'd walked through her front door from the airport. It was as if her body was saying *welcome fucking home.* The house was quiet, and she'd found Colin sprawled across their bed with the sheets kicked down around his feet. She'd paused in the doorway and listened to his breathing, wondering why he hadn't waited up. They'd talked briefly before she'd boarded her flight home from New York, Gabriela apologizing for hanging up on him and ignoring his calls, but he'd still seemed detached, offering nothing more than apologies that the IVF hadn't worked again. Gabriela felt more like she was talking to her doctor than to her husband.

She'd pretended to be engrossed in the romantic comedy playing on the airplane on her flight back to Los Angeles, wanting to turn to Claire and make things right between them, but not sure where to start. She didn't know if it was pride or fear, but she couldn't seem to swivel her body toward Claire's and tell her the real truth, the deep secret that swelled inside of her like a current about to pull her under—that she wanted a baby more than she wanted *anything,* maybe even a writing career. *Maybe.*

Claire might have a child, but she had no idea what Gabriela was going through, no clue what it felt like to fail, over and over again, at becoming a mother. Both she and Jessie tried to find the right words to make her feel better, consoling her when she confided her sadness about not being pregnant, but nothing they said could fill the ache in her gut. Claire's pregnancy had been a surprise and Jessie had become pregnant with twins naturally and then had a third baby when she was almost *forty,* despite her lazy ovary. Gabriela honestly felt more connected to many of the women in the TTC chat rooms than she did to her best friends. Her quest to become pregnant was consuming her, thoughts of it always sitting at the top of her mind, the words to discuss it always at the tip of her tongue.

When Gabriela had met Jessie for lunch in the park the other day, Jessie had seemed jittery, blaming her disposition on a swarm of bees, but Gabriela knew she wasn't telling her everything. And Claire had seemed like she was holding something back when she'd talked about Emily's trouble at school, as if there were more to the story. Their friendships had felt impenetrable before. But this time, Gabriela didn't feel as protected by them as she once had, and she wondered if they felt the same way about her. How had this distance grown between them?

Gabriela picked up the tampons one by one and shoved them back into the box and placed it beneath the sink, wondering if she should call her doctor in the morning and talk to her about starting a third IVF cycle. She placed her hand on her abdomen as she looked in the mirror and wondered if there would ever be a baby growing inside of her. She knew she should go to her office and write, even just a few sentences, but she was petrified to turn on the computer and have to face that blank screen, the one that seemed to match her mind. So she kept walking, but not to her bedroom. Instead she opened the door to the room at the end of the hall, the one where visitors slept, and slid under the comforter, thinking of her husband who had left her alone with her loss and wondering why she felt like a guest in her own home.

• • •

Jessie had spent the night tossing and turning, Peter's face working his way into her mind every time she squeezed her eyes shut. Finally, she'd given up on sleep and tiptoed down the hall to check on the children, something that always seemed to calm her since she'd traveled back—they were all still here, under one roof, in the home she shared with Grant. She hadn't screwed it up, yet. She'd peered into the twins' rooms, pulling the covers tightly around Madison's chin and putting the *Wings of Fire* book she'd been reading on her night stand. She'd always been a sound sleeper, Grant once joking Madison wouldn't wake up even if a train drove through her bedroom. Conversely, when she'd cracked open Morgan's door, Morgan rolled over from the slight sound. Jessie remembered the spot on the carpeted floor of her nursery, the one she'd try with all her might to avoid but somehow always seemed to step on, causing Morgan to wail nonstop until Jessie finally gave in and picked her up.

Jessie always saved Lucas' room for last. As she peered into his crib, she pictured Peter's face. There was something in the way Peter's mouth formed a tight line after he'd not so subtly threatened her that had pierced Jessie. She felt her chest burn as she thought of Peter's words, that he couldn't keep their secret if he couldn't see his son. If he followed through, he'd be destroying two families. And the idea of ever having to share Lucas with a man who would consider that made her feel sick.

She was suddenly overcome with the cruel reality that things could turn out even worse than before—that divorce from Grant could be minor in scale compared to the aftermath of Peter exposing the truth. If she couldn't figure out how to appease Peter soon, it would be worse than losing Grant all over again. She might also lose Lucas.

• • •

The next morning, Claire opened her front door, her skin sallow and her eyes bloodshot. "I know," she said before Jessie could speak. "I look like hell. Only got three hours last night."

"You lucky bitch, I only got two!" Jessie set the car seat down and hugged Claire, who inhaled Jessie's fruity shampoo, wondering when she'd last embraced someone. She hadn't seen Mason since she'd been back from New York. But even before that, their dates had dwindled to maybe one a week. She knew he wanted to see her more, but even when she was with him, she was preoccupied and felt terrible every time she'd asked him to repeat what he'd just said, constantly lost in thought. "Hey, I brought the girls. Hope that's okay?" Jessie added, looking over her shoulder as Madison and Morgan walked up the sidewalk.

"Come in! Hi, girls," Claire said, squeezing the twins. "Here, let me take that," Claire offered as she picked up the car seat and made kissing faces at Lucas. "I forgot how heavy these fucking things are! I mean freaking things," Claire said, laughing as the twins rolled their eyes. "Coffee?" she asked Jessie once they were inside, who nodded vigorously in response. She grabbed her own cup, which she'd already refilled three times. "Emily! Morgan and Madison are here," she called as she started pouring grounds into the filter.

Jessie lay back in Claire's dad's recliner as Emily came out of her room and grabbed the twins. She watched them, smiling as the door shut behind them, happy she'd decided to bring them over. She realized she'd been selfish before, keeping them away from Emily. This time, she decided the girls probably needed each other, much the same way she needed Gabriela and Claire. Maybe this could end up being a lifelong friendship just like theirs. "This chair is so comfortable, maybe I should get Grant one of these," she remarked as she pulled the lever to extend the footrest.

"Be warned that if you do, he might not ever get out of it. My dad sits in that thing for hours every night. Even sleeps in it!" Claire smiled and handed Jessie a steaming mug of coffee.

"Oh, then I'm definitely out—I don't want to give him any excuses not to sleep in our bed!" Jessie laughed as she accepted the cup and took a long sip. "Where is your dad, by the way?"

"He took my mom to the doctor."

"Is that why you were up all night? Because of your mom?" Jessie asked, lowering her voice. "Or is it Emily?"

Claire thought about the letters Emily's dad had written her and decided now was definitely not the time to tell Jessie the truth, especially in light of her own situation. Hearing the laughter coming out of Emily's room, she was so thankful Jessie had brought her girls over. She didn't want to do anything to make her snatch them away, to make her want to keep them from Emily, much like she had in the other version of their lives. Claire had never said anything outright to Jessie, but she knew her friend had made excuses for why the twins couldn't come over, not wanting Emily's bad attitude to rub off on them. And while Claire could understand that, she was still hurt. Her daughter wasn't a bad person, she was just a kid with an absent father.

Claire wished she could explain to Jessie that withholding Lucas' dad would eventually have consequences, no matter how good her intentions were. Now that Claire had seen Emily's reaction to what she'd done, she was beginning to realize that it probably hadn't been her decision to make. But she knew Jessie wasn't ready to hear that.

"She's doing okay. We took the apology letter she wrote to school today and she gave it to the girl she bull—" Claire's voice broke slightly and she sucked in a sharp breath as if trying to stop herself from crying. "I'm sorry, I can't even say the word. It's just so crazy to think Em would be so"—she dropped her voice to a whisper—"mean." She sighed. "Or at least, mean to someone other than me," she added, laughing weakly.

Jessie thought of Madison and Morgan. They were just two years younger than Emily, but still playing with Pokémon cards and watching cartoons. She'd do anything to maintain their naïveté. If Peter decided to reveal he was Lucas' father, her daughters would know the *real* reason their parents were breaking up: their mom had betrayed their dad with one of their classmate's fathers. They would hate her and she would lose them. She was sure of it. Last time, after months of the girls' acting out, she'd finally found a counselor they could talk to. And it had helped. In fact, the woman had probably saved them from going down a bad path—a path not unlike the one Emily had taken.

Just yesterday, Madison had suggested they bake chocolate chip cookies. Jessie had placed Lucas in his high chair and pulled him up next to the counter. Morgan had spread flour across his tray and he'd traced his fingers through it in awe, Madison leaning over and kissing her baby brother on the cheek. Jessie watched her children, so blissfully ignorant, and thought of their alternate life, the one where door slamming and glares were the way they communicated their displeasure. Jessie wanted more than anything to avoid going through that again. She didn't want to be separated from her children every other weekend, nor answer her daughters' persistent questions about why she and Grant couldn't get back together.

"Emily is not a mean girl. Even when she was at her worst during those teen years, she never turned her anger on her peers," Jessie whispered. "What's different this time?"

Claire thought about the letters again. Even though Emily had only just admitted to discovering them, she wondered how long she'd had them. "That's what's so hard about all this, Jess. I wish I knew for sure! It seems like *more* problems are coming up. Just when I think I'm getting rid of one, another pops up in its place. Sometimes it feels like I'm playing that arcade game Emily used to love. Do you know the one I'm talking about?"

"Whac-A-Mole," Jessie said with a smile, remembering Lucas pounding the moles with a felt mallet. She followed Claire's gaze to a blue jay that had landed on a tree branch. He stared hard at them before spreading his wings and flying away. "Maybe this is why people say what's meant to be, will be."

"I know what you mean." Jessie sighed.

"What does Emily have to say about why she did it?"

"She says she doesn't know," Claire responded, opening her mouth and then shutting it quickly, leaving Jessie wondering what she'd decided not to say.

"And the apology? How did it go over?"

"The girl accepted it, but she's very shy—she barely looked up." Claire paused for a moment, seeing Emily's classmate in her mind again. The scuffed tennis shoes. The torn fingernails that had been chewed endlessly. The tears sitting in the back of her eyes. "At that age, it's hard enough to get these kids to talk to an adult on a good day, let alone when they are in the vice principal's office. I just felt so terrible sitting there. That my daughter had done this to her."

Jessie nodded. The Emily she remembered had been hard on Claire, but never on other kids. "What about her mom and dad?"

"They were sitting on either side of her and were so close that I thought they were going to squish the poor girl." Claire thought about how her dad kept his arm firmly around his daughter's shoulders the entire time and her mom had kissed the top of her head over and over. As angry as she was with Emily, her heart broke as she watched Emily watching them—this girl had a mom *and* a dad.

"Claire?" Jessie's voice interrupted her thoughts.

"I felt like such an ass. The single mom with the problem child. So cliché, right?"

"Any kid can be mean—being a single parent has nothing to do with it," Jessie assured her.

"Even so, I could barely make eye contact with her parents. I knew they were silently blaming me. And maybe this is my fault."

Jessie shook her head. "Emily might be young, but she's still responsible for her own actions. You have been a great mom to her."

"But I've failed her," Claire said.

"No, you haven't. You're doing your best."

"I just keep thinking I could've done better." She'd tried to explain to Emily the other night that she was only trying to protect her from getting hurt, but Emily had scoffed and headed to bed.

"Maybe we can always be better, but we can't be perfect. Look what a mess I've made of everything—twice!" Jessie said, thinking about Peter's threat. If someone had told her the day she married Grant that she'd one day cheat on him and get pregnant with another man's baby, *a married* man's baby, she would've responded with an emphatic, *There is no way that will ever happen!*

"Have you heard from Peter since last night?" Claire asked.

"No. But I was up all night freaking out about the next time he's going to pop up."

Claire felt goose bumps prick her arms. "Have you considered telling Grant the truth? Wouldn't it be better if he heard it from you?"

"No! We already know how that version of the story turns out."

Claire thought for a moment. "Not necessarily. This time, you're telling him much later—Lucas is how old now? Seven months?"

Jessie nodded.

"You've said this extra time has made your marriage stronger. That you're stronger. Maybe it's possible he'd forgive you?" Claire said hopefully.

"And agree to share custody of Lucas with the man I cheated on him with? I doubt it. And like you said, our problems seem to have mutated this time. Who knows how horrible it could get if Grant finds out. I'm worried he'd fight me for full custody of the girls."

"Okay, then what's the alternative? What are the chances Peter will actually tell him?"

"I don't know. He was pretty adamant." Jessie rolled her shoulders back to release some tension. "It's so weird to think this is the same man who made me feel so giddy and alive," Jessie said with a bitter laugh. "How could I have been so wrong about him?"

"It's all fun and games till someone gets pregnant." Claire smiled to let Jessie know she was kidding, but thought of David and how in love they'd been, or so she'd thought, until she announced her own pregnancy. Then he showed his true colors. "But all bad baby jokes aside, I think when it comes to children, parents will do almost anything for them, even things that might surprise you."

Jessie nodded. She'd given up her marriage by giving birth to Lucas.

"So if you do think Peter is unstoppable, wouldn't it soften the blow if *you* told Grant before he could?"

Jessie shook her head, her gaze falling to the floor. "I can't," she said softly. Claire wasn't about to push. She wouldn't have wanted someone so much as nudging her in any one direction when it came to David and the decisions she'd made. That's why she hadn't told Gabriela or Jessie about the letters. Right or wrong, she hadn't wanted a second opinion.

"But maybe there's another way to fix this," Jessie said suddenly, looking back up.

"How?"

"Give Peter what he wants."

"But I thought you said telling Grant wasn't an option?"

"It's not. I mean acquiescing, but on *my* terms. I could tell Peter he can see Lucas once a week, but only if he agrees to keep it a secret. He can be in Lucas' life and Grant will never have to know."

"Do you think he'd agree to that?"

"I do. At least for a while. He might genuinely be unhappy with his wife, but I'm going to bank on the fact that he doesn't want to risk losing custody of his *other* son. I'll convince him that this way, we can both keep our families together and he can have time with his baby."

Claire took a deep breath before responding, choosing her words carefully. "Okay, but what will happen down the road, when Lucas starts talking?"

"Well, number one, I don't even know if I'll be here after Lucas' first birthday. There's always the possibility we'll go back, right?" Jessie looked at Claire, who shrugged. "But I don't think we'll get that far anyway. Don't forget that last time, he wanted *nothing* to do with Lucas. So I predict he'll eventually lose interest and move on, back to Cathy and his family."

Claire looked into Jessie's hopeful eyes. Her plan had so many uncertain variables and Claire was beginning to understand that the truth seemed to leak out anyway. But Jessie wasn't ready to give up on her new life with Grant, and Claire understood why, thinking of Mason. When love finds its way back to you after being lost for so long, you never want to lose your grasp on it again. "Okay," she said. "I know this is what you want, and I'm not going to stop you. Just please be careful, Jessie."

"I know it's risky, but it's the only solution. I'll never forget the look on Grant's face the first time I told him about Peter. I'd do pretty much anything to never see it again."

CHAPTER TWENTY-ONE

....

"Whee!" Jessie called out as she launched Lucas down the small red slide, where Peter's outstretched arms awaited him at the bottom. Lucas squealed in delight as Peter caught him and swung him up by his arms, and Jessie felt the conflict arise in her heart, that Lucas' joy meant that her own might end soon.

She and Peter had been secretly meeting once a week for two months at a playground about twenty minutes south of Redondo Beach. Two months of playdates filled with building sand castles and driving foam bulldozers together through the sandbox. Two months of taking turns pushing Lucas in the swing, his chubby legs flying through the air carelessly as he laughed in delight. Two months of watching a man bond with his son, of seeing them become more than just two strangers.

"How's the teething?" Peter asked as Lucas heaved himself up on the bench. He was so close to walking, attempting it almost every day, eager to keep pace with his older sisters, who'd just started their soccer season, Lucas watching excitedly from the sidelines, trying to crawl onto the field.

"Not too bad. He's just very drooly, as you can see." Jessie smiled wryly and pointed to the never-ending cascade of saliva that propelled from the corners of his mouth.

• • •

The first week they'd met at this park, Jessie had sat stiffly at the picnic table as Peter self-consciously bounced Lucas in his lap. Lucas kept reaching his hands to his mother, and Jessie felt satisfied that Lucas was rejecting Peter and was hopeful it would deter him from wanting to see his son again. But the next week, he'd been waiting for them with a basket of sand toys, the price tags still hanging from them. "I thought we'd switch things up a bit," he said simply, and had sat for thirty minutes in the sandbox with Lucas, who only reached for his mother once. Slowly, with each passing week, Lucas, and eventually Jessie, would warm up to Peter a bit more. One day, Jessie found herself not feeling sick as she pulled into the parking lot, and was even able to meet Peter's eyes when he said hello and reached for their son. As Lucas began to accept Peter, a small part of Jessie begrudgingly did also, finding it almost impossible to despise someone who put so much effort into knowing Lucas.

"How are things with Cathy?" Jessie asked. "Any better?" Jessie had drawn the courage a few weeks ago to bring up the state of Peter's marriage, hoping that if she could help convince him it was worth saving, he'd reconsider what Lucas' presence might mean for that.

"She's pissed at me again. Apparently I'm not attentive enough."

"So pay more attention to her," Jessie said, and rolled her eyes. Since initially asking, Peter had opened up, telling Jessie all the ways he felt Cathy belittled him, making him feel more

like her assistant than her partner. Before, when she was traveling, Peter had the freedom to run the house how he saw fit. But
now that she was home by dinnertime each night, she'd begun
to micromanage each decision he made, causing him to grow
increasingly frustrated. Jessie counseled him, which felt weird
and inappropriate. But if she was going to save her own marriage,
she was going to have to fix Peter's first.

"It's not that easy. It's like everything I do is wrong. Last night,
she was upset because all the plates in the dishwasher weren't
facing the same way. I had made dinner and cleaned the entire
kitchen before she even got home. And instead of a thank-you,
all she did was complain."

"You sound like a wife," Jessie teased lightly.

"Well, that makes sense, because I feel like she's cut my balls
off." Peter laughed bitterly and Jessie thought about how different he was from Grant. As she let herself get to know Peter, she
found him to be confident on the outside, but wildly insecure
on the inside. And something about Cathy's behavior seemed
to flip a switch in him, making him angry and insolent. Jessie
boldly asked him if he still loved her, and he'd paused for a full
minute, Jessie picking at her cuticles as she waited anxiously for
his response, praying that he'd say yes. She needed him to love
her. Or at least care enough to not want to destroy her.

"I don't know anymore," he whispered finally. "Do you love
Grant?"

"Yes," Jessie said without hesitation.

"How do you know? After everything that's happened?"

"I just know." Jessie thought about kissing Grant good-bye
that morning. She'd sucked on his lower lip, then let her tongue
find his, not allowing herself to be distracted by Lucas' squeals
or the girls calling for her to help them find their field trip forms.

"Because I want to be better. For him. For us. Because at the end of the day, the core of my heart belongs to him. That's why I don't want to hurt him."

"Or yourself. You don't want him to leave you."

"Or my kids," Jessie conceded. "Because it's not just about me. The truth will hurt them too. You might not care how it affects Cathy, but what about Sean?"

"Of course I've thought about him. But Lucas is his brother. And as an only child, he deserves to know he has a sibling."

Jessie felt faint as she'd listened to his argument. She'd been bending over to grab the diaper bag from under the picnic table, and she'd had to squeeze the edge to stop her hand from shaking. In all the times she'd turned the scenarios over in her head, that one hadn't occurred to her. She looked at Lucas' onesie with #1 Little Brother printed on the front, remembering how Morgan had dressed him in it, calling out to Jessie that she had finally mastered the snaps at the bottom. She and Madison got to spend time with their brother every day. Sean deserved the same opportunity, but at what cost?

"You're right, they are brothers. But would it really be better to tell him he has a sibling if it meant breaking up your marriage to do so? I can tell you that divorce is hard, really hard."

"How would you know?"

Jessie backtracked, realizing her mistake. "I know people who've gone through it and it's terrible," she said truthfully. Remembering the searing pain inside of her as she'd signed her name on the bottom of the papers, her attorney looking on with feigned empathy.

"Well, I honestly believe divorce might be better than Sean thinking my marriage to his mom is what marriage really looks like. He hears us fight, Jessie, a lot. I'm not proud of that."

"Couples argue," Jessie said quickly. Last time, before Grant moved out, they had done their best to talk when the girls weren't home about Jessie's infidelity, but sometimes they'd end up in their bedroom, voices raised, and she wondered if the girls had overheard.

Peter made a face. "Someone needs a new diaper."

Jessie reached for Lucas, but Peter waved her off, pulling a diaper out of the bag and changing Lucas so quickly she almost thought she'd missed it. It was becoming harder to deny that he was a natural father.

Jessie thought hard. "You could go to counseling."

"Tell you what. I'll go when you go. You're talking a good game here, but you weren't exactly hesitating in that hotel lobby. Obviously you wouldn't have jumped into bed with me if your marriage was as rock solid as you're trying to make it sound."

"It's far from rock solid. But it's also not broken. I made a mistake. I was an idiot to sleep with you," Jessie said, remembering her boldness as she'd held the pool cue.

Peter shot her a look as if to say, *Gee, thanks*, which Jessie ignored.

"I didn't leave that bar with you because I didn't love my husband. It's just that you made me feel wanted. It had been a long time since I'd felt that way with Grant." She avoided eye contact as she started shaking the sand out of the buckets and stacking them. "And so I convinced myself that something was wrong with him, and with us. But I was the one who was wrong."

"I don't think it's asking too much to want to feel wanted by your spouse *after* the honeymoon period is over," Peter said as he handed her a yellow shovel that was hanging over the edge of the sandbox. "Even after having kids," Peter added, and Jessie wasn't sure if he was talking to her or to himself.

"You're right, but the reality is that couples get lazy, putting all their energy into children and careers and then blaming the disconnect on each other when, in reality, they're choosing—*you and I were choosing*—the easy way out. We turned to each other when we should've turned to our spouses. I wasn't choosing Grant. You weren't choosing Cathy. And we have to take ownership of that." Jessie stretched out a mesh bag and placed the buckets inside. "I'm choosing to fight for my marriage. And I think you should too."

"Maybe." Peter reached for Lucas' hands as he pulled himself up, letting go as soon as he balanced himself. Lucas flashed a grin and tentatively took three steps before toppling over.

"Oh my God." Jessie's hand flew over her mouth. "He just walked. Those were his first steps!" Jessie ran over and picked him up. "Good job, buddy! Walking at nine months, that's a new record!"

"I'd like to think that dexterity comes from my side of the family. I walked very early too." Peter came over and rubbed Lucas' back. "Great work, son!"

Jessie half smiled, not sure how she felt that Peter was the father who got to witness Lucas' milestone. But there was one thing she now knew for certain as she beamed at Lucas. Peter wasn't going anywhere, anytime soon.

• • •

"What's that?" Colin asked as Gabriela heaved a box into the house, pushing it through the doorway with her foot when she couldn't carry it any longer. "My anniversary gift?" he joked tersely. It was March 12 and neither of them had mentioned the upcoming date.

"No." Gabriela offered him a partial smile. "The drugs for the next cycle."

Colin frowned as he grabbed the box off the floor. "Last time I checked, you needed *my* sperm and *my* approval for another round." Colin's voice bristled with anger. The morning after she'd returned from New York two months ago, she'd gone to see Dr. Larson without Colin, working out the details of the third cycle, nodding mildly when the doctor inquired if Colin was still on board, then coming home and announcing matter-of-factly that *she* was starting again. Colin had flashed her a look of pity and muttered, *What happened to* we? before heading out for a run.

"What are you saying?" Gabriela's voice shook and she rubbed the goose bumps on her arms.

"This will be round four in less than a year. Shouldn't *we* take a break?"

Gabriela clenched her jaw, ignoring his dig. When she'd found out she wasn't pregnant *again*, for the third time, she hadn't gotten out of bed for five days, sobbing into her pillow so much that she'd given herself a rash on the side of her face.

"Taking some time off from this will help you—*us*—relax a bit and give your body a chance to rest."

"You're acting like I should take a vacation. Maybe go somewhere warm and tropical and frolic on the beach. How about Bora Bora or Turks and Caicos? Like that would make everything okay, Colin. I could *never* do that right now. *That* would stress me out. Not being here. Not trying to make this happen. Don't you get that?"

"Not a vacation. I was thinking maybe more like focusing your energy on something else, like your writing."

The truth was, she had only turned on her computer once in the last two months. And when she had, she'd written just three terrible sentences. As her fingers rested on the keyboard, she'd felt as if someone were sitting on her chest, and she'd gasped for breath, her heart racing, her fingers tingling. Jessie had suspected it was a panic attack when Gabriela confided in her, but she refused to go to the doctor to find out, afraid they would prescribe her a medication that would interfere with her ability to get pregnant. Or worse, they'd suggest she take some time off from IVF. And that, she was not willing to do.

"I've been writing here and there," Gabriela lied. She had found it easier to tell everyone she was writing, to avoid the concerned looks they were sure to dispense. *Two thousand words just today!* she'd written in an email to her editor, her stomach clenching as she'd pushed send. She hated to mislead her, but she kept thinking about Sheila's plea that Gabriela not let her down. She prayed the words would come, that she'd wake up one morning and the book would rush out of her. The last time she'd penned the novel, she'd done so in less than ninety days so she knew she was capable of making the deadline if she could just get the words to form in her head soon. Because it wouldn't be long before she and Jessie and Claire would have to decide if they were going back or staying here.

"Can I read any of it?" Colin pressed. "You used to give me pages every night. I haven't seen anything in almost a year."

"I'm keeping this one really close to my heart. I think it's going to be better that way. But I promise to show you something as soon as I feel it's ready." And that was the truth. She wanted so badly to have something to show him, something that was worthy to read and she knew if she could just get pregnant, the book would be unleashed onto paper.

Colin's face contorted. "Can you at least admit that agreeing to *another* round without talking to me isn't fair? Especially when you know my health insurance won't cover a fourth cycle."

"How can you bring money into this? We're trying to make a baby, not buy a car!" Gabriela spat.

"Well, you're treating this like it's a pricey pair of shoes you bought without telling me and then hid in the back of the closet. It's a *baby*, Gabriela." He drew out the syllables of the word slowly, as if she couldn't understand them otherwise.

"I get that, Colin. Believe me, I'm obsessed with the *baby*," she yelled, then kicked the Styrofoam box of medication. "The question is, why aren't you?"

Colin took a deep breath. "I don't know who you are anymore. The woman I'm looking at right now, she's *not* the one I married."

Gabriela watched him walk out of the room and heard their bedroom door close softly behind him. She knew she'd be sleeping in the guest room again tonight, where she'd been for most of the past two months. She waited for the tears to come, for the feelings of panic to arise in her heart that she could be losing her husband, but she felt numb. So she concentrated on the one thing that seemed to matter. She tore the lid off the top of the box and started sorting through the fertility drugs—Repronex, progesterone, Follistim—plus the packages of needles that she hoped would help bring her the baby she wanted so badly.

CHAPTER TWENTY-TWO

....

"Again?"

Claire could picture Mason on the other end of the phone frowning, disappointed that she was canceling another date, the second one this week. "I'm sorry, but my mom's not eating. And I wouldn't feel right going to dinner while she's in this condition."

"I'm really sorry about your mom, but I miss you. Isn't there any way I can see you? I could bring her some chicken noodle soup."

"She doesn't have the flu, Mason. She has cancer," Claire snapped, immediately regretting her words.

"I know. I know. I can't imagine what it's like for you."

"It sucks," Claire whispered, and felt tears in her throat. "But I shouldn't be taking it out on you. You don't deserve that. We'll see each other soon. I promise," Claire said, but wasn't sure she could deliver on it. The more ill her mom became, the more Claire seemed to cling to her.

"It's okay," Mason said.

"No, it's not," Claire said. "I wish you didn't have to see me like this. I wish you could know the happy Claire." Last time, Claire and Mason had enjoyed six uninterrupted months together before Mona's diagnosis. They had been carefree and fun, and it had been a solid foundation for when things got tough the next year. This time, Mason had barely glimpsed that Claire. The only version of her he knew was stressed and frazzled and distant.

"I like this Claire," Mason said firmly, and Claire's heart melted.

"I'm glad you do, because I can't stand her." Claire laughed feebly before saying good-bye and putting her head in her hands. As she listened to the ticking of the clock in her parents' kitchen, she speculated why she had kept Mason at bay this time. Sure they laughed, both having a deep love for *Seinfeld*'s humor; they watched basketball games on TV, Claire's legs slung over Mason's lap; and they'd talked, but Claire kept the conversation centered around lighter topics, skirting his questions about her mom's health or Emily's situation at school. She knew she was holding a big part of herself back. She felt conflicted about Jared—whom she was missing less each day—and about her feelings for Mason, which were deepening each day. It was hard to stop herself from falling back in love with the one that got away.

Last week, when she'd gone home to get her mail, noticing the front porch light and four other bulbs had gone out, she'd complained to Mason that since she'd been practically living at her parents' house, she'd been neglecting her own, only going home to water the grass or grab some more clothes. An hour later, Mason was on her doorstep holding a plastic bag from Lowe's. She'd thrown her arms around his back, buried her chin into his broad chest, feeling his lips brush the top of her head, then cried out, "Let there be light!"

"I love you, Claire," Mason whispered into her ear, the way he used to, and Claire's breath caught in her chest. When they broke up, and she'd watched him walk to his car, his shoulders hunched in a way that made him appear to have lost several inches of height, she was sure she'd never hear those words from him again. And now, his *I love you* felt like hearing her favorite song playing on the radio.

But she already had a man back home in 2015, whom she loved and was planning to marry. And even though she knew that in this alternate time she and Jared weren't together, it still felt wrong to say it back to Mason, especially since she'd been telling herself she was returning to her old life when the year was up. So she stayed silent. Because the relationship they had in this life was not built on truth. Mason had no idea who she really was, where she had been, and where she was going in just three short months. She wished she could tell him everything. That it had shocked her how easy it had been to fall back into step with him, that the love she felt for him rekindled faster than she'd been comfortable with. That it made her think she didn't love Jared as much as she thought she had. That this realization scared her most of all. But she didn't say any of that. Instead she sat in place, her lips glued shut as Mason held her gaze expectantly, kicking the welcome mat with his toe.

Finally he'd mumbled something about an appointment with a general contractor, gave her a quick peck on the lips, and hurried to his car. It hadn't come up since, but had hung in the air during each conversation. Claire knew she needed to address it, that he deserved to know why she couldn't love him. Or at least why she was unable to say it. But she just wasn't ready to go there yet, to let him down. So she allowed the elephant in the room to hang out with them—in the spaces of silence during their phone conversations, in the backseat of the car as they traveled to dinner, on the couch next to them when they watched TV—praying he wouldn't bring it up again before she was ready to let go.

. . .

Mason hung up the phone and popped the top on a can of Budweiser. He took a long drink, wondering if Claire was distancing herself from him because of what he'd said. He knew it was probably too soon to have told Claire he loved her, but the words were out before he could stop them. And even though it had stung when she hadn't said them back, he wasn't sorry he'd told her. Because he'd wanted her to know—from the morning after they'd slept together if he was being completely honest.

When he'd first noticed Claire standing by the chocolate fountain at the birthday party—watching her tuck a piece of hair behind her ear before she glided a strawberry through the fudge, laughing as she'd popped it into her mouth—he'd felt something almost physical in his chest. He'd felt his feet moving toward her, his boldness surprising him. But he had to meet this petite woman with the large laugh. And then he'd pressed his business card into her soft hand and squeezed, feeling an electric current run up his arm. And when she'd called him the next night, he couldn't believe his luck. Women like Claire didn't go for men like him. He knew she was out of his league. Claire was gorgeous—reminding him of a porcelain doll with her fair skin and large brown eyes. He knew from their brief chat at the party that she was a successful real estate agent and a single mom. Although he had height on his side, towering over her at six foot four, his hair was thinning and he had a few crooked teeth his parents couldn't afford to fix with braces. People sometimes told him he reminded them of a skinnier and taller version of the guy from *King of Queens*. He'd take it! He was a carpenter who hadn't finished college, but he was a hard worker with plenty of money in the bank.

At first, she'd flirted with him tentatively on their date, pausing every few minutes to take a work call with an apologetic smile. But as the night wore on, she'd finally relaxed as she sipped her wine, and eventually slipped her phone into her purse, letting it vibrate without answering. And when the bartender announced last call, they'd shared a tequila shot right before she'd blushed furiously and shyly invited him home. He'd practically jumped into the busy street to hail a cab and they'd made out in the backseat, Claire only coming up for air to give the driver directions. Once there, they could barely get inside the house before their clothes were off, then he'd picked her up and carried her into her bedroom, her laughing and directing the way. He figured, to her, it would be just a one-night stand. A busy mom with not much of a dating life—she'd told him that—letting off some steam after having some liquid courage.

The next morning, he was mystified. She wasn't the same woman he'd met at the party or even talked to on their date or the one he'd gone to bed with. The one he'd met at the party was sweet, but very reserved, buttoned up, focused—maybe too much so. But this version of Claire—the one who woke up beside him and let her guard down, who acted frazzled, who forgot who the president was, who'd looked at her phone like it was a foreign object—he liked a lot more. She seemed more real, more human, more like a girl he'd want to get to know better.

And it was the strangest thing: even though they hadn't gotten to know each other as well as he would've liked—Claire always turning the conversation away from serious topics and thinking he didn't notice—he felt like somehow he knew her, like he'd known her for years.

• • •

The front door of her parents' condo opened and Claire jumped at the sound.

"Mom?" Emily called out.

Claire looked at the clock. She'd lost track of time since hanging up with Mason, realizing she'd been sitting at the kitchen table for over an hour. "In here," Claire answered, a smile crossing her lips. Things between her and Emily were better than ever. Recently, they'd started watching the show *Gilmore Girls* together once a week, Claire drawing hope and inspiration from the fictional mom and daughter who lived in an idyllic town and, despite their problems, always seemed to figure things out. Emily had also been helping to care for her grandmother more and more. Mona even taught her to play cribbage on one of her better days.

When Claire felt enough time had passed after their argument about the letters Emily's father had sent, Claire had carefully broached the subject of the classmate she had bullied and asked again why she had done it. Emily had dissolved into sobs, finally stopping and making Claire promise she wouldn't be upset. Claire had nodded, hoping she could handle whatever was coming.

Slowly, the story spilled out that the girl had made a snide remark to Emily about having a single mom, asking her what she'd done wrong to make her dad leave. When Claire pressed Emily on why she hadn't just told her what the girl had said, her heart dropped when Emily confessed she'd been afraid to tell Claire because she didn't want to hurt her feelings.

Claire was livid, of course. It took all her strength not to phone the girl's parents and tell them what had really happened. That their child didn't deserve that perfect kiss on the head they'd given her. But she didn't, because it was the sadness that dominated. Sadness that Emily had to carry the burden of having only one parent. Of course, Claire said all the right things—that even though that girl had been cruel, it wasn't okay to fight back that way. But inside, guilt overpowered Claire—she could feel it from the buzz in her head to the twitch in her toes.

But then Emily had hugged her, hard, folding her body into Claire. And instantly, the twitching and the buzzing and the anger all fell away. She decided to focus on the positives— Emily's grades were improving and she'd made two new friends that she now hung out with often. Claire had met them both and had been incredibly relieved that they seemed kind and sweet and had normal-colored hair.

Things had been going so smoothly that Claire had almost convinced herself that Emily might never bring up her dad again. But then just last night, there had been a commercial on TV, a father wrapping his arms around his daughter at her high school graduation, and Emily had said sarcastically, in not much more than a whisper, *How sweet for them.* Claire had known she should turn the TV off and talk to Emily about it, that she was testing the waters, wanting to see if Claire had softened her position about her dad's involvement in her life. Claire had opened her mouth to answer, but no words came. She knew she needed to be brave, that she needed to have a discussion about Emily's father, and that her daughter deserved a say about whether or not to let him back into their lives, for better or worse. But instead she told herself it wouldn't matter in three months, she would disappear back to a life where Emily had no idea the letters existed. So instead, Claire was a coward and said nothing, ignoring the burning in her gut telling her to do otherwise.

"How's Grandma today?" Emily said, dropping her backpack on the floor and grabbing a bag of Lay's potato chips out of the pantry.

"She's sleeping. But she still has zero appetite."

"I'll try to get her to eat when she wakes up."

"Thanks. How did you do on your Spanish quiz?"

"I got an A!"

"That's great, Em. I'm proud of you."

"Thanks, Mom."

"Do you have homework tonight?"

Emily nodded. "Science and current events."

"Okay, get started on it. I need to write up an offer and get two listings into the Multiple Listing Service. By then, your grandmother will probably be up." Claire started walking toward the den.

"Hey, Mom?"

"Yeah?" Claire said, turning around.

"I wrote something, and I was wondering if you'd read it."

"Sure, what is it?"

"It's a letter," Emily said, stopping to chew a chip. "To my dad."

Claire quickly readjusted her face from a shocked expression into a smile. "I'd be happy to." She accepted the two sheets of folded notebook paper from her daughter, wondering whether Lauren Graham's character in *Gilmore Girls* would have done the same.

• • •

"So how's it been going with the men in your life?" Claire asked Jessie the following night after their waitress left to get their drinks from the bar.

"Things are so much better with Grant." Jessie smiled.

"And the other one?" Claire asked.

"Lucas? He's doing awesome!"

"Nope. Not that one. The one you don't like to talk about."

"He's fine." Jessie frowned.

"If he's fine, then why do you have that look on your face?"

"Dammit. He's just so great with Lucas."

"And that's a problem?" Claire laughed, then wished she could pull it back the second she saw the defeated look in Jessie's eyes. "Sorry, I didn't mean to be flippant. I get it. You want him to be terrible. You want him to go away."

"Do you get it? Because I feel a little weird talking to you about this. It's like you're biased."

"Why? Because I'm a single mom and my daughter's father has been MIA?" Claire said. "So you think I can't be objective?"

"Sorry, but that's exactly why. Be honest, are you *really* being objective?"

Claire nodded as the server delivered a glass of red wine to her and a dirty martini to Jessie. "Of course. And I'm sorry if I've made you feel otherwise." Claire knew her own issues were starting to cloud the way she viewed Jessie's.

Jessie took a sip of her drink before continuing. "Okay, here it is. Despite the fact he's clearly a good father, I wish he weren't; every time we meet, I watch him getting closer with Lucas, and it scares the hell out of me."

Claire's stomach twisted, knowing now was the time she should tell Jessie the truth about how she'd kept Emily and her biological dad apart. How there had been a man, despite his flaws, who wanted to be a father to his daughter and Claire hadn't allowed it. Maybe if Jessie could see the outcome it had on a child later, she might make different choices now, even at her own expense. Claire had read Emily's letter over and over last night, sobbing as she took in the words. Some of them seemed so young, but others conveyed a wisdom far beyond her years, leaving Claire scared shitless. If she sent it to David as Emily had requested, he might never respond—or even scarier, *maybe he would.*

Claire pictured her daughter's loopy cursive handwriting. It was near perfect, as if she'd been trying to show him her best penmanship, trying to impress him.

Dear Dad, Daddy, Father?

    What would I have called you? I guess we never got to find out, did we? I'm sorry we don't know each other. I wish we did. More than ever after reading your letters. I was always curious about you. I wondered what you looked like, what your favorite sports team was, what you liked to do for fun. But I knew Mom didn't want to talk about you. I tried, but bringing you up made her sad and I didn't want that. I figured you would've been in my life if you wanted to be. Because you're my dad. But I'm smart (my mom always tells me I'm wise beyond my years) and I know that dads bail sometimes. It happens. So I decided that's what you'd done. That's why Mom was upset. But after reading your letters, I'm more confused than ever. Because it sounds like you wanted to see me. And Mom wouldn't let you. Mom explained that she was doing what she thought was best. But it was MY decision to make. Wasn't it? You're my dad, not hers. I don't know what's going to happen from here, but I want to get to know you. I hope you still feel the same. By the way, I've enclosed my most recent school photo (ignore

*the braces!), my favorite sports team is the Dodgers, and I
like to go to the mall for fun.*
Love, Emily

Claire took a drink of her wine and started to tell Jessie about
all the letters when her cell phone interrupted her. When she
saw it was her father calling, her heart rate escalated, worrying
as she always did when he called. "I have to get this," she said to
Jessie, taking a deep breath before answering.

"Claire?"

"Hi, Dad, everything okay?" Claire said hopefully, telling herself she was imagining the edge she heard in her father's voice.

"It's your mother. We're at the hospital."

As her father's words sunk in, Claire felt her faith begin to
falter. She squeezed the phone in her palm, still not understanding why, even though they'd caught the cancer earlier,
her mom's health seemed to be disintegrating faster, along with
her resolve. Last time, she hadn't gotten so sick so quickly.
This time she was in bed more than she wasn't, unable to eat,
and literally shrinking away in front of them. The doctors had
tried everything, even suggesting that Claire pick her up some
medicinal marijuana. But even while high as a kite, consuming
food was a battle for Mona. The doctors had warned Claire
that inserting a feeding tube was next, and she knew her mom
was going to fight them every step of the way. She'd pleaded
with Claire to please not call the doctors and tell them her
appetite was virtually nonexistent, that she'd do anything to be
at home with her family, not in a sterile hospital with scratchy
bed sheets. And so far, Claire and her father had acquiesced,
but tonight he'd been forced to take her to the emergency room
when he couldn't wake her from her nap.

"What is it?" Jessie asked.

"It's my mom, she's at the hospital. I have to go."

"I'm coming with you," Jessie said, grabbing her purse and Claire's hand as they hurried out the door, Claire squeezing it so tightly that Jessie winced, but she still didn't lose her grasp.

CHAPTER TWENTY-THREE

....

Gabriela inched away from Colin on the couch, hoping he'd think she was just adjusting. And in many ways she was. *Adjusting* to the reality she may never have a baby. Or be a bestselling author. Or have a solid marriage.

Even though she was deliberately putting distance between herself and Colin, her recoil from his touch felt involuntary. Gabriela had always considered herself emotionally independent, learning not to need others to fill the void she felt when her mother died. But she'd always had a strong appetite for Colin's touch, slipping her fingers through his or curling up into him in bed, the warmth of his body bringing her comfort. He used to joke that she couldn't keep her hands off him, and in many ways it was true, as if she had to remind herself that he was still there. Her therapist announced years ago her behavior was a by-product of losing her mother so early, but Gabriela believed it was much simpler than that. There was something in the way Colin's skin felt under her fingers, the way his full lips brushed hers when she wasn't expecting it, the way he'd wrap his arm around her tightly, like he wanted to let the world know she belonged to him. Being possessed by Colin had always brought her comfort. *Until now.* Her relationship with him was spiraling quickly. The worst part? She wasn't sure she wanted to tighten her grip.

"Are you coming to my appointment tomorrow?" Gabriela asked, inching even farther away as she uttered the words, her body already anticipating his answer.

Colin grabbed the remote and paused the TiVo before turning to face her. Gabriela glanced down at her oversized V-neck and yoga pants and thought how often Colin must wonder what happened to the old Gabriela, who wouldn't have been caught dead in a T-shirt. She couldn't blame him, having contemplated the same thing several times herself.

"No, I won't be going. And I don't think you should be either."

Gabriela turned her head toward the frozen figures on the screen, the ones they had been pretending to watch together, refusing to look back into his eyes, not sure if she'd see compassion or anger or even love in them. It was much easier to think Colin was numb toward her, that he'd abandoned her without a second thought. It made it less painful for the next words to spill out of her lips, the same lips that she used to run all over his body to wake him before her morning run each day. Before she'd used them to say things that could never be taken back, like she was about to do now. "I can't do this anymore," Gabriela whispered.

• • •

Jessie paused in the doorway as she watched Claire hurry into her mother's hospital room and throw herself into her father's arms. Jessie took the moment to take inventory of Mona, who lay with her eyes closed, the beeping of the monitor reassuring them that she was still with them. But the doctor wasn't sure if she'd awaken from the coma she'd slipped into earlier. Emily was slumped in a chair, her body soft like a rag doll as she stared outside, raindrops aggressively pelting the window. As Claire and her father stepped into the hall to discuss Mona's condition with the physician, Jessie tentatively took the open seat beside Emily.

"You doing okay?" Jessie touched Emily's forearm gently, not wanting to come on too strong. She'd never been close to Emily before, her protective feelings toward Claire and how Emily treated her always creating a silent wall between them. But this time, Jessie noticed a marked difference in Emily. Everything about her seemed softer. Even her posture was relaxed and open—before she'd always sat with her arms wrapped tightly around her chest as if they were her armor.

"I'm not ready for her to leave yet," Emily said as tears welled up in her eyes.

Jessie scooted her chair closer and wrapped her arms around her. "I know you aren't. None of us are. But some things in life are out of our control." She thought about how little control they'd had since returning. Jessie had assumed that she'd take back the reins of her life by making different choices. But all it had done was create new and different problems.

"But we aren't done yet," she whispered, and nodded in the direction of a book on the nightstand that Jessie realized was Gabriela's debut novel. She had dropped off copies of all of her books after Claire told her Emily had been reading them to her mom. "She really wants to know how it ends."

Jessie eyed the book, knowing exactly how it ended, that the daughter and her mother were finally able to forgive each other after years of fighting over a terrible secret that had been revealed. Jessie smiled sadly. It was her favorite of Gabriela's novels. And she wondered in the wake of yet another failed IVF attempt if Gabriela would be able to find her voice again, bring magic to the page again. Everything about her seemed heavier, not just her physical body, but her spirit as well. Jessie felt terrible. Out of all of them, it seemed as if Gabriela was having the hardest time.

Jessie glanced at Claire and her father, who stood nose to nose in the hallway speaking in hushed whispers. Claire seemed to sense Jessie's gaze and looked over, shaking her head slightly as if to say, *things aren't good*.

Jessie turned back to Emily. "You know, they say that people can hear you, even if they are in a coma."

"They can?"

"Yes," Jessie continued. "I had a cousin who slammed her car into a tree and was in a coma for six weeks."

"Six weeks?"

"Yes. And I would visit every few days and read from all her favorite gossip magazines. Oh man, how that girl loved her celebrity scandals!"

"You'd just sit there and read to yourself? You didn't feel stupid?"

Jessie laughed. "Maybe a little bit, at first. But then it became really comforting, like I was doing something to help."

"What happened to your cousin? Did she ever wake up?"

"She did. And to this day, she swears she was awake each night I came to read to her. She even remembers most of the articles, and in her own mind, was responding to me."

"Seriously?" Emily's eyes widened and she stole a look at Mona. "So you think my grandma will do the same thing. That she'll hear me?"

"I do." Jessie smiled. "And it can't hurt, right? Don't you want to discover the ending together? I hear it's really good." She walked over and picked up Gabriela's book, running her thumb over the cover before placing it in Emily's lap. "I'll give you some privacy."

Emily held the paperback tightly for a moment before sliding her chair closer to Mona's bed, lifting her hand gently and kissing it before beginning to read quietly.

"What's that all about?" Claire asked as she hovered in the doorway watching Emily while her father went to find a cup of coffee.

"Emily wants to make sure your mom gets to the end." Jessie nodded at the book, her voice cracking slightly, both of them knowing she probably wouldn't. Jessie was sad that Claire was on the brink of losing her mother—again. But there was a part of her that also felt joy because Claire and Emily were finally finding each other. And as Emily's soft voice read the words aloud, Jessie felt sure that Mona was listening to every word, her heart bursting that she had been the conduit.

• • •

"What are you saying?" Colin asked Gabriela.

"I'm done. With this," Gabriela said, and made a sweeping gesture. "Us."

"Gabs," Colin said in the tone he usually reserved for her when she had too many mojitos and spoke loudly at parties. "Be reasonable. Are you honestly saying you're choosing in vitro over our marriage?"

"No. I'm choosing a child over this marriage. And that's the whole problem—you just see this as a process, like it's a business transaction."

Colin flinched at her words and wrapped his hands around hers. "Listen, I get how hard this has been for you. And whether you believe it or not, it's been hard on me too. You aren't the person you were a year ago. Can't you see that?"

"Yes," Gabriela admitted. "I just thought this time things would be different," she said more to herself than to Colin.

"What do you mean, this time?" Colin asked, Gabriela quickly realizing her slipup.

"I just mean that last round of in vitro. I did everything right. I don't know why it didn't work."

"Have you ever thought it's just not meant to be?"

"No," Gabriela said definitively.

Colin looked down. "I still don't get why you had the change of heart. You didn't want a child for so long, and then suddenly you did. And you want one so much you'll let everything else in your life fall by the wayside, including us?"

Gabriela sighed, thinking back to their wedding day, how light and free she'd felt as they swayed on the dance floor, the rest of her life ahead of her. Now it seemed there was more behind her than in front. She knew Colin was right. She hadn't been herself, she wasn't writing, she couldn't be a wife to Colin, and she'd hardly been there for Claire, whose mother was dying. All that seemed to matter was this baby. It was impossible to explain everything to Colin without telling him the truth. And of course he'd never believe that. "Look, it will work. It has to."

"And what if it doesn't?"

"It will."

"But what if I don't want to go through it again? What if you are more important to me than a baby I've never met, I may never meet?"

Gabriela shrugged. She didn't have an answer for him. Not one he'd want to hear anyway.

"So you're willing to sacrifice me for this baby?" Colin brushed her knee with his knuckle as he said it, his eyes downcast. Gabriela already knew the answer, but she was afraid to say it out loud.

She waited several beats before saying the words she couldn't hold back any longer. "I want a baby. And if you don't, then this isn't going to work." Gabriela bit her lip, waiting for Colin to look up and see that she didn't want to hurt him, that she loved him and wished they could do this together. But he never did. He got up slowly from the couch and walked out the door without saying another word.

CHAPTER TWENTY-FOUR

....

Claire stood stoically at the end of the receiving line at Mona's funeral. She bobbed her head up and down and curved her mouth into something between a smile and a frown for each one of them—the woman who had worked beside her mom for years in the superintendent's office, the man who had delivered her mail and looked forward to Mona's famous holiday fudge cookies, and the gaggle of fit elderly women who had religiously Zumbaed with her until her diagnosis.

As Claire felt one clammy hand after the next grip her fingers, her mind drifted to earlier that morning. She'd spent the night with Mason, after weeks of making excuses for why she couldn't sleep next to him, not able to articulate why it was easier to lay her body on the stiff mattress on the pullout couch in her mom and dad's guest room each night than to drive over to Mason's house to curl up next to him. That she wanted to be just a room away from her dad in case he needed her; that she liked the smell of her mom's afghan that she wrapped around her shoulders as she looked through old photo albums remembering the years she hadn't appreciated; that she felt safe between her mother's walls, seeing herself as a kid, riding her bike or her mouthful of braces, in her old school pictures staring back at her; that if she wasn't at the hospital sitting at Mona's bedside, Claire felt she should be at her house, doing something, *anything*.

But a week after Mona died, her father found Claire sobbing into a pile of laundry she'd discovered in the dryer, her nose buried in her mom's favorite orange sweater as she wondered how she would be able to get through the funeral, which was the next day. Her dad told her she should get out of the house, maybe see that Mason fellow. He'd arched a gray eyebrow at her and there was a twinkle in his eye. He knew she cared about Mason, despite how hard she'd tried to hide it. Claire had started to argue, to ask her father what he was going to do without her help—who would make his dinner or iron his shirt for the memorial service? Her dad had stopped her midsentence and said that he was okay, that he could take care of himself, that after forty-two years of marriage to Mona, he could still feel her with him, and that right now she was probably scolding him from above for forgetting to take his blood pressure medication.

"What about Emily?"

"She'll be just fine. Believe it or not, we know how to take care of ourselves when you aren't around." He smiled and squeezed her arm gently. "I insist. Fussing over me isn't going to bring her back. And as much as I love having you here, you need some fresh air."

Claire shook her head again. How could she leave her family now?

"Mom." Claire turned toward Emily's voice. "Grandpa's right. There's no more laundry. The refrigerator is sparkling. The floors are shining. There isn't one more thing to do here."

"Don't you need me?" Claire asked in a small voice.

"Of course I do. But Grandma would want you to make some time for yourself. And she'd want you to go see Mason. We'll be okay, I promise."

"I'm planning on kicking Emily's butt in Uno the minute you walk out the door anyway." Claire's dad smiled and pointed toward the kitchen where there was always a deck of cards on the kitchen counter. "And I don't think you want to be here to see that. It's going to be ugly."

Claire finally acquiesced, because the truth was she missed Mason, and it frightened her how much she was struggling to remember the love she'd felt for Jared, which now felt so far away. So she'd left Emily with her dad and shown up on Mason's doorstep, her simple black dress for the funeral in her bag. When he opened the door and squeezed her hard, blinking back tears in his eyes, she decided waking up next to Mason on the day she would bury her mother was going to make it a little less awful.

Mona had woken only once before she slipped away. Her eyes had flown open with purpose on a crisp morning last week, Claire jumping up from her chair in surprise. The doctors had told them not to get their hopes up that she'd wake again, but Claire had been praying nonstop for a chance to have one final conversation with her, bargaining (agreeing to attend church every Sunday) and pleading (closing her eyes and begging until she fell asleep) and even demanding loudly that God give her an opportunity to say a proper good-bye, the nurse turning her head politely as she walked by the room, having seen it all before.

"Mom."

"Hi," Mona said simply, as if she'd just returned home from Costco, not awakened from a three-day coma.

"Hi," Claire said. "You've had us pretty worried."

Mona had moved her hand to Claire's head, running her hand through her dirty hair. "I love you," she said, her voice low but strong.

"I love you too," Claire had replied, and wished her father and Emily were there. They'd finally gone home to take showers and sleep, the exhaustion having begun to take its toll. She glanced at her phone sitting on the bedside table, wanting so badly to call and have them rush back, but not wanting to break the moment of clarity with Mona.

Mona motioned to the water pitcher, and Claire quickly poured her a glass and helped her take a few sips, her lips dry and patchy. "Mom, I have to tell you something," Claire let the words slip from her mouth before common sense could stop her.

Mona took another sip of water and nodded to give Claire permission to go on. "You may not believe what I'm about to tell you. Hell, I still don't believe it sometimes. But you've always been honest, even if it wasn't what I wanted to hear. And right now, I need that candor more than ever."

"Tell me," Mona whispered.

And so Claire unleashed her story in great detail, explaining to Mona how she ended up living this year all over again. She confided why Jessie was so adamant they return. How Claire feared Gabriela's writing career might never recover. She told her how guilty she felt about her feelings for Mason, and at her mother's prompting, told her about Jared as well. And finally, she admitted her biggest fear. That she'd somehow shortened Mona's life by returning.

"Claire." Mona's eyes were clear. "You have to stay. Here. In this life." Mona's eyes fluttered slightly, as if the conversation was exhausting her. Claire felt her time with her mother slipping through her fingers like flour through a sifter.

"But what if I made things worse by coming back? I thought I could save you this time. But here we are, again. I couldn't stop it from happening." Claire choked as she said the last words—the ones that had been playing on repeat in her head, torturing her. "If anything, the cancer is taking you so much more quickly. I failed."

Mona gestured for Claire to come closer and lifted her hand to cup Claire's chin. "You didn't fail at all. Some things aren't meant to be fixed. If you came back a thousand times, you still couldn't change this."

"But I'm not ready for you to go." Claire let the tears fall silently into Mona's hand.

"Listen to me." Mona's voice was weaker. "The last nine months with you have been amazing. And now I can go, because I know Emily is going to be okay. She has a mother who came all the way back in time to help her."

"So you believe me?"

"Of course I do. You never were much of a liar." Mona smiled frailly. "But promise me one thing."

"Anything."

"Now that you've helped Emily, it's time to do something for yourself."

"What?"

"Don't waste your second chance for true love."

"I'm not sure what you're talking about."

"Yes, you do, Claire."

"Mason?" Claire asked.

Mona nodded, closing her eyes.

"Mom?" Claire shook her arm slightly and Mona's eyes blinked open again. "Thank you. For everything. I love you. I'm so happy I got another chance."

Mona locked eyes with Claire. "You've always been such a

good girl. Go. Be happy. It's okay. I'll always be here for you—just be sure to watch for the signs. And, Claire?"

"Yes?"

"Tell Emily I agree with her about the ending of Gabriela's book. Mothers and daughters should forgive each other; life is too short not to," Mona said softly, smiling serenely before closing her eyes for the very last time.

• • •

"Your mom was an amazing person. She will be missed." A tall woman whom Claire vaguely recognized from the bakery downtown was clasping her hand, removing her from her thoughts.

"Yes, she sure was," Claire responded. "Thank you for coming." After she had moved on, Claire turned to Emily, who was standing to her right. "You okay?"

"My feet are killing me, and that last woman had the worst breath ever. She kept talking about how Grandma loved the butter croissants at her bakery. But other than that, I'm doing all right." She smirked slightly.

Claire laughed. "Her éclairs are pretty spectacular too."

"She keeps staring at Grandpa!" Emily rolled her eyes. "She just handed him a big basket of baked goods!"

Claire nodded toward her father, who was deep in conversation with Jessie, the lines in his face etched even deeper than usual, a side effect of little food and sleep. But he was a handsome man, and she wasn't surprised the vultures were circling. And she knew Mona would approve, that she'd want him to move on, to be taken care of—maybe not *at* the funeral, but in the near future. Before, he had never really embraced the idea of another woman after she passed. This time, Claire planned to make sure he did. "We should get Grandpa home. He looks exhausted."

"I'll go get him," Emily said, and Claire noticed again how much more mature she seemed than even a month ago. After Claire had mailed the letter to Emily's father, she'd held her breath for what felt like weeks, every time the phone rang, feeling a shiver of fear go through her—how would she handle him reentering her daughter's life? But so far, they hadn't heard from him, and Claire felt herself growing more comfortable with the idea that they probably wouldn't. Emily hadn't brought him up again, so maybe the simple writing and sending of the letter was enough.

Emily had taken Mona's death better than Claire had expected, her tear-stained face beaming when Claire pulled her aside at the hospital and revealed that Mona had heard every word she'd read to her, that she'd been listening until the last page of the book. Emily had given a moving eulogy earlier when Claire realized she couldn't do it, that the words she wanted to say about her mom clung to the back of her throat. As Emily articulately shared her poignant memories of her grandmother, things Claire had even forgotten, like the time Mona had taught Emily how to crochet a beret for her doll, Claire cried happy tears. She was proud. Proud that her daughter stood up—when Claire couldn't—and showed love. For her grandmother. For Claire. And for herself. The change in Emily between this funeral and the last was striking. Before, Emily had sat, arms crossed and insolent, unwilling to let any of the emotion she was feeling escape, instead allowing it to seethe inside her until it exploded. Claire knew, as she watched Emily at the podium, that Mona had been right, Emily was going to be okay.

"Claire!" Claire heard Jessie call her name as Mason walked her to her car, her dad having already left with Emily. He had insisted on driving himself that morning, claiming he didn't need to be babied, and then pointing up at the sky and winking. Claire had smiled and let him go.

She turned to see Gabriela and Jessie hurrying over. "Your dad almost hit me pulling out of the parking lot," Gabriela said, smiling. "Glad to see this isn't going to slow him down."

"Literally," Jessie added. "He was hauling ass. Emily was holding on to the 'oh shit' bar for dear life!"

Claire paused and watched in amusement as Mason's face paled. He hadn't spent a lot of time with Gabriela and Jessie and had no idea this banter was exactly what Claire needed. That if they felt sorry for her right now, she'd break into tiny pieces all over the blacktop. She needed to laugh. She needed to get out of her own head. She needed her friends.

"Did you see the way those Zumba women were circling him like sharks?" Claire said, perking up. "I mean, my mom's body is barely cold, and they're already treating him like man candy! What's next, a Tinder profile?"

"What's Tinder?" Mason asked, and the girls exchanged a guilty smile, Claire remembering the few times she'd used the matchmaking app, finally deleting it after a man she swiped *yes* on sent her a message asking if she'd suck his toes. She'd met Jared shortly after and recalled sighing in relief at the end of their first night out, when the only thing he'd ask her to suck was his straw to taste the drink he'd ordered.

"I wasn't going to tell you this, but I had to wipe some magenta lipstick off his cheek when I saw him," Jessie said sheepishly, ignoring Mason's question about the dating app. "That widow that runs the bakery planted one on him right before I walked up!"

"Slut," Claire deadpanned, and they all broke into laughter as Claire released her anxiety, sadness, and disappointment with every breath. For the first time in as long as she could remember, she felt free. "She also gave him some sweet treats!"

"I bet she wanted to give him a lot more than that!" Jessie snorted.

Claire was laughing so hard she almost didn't notice the large monarch butterfly that appeared, circling and flapping its wings slowly.

"Wow," Mason said as the butterfly landed on Claire's shoulder.

"That's the most beautiful butterfly I've ever seen," Jessie said, staring at the orange and black creature.

"You know that's good luck, right?" Mason said.

Claire only smiled, looking up at the sun peeking through the clouds, teasing them with slivers of sunlight. "Thank you, Mom," Claire said quietly, right before the butterfly took flight, disappearing a few moments later.

• • •

"So do you think Mona really believed you? About us?" Gabriela asked between breaths as she, Claire, and Jessie power walked the next morning down The Strand toward her house, surprised, as she often was lately, how breathless any kind of exercise made her. Was she still the same person who ran a half marathon in under two hours? Most days, she didn't feel like it.

"I do," Claire said with confidence. "All I know is that my mom told me to stay. That I *had* to."

Jessie and Gabriela shared a look. Colin had moved out the week before, Gabriela watching silently as he and his best friend, Dan, carried off the bed they'd slept in for fifteen years, Gabriela insisting he take it. She'd been sleeping in the guest room so often that the luxe king mattress didn't even feel like hers anymore. She lay in the double bed with the bland oatmeal-colored comforter tucked under her neck that first night Colin was gone and watched *The Notebook*, crying until her eyelids swelled shut. She had come back with a purpose, and she had to see it through, even if she had to do it alone.

"So you want to stay?" Gabriela asked, absentmindedly putting a hand on her abdomen, praying there would be a baby in there this time. She had recently started her fourth round of IVF and, at the insistence of the women in the TTC chat rooms, she'd found a new nutritionist and had changed her entire diet *again*. This time, she was eating *more* red meat and not consuming any cold liquids. She was also diligently taking her fertility drugs and now giving herself the shots that Colin once had. She had an ultrasound the next day to gauge how many follicles were growing inside of her and then they would start planning for the egg retrieval.

Claire paused, thinking about her life since she'd been back. How, even though things seemed more complicated, she felt a clarity she'd never achieved before. "I do," she answered matter-of-factly as they approached Gabriela's front door. "What about you guys?" she asked, studying their faces.

Ironically, even though her mom had just died, she felt more content with her life than the others did. Jessie had the complication of Peter's involvement in Lucas' life and worried if he would eventually confess their secret to Grant. Jessie had admitted to Claire recently that she'd be willing to risk him finding out later if it meant she'd get a few more years with Grant, knowing she couldn't convince Peter to be the silent father forever. And Gabriela. If she stayed, there was still a chance she could get pregnant. Or become a bestselling author. Maybe even work things out with Colin, as Jessie and Claire had implored her

254 liz fenton and lisa steinke

to try to do. But there was also the risk that she'd end up with nothing. No baby. No career. No Colin.

Gabriela opened the door of her house to the sound of her phone ringing. "I've got to get that, it might be the doctor's office," she said, and ran inside.

"What about you? Do you know if you want to stay?" Claire asked Jessie as they followed Gabriela inside and eased into two chairs in the kitchen and took off their shoes.

Jessie sighed, rubbing the sole of her foot. "It's so convoluted. There's no way I can have the life I want whether I stay or go back. It's like choosing between the lesser of two evils."

"Because of Peter?"

Jessie nodded. "I'm still hoping I can get Peter to work things out with his wife. I've kind of been playing matchmaker between them."

"Awkward," Claire sang in a high voice, and shook her head.

"I know, right? I actually forced him to take her to dinner the other night and I watched their son, Sean. Lucas came with me. I took them for ice cream and Sean was really cute with Lucas. And I kept thinking, they are brothers. If I go back, Sean will miss out on all that time with him."

"I sense a *but* coming," Claire said, trying not to think of all the time Emily's father had missed with Emily.

"But . . ." Jessie said slowly.

"Yeah, *but what*, Jessie?" Gabriela demanded, her arms crossed over her chest. "Please tell *us*."

Claire's eyes widened and Jessie felt her stomach drop to the floor with the force of a falling elevator.

"Oh, don't stop talking on my account. Please, go on," Gabriela fired back.

"Gabs." Jessie rose to her feet.

"What the fuck, Jess? How could you not tell me this?" Gabriela's eyes flashed with anger as she looked from Jessie to Claire. "How could you both keep this secret from me? You don't trust me?"

"No, it's not that at all, Gabs," Claire said. "It's much more complicated than that."

"No, it's not, Claire," Gabriela said, turning toward Jessie. "Why, if we are all supposed to be best friends, didn't you tell me who the real father of your son was?"

Jessie bit her lower lip. She had planned to tell Gabriela after they returned to this year, but the timing had never been right, especially when she hadn't been able to conceive.

"And you," Gabriela shot at Claire. "When did you find out?"

Claire's face contorted as she tried to formulate an answer.

"You already knew about this? From the first time she had Lucas?"

Claire nodded slowly.

"I can't believe you supported this, especially after everything with Emily's dad. Your daughter didn't get to grow up with her father, and she had so many problems as a result. And now you're both sentencing Lucas to the same fate?"

"But he has Grant," Jessie said quietly.

"Until he finds out, Jessie. God, this is why Grant left you last time. This is why you were dying to come back. To cover your tracks better."

"It's not like that," Jessie began, but Gabriela cut her off.

"I came back here, not only for me, but for you, both of you," she said, pointing at Jessie, then Claire. "I trusted you enough to come back in time, and you couldn't even bother to tell me the truth about your intentions?" Gabriela wiped the tears that began cascading down her face. "My life has gone to hell, but hey! At least Jessie gets to hide her son's paternity from the man she supposedly loves. Happy ending, everyone!" Gabriela's voice was shaking. Rage burned inside her as she thought of how it had been Lucas' birth that had convinced her to finally try to have a baby. Lucas. A baby conceived in infidelity. A baby that had made her so passionate to become a mom that she'd pushed her own husband away.

"Gabriela," Jessie started once more, then stopped, hit hard by the fact she couldn't give Gabriela answers when she didn't have them for herself.

Gabriela held up her hand. "Just go."

Claire took a step forward, but Gabriela jumped back in response. "Go. Please."

Jessie grabbed Claire's hand and their shoes and pulled her toward the door, both of them giving Gabriela one last look before clicking the front door carefully so it didn't slam shut.

CHAPTER TWENTY-FIVE

....

June 2006

The hot June sun shone through the window as Gabriela hung up the phone, her shoulders shaking violently as she curled into the fetal position. She wanted to somehow feel closer to the baby she was now convinced would never be growing inside of her, the emptiness in her abdomen feeling cavernous. Three more months had passed and she was still no closer to becoming a mom. In fact, she felt further away from it than she ever had.

Dr. Larson had called her personally this time to tell her the fourth round of IVF had failed, Gabriela breaking into sobs the moment she heard her sympathy-laced voice. *It didn't work.*

Dr. Larson reeled off the statistics of the likelihood of Gabriela ever carrying her own child, and as Gabriela contemplated the percentages, she decided she had a better chance of dying in a plane crash than conceiving. The doctor had talked about Gabriela's uterine lining and how she now believed it wasn't thick enough to support the implantation of an embryo, no matter what drugs she prescribed to strengthen it. That, in combination with her low-grade egg quality, was going to make her odds even slimmer. The doctor never said *never*, but suggested looking into a surrogate and egg donor. Gabriela almost laughed out loud through her tears, wanting to say she'd also need a sperm donor now that Colin was gone. The doctor had no clue that she and Colin were separated and that he had warned Gabriela that she did *not* have his permission to try again if this cycle failed. He hadn't even gone with her to the last egg retrieval or implantation surgery, calling at the last minute on both days with an excuse about work. Gabriela knew he was hurt after she insisted he move out ninety days ago, and this was his way of distancing himself.

After Gabriela finally picked herself up off the floor, she'd stared blankly at the gaping holes in her living room where the pieces of furniture Colin took when he left once stood, the indentation marks in the carpet still slightly visible. If someone walked in and saw the simple love seat and television that remained, they'd think Gabriela was also in the process of moving. *Maybe she should.* Rowan had come by earlier that week to check on her, a fresh stack of inspirational books under her arm.

"How are you?" she'd asked as her eyes darted around the room, no doubt surveying how depressing the once vibrant space had become.

"I'm okay," Gabriela lied. She was not even close to okay.

"Have you seen Colin?" Rowan asked. "I really think—"

"Rowan," Gabriela interrupted. "I love you, but please don't."

Rowan sighed. "I'm sorry. I just feel so helpless."

"I know." Gabriela looked at the deep frown lines around her mother-in-law's mouth. She was hurting too. Gabriela knew she had the ability to take some of that pain away, even if only temporarily. So she walked over to the stack of books Rowan had carried in and pulled out Eckhart Tolle's latest.

"Tell me about this one," she asked, and watched Rowan's eyes spark as she began to read aloud.

• • •

Tomorrow was Claire's birthday and the year anniversary of meeting Blair in Las Vegas. Gabriela's fortieth had passed the month before unceremoniously, despite Jessie and Claire's best efforts to draw her out. Gabriela glanced at the invitation to their joint birthday party on the coffee table and wondered why they were even bothering. Gabriela's mind was made up, or maybe the decision had been made for her, but either way, tomorrow night she planned to return to the age of fifty. To Colin, and to the relationship they used to enjoy. If she couldn't have a child, she at least wanted her husband back, even though she worried she might resent him for leaving her in this life. She wasn't sure being an author was the career she still wanted when she returned back home. But Colin had always been a constant, a steady force in her life. Gabriela recognized she hadn't exactly made it easy to support her, even aggressively pushing him away—*literally*—in her feverish attempt to get pregnant. Thankfully, he would never remember, but she would. She was just hoping she could learn to forgive both Colin and herself, even if she couldn't forget.

Tomorrow also marked the deadline her editor had given her. Gabriela's stomach twisted tightly each time she thought of how she'd only managed to squeeze out about half of the book Sheila was expecting. How could she ever explain to her that all the changes in her life had influenced her writing, and somehow she'd lost the magic she'd needed to craft the bestseller that once sat inside of her? She hadn't told anyone yet, but the day Colin moved out she'd abandoned that manuscript and started a whole new one that was nearly finished, staying up until all hours of the night in her empty house typing nonstop. Although she had little hope her new work would ever be published, it had surprised Gabriela how cathartic it had felt to write without anyone else's expectations weighing her down. She had sat at her desk late last night, staring at the keyboard, pondering how the story would end.

Gabriela had no idea if Jessie or Claire planned to stay or go back. She had accepted their rapid and insistent apologies, but had avoided seeing them in person—even on her own birthday— when they'd wanted to take her out for drinks, telling them she needed to work on her book, the sting of what happened still pricking her. Gabriela understood Jessie hadn't done anything directly to her, but she still felt betrayed, as if the last ten years of their friendship had been based on a lie. Not to mention she worried what would happen when Grant discovered the truth this time. Because Gabriela knew that the facts always had a way of working their way to the surface, no matter how hard one might try to push them down.

She'd passed on attending Lucas' baptism, feeling she'd be a hypocrite if she attended and helped perpetuate the lie to Grant. But selfishly she still wasn't ready to look into Jessie's eyes, unable to accept how Jessie had *accidentally* gotten pregnant with her third child while she couldn't even conceive her first. She hated to admit it, but it did bother her that the universe had rewarded Jessie's bad behavior with a baby, yet refused to grant one to Gabriela, who wanted it more than anything in the world.

She'd agreed to attend the birthday party via email because they'd long ago made a pact that nothing would ever come between them and celebrating together. And despite their splintered friendship, Gabriela knew they still needed each other.

She caught herself picking up the phone so many times the past three months, only to set it back down again, letting her hurt feelings create an invisible wall between them. But tomorrow they had a choice to make, and she hoped they'd all agree. It was time to get back to the lives they were meant to live—the ones they had left behind a year ago.

The only person she'd been seeing regularly besides the pharmacist at the drugstore she frequented was her father, who insisted she come to dinner at his restaurant every Thursday night. She'd wanted to say no, but agreed, having been so busy last time around, often canceling their weekly dinner dates, ignoring the disappointment in his voice as she'd rattled off her excuses about writing deadlines.

She always forced a smile as she dipped her salty tortilla chip in the salsa, refusing to admit how much the jalapeño peppers were burning her tongue as they always did, knowing her dad would mock her for not being able to handle the hot stuff like a true Latina, her mother no doubt rolling her eyes from Heaven. Last week, he'd asked about Jessie and Claire, and Gabriela had lowered her eyes, not wanting to lie. "What's going on?" he asked when his question was met with silence. "Those are your best friends. And it would seem like you need them now, more then ever."

"It's a long story," she had said, and smiled, hoping he'd drop the subject.

"It always is, *mija*," he'd laughed.

"Can I ask you something?" Gabriela leaned in, the margarita she'd been sipping giving her the courage to seek the answer she'd always craved.

"Yes, of course. Anything."

"How did you get over losing Mom?" When he didn't answer

right away, his black eyes boring into hers, she had stuttered, "I'm sorry, I wasn't trying to say . . ."

He held his hand up. "It's okay. I understand what you're asking." He rubbed his mustache thoughtfully. "The thing is, Gabriela, is that you never really get over losing someone or something you love. But the world keeps moving and you have to also, or you'll get lost. Learning to accept things and move on isn't a weakness. It's a strength. And it's what your mom would have wanted, for you to learn to persevere, even when life fails you."

Gabriela sniffed hard to hold her tears. There had always been a part of her that felt like if she let go of the pain of losing her mom, then she was letting go of her altogether. That she'd fade further and further from Gabriela's memory until she disappeared. "I still miss her," Gabriela whispered. "Every day."

"So do I," her father admitted as he placed his hand over hers. "But don't ever let that stop you from moving forward."

• • •

"Mom? Which one do you like better?" Emily stood in the doorway of Claire's bedroom holding up two dresses.

"They're both nice, Em," Claire said as she looked them over.

"Nice?" Emily frowned. "You might as well say *totally boring!*"

"What's gotten into you? It's just *my* birthday party with *my* friends you've known all your life. They always think you look beautiful."

"But *I* care, okay? I want to look good."

Claire took a deep breath. She was worried about Emily. Lately, she'd seemed to slip into some of her old patterns, being secretive and elusive. And whenever Claire asked her about it,

Emily told her nothing was going on, that everything was *fine*. She'd followed up with her teachers and they agreed that all was going well. But Claire felt that familiar tug in her gut, the one that told her Emily was not being honest.

"Mom, I need you to help me choose one—*please*," Emily pressed.

"Okay, I would go with the blue," Claire said as she eyed the navy cap-sleeved dress with the black patent leather belt.

"Not the red?" Emily cocked her head toward the short red sleeveless shift dress with the jeweled buttons on the back.

"The red is ni— I mean, really cute too, but the blue one will bring out your eyes more."

"Thanks," Emily said tentatively. "I think I'm going with the red," she added, and hurried out of the room.

Claire shook her head, ironically having no clue what *she* was planning to wear to the party tomorrow, on undoubtedly the most important day of her life. She'd tried to put most thoughts of the party aside, letting Jessie handle the majority of the planning. She had made her decision. She wanted to stay. Despite Emily's secretiveness, their relationship was sturdier than it had ever been. And things with Mason were stronger than ever. In fact, she sensed he was going to propose soon. But she wasn't sure where Gabriela stood, and because of that, she wouldn't let herself get too attached to the idea of staying here, even though the thought of going back to her old life made her ache each time she imagined herself in it.

She'd still been unsure until she'd driven to Jared's house, deciding she had to see him, she had to know for sure. Even though there was no way he would recognize her because they hadn't met in this life, she'd still kept out of sight, stealthily sipping her Starbucks and reading a book until he arrived home from work to his house in Anaheim. As he'd stepped out of the car, his front door swung open and a little girl ran out and threw her arms around his neck, squeezing hard. Even though he'd eventually gotten divorced, she remembered he'd told her these years, when his children were little, had been his happiest in his marriage, before they'd started to drift the way people often do, when they forget all the reasons they fell in love in the first place. Claire had felt nothing more than a strong affection for him, realizing maybe that's all it had ever been. At fifty, the old Claire had needed, or thought she'd needed, a man who'd simply loved her unconditionally. But now, after being back in Mason's arms, in his bed, she realized she needed much more, and it was something only he could give her. She decided if she went back, she'd break off the engagement. And if she stayed here, she'd leave an anonymous letter in Jared's mailbox, urging him to appreciate his marriage and his family. Maybe, it would help. Just maybe.

• • •

Jessie handed Lucas to Peter and watched as he raised him above his head and blew bubbles on his stomach. She laughed as Lucas giggled in response, glancing around the chain restaurant where they were about to eat, feeling less fear about getting caught than she used to, becoming more accustomed to meeting with Peter in public and deciding people would probably never suspect anything because they were with Lucas. Who would bring their toddler to an illicit meeting? As she caught the eye of another mother who smiled at her, she realized the woman was probably mistaking the three of them for a family. And in many ways, over the last six months, they had become one.

"Grant invited me to your party tomorrow night," Peter said casually as they looked over their menus.

"What?" Jessie said quickly. "When?"

"I saw him a few days ago at the athletic complex. I didn't know he played basketball there."

"And my party came up how?" Jessie frowned.

"We were shooting the shit and he mentioned it. In fact, he thought Cathy and I were already coming," Peter said, raising his eyebrows. "I didn't know you'd told him you watched Sean so Cathy and I could go out. What else does he know about *us*?"

"First of all, we are not an *us*," Jessie scolded. "This thing we're doing," she said, holding her hands out, motioning toward the table, "is about *him*." She nodded at Lucas, who was gnawing on a rubber giraffe. "And the answer is, Grant knows enough. I told him you and I were volunteering together in the classroom, which is true, we have several times, and that I'd seen Cathy around a lot more since she's not traveling."

"Jessie, calm down. I realize we're not a couple, but we are Lucas' parents. And we are real friends, *aren't we*?"

Jessie thought for a moment. This relationship with Peter was like a delicate dance, and she was constantly trying not to misstep. And she had to admit, she liked him. He'd always been kind and understanding until she'd gotten pregnant, and then he'd transformed into someone she barely recognized. But this time, they'd gotten to know each other on a much deeper level. Because Lucas couldn't yet talk, they had a lot of silence to fill. So they'd broached other topics, and Jessie was surprised how little she had known about him, like the fact that he'd grown up with a single mom and had never known his own father. Sometimes she wanted so badly to tell him what a great kid Lucas turned out to be, at least in her other life—that he was gracious and sweet with a wicked sense of humor. And now that she really knew Peter, she had to attribute some of those traits to him.

"Yes, we're friends, Peter. Of course. But that doesn't mean you should come to my birthday party." She still didn't know what was going to end up happening, if she was going to stay here or go back, but having Peter there, the person who'd come between her and Grant last time, would only complicate things.

"It's too late. I already told him I would. And honestly, I want to. Cathy would love it too; things are going better with her."

"Because you're actually making an effort," Jessie said, and cocked her head at him.

"You don't have to rub it in that you were right," he said, referring to Jessie's advice about fighting for his marriage. "So, can we come? Please?"

Jessie considered it. Maybe it wouldn't be the worst thing to let him attend. Plus, she was always looking for ways to help get his marriage back on track, and if this was going to help, so be it.

"Okay, you can come. But you better bring a kick-ass gift!" Jessie said, wiping some drool off Lucas' chin.

"I promise to be on my best behavior," he said, and held up his right hand.

"Whatever." Jessie rolled her eyes playfully. "Just stay on your own side of the room."

"Don't worry. I'll let you have your night," he said, reaching over to brush Lucas' hair out of his eyes. "Can't believe the little man is almost one! Time is really flying."

Jessie studied the menu. "Yes, it is," she answered, thinking how quickly the year had passed. How far she and Grant had come in the past few months. How much she had learned. About herself. About marriage. About life. But would those lessons be enough if or when her world came crashing down again? She looked at Peter's angular face, pushing aside the tinge of worry she felt inside, ignoring the feeling that she was going to regret letting him inside their home.

CHAPTER TWENTY-SIX

....

"You can put them over there," Jessie called out to the florist, who was carrying two boxes of yellow tulips across her lawn the next morning. "I'll arrange them on the tables later. As long as it doesn't rain," she muttered as she sipped her coffee, tipping her head toward the sky that was peppered with dark clouds. The forecast called for thunderstorms that evening, a weather pattern that hadn't been seen in the month of June in years. Jessie hoped it wasn't an omen.

"Crazy, isn't it?" Grant walked up behind her and pointed to the sky. "I can't remember the last time we had heavy rain this time of year." He set his hands on her shoulders and began to rub as they both stared at the looming clouds. "Don't worry, no matter what, it will all work out."

Jessie leaned into his strong hands as he massaged her. "Promise?" she asked, her voice cracking slightly. She'd woken with trepidation an hour earlier, pulling Lucas into bed with her and trying not to think about the choices they all had to make that evening. The thought of leaving baby Lucas, even if it meant she'd be returning to ten-year-old Lucas, devastated her. Eventually, her mile-long to-do list for the party propelled her to get up, but she still felt off, like she already had her postparty hangover.

"I promise." Grant turned and kissed her neck and Jessie closed her eyes, memorizing the way his hands felt against her skin, knowing if she returned home, to the way things were before, she would never again feel his touch. That he would be back with Janet, his fingers grazing her high cheekbones and his hands caressing her model-like body. "Rain or not, this night will be magical. Just wait and see," he said before walking back into the house.

"That's what I'm afraid of," Jessie murmured to herself as she stared at the pile of tables waiting to be assembled, the sound of distant thunder rumbling through the sky, deciding she'd better order a tent.

• • •

Gabriela wrestled with the zipper of her favorite violet dress, the one that used to hang loosely and now clung to her hips like plastic wrap. Frustrated, she peeled it off, throwing it on her bed along with the other discards, finally settling on a shapeless black dress that reminded her of a potato sack. "It will have to do," she said to her reflection in the mirror, running her finger under her eyes, hoping she'd be able to disguise the dark circles there. Ironically, she probably looked closer to fifty today than she did when she was actually that age, the lack of sleep having taken a serious toll. She'd barely slept the night before, her *abuela* making an appearance in her dream when she did finally fall into slumber. Her grandmother, with her long silver hair and gray eyes, would beckon Gabriela over, but when Gabriela would get close enough to hear what she was trying to say, she'd fade away into the darkness, Gabriela feeling like she was running through waist-deep mud to find her. Finally, right before she woke, she got close enough to wrap her arms around her, squeezing tightly as she felt the tears on her cheeks, not realizing how much she had missed her. As she rested her head against her shoulder, her *abuela*'s voice materialized, like a soft breeze brushing your ear. Gabriela bolted up in bed with one word playing over and over in her head: *Stay*.

Had she meant to stay here? In this life?

She'd been so sure she wanted to go back. Colin had stopped by unexpectedly to give her an early birthday present, explaining that he hadn't missed giving her a gift in over fifteen years and despite their separation, he wasn't planning to start now. Her eyes filled with tears as she watched him stand awkwardly in the doorway clasping a small box in his hand, waiting for her to respond. She'd smiled, the corners of her lips quivering as she waved him inside, her hands shaking slightly as she untied the bow, slid off the top, and pulled out her grandmother's necklace. She'd gasped, the gold chain and locket slipping from her grasp. She and Colin had bent down at the same time to pick it up, their hands brushing. She'd lost the beloved necklace several months before, scolding herself because she'd known the clasp was loose, tearing her house apart looking for it. Finally, after days of searching and retracing every step she'd made, she'd given up the hunt, deciding it must be a sign that she didn't belong in this life. But it had resurfaced, and so had her *abuela*, and now she was more confused than ever.

"How did you . . ."

"I found it wedged between two pairs of my running shorts. It must have fallen into the dresser drawer before I moved out."

"Thank you," Gabriela said as she fingered the chain.

"I was worried you might be lost without it."

"I was," Gabriela said, stealing a small glance at him before looking down, knowing she was talking about so much more than the locket. Still surprised that their long marriage was able to unravel in such a short amount of time.

"I hope this helps you find your path again," Colin said, and touched her arm, the feel of his hand sending a shiver through her. She stepped backward, hoping he hadn't noticed how much his touch affected her.

Desperate to change the subject, Gabriela found herself confessing to him that she wasn't going to meet her editor's deadline. That she'd sent Sheila an email with the news just that afternoon and had attached, in its place, the other manuscript she'd been working on, that she'd finished that morning, finally deciding on how to end the story. She admitted her career might be over, but that she was at peace either way. Of course, she couldn't tell him that it wouldn't matter in twenty-four hours when she returned to her former life, that she'd be signing copies of her bestsellers and doing TV interviews again, that this new manuscript she'd crafted, the best thing she'd ever written, would likely never see the light of day. Maybe that's why she'd sent it to Sheila. She wanted someone to read it before she left, even if she'd never remember doing so. Colin had listened silently as the story spilled out of her, finally taking her in his arms and saying he was sorry, that he knew this year had been hard and he wished he could take a magic eraser and make it disappear. This time, instead of pushing him away, she let her head melt into his chest and felt his fingers thread through her hair and smiled—an eraser like that did exist. And it was in the hands of a magician named Blair Wainright.

Long after Colin left, brushing her cheek with his lips before whispering that he'd see her tomorrow at the party, Gabriela had sat, curled up in the lonely love seat in her living room, more excited than ever at the thought of returning to her old life, to the solid marriage they'd had before, the one she'd taken for granted. She'd fallen asleep with her hand clasped around her locket, thinking of how it used to feel to have her husband's body lying beside her. This life had worn her down to a stub of what she used to be, like the lead of a dull pencil. But then her *abuela* had appeared in her dream and told her to stay. The question was, why?

• • •

Claire slid into her new Mercedes and smoothed her dress. Because she hadn't been scared to take financial risks this time, she had borrowed money from the bank and flipped three properties in the past two months for a substantial profit and had purchased the sleek silver sedan last week. She'd hoped that having an upgraded car would give her clients more confidence in her and ultimately increase her business. But she also realized that leather seats and a sunroof weren't going to be enough— she'd have to do the hard work too. She'd also called the hospital last week and paid all of her mother's medical bills, a financial burden that had weighed heavy on her father last time, causing him to fall deeper into depression. She had been granted a fresh start, and she wanted to create one for him too.

"Ready for a great night?" She glanced over at Emily as she backed carefully out of the driveway, double-checking her mirrors as she inhaled the glorious new-car smell.

"Sure." She'd pulled down the visor and surveyed herself in the mirror, but said nothing more.

Claire relished the silence in the car, taking the time to

daydream about Mason, feeling her cheeks flush at the thought of seeing him tonight. Their relationship had escalated rapidly once Claire finally burned down the wall that she'd been holding up between them, and her stomach fluttered as she remembered how deeply he'd kissed her when she whispered that she loved him the night after Mona's memorial. After her mother died, Claire had decided to stop holding back with Mason, to stop worrying about where they were headed and just let herself fall. It felt amazing to become lost in him, to swim in his embrace, never wanting to let go, to talk for hours about everything and nothing at all. And for the first time, she knew with 100 percent certainty where she wanted them to end up. Together. In *this* life.

Claire's mind moved on to seeing Gabriela for the first time since they'd argued over not telling her the truth about Lucas' biological father. She'd tried to talk to Gabriela several times to explain why she'd kept Jessie's secret, but when she did reach Gabriela by phone, she was short and refused to discuss it, saying she understood, even though it was clear from her clipped tone she didn't. When she'd emailed that she would be at the party, Claire had exhaled in relief. She couldn't be *that* mad anymore if she was going.

But when Claire had replied and asked her if she'd made a decision about whether she was going back, she hadn't responded, leaving Claire with a knot in her stomach. Blair had said they'd all have to be in agreement about whether to stay or go, but the truth was, they'd never been further apart. And Claire suspected she might be the only one who wanted *this* version of their lives. Claire shuddered slightly as she pulled her car in front of Jessie's house. One of them was going to have to compromise her dreams for the others. Claire thought about all the things she'd sacrificed for Emily, the secrets she'd kept for Jessie at the expense of her other friendship, the way she'd supported Gabriela even when she didn't agree with her choices. Wasn't it time they did something for her?

• • •

"Jess?"

Jessie let out a squeal and twirled around to face Grant. "Oh my God, you scared the shit out of me!"

Grant shook his head as Jessie dramatically covered her thumping heart with her hand.

"I was just coming to tell you Claire is here to help set up."

"Oh, thanks," Jessie said sheepishly.

"What were you just thinking about? I must have said your name three times before you screamed bloody murder."

"Tonight," Jessie said truthfully as she picked up her blush brush and applied more color to her now pale cheeks.

Grant crossed his arms over his broad chest. "What is it about this party that has you so high strung? Is it the storm?"

Jessie looked out the bedroom window splattered with rain-drops, thankful she'd found a company that could bring a large tent to cover the tables and dance floor in her backyard at the last minute—the party business had just received a cancellation, someone not willing to risk the rain ruining their event. Jessie didn't have that luxury. Tonight was *it*. She stared at the tent—the only one that had been available was red with thick white horizontal stripes, making it look like it belonged at the circus. Although maybe it would end up being perfect for the sideshow Jessie was now very worried could take place tonight.

Yesterday, after they'd had lunch, Peter and Jessie had taken Lucas to the park, and as they both trailed behind him, hunched over with their arms outstretched like nets that would break his fall, Peter had brought up Father's Day. Jessie's throat tightened and she'd reached up to grab it, feeling as if she only had a tiny hole where her breath could force its way through. Peter asked what she and Grant and Lucas planned to do to celebrate, and she was afraid to meet his eyes, what she might see in them if she looked. The truth was, she didn't know. Because there was a strong chance that she might not be here in a week, that she'd be back in a life where Father's Day felt like a foreign holiday, one she didn't participate in. One where she'd help Lucas and the twins purchase a gift for Grant and wrap it, always saddened that with each passing year she had a harder time helping Lucas pick one out. A life where her heart would thud each time Lucas told her about a new interest of Grant's—how she'd obsess whether or not Janet had been the one to introduce him to it. Where she would drop him off at Grant's for the weekend as she sucked in the wave of sobs that fought to crash out of her.

"I'm not sure. What are you, Cathy, and Sean planning?" Jessie finally said, deciding to deflect his question with one of her own. "I hear that new Italian restaurant on Third Street is pretty good."

"Jess."

Jessie pretended Lucas was about to topple over and grabbed his arm, guiding him toward the sandbox. "Do you guys celebrate with your dad too? Doesn't he live up in Pomona?" Jessie asked, hoping to steer the conversation away from where she knew it was headed.

"Jessie, you know I'm not making small talk here. You know why I'm asking."

"No, Peter, I really don't," she said as she pulled action figures out of her bag and struggled to separate them from each other.

"It feels strange. Thinking of Grant being with *my* son on that day."

Why didn't it bother you last time? Jessie thought, knowing exactly why. Last time, Lucas was just an idea, one he was able to push away because he never had his little hand wrapped around his finger, he never saw him take his first steps, never held him when he was sick. How could she have been so naïve to believe that letting Peter spend time with his son would actually keep him from wanting to actively be his father?

"I get it, Peter, but let's be fair. Grant is also very much his father—he's the one who puts him to bed each night, the one who's been there each and every day since he's been born." Jessie said the last words gently, trying to take the sting off them. "I understand this is complicated—for all of us. What if we met up with you the next day? He would never know the difference."

Peter crouched down next to the sandbox and handed Lucas a shovel. "But *I* would."

"So what do you want me to do? Tell Grant I have to take Lucas to celebrate with his *real* father? Thanks for all the diaper changes and sleepless nights this past year, but now Peter's decided to step in and we won't be needing your services anymore?" Jessie scoffed, looking up at the overcast sky.

"Of course not. But I don't think it's too much to ask to see my son on Father's Day. Even if he doesn't know the truth, I do. And I want to be there for him." Peter reached out and grabbed Jessie's arm, turning her toward him. "Jess, isn't this what you wanted when you met me at that dive café to tell me you were pregnant? Because you could have just kept it to yourself. I never would have known."

But I would've known, Jessie thought, repeating Peter's words from earlier in her mind. And one day if Lucas found out, she'd have to explain why she hadn't told his father.

"I couldn't *not* tell you. How would I have explained that to Lucas? I couldn't tell another lie," Jessie finally answered.

"You've been lying to Grant for months. How is that any different?"

"I know." Jessie looked down. "But those lies have allowed you to get to know Lucas."

"With limitations."

"True," she finally answered. "But you didn't want anything to do with your son until our little run-in at the coffee shop, *with your wife*. Then you suddenly decided being a dad to this baby was important. How do you explain that?"

Peter's face had turned sheet white and he'd looked down for several seconds, as if trying to collect his thoughts. "I don't know, something just happened to me—seeing him changed everything. Honestly, if I hadn't, I'm not sure we'd be here right now. Isn't it weird how a chance meeting like that changed everything?"

"Yes," she answered quietly, knowing that chance hadn't had much to do with it. She felt a lump form in her throat as she thought about the decade of Lucas' life Peter had missed before, even if it had been of his own doing. If she returned, she'd be taking that from him all over again. She heard herself telling him she'd figure out a way for him to see Lucas on Father's Day, knowing if she decided to stay, life was about to get even more complicated than she realized. The life she left behind may have been lonely, but at least she knew what to expect. Here, she was realizing, anything could happen. "Maybe you and Cathy should skip the party."

Peter shook his head. "Cathy already knows about it. It will

be harder to come up with an explanation for why we're canceling than it will be to go."

"Okay, but will you please steer clear of Grant? A lot of
people will be there, so he'll never take it personally if you don't
come over and say hi."

"What do you think's going to happen if we do talk, Jessie?"
Peter's face had transformed, suddenly looking more like a little
boy than a grown man.

Jessie backpedaled. "I don't know, but he might pick up on
something, sense something. You never know; I'm just trying to
be cautious. Like you so kindly pointed out, I've been lying to
him for months."

"And obviously he doesn't have a clue, Jessie."

"I hope you're right." Jessie shrugged, thinking about how
Grant had peppered her with questions a few weeks ago when
she'd taken Lucas to meet Peter at the children's museum. She
was pretty sure he'd just been curious, but each inquiry felt like a
bullet to dodge, and she didn't know how much longer she could
make up stories and keep track of them. Even though the truth
about Lucas' paternity and their split had devastated her, at least
Grant knew the truth and he'd chosen to be Lucas' father anyway, because that's the kind of person he was. Jessie wondered
if she chose to stay here, how long she could manage the double
life she'd created for herself. "What about Cathy? How can you
be so sure she doesn't suspect something?"

"She doesn't know a thing. I always meet you when she is at
an appointment or a meeting, when I'm absolutely sure there's
no risk of running into her."

"And the night I babysat? She didn't suspect a thing?"

"Nope. She was just thrilled I was taking her out."

"How can you be so sure?"

"I could ask you the same thing about Grant. After all these months, why are you freaking out about this now?" Peter frowned. "Don't you trust me? I know what I said to you at the auction. But things are different now. I would never want Cathy *or Grant* to find out the wrong way."

The problem was, Jessie did trust him. She trusted that he had changed from the first time around, that he truly wanted to do the right thing, to have a relationship with his son. And because of that, she wasn't confident he would keep their secret for much longer. For that reason, she knew her life as she knew it was in jeopardy. "I do," she finally answered before standing to leave, closing the door on their conversation. She'd be deciding soon enough if she'd even be here on Father's Day.

• • •

But now, as she stared at the rain pounding against the circus tent outside, she was still conflicted. Her choice would affect so many more people than her. "I just want to have a good night with you," Jessie said as she walked over to Grant and laid her head on his chest, tucking the memory away to reference later, in case this was the last night he was hers.

"Every night is a good night, as long as we have each other," Grant said, leaning against the doorframe. "Right?"

"Do you really mean that?" Jessie asked. "Even the ones when Lucas is puking and the girls are whining and I'm wearing the same shirt as the day before? You're still satisfied?"

Grant grabbed her hand and placed it on his chest. "I think the one thing I've learned this year is that if you keep waiting around to discover what makes you happy, then you probably never will be."

"You have to just find your happiness in what you already

have," Jessie added, thinking about how often she used to think if she only had *this* or *that* that she would be satiated. She'd never really concentrated on loving the life she already led.

"Remember that night that you told me you wanted us to still like each other ten years down the road? So what's the verdict? Will we? Do I still make you happy?"

"Yes," she said, and thought of how little she had slept that week, of how disorganized her closet was, of how her hair still frizzed out at the top, no matter how much hair spray she piled on. She thought of how Lucas had bit her on the soft spot of her arm earlier and left a mark, how annoyed Grant had been with her when she'd lost her keys *again,* and how frustrated she had been with Goldie, the puppy, when she'd chewed up Jessie's favorite pillow on the couch. Yes, her life was a mess most of the time. But it was hers. And she finally realized it made her happy, no matter how messy it was.

• • •

An hour later Jessie locked eyes briefly with Gabriela across the room, and she smiled lightly before looking away. She scanned the crowd until she found Claire, who appeared to be listening to a story one of Grant's colleagues was telling, but her eyes were darting around as if she was searching for something.

Jessie and Claire had briefly talked to Gabriela when the party first started and they exchanged awkward hugs, Gabriela stiffly leaning into their embraces, making it clear she still had her wall up. "We need to talk," Claire had said under her breath.

"Agreed. Let's go somewhere more quiet," Jessie said, eager to sort out their plan.

Gabriela had nodded. "Yes, but not right now. I need a drink first—now that I can have one." She half smiled as she placed her hand on her stomach. Claire noticed her boxy dress, thinking it was not at all like the bold, figure-flattering ensembles Gabriela would've worn in her alternate life, then realized that Gabriela's smile didn't make its way up to her eyes, the way it always used to. Claire couldn't remember the last time she'd seen her friend's sultry grin or her flirtatious pout. She seemed a shell of herself and Claire wondered, would staying here take away what was left of the Gabriela she'd known for thirty years?

"You okay?" Claire asked Gabriela, putting her hand on her arm, noticing her flinch a tiny bit.

"I'm fine. Just need to take the edge off. I'll find you guys later," she said, turning to walk away.

Jessie and Claire exchanged a look and Jessie started to say something, but sucked her words back as Grant approached, grabbing Gabriela's hand and pulling her into a bear hug. "Here they are, the birthday girls!"

Gabriela pursed her lips as she tried to squirm out of his grip.

Grant, oblivious, wrapped his other arm around Jessie and Claire, and Jessie noticed his eyes were already glassy from the Fireball shot she'd seen him take a few minutes earlier. "I wasn't going to say anything, but what the hell, you know I can't keep a secret from you, Jess! We tell each other everything." He released his arms and stepped back, giving Jessie a knowing look, Jessie forcing herself to meet his gaze, deciding his words had to be purely coincidental, that he didn't know anything. "I have something planned for you guys later. You are going to love it!"

Gabriela, Jessie, and Claire exchanged nervous glances, all of them thinking the same thing as they studied Grant's wide-eyed expression—what could he have planned that could top their own surprise at the end of the night? "We can't wait to find out what it is, babe," Jessie finally said, breaking the awkward silence, giving Grant a kiss and squeezing his hand as Gabriela and Claire nodded their heads in agreement.

Grant smiled and checked his watch. "We still have some time before the big reveal. Let's get some pictures."

They'd stood under the birthday banner and posed for photos, all of them glancing at the front door—Jessie wondering when Peter and Cathy would walk through it and wishing when they did, nothing bad would happen; Gabriela wanting to see Colin, praying he didn't have a change of heart after their conversation the night before; and Claire, anxious to see Mason, her heart fluttering at the thought of kissing him, hoping the others decided to stay here so she could have the life with him she didn't get the first time around.

CHAPTER TWENTY-SEVEN

....

Gabriela clinked Grant's glass and tipped hers back into her mouth, letting the warm liquid slide down her throat before pounding the shot glass down on the bar, laughing as Grant lifted his hand to high-five her. "I told you it would go down smooth as silk," he said, having followed her to the bar after he'd announced he had a surprise for them later. Gabriela found herself laughing at his use of the cliché phrase despite the tension that was gripping her chest with each passing hour, her watch now indicating it was 9 p.m. Never in her life had she wanted time to go slower. Colin still hadn't arrived and she feared he might not. She needed to see him one more time before leaving, even though she was going back to the version of Colin that seemed to like her much better.

She searched Grant's open, delighted face, pondering whether or not he really had no clue Lucas wasn't his. Gabriela had known Jessie for thirty years—and was shocked Jessie was capable of pulling off that kind of deception, of hiding it from not just her, but from her own husband. That constant thought was the reason she hadn't been able to completely let go of the anger she felt toward both her and Claire.

Gabriela thought about Colin—how she had felt that light in his eyes go out when he looked at her this past year. With him, it had been more of a slow leak that drained until it was empty. She knew the reason Jessie and Grant had gotten divorced last time hadn't been because they grew apart or fell out of love or whatever half-truth Jessie had told her, but they'd split because Grant couldn't continue on in their marriage after what Jessie had done. So Gabriela could almost understand why Jessie would do just about anything not to let it happen again with Grant in this life, why she might keep the truth from him this time.

Gabriela was putting off talking to Jessie and Claire, deliberately avoiding them since seeing them earlier that night. She knew it was cruel, that their fate was intertwined with hers and it wasn't fair to make them wait to hear what she was thinking. She was still determined to return to the night one year ago when they'd held hands and took the leap of faith in Blair's dressing room. And judging by the way Claire was embracing Mason, who had just walked through the door, and by what she knew of Claire's newfound relationship with Emily, she suspected she wasn't on the same page. There was a part of Gabriela that wanted to give this one to Claire, that wanted to hand her the happiness that seemed to elude her before. No matter the secrets she had kept, Gabriela still loved her and wanted the best for her friend. But the taste of failure in this life, something she'd never dealt with before, felt stronger than her need to help Claire. And she hated herself for that. Sure, she'd had her share of hard times, but she had always managed to rise from the ashes and let the pain strengthen her. For that reason, she'd been appalled at how weak she'd become, how she'd managed to lose everything that was important to her this past year—her husband, her career, and the dream of having a child. No matter what her *abuela* had whispered the other night, a dream that had been playing in a loop in the back of her head ever since, she knew it was time to go back.

She was less sure of Jessie's choice—there was so much to lose if she stayed. But then again, she had gone through it before and survived, so maybe she was willing to take the risk again?

Blair had warned them if they weren't in agreement about staying that he would send them back. Gabriela swallowed hard, knowing she was likely to be the holdout, and that her voice wasn't going to be loud enough to change her friends' minds. Unless she did something drastic, something that forced her friends to want to return, she worried they may end up resenting her for being the catalyst for sending them back. Grant slid another Fireball shot across the bar and raised his eyebrows in question, pulling her from her thoughts. She wrapped her fingers around the glass. She couldn't gamble her friendships just to get back with Colin and put her career back on track, could she? She eyed the shot, knowing she should say no, that being sober was critical when she would be making the most important decision of her life, but instead she smiled wryly. "Why not?" she said, then kicked it back, wiping her mouth afterward.

Grant laughed. "Just don't blame me for your hangover tomorrow."

Gabriela only smiled, not wanting to think about where she'd be waking up the next day or the feelings that would come along with it.

• • •

Mason spun Claire around on the dance floor and dipped her dramatically as she watched helplessly as Gabriela powered

down another shot. Great, all they needed was for her to get
wasted on the most important night of their lives. Gabriela
hadn't said outright that she wasn't going to stay, but Claire knew
her friend, and she could see it in her inability to look at them,
feel it in her awkward embrace. She needed to get to her, to
make her understand why it was a bad idea to go back, why their
lives would be far better if they stayed here. Only she wasn't sure
Gabriela's life would actually be improved. By what she'd seen so
far, it had only gotten worse.

And then there was Jessie. She had whispered in Claire's ear
earlier that she was leaning toward staying. Claire had squeezed
her hand and thanked her, Jessie quickly adding not to thank
her yet, that the night wasn't over. This caused Claire to wonder, again, what had happened to the three of them, that they'd
seemed to have lost the blind trust they'd once had, back when
they were just three girls who worked in a restaurant, with big
dreams and hopeful hearts. No matter what happened tonight,
she vowed to rebuild that, no matter how long it took.

"What time is it?" Emily's voice snapped her back into the
moment.

"Nine thirty. That's the third time you've asked since we got
here. Everything okay?" Claire asked, studying Emily's face. "You
bored already? It looks like there are some kids around your age
over there," Claire said, pointing in the direction of a group of
teens drinking sodas near the dance floor, and Emily rolled her
eyes and walked in their direction.

Claire glanced back at the bar, where Grant was now sitting
alone. She scanned the room until she found Gabriela, sipping
champagne and looking melancholy as she watched the crowd.
She'd mentioned earlier that she thought Colin was coming, but
there was still no sign of him. Claire knew she should go talk to

her friend and make her feel better, but instead, she let her hand fall from Mason's and started to walk in the opposite direction of Gabriela, an idea forming in her head. They didn't have much time left and there were things Claire needed to say. That way, no matter what happened, she wouldn't have any regrets.

She had made it only a few steps when a strong hand cupped her shoulder. Later, she'd tell Jessie there was something familiar about the way his fingers felt, that maybe she'd even known who it was before she turned around. But even so, her stomach still fell to the floor when she turned to see Emily's father, David, standing right in front of her.

• • •

Jessie twirled each of her daughters on the dance floor and tried to stay present, to embrace the moment, the way Madison's head tilted back as she sang the chorus to "Hollaback Girl" and how Morgan jumped up and down unapologetically. She saw Madison smile and wave to Emily as she walked up, thrilled the twins had both grown close to Emily after the day she'd brought them over to Claire's. Emily had told Claire that she'd loved how the twins were constantly asking her advice on things like how to get the cute boy in their class to play dodgeball with them at recess. And Jessie thought of Lucas sleeping soundly in an upstairs back bedroom with a babysitter looking in on him. She ignored the temptation to turn toward where Peter and Cathy stood. She could feel Peter watching her as he drank the expensive scotch he held up like a trophy to Grant when he'd arrived. But so far, that had been their only interaction, Jessie discreetly monitoring Peter's every move since he'd arrived, just in case.

Claire had been anxious earlier, wanting a commitment from Jessie to stay. And oh how Jessie wanted to give it to her.

Although she'd fantasized about it often in her old life, she'd forgotten the pureness of the way Grant loved her before he found out about Peter. So many nights, Jessie lay in bed and tried to pinpoint when she'd decided his love wasn't enough for her, why she'd let Peter give her something she'd *thought* was missing. At the time of the affair, she'd blamed Grant. She'd confused his contentment for complacency. And later, she'd harshly chided herself for her selfishness. But lately, she'd come to the conclusion that the way it had played out before may have been part of the journey she was meant to endure. That maybe the only way people could know how much they loved something was to be faced with a chance they might lose it. It didn't mean you should live in constant fear, but rather it should serve as a reminder that love should never be squandered. Now she understood the value of Grant's love and the love of her family—and whether she stayed here or went back, she would never forget to appreciate the power of love.

• • •

"What are you doing here?" Claire tried to catch her breath as she took in the man in front of her. The man who had walked out of their lives years ago, the same one she'd tried to keep away ever since.

David cocked his head toward Emily, who had come back from the dance floor, her face contorted with a mixture of excitement, happiness, and apprehension. "I got the letter you sent me from Emily. We've been exchanging emails and a few phone calls since then—that's when she invited me."

"Why didn't you tell me he responded? Why did you go behind my back?" Claire surprised herself by the loudness of her voice, deliberately not looking at Mason, not wanting to see his expression. She thought of the last time she'd been with him, how the drama with Emily had always bothered him and eventually sent him away, even without David's presence. Claire cringed to think what that added stress might to do to their relationship in the long term.

"He's my dad, Mom. I have a right to see him. And I didn't want you to get in the way of that. Again."

"Not like this, Em. To bring him here, of all nights. It's not fair," Claire said, looking around to see if anyone was watching. But all of the party guests seemed immersed in their own worlds, as if this scene—one Claire had been petrified of for years—wasn't unfolding right in front of them.

"What do you know about fair, Mom? You lied to me. You said he wanted nothing to do with us. You made me believe he didn't love me." Emily cast her eyes downward, filling Claire with both rage and shame.

There was truth to her words, of course. Claire *had* pushed David away. But she'd done it to protect Emily. Or maybe herself. She wasn't sure anymore. All she knew in this moment was *she* had raised Emily. *She* had been there every day of her life—nursed her through fevers and flus, supported her through sadness and heartbreak, taught her right from wrong. She wasn't going to let this man waltz in here and take those years from her.

"I was just trying to protect you." Out of the corner of her eye, Claire spied Jessie flying in from the outside, her eyes widening as she spotted David standing in her foyer, walking over and standing next to Claire.

"Are you okay?" she asked, nodding a greeting to David before grabbing Claire's hand and squeezing it tight.

"Hi, Jessie," David said quietly, not taking his eyes off Claire.

290 liz fenton and lisa steinke

"No, I'm not okay," Claire replied, still unable to look at Mason.

"Let's all calm down." David reached out to touch Claire's arm and she pulled back as if she'd been burned. Claire took him in, his chocolate eyes that matched Emily's, his thick shaggy hair that needed a handful of pomade to behave, the ten pounds he'd put on since she'd last seen him.

"Don't tell me what to do," Claire hissed. "How dare you come here without asking!"

"Are you really going to judge me? After you kept my letters from Emily for all these years?"

"I thought I was doing the right thing. And I did send her response. Eventually," Claire said quietly.

"*After* she found the letters you had hidden."

"True," Claire said. "I wanted to protect her," she said again, finally meeting Mason's eyes. She'd told Mason the truth just last week, deciding if she did stay here, she couldn't keep that from him. She needed to know he wouldn't judge her. And he hadn't—he'd seemed to understand her need to shield Emily from David. Or at least the David she used to know.

"I'm not trying to cause drama here. Emily told me she was going to tell you I was coming," David said, glancing at Emily, who looked away. "Obviously she didn't. I'm sorry, Claire. I know this isn't the best timing. And I realize I haven't always done the right thing. But the fact is, I'm here now. And I want to be a part of my daughter's life. And obviously she wants me to be a part of hers. So are you really going to stand in the way of that? Especially when she's telling you it's what she wants too?"

Claire sucked in a deep breath before answering, feeling as if the room were spinning. And then she felt Mason place his hand firmly on the small of her back in support and she felt herself exhale. She locked eyes with Jessie, remembering their conversation from yesterday. Claire had gently suggested that maybe it wouldn't be the end of the world if Peter did become a bigger part of Lucas' life, that it didn't sound like Jessie was going to be able to hold him off for much longer if they ended up staying here. Jessie had mumbled something under her breath and quickly changed the subject. Claire hadn't pushed it, knowing her advice would sound horribly hypocritical, considering her own choices.

Jessie's jaw fell open as she realized she wasn't the only one with secrets, discovering just how far Claire had been willing to go to keep David from Emily. Before, when Jessie found out she was pregnant, Claire had told her repeatedly that she should tell Grant the truth because it had a way of finding its way out. Jessie wondered why she hadn't taken her own advice.

Claire debated what to do, what to say. Now, if she stayed, she'd have to deal with David and the negative impact he could have on Emily's life. Even though he stood before them now, resolving to be the father he'd never been, she worried he would revert to his old ways. She'd finally helped Emily get to a good place in her life and she knew Mason could be the father figure she needed. Claire glanced at Emily, whose large eyes were shining as she stared at her dad. Claire certainly didn't need David. But maybe Emily did.

She saw Gabriela across the room and wondered if she was aware of what was going on. Gabriela shot her a questioning look before being distracted by something out the window. Claire followed her gaze to see Colin coming up the winding driveway. When Claire had begun to walk away earlier, before David grabbed her shoulder and changed her life, it had been to search for Colin, having convinced herself that Colin was the only person who could affect Gabriela's decision to stay. She planned to plead with him not to give up on becoming a parent. Her earlier motivation was fueled to convince Gabriela to stay. Now she wasn't sure she belonged here either. Claire was still thinking when, to her surprise, Gabriela turned in the opposite direction of her husband and beelined back toward Grant, who was still leaning comfortably against the bar. Claire drew in a deep breath as another man carefully filled his scotch glass to the brim, before slinging an arm around Grant's shoulders. She watched in horror as Peter leaned in close, as if he had a story to tell. Claire swallowed hard as she watched Grant sit on the stool and bend his ear in to listen.

Jessie followed Claire's gaze across the room, landing on her husband and her onetime lover. "No!" she heard her stammer as she ran toward them.

CHAPTER TWENTY-EIGHT

....

Jessie's heart hammered as she hurried across the tent to where Grant and Peter were huddled together. Feeling like she was sprinting toward a finish line, her adrenaline powering her body forward with full force, she darted around her party guests, nearly colliding with a server carrying a tray of crab cakes.

"Sorry!" she blurted to the waiter as she approached her husband and the man who would bring her entire world crashing down with just four words—the same four she'd let slip from her lips when she'd told Grant last time: *Lucas isn't your son*. Her life flashed through her mind like snapshots in a photo album: her pregnancy tests piled up in the Starbucks bathroom trash can; being hunched over the toilet with her head in her hands as she contemplated what she'd done; confessing to Peter that she was pregnant, his face peaked; the contrast when she revealed the same information to Grant, his face flush with excitement; the next nine months, when her anxiety expanded along with her belly; Lucas' birth; Grant's grieving face as he processed the fact that Lucas wasn't his son; her sobs as she watched Grant throw his belongings haphazardly into a ripped navy blue duffel bag; her heart breaking in half as she signed the divorce papers, the black pen leaking all over her fingers and onto her skirt.

And now she studied her husband's open face—not wanting to watch as his expression shifted, not wanting to see his brow knot, his eyes narrow, his lips frown, wishing she could skip over this part somehow—the moment where he discovered Jessie had been lying to him. As she threw herself frantically toward him, she decided she couldn't and *wouldn't* let that happen. Not this way.

• • •

Gabriela also raced toward Grant and Peter, her kitten heels sliding on the dance floor, nearly tripping over a chair, but regaining her balance. She watched Peter lean in closer toward Grant and imagined the words spilling out of his mouth in urgent whispers. *I am Lucas' real father.* She focused on Grant's face as he rested his chin on his hand and listened, likely expecting a piece of gossip or an anecdote, never imagining Peter was about to bring his world to a screeching halt.

Gabriela remembered the day she found out her mother died. She'd received an A on her art history test *and* she'd been asked out by Nate, a quiet but cute and smart water polo player. She ran that day too, all the way from her last class to her used Honda Accord hatchback in the parking lot of the high school, then from the street in front of her house to the kitchen, where she was sure she'd find her mother as she always did, preparing that night's dinner. But she wasn't there. Gabriela would find out from a neighbor that her dad had said to meet her at the hospital, that there'd been an accident. Gabriela's heart pounded as she jumped into the driver's seat, not bothering with her seat belt, racing through red lights, parking in a tow-away zone in front of the emergency room. She'd been just a few minutes too late, her mom dying from injuries sustained in the accident just moments before Gabriela could say good-bye. Her dad was there, tears streaming down his face. Gabriela grabbed her mom's hand, still warm, and kissed it, not knowing how she'd manage a life without her mother, her best friend.

"Please, Peter, don't do it!" Gabriela looked up to see Jessie reach Grant first and stopped in her tracks as she heard Jessie bellow her plea.

Peter and Grant both whipped their heads around in surprise, Jessie's eyes welling with tears as she stood before them, breathing hard. Gabriela ran up beside Jessie and absorbed the scene. Grant's face was unreadable but Peter was stoic. Had Peter already told him?

"What's gotten into you? What don't you want Peter to do?" Grant asked, getting off the stool he was sitting on and approaching Jessie. Jessie stammered a response, but nothing comprehensible came out of her mouth. She looked with pleading eyes to Gabriela, who took a deep breath before speaking.

• • •

Claire stared hard at David, suddenly picturing him not as the forty-year-old clean-shaven man with the crewneck sweater standing in front of her, but as the twenty-seven-year-old with the lopsided grin and goatee who smoked Marlboro reds and liked to show off his eagle tattoo on his right arm. They'd met at a bar where he'd been the drummer in a punk band. They'd locked eyes during the performance, Claire's body moving to the beat. And after the set, he'd approached her. He wasn't at all her usual type, but there had been something magnetic in the air between them. They'd fallen in love hard and fast, and she'd ended up pregnant after just a few months. Looking back, how could she have expected him to be ready to be a father, when she wasn't at all ready to be a mother? He'd never told her he wanted to settle down, and for the most part they'd been careful with birth control. But Claire had been young and stupid and caught up in the way he made her feel, and hadn't thought much when she'd forgotten to take a pill. Missing only one day wouldn't matter, right? Turns out, it did.

As she searched for the right words to explain why she hid his letters from Emily, she wondered why, in this version of their lives, her daughter had discovered them. Had she been so distracted with work that she had been careless when she put the letters away, allowing Emily to find them easily? She wondered now if the universe had been guiding her in that moment. If the powers that be knew she would have never had the courage to let David back into their lives otherwise.

Blair had hinted that having the power to change their lives would improve them. Or had they just assumed that? There wasn't much time to find the answer.

• • •

"Jessie! I *told* you not to drink that third martini!" Gabriela blurted as Grant stared at Jessie, confused. "You know you can't handle your alcohol, girl! And everyone knows, one martini is fine, two is pushing it, and three is just asking for trouble," she added with a high-pitched laugh.

Jessie looked at Gabriela in surprise, then smiled faintly. "Yeah, I should have listened to you," Jessie replied, and then leaned against Grant. "I'm feeling pretty hammered."

"Are you sure that's all this is?" Grant gave Jessie a knowing look. "Because you said you wanted Peter to stop. Stop what exactly?"

"Well," Jessie stammered again, not wanting to lie, not after all the lies she'd already told. She was done being dishonest. She had to be.

"Peter was just about to tell me a story. One he said I would never believe."

"Really?" Jessie swallowed hard, forcing herself not to look at Peter and to stay focused on Grant, shocked that Peter chose tonight of all nights to tell Grant the truth about Lucas, with his own wife just across the room. When he'd just assured Jessie yesterday that he wouldn't. She looked at the bar in front of him where a half-empty bottle of whiskey sat and wondered how much he had drunk.

Gabriela stepped closer to Jessie. She shook her head, unable to believe just minutes ago *she* had contemplated telling Grant the truth about Lucas to force Jessie to have to go back to their old lives. It made her feel ill that after so many years of friendship it had even crossed her mind. "Jessie thought Peter was coaxing you into doing shots with him and she didn't want you to get you so drunk you would forget about our surprise. You know how much that girl loves her surprises—remember that time she accidentally found out about the baby shower we were planning for the twins, then bawled for hours because she'd ruined her own moment?" Gabriela locked eyes with Grant, refusing to look away, shocked at how easily the lie slipped from her mouth, and instantly understanding why Jessie had kept the truth from her about Lucas' paternity last time *and* this time. Jessie had been protecting her from having to lie for her. Whether or not Grant was meant to discover the truth this time, Gabriela was certain it wasn't supposed to be from the man Jessie had slept with. From this vantage point, Gabriela was beginning to see that forces much larger than themselves had been at work during this past year.

"So, let me get this straight. Jessie can have three martinis, but I can't have a few shots? She's never cared how much I drank before," Grant said to Gabriela, then gave Jessie a long look. "I don't know what's gotten into you two," he said, nodding at Jessie. "Can I talk to you alone for a second?"

Jessie stiffened as Grant led her toward the house. Gabriela watched Peter as his eyes trailed them. He'd remained quiet during the whole exchange. She kept her eyes on him as he polished off the rest of his drink and poured himself another.

• • •

"Gabs?"

Gabriela spun around and threw her arms around Colin. "You came!"

"Of course I did. I said I would." Colin gave her a puzzled look. "You okay?"

"Not really," Gabriela answered honestly, thinking about the night so far, all the drama that had unfolded. "I feel like I'm just getting through."

"Getting through," Colin repeated thoughtfully. "What's on the other side?"

Gabriela thought for a minute. "The old me. The me that used to get things right. The me that was easier to love." She'd never been very good at revealing her weaknesses, but she knew she could be leaving in a few hours. And she had just witnessed the damage lies could do to a marriage. So she decided to let herself be vulnerable, finally, hoping she wasn't too late.

"Gabriela, I love *all* versions of you. Granted, some of them a lot more than others," Colin said, his eyes smiling.

"I feel like all the good versions are buried so deep I'm not sure I could even find them if I wanted to. Let's face it. I came apart this year and you gave up on us. Not that I blame you. But still."

Colin ran his hand through his hair. "That's the thing you don't get. I never gave up on you, or us."

"That's funny. Because I'm not the one who left," Gabriela said, her tone becoming sharp. The conversation suddenly felt suffocating and she began to walk away. That's what this year had turned her into—a woman who ran away from her own life when it got tough.

Colin grabbed her wrist. "Don't leave. Let's finish this conversation. Please."

Gabriela nodded, forcing herself to swallow her quick temper.

"Listen. I left because *you* asked me to. We fell apart because *you* refused to accept that getting pregnant might not happen."

"But you didn't want it to happen," Gabriela whispered, and let a tear escape from her eye.

"That's bullshit! I'm sorry, but I won't let you tell yourself that anymore. I won't let you blame me anymore. I've tiptoed around you all year because I thought that was the best way to be supportive. But now I realize I did you a huge disservice. I should have told you the truth."

"And what's that?"

"That maybe we were meant to fail at having a child."

"How could you say that?"

"Just listen to me, Gabs. You let your obsession with getting pregnant take over every aspect of your life. You let it destroy you. Destroy us. How can that be a good thing?"

Tears began to spill from Gabriela's eyes. She knew he was right. She'd treated her IVF like a battle she could not afford to lose at any cost, even over her own marriage. With each cycle, she upped the ante, falling further each time it didn't work, until she hit rock bottom. "I'm broken," she whispered, and burrowed her head into his chest.

Colin wrapped his arms around her. "Let me help put you back together."

Gabriela pulled back and wiped her nose. "Do you really believe that's possible? Because I was so sure we were meant to be parents. How could I have believed something so strongly and been so wrong about it?"

Colin wiped the tears from her cheeks. "Who said we're not meant to be parents?"

Gabriela stared at him blankly. " What do you mean? We tried four times—"

"To get *you* pregnant," Colin said, interrupting her.

"Yes, to get *me* pregnant," Gabriela repeated, pointing to herself, not understanding where he was going with his thoughts.

"All I'm saying is, there are other ways to become parents," Colin said, smiling.

"What do you mean?"

"I mean I haven't closed the door on becoming a father. There's adoption, fostering. I don't know how or if it will happen, but I'm open. The question is, are you?"

Gabriela took a deep breath. She'd been so laser focused on conceiving that she'd never considered those alternatives, let alone whether Colin might be open to them. She'd convinced herself he didn't want to be a dad, but maybe he just hadn't wanted to become a parent if it meant they'd lose themselves along the way.

"You would still want me and to potentially become a parent with me after all this?"

Colin nodded. "What can I say? I know you're still in there. It's hard to explain, but it's like you just got off course."

"But how do we get back on track? Back to who we were?"

Colin studied her face. "Maybe we aren't supposed to be those people anymore."

Gabriela let Colin's words permeate her, realizing he was more right than he could ever know. She thought of the relationship she had felt desperate to get back to. It had been easy—maybe too easy. It glided along so effortlessly that it often took a backseat to the stressors of her career or the issues in her friendships. Maybe, she realized, that was because she'd never had to fight for it.

"Gabriela," Colin continued, "stay here with me. We'll get it right one way or another. I promise."

Gabriela's mouth fell open. "What did you just say?"

Colin frowned. "I asked you to give us another chance."

"You said to stay. That you wanted me to stay." Gabriela's head was spinning. *Did Colin know?*

"I just meant I want us to stay together," Colin answered, perplexed. "I came here with the intention of not letting you leave until I told you how I felt."

"Leave?" Gabriela was struck again by his choice of words.

"Leave the party. I didn't want you to leave the party without you knowing how I felt." Colin's face fell. "Was I wrong to think we still had a shot here?" He bowed his head. When Gabriela didn't answer immediately, he took a step toward the house.

"Wait!" Gabriela grabbed his arm. "I'm sorry. It's just a lot to take in." Gabriela considered Colin's declaration that he'd adopt a child or foster one, knowing that process was sometimes just as stressful as trying to conceive. She imagined herself becoming obsessed again, this time with choosing a country to adopt from and filling out the perfect application. She wondered if she was just trading one obsession for another. And she wasn't sure her psyche or their relationship could handle another failure.

• • •

Just then, Grant's voice boomed through the tent, and Gabriela swiveled her head to where he was standing on the stage holding a microphone. "Where are the birthday girls? Get on up here!"

Gabriela stood frozen in place, searching for Jessie. She had been worried for Jessie when Grant took her away to talk, concerned that she was going to be forced to tell him the truth tonight. But Grant was up onstage, looking happy and calling for them, so she assumed that he was still in the dark.

"I have to go up there," Gabriela said to Colin, then kissed him quickly, and his eyes lit up in surprise. "Don't go anywhere, I'll be right back." Jessie and Claire caught up with Gabriela and looped their arms through hers as they made their way toward the stage.

Gabriela leaned into Jessie and whispered, "Are you okay?"

Jessie nodded. "For now," she sighed. "Grant started to grill me about what happened back there with Peter and then some contractor he works with came up and interrupted us, thank God. After the guy finally left, Grant said it would wait until after the surprise." Jessie bit her lower lip. "I feel like my crazy outburst stirred something in him, like all of a sudden he was connecting dots he never had before."

"Really? But he seems fine right now," Gabriela said as Grant told the band to start a drum roll and called for them to come up onstage again.

Jessie took a deep breath. "I hope you're right. But it's possible he's just putting on a happy face. He has to. There are over 150 people here."

"I think I want to stay," Gabriela whispered quickly before she could take it back, surprised when both of her friends' jaws went slack. "What?" Gabriela countered. "I thought this was what you guys wanted?"

"I'm sorry. I know I told you I definitely wanted to stay, but now I'm not so sure. You saw what happened earlier with Grant. Even if he still hasn't figured it out, it's obvious Peter intends to tell him."

Gabriela drew a deep breath and looked at Claire. "What about you?"

"Long story, but Emily's dad is sitting in the kitchen."

"What?" Gabriela exclaimed. "That's who you were talking to? I didn't even recognize him." Her nose scrunched up. "Not that I have any right to talk, but he's really gained weight."

"Ladies, let's go!" Grant called again. "You can gossip later!" he said, and the crowd laughed.

Claire, Jessie, and Gabriela stepped up onstage, holding hands tightly. Gabriela stole a look at her watch. It was already 11 p.m. Where had the time gone? Where had the year gone?

"So, now that she's finally up here . . ." Grant paused as people laughed and cheered again. "I had promised these ladies a magical night," Grant began, looking sideways at the three of them with a glance that Gabriela couldn't read. "Please give a warm welcome to an up-and-coming magician that will amaze you. They're calling him the next David Copperfield. Here he is, Mr. Blair Wainright!"

Gabriela gasped as a young Blair made his way from the back of the crowd and took her hand, kissing it. "Hello, ladies." He tilted his head toward the crowd before glancing at his watch and whispering, "Meet me in Jessie's bedroom at 11:45 p.m."

Claire let out a snort. "And until then?"

"Be prepared to be amazed!" Blair shouted in response, the crowd growing silent, and then applauding loudly as he levitated off the ground.

"Show-off," Jessie said, but quickly feigned a smile for Grant, who was staring intently at her from across the stage, his eyes clear and glistening. Jessie held his gaze and silently prayed she had the strength to make the right choice.

• • •

"Where is he? He said 11:45 and it's 11:57!" Gabriela hissed as she, Jessie, and Claire stood in Jessie's darkened bedroom, Jessie insisting that they not turn the lights on, terrified that Grant was going to find her. After the show, Claire had grabbed her hand and yanked her from the crowd, dragging her up the stairs as Gabriela trailed behind them. Jessie had paused outside of Lucas' bedroom, holding up a finger before tiptoeing in and kissing him softly, not sure if it was the last time she'd kiss his sweet baby face. Earlier, she'd drawn the twins in for a tight hug, both of them wriggling out of her arms and exclaiming, "Mom!" in unison.

"I'm right here," a voice came from the shadows of the bathroom, and they all jumped.

"Jesus!" Gabriela said as Blair appeared in front of them. "Have you ever heard of knocking?"

"It's a pleasure to see you too, Gabriela," Blair said, the moonlight showcasing his smug smile. "Good year?"

"Oh shut up. You know exactly how *not* good this year has been."

"I'm sorry," Blair said calmly.

"Are you?" Gabriela shot back. "Or have you been laughing at us from whatever godforsaken place you come from?"

"Being angry with me isn't going to change anything, Gabriela. I simply gave you all the opportunity you wanted—another chance at the year you turned forty. What you did with it is on you, not me."

"What kind of game is this?" Claire asked, her voice low but filled with emotion. "Do you get off on fucking with people's lives?"

Blair ignored Claire's question. "Ladies, you now only have three minutes to decide if you are staying or going."

"What if we don't know?" Jessie squeaked. "What happens if we can't decide?"

"It's a very difficult choice to make. That's why your heart will make it for you."

"What do you mean?" Claire blurted as her hands started to shake.

"As humans we often let our egos rule our decisions. We let fear stop us from reaching our true potential. We forget about love. But the heart? It never forgets. No matter what happens, no matter how hard things get, it always remembers."

"Wait, so we aren't going to tell you what we want to do?" Gabriela whispered. "I don't understand. I've been stressing this whole time and I don't even get a vote?"

Blair reached through the darkness and took her hand. "You are going to tell me, but not with words. In just one minute, you are each going to close your eyes and let your heart answer the question. Trust me, Gabriela, it will be the right one."

"How can you know that? What if it's not?" Jessie cried.

"If you learn one lesson from this, Jessie, I hope it's that your heart is pure and true. Trust it, and trust yourself." Blair glanced through the window at the glowing moon, the threat of an impending storm having disappeared. "It's time, ladies."

Gabriela reached for her friends' hands and gripped them tightly, willing her heart to make the choices her mind could not. Tears streamed down Jessie's face as Blair's words sunk in and she realized how little she trusted herself anymore, and Claire exhaled and thought of her mother, and what she had asked her to do on her deathbed.

"And so it is." Blair's voice threaded through their minds like a heavenly song, calm and beautiful and hopeful all at the same time. It was the last thing they heard before everything went dark.

EPILOGUE

....

Nine years later

Gabriela's feet burned as she flew across the white Cabo San Lucas sand, each touch scorching her a tiny bit before she lifted one foot up and pounded the other down, the heat providing the perfect balance of pleasure and pain as she propelled herself toward the casita. She reached the open glass French doors and put her hands on her thighs, breathing hard, but smiling widely. Running hard always made her feel alive.

"You still got it, girl!" a voice rang out, and Gabriela turned to see Claire watching her through oversized sunglasses from a blue-and-white-striped chaise longue next to a private pool, where they'd drunk too many margaritas the night before, laughing and telling stories until long after the sun had set.

"I'll take that as a compliment." Gabriela dipped her foot in the cold pool and kicked water at Claire. "And happy birthday, by the way."

"Thanks, I'm really feeling my age after last night," Claire moaned. "I can't believe you went for a run! It's already so hot, how can you do it barefoot?"

Gabriela lowered herself down and dangled her feet in the infinity pool. "There's something about the heat that makes me run faster."

"Even after all those shots we did?" Claire shook her head. "I could barely get myself from the bed to this chair! Is that how you stay in such amazing shape? Running even when you're hungover?"

Gabriela shrugged. "How can I resist that glorious beach when it's just ten feet away? Plus, I feel pretty good, considering."

"You look pretty damn good too," Colin called from the other side of the pool. "Get over here, woman!"

"I'm all sweaty!" Gabriela laughed.

"Just the way I like you." A sly grin spread across Colin's face.

"Gross!" Claire lifted her magazine to block them.

Gabriela perched on the end of Colin's chair. "I can't believe we're all fifty," she said, then muttered, "again," thinking about how they'd let their hearts decide their fate that night nine years ago today.

Gabriela had awakened with a start the morning after the party. She'd shot up in bed, frantically searching her surroundings to understand where she had ended up—where her heart had decided she should be. She had felt both elated and terrified as she walked into her half-empty living room. *They had stayed.*

Gabriela's iPhone pinged on the ceramic table. It was a message from Angelina, her agent. She was ready to send over the contract for the three-book deal Gabriela had just been offered by her publisher.

"Who's looking for you all the way down here in Mexico?" Colin asked as he applied sunscreen to his already reddened face.

"You should grab a hat, my fair-skinned Brit!" Gabriela tossed her wide-brimmed straw hat at him. "It's Angelina. She's going to email the contract for me to sign today."

Colin grabbed her hand and kissed it. "I'm proud of you."

"Me too," Gabriela said, more to herself than to him.

Nine years ago, the morning after the party, Sheila had called her, breathless, having finished Gabriela's manuscript in one sitting. Gabriela was shocked, never expecting anyone to read it, sure she was going to end up back in her old life, not still living the one she'd restarted. She had pounded out a memoir about how she lost herself so completely in the race to get pregnant. It was raw and honest (save for the part about how she'd time traveled), Gabriela not holding back even the slightest about what her quest for a baby had done to her psyche and her marriage, not to mention her body. *When Will My Baby Find Me?* had spent twenty weeks on the *New York Times* bestseller list the following year. It wasn't the fictional story Gabriela had originally written the first time she'd been forty, but that was okay. She wasn't that person anymore.

Her follow-up memoir focused on her reconciliation with Colin and the foundation they began together, one that provided support, both mental and financial, to those trying to become parents. In vitro, adoption, fostering, it didn't matter. Their goal was to help other families get through the process without imploding, the way Gabriela and Colin almost had.

After many sleepless nights and arguments, they finally agreed not to adopt or foster a child, instead deciding they'd much rather throw their energy into helping others find their baby instead of risking their still-fragile marriage all over again. It was hard to explain, but helping others not have to go through the pain they did was enough. And as much as she had loved the virtual friends she'd met on the message boards while she was trying to conceive, she wished she'd had more of a personal connection. That's what their foundation aimed to be.

Gabriela leaned in and gave Colin a quick, salty kiss as she looked out over the Pacific Ocean. It hadn't happened overnight, in fact it had taken years, but they had finally worked themselves back to a happy place—in some ways even happier than they'd been before. Their relationship now had some scar tissue—but in Gabriela's eyes, it only made them stronger.

"You guys kept me up with all your partying last night!" Emily said as she walked out from the house, with an arm full of textbooks, her long blond hair pulled back into a neat ponytail. "Aren't the twins and I supposed to be the ones boozing it up, not the fifty-year-olds?"

Claire reached out and swatted Emily's leg with her magazine. "It's not our fault *you're* the one acting like an old lady!" she teased, grinning wildly and eyeing her books. "Always studying—even on this trip!"

• • •

Claire had woken up that morning nine years ago tangled in Mason's arms. *We have a second chance,* she thought as tears slid silently down her face. She had jumped out of bed quickly and jogged down the hall to Emily's bedroom, creaking the door open and watching her sleep peacefully for a few minutes before shaking her awake gently. "Hey," she said when Emily's eyes opened.

"Hey," Emily repeated, propping herself up on her arm.

"I'm sorry about last night. I was wrong to keep those letters from you. And even when I sent your response, there was a huge part of me that didn't want him to respond. I didn't want to share you."

Emily's eyes welled up with tears. "I just want to have a dad, like everyone else," she said, the last words barely a whisper.

Claire fought back her own tears as she thought about her relationship with her own dad, unable to imagine a life without him, especially now that her mom was gone. "I know that now. I thought I was protecting you. But I think I was trying to protect myself even more. And I'm sorry for that. It was selfish."

Emily smiled. "So I'm not in trouble for going behind your back?"

Claire laughed. "In this case, I think it's understandable. And I promise we'll work out something with your dad, so you can start spending time with him. Okay?"

"Okay," Emily had said before lying down and closing her eyes again, Claire playing with her hair until she fell back asleep, then crawling back into her own bed and inserting herself back into Mason's strong arms, where she knew she belonged.

David had stayed true to his promise to be an active part of Emily's life. Claire had met with him a few days after the party and laid out her conditions. He couldn't be a fair-weather father, he had to promise to be a participant in her life and let her be one in his. Claire had brought photos of Emily from over the years and filled David in on all she could about her childhood. As David studied the school pictures, Claire could see the regret in his eyes over all the time he'd missed, then he'd looked at Claire and vowed not to leave again, revealing he had remarried last year and couldn't wait for Emily to become a part of their family too. He and his wife lived two hours south, but David drove up every other weekend, and he and Emily and sometimes Claire and David's wife, Gretchen, began to slowly get to know each other. Claire liked Gretchen immediately, and couldn't help but wonder if she was the influence David had needed.

Claire still couldn't believe the contrast between this Emily and the one from her former life—this version of her daughter had just graduated from UCLA and was studying to take the GRE in preparation for her grad school applications. This Emily was kind and selfless at times—and Claire knew that a big part of the change had been David's presence in her life. And Mason's—he'd accepted David unconditionally from day one and also proved to be an important role model in Emily's life.

Emily had stood by Mason's side the night he proposed to Claire. Claire had looked to Emily, who had nodded her head vigorously before Claire whispered yes and said a silent thank-you to Blair Wainright, wherever the hell he was.

• • •

"Where's Jessie?" Claire asked, looking toward the house.

"She woke up early and went into town with Lucas and the girls," Mason said as he walked up.

"More shopping?" Claire laughed, thinking back to the orange-and-brown-striped poncho she'd bought Lucas earlier in the week, and the confused look on his face when she'd given it to him.

"Grant went with her—for damage control. He said they were already going to need another suitcase just to cart home all her trinkets."

Claire laughed and caught Gabriela's eye, both of them knowing her road had been the hardest.

Jessie had forced her eyes open the morning after the party, not sure which reality she was waking up in, not sure which reality she *wanted* to wake up in. She rolled over to find Grant awake, staring at her, his lips pursed in thought. Her chest soared and then dropped with a thud to the floor. Grant was still hers, but it wasn't worth keeping him if it meant she had to continue to lie. It wasn't fair to Grant, and it wasn't fair to Peter, and it definitely wasn't fair to Lucas or her girls. So she ran her hand along the profile of his face and began to tell her story, not surprised at all that her heart broke into a million pieces all over again just like it had the first time she'd broken his.

Before, when Jessie had confessed to Grant, she'd become a shell of herself, thinking she didn't have a right to fight for him, for her marriage, for her family.

This time, Jessie fought. She made him talk to her, even if she didn't want to hear what he had to say. Instead of crying endlessly and telling Grant she loved him, she *showed* him—she stopped by his job site on the hottest day of the year with a cooler of Gatorade for him and his crew. She re-created their first date on their anniversary, right down to the dress she wore, which she had miraculously kept and did a three-day juice cleanse that nearly killed her to fit into it. She challenged him to stay. Yes, for the girls and Lucas. But for her too—reminding him that they had both given up a bit on their marriage. Grant may not have cheated, but he'd let Jessie believe she wasn't important anymore. So she asked him not to let the biggest mistake of her life define her, or define them.

The initial shock of her betrayal hit him the same way it had last time. He grabbed the same duffel bag and haphazardly moved out. They even legally separated and lived apart for almost a year and a half. Even though they were in therapy once a week at Jessie's insistence, there were times she was sure they'd never reconcile. It was messy and complicated and sometimes even ugly. She'd often jog to her car after and simply rest her head on the steering wheel until she felt strong enough to go home to her kids. Then Grant had met Janet, all over again, just as he had before, in a coffee shop. Only it was much, much sooner. When he'd told Jessie maybe they should start dating other people, her heart folded in half and she'd panicked—was this it? Would Grant meeting his future wife ruin any chance he had at reconciling with his current one? She wasn't about to find out. She'd shown up at his apartment late one night.

"I don't want to live in limbo anymore. Either forgive me and we try to move on, or file for divorce. I *can't* take back what I did. But I *can* spend the rest of my life showing you that you can trust me."

Grant raked his hands through his hair. "I want to believe you, Jess, I really do. Why do you think I haven't filed already? We built a life together and I don't want to throw it away."

"Then don't," Jessie pleaded.

"I think I can forgive you. Maybe I already have . . ." He trailed off.

Jessie's heart lurched. She'd been waiting to hear Grant say those words for so long but she could feel his hesitation. "But?"

"But," he repeated slowly, "how can I be sure you won't do it again?"

"Because I won't!"

Grant offered her a sad smile. "How can I stop my mind from wondering every time you go away with the girls or you smile at a dad in Lucas' class. I can't live like that." He shook his head.

Jessie wrapped her jacket tighter around her nightgown. "I get that, Grant. I do. But promising you won't be enough. You have to let me *show* you that our marriage will be my priority; that I won't step outside of it; that I won't hurt you again. So you either choose to take a leap of faith with me or you don't. It's that simple."

Before he could answer, she took her own leap of faith and did something she hadn't done in almost two years—she'd kissed him. And to her surprise, he'd kissed her back, both of them realizing they needed that physical connection again more than they could have known. And then he came home. And eventually, he forgave her. The time in between was almost unbearable, but his forgiveness appeared fast and furious, and Jessie exhaled for the first time in what felt like years.

Unfortunately, Peter's wife didn't feel the same way. Cathy asked him to move out the day after he confessed. Peter could only afford a sparse condo across town, but he said he felt good knowing his son, Sean, could still live in his home.

Telling the twins that Lucas had another father was almost as heartbreaking as telling Grant, the blind trust they'd always held for their mother shattering in an instant. They were angry, and Jessie couldn't blame them. They either gave her the silent treatment or said terrible things Jessie prayed they didn't mean. Jessie would call Claire for advice and she guided her. *Don't let your guilt dictate your choices. Stand strong. You made a mistake, but you're still their mother.* So Jessie had done just that, and eventually they got on the right track, especially after Grant moved back in.

When they felt Lucas was old enough, Jessie, Grant, and

Peter told him the truth together with the help of a counselor. And Lucas eventually came to accept that although his situation might be a bit different from his friends', he had two dads who loved him. Grant, as much as he resented Peter for the betrayal, was grateful for Lucas, and didn't want to deny Lucas his biological father. Grant and Peter never became friends, but they tolerated each other for Lucas' sake. And that was more than enough for Jessie.

Soon after Jessie and Grant had officially reconciled, Claire and Jessie had taken their kids to the beach. As they leaned back in their folding chairs and watched Emily and the twins burying Lucas in the sand, Jessie had asked Claire if she thought it was fair.

"Is what fair?"

"That we got a second chance. Most people don't. They have to live with the consequences of their actions. Is our karma going to be all screwed up now? Are we going to die in some freak accident?"

Claire tipped her sunglasses down her nose. "I told you not to watch that stupid movie!"

"*Final Destination*? I had to!"

Claire shook her head. "I don't get your fascination with horror movies."

Jessie rolled her eyes. "Will you listen to me, please? I had a nightmare about this last night. What if the universe is going to punish us in some way? For not having to pay the price everyone else does?"

Claire took a sip of her water before answering. "I don't know, Jess. I think we've faced plenty of demons in this life too." She nodded toward Lucas, the girls begging him to stop putting sand in his mouth, then giggling when he didn't. "You fought like hell for your marriage and your family. You had to sit your daughters down and tell them you had a baby with another man. You had to face the rage of that man's wife."

"I did." Jessie took a deep breath. It had been incredibly difficult, but confronting her secrets had been her penance, and the only way to truly start over. "And you still lost your mom all over again." Jessie squeezed Claire's hand. "And Gabs never did get her baby."

"I've thought about it a lot. And I think the point of going back to that year wasn't to make everything perfect. It was to learn how to face things head-on, instead of running from them or hiding from them. *Every single secret* we held came out. And you know what? We're all stronger for it." Claire paused, thinking about Mona again. Even though it was devastating to go through her death a second time, she wouldn't have given up having that year with her again for anything. And she got to fix the mistakes she made with Emily, giving her daughter the life she always deserved.

"Did you guys start the festivities without me?" Jessie's voice rang out from inside. She watched as Lucas barreled toward the pool and dove in, Gabriela laughing as water sprayed her. Jessie dumped all her purchases except one on the counter and grabbed a pitcher of mimosas from the fridge, while Grant helped Madison and Morgan pull plastic cups from the cupboard. Morgan's blond hair had recently been chopped off into an asymmetrical bob, yet another new haircut in a matter of months, but Madison's was still long and parted down the middle, the way it always had been. The girls remained so similar to the way they'd been as little girls—Morgan outgoing and direct, never mincing words to make her point, Madison more reserved, saving her voice for when it would be impactful. But both laughed and rolled their eyes when their father teased that he should make them a virgin cocktail, even though they were twenty years old and the legal drinking age in Mexico was eighteen.

"Happy birthday, Claire!" Jessie said as Grant poured the drinks and handed them out. "To fifty! It's the new twenty-five, right?" Jessie said, looking at Emily, who was nearly there, and everyone held their drinks high in the air.

"I wouldn't go that far!" Claire said. "My headache would argue otherwise!"

"Whatever, lady! Drink up. Hair of the dog, right?" Jessie laughed, then added, "I have presents!"

"I don't need a set of maracas, Jessie," Gabriela teased.

"Oh shut up!" Jessie said. "Seriously, both of you come over here."

Gabriela and Claire sat down next to Jessie and waited patiently as she carefully unwrapped the tissue paper to reveal three necklaces, each with a small bottle of sand and a charm with the number forty dangling from it. "So we'll always remember the year we turned forty," Jessie said, so quietly only her best friends could hear her.

Each woman picked up her necklace and let it dance between her fingers, reflecting on the journey that had led them to exactly where they were today. Gabriela learned to fail and rise back up, stronger than she was before. Claire discovered she didn't have to sacrifice her own happiness for everyone else's. And Jessie found out that sometimes you have to fight like hell for something, even when you doubt whether you still deserve it.

"Wait," Emily said as she leaned over Claire's shoulder. "You messed up. That says forty. You're fifty!" She glanced at Morgan and Madison and smirked. "God, I hope early senility doesn't run in our families!"

"No, it's perfect, just the way it is," Jessie said, glancing back at Grant before grabbing Gabriela and Claire and pulling them into a group hug.

Madison shook her head. "I don't get you guys sometimes."

"That's okay," Claire said, wiping the tears from Jessie's cheeks with her thumb. "We get each other. And that's all that matters."

Acknowledgments

What a fun ride this has been!

Thank you to Greer Hendricks for taking a chance on us four years ago. You didn't have to read our manuscript, but you graciously did. We'll always be thankful to you and our wonderful publisher, Judith Curr, for believing in us.

Sarah Cantin! How can you continue to be so incredibly fabulous *and* nice? It really doesn't seem fair. Thank you for always advocating for us. We want to be you when we grow up.

Elisabeth Weed, you continue to be the best agent anyone could ask for. We appreciate when you discreetly look away when we get into arguments in front of you. At dinner. After a bottle of wine. (Long story!)

And Dana Murphy—you are outstanding and we heart you.

Ariele Fredman, we are so in love with you. Can you feel it? You are amazing and we are so thrilled with everything you and the lovely Kathryn Santora have done for TSOAT.

To our friends and family—thank you for preordering our books and hauling your bad selves to our book signings. One day, we promise to have people we *don't* know in those seats and you'll be off the hook.

To the incredible book bloggers who have championed us along the way—it's hard to put into words the gratitude we feel. Word of mouth is everything and we appreciate every single mention. Hugs to Jennifer Tropea O'Regan from Confessions of a Bookaholic; Andrea Katz from Great Thoughts, Great Readers; Natasha Minoso from Book Baristas; and of course, Melissa Amster from Chick Lit Central—we owe y'all some serious cocktails!

To our readers—thank you doesn't seem like enough. We are literally nothing without you. We love to hear from you and read your reviews. Keep 'em coming!

Liz would like to send love to her father, Bill, who passed away while writing *The Year We Turned Forty*. You always said tough times build strength, and as usual, you were right. You are missed every single day.

And last, but not least, thank you to Mike and Matt. You guys could've told us this would never happen. But instead you encouraged us to dream big. You could have asked us to quit to make your lives easier. But you never did. Know that every word we write is because of you guys. We love you! PS: Now let's go to Vegas! (After a shout-out like that, we deserve it, right? #stringsattached #sorry #notsorry #weloveyouthough)